A Night of Pleasure and Wrath

A SHARED SINS STANDALONE

VICES AND HEDONISM

MADDISON COLE

Copyright

Dedication

To every husband who suddenly finds themselves as the sub...

Your woman is a queen, and it's her royal duty to dominate
you. Order some restraints, get the blindfold ready, consider
your pain threshold level and tell your buddies you won't be
online tonight.

RULES
Whips are mandatory; edible lube is optional.
Now strip, lie down, and let your woman get to work.

You are very welcome.

Author's Note

Welcome to a Night of Pleasure and Wrath, where there are no safe words, and your inhibitions need to be left at the door. *This a standalone novel* between Harlow and a gang of MMA fighters who use her body for one purpose only - *to show her the lengths she'll go to in order to achieve her deepest desires.*

Welcome to a Night of Pleasure and Wrath, where boundaries are pushed and restrictions are abandoned. The story follows Harlow and a group of MMA fighters who use her for their own pleasure, pushing her to explore her limits and uncover her innermost desires.

Due to dark themes and BDSM connotations, this book is inappropriate for those under 18. Expect excessive amounts of steam, pushing boundaries, violence, and cursing throughout.

This reverse harem includes a female character, so please be aware of the F/F romance included.

Now, please sign your NDA, hand over your phone, and come on in. The Bloodied Skulls are waiting for you.

The ancient clock in the conference room seems to tick on the same second over and over while the big boss drones on and on about overheads and setbacks. The stuffiness in this room sends my eyes drooping, my blinks getting longer with each torturous moment, and it's an effort to stay awake, even from digging my nails into the palm of my hand.

Sarina, the manager of my department and all-around ass-kisser, stays bolt upright and alert, soaking up every boring word being said by the insipid man in front of me. Her beautifully shiny coffee-colored hair – not from a box, but a gorgeously expensive salon – is totally put together, every strand wrangled into submission and held in a severe bun.

Meanwhile, I had to borrow a cardigan from one of my colleagues to hide the coffee stain down my left tit. Of all the days, I had to wear a white shirt with a black bra. The fucking alarm decided not to work this morning, and my boyfriend, Ricky, had already left. He's been working all the hours lately to close a huge deal at his marketing firm, but hopefully once I get this promotion, we can both work less hours. Then we will have the time to take that holiday I've been so desperate for, and I'll be claiming Fridays as *'me'* days to spare these boring meetings.

"Harlow, do you understand what I am saying?" The Boss, Mitch, asks with a quirked brow. Sarina pauses her furious scribbling with the pen poised above her notebook and scrutinizes me, her lip curling at the state of my face wearing last night's makeup. Again, I thought maybe I could get away with not reapplying it as I crashed out so late last night but waking up late has royally fucked me over.

I plaster a wide smile on my face, sitting up a little straighter, not wanting him to know my thoughts had been about lying on a beach with some cocktails, rather than this suffocating office. "Yep. All clear Mitch. I can't wait to get started." It's hard, but I interject as much enthusiasm into my voice as possible, despite the fact I want to go home and nap like a queen.

But the fake smile slips off my lips when the room stays silent. That shitty clock mocks me on the wall with its broken ticking, and I suddenly get the impression that somewhere along this conversation, I seriously fucked up.

Sarina clears her throat delicately, placing her hand over mine and it takes everything in me not to jerk out of her fake condescending grip. "Harlow. What Mitch has been saying is that we must let you go. It's nothing personal," she chuckles, finally pulling back her hand to smooth back a non-existent hair. "We haven't got the budget to keep you, and it's last in – first out." Mitch gives me a tight nod, but all I can do is blink in confusion.

"Wait. So, this isn't a promotion?" I stumble over my words.

He grimaces, jowls wobbling when he shakes his head. "No. I am sorry, but we have to terminate your employment. Best of luck in the future." He gives me a limp handshake, and on a final nod, sweeps his mundane ass from the room.

"What the fuck?" I turn to Sarina who's gathering her things together. "He just left, after firing me."

She gives me a pitying smile, "Honey. He's important in this business and time is precious, but he took the time out to come and speak to you." Her response makes me see red, and before I even have a chance to process what I'm doing, my chest is against hers, and my finger is poking her in the face.

"Are you for fucking real?" I growl, moving forward with her when she takes a step back. "So, I should be grateful for him taking time out of his busy schedule, probably getting his tiny limp dick sucked by you, to fire me when I have been here for years?" She gives a shocked gasp, puckering her mouth into an asshole, but I'm on a roll. "There have been others that came in after me, and had a promotion, but I bust my ass off for you, and now what?" I step back from her, picking up my glass tumbler and smashing it onto the floor.

Sarina rushes over to the glass door, which offers a view of the open-plan office. "We need security assistance please!" she barks, getting everyone's attention on us. All heads turn in our direction, and my anger dissipates into a sick twisting in my stomach.

Two of the building's security stride over, and calmly stand there while I register everyone looking at me, shame coloring my cheeks. Fuck, this is embarrassing. I swear Chad over in the corner is filming me, so I turn and flip him off when the security guard grips my forearm.

"Get your fucking hand off me," I snarl, pushing him back and stepping into his space.

"Calm down," the other man orders quietly, like a warning I

should heed while shuffling me onwards. But the man who holds me, curls his lip and my stomach flops painfully.

"Are you assaulting a security guard?" he questions rhetorically. "I think you are." He then yanks my arm behind my back, ignoring my shocked gasp, and marches me all the way to the elevators, keeping his bruising hold on me. We cross the foyer, and of course, it's busy as hell. Everyone stops to watch as I am carted out like a criminal. Could this day get any worse?

The answer to that is a resounding yes, as the heavens decide to open, soaking me to the skin in seconds, leaving my black bra in full view under the white shirt. I fish out my phone in my purse and try dialing Ricky to come and pick me up. We recently made the decision to share a car so we can save for a new house. But in times like this, I really regret it.

As luck would have it, the phone goes to voicemail. I try calling a few more times, huddling in a doorway, but it's no good. I'm going to have to walk the ten blocks home.

Normally, I wouldn't mind, but with the rain and my mood I just want to get the fuck home and curl up on my couch feeling sorry for myself.

My shoes rub my ankles to shreds and I grit my teeth against the pain, hobbling back to our apartment. It's in a nice area, full of shops and restaurants that we frequent. Lately with our workloads, we haven't been out as much. But I am going to spend my time in that cute little café on the corner, applying for jobs.

Finally, I make it up the steps, and put my key in softly to surprise Ricky. Hopefully, he won't mind too much that I'm suddenly unemployed as I have a tiny amount in my savings, and it shouldn't take too long to get another job.

The apartment is quiet when I enter, so I don't call out his name, figuring he's still at work. Flicking on the coffee maker and throwing off my shoes, I drag my sorry ass upstairs, desperate to get comfy and wallow in self-pity. I swing the door open, and –

What the fuck?

Ricky is kneeling butt-naked on our bed, screwing his dick into an ass tilted in the air. Hands grip our headboard, holding it away from the wall so it doesn't bang. When a moan sounds from the person on all fours, I have to grip the doorframe to keep upright. *That's not a woman.*

They're in the middle of it, and neither have noticed me, too engrossed in each other. I can't even process what's happening at this moment. My brain has gone on some sort of meltdown, and I just can't cope. I must make a noise because Ricky's eyes swing to mine, and he jumps back, giving me a view I didn't need to see.

"H-Harlow," Ricky stammers, "Wha...what are you doing home?" He reaches over the bed, grabbing his underwear in an attempt to cover himself on his way over to me, while I remain frozen. The man on the bed uses *my* fluffy throw to shield his dick, but I saw it. Shrivelled, like the sagged ballbag underneath. Grey peppers his hair and when I double take at his face, he has the audacity to wave a hand at me.

"Hey, Harlow." My mouth drops even wider, my eyes flying to Ricky.

"You're screwing your boss?! Could you be anymore fucking cliché?!" Ricky has the decency to blush, lowering his head like a dog who shat on my favourite rug. But this is so much worse. Ricky blocks my view of the man I've only met at a BBQ once, hastily dressing, and puts his free hand on my shoulder. I lose it.

Swiftly lifting my knee, I happily connect it with his dick for one last time and he topples over in pain. His boss tries to edge around me, but I grip the back of his head in my hand and yank his face down to also smash my knee into his nose.

Double win for the kneecap today. He screams and drops to the floor like a sack of shit, blood spewing everywhere.

I don't even care if it stains the cream carpet, and I'm not going to stick around to find out. Grabbing my oversized handbag stuffed in the corner, I start filling it with clothes from the drawers. Some of mine, most of his so I can enjoy creating a bonfire later. A piece of card hidden in the underwear drawer gives me a nasty paper cut as I stuff it in too, spotting the older man edging out of the room.

"You're a psycho," he spits, disappearing out the door.

"Yeah? Maybe." I call after him, grappling for something witty to say. There's nothing. All my anger currently rests with Ricky, the pathetic cunt. Feet can be heard stomping down the staircase and the front door slams, leaving me alone in the loaded silence with my cheating asshole ex-boyfriend.

"Honey, I swear he doesn't mean a thing to me. I love you. Please," Ricky urges, standing half upright to hover behind me.

"I suppose that promotion you didn't deserve or work for just fell into your lap then?" I cringe at the double meaning I didn't intend to make. Honestly, I have no idea how I am so calm. I think this has lifted me above my bullshit-I-can-handle meter. Ricky reaches out a tentative hand again. I shuffle away before it makes contact, and he has the nerve to look annoyed.

"Harlow. I swear, it's only you. You're always busy and I was staying late at the office anyway. It sort of just...happened..." he trails off when I spin back towards him, pushing him out of my personal space.

"That is no excuse. Actually, only a weak, pathetic asshole would try to blame me for your wrongdoings. Three years I've been wasting my time with you." I hastily shove more things into my bag. I'll come back another time and grab the rest.

I barge in the hallway and take one more look at him standing there, looking utterly pathetic. "Your cheating cock is fucking tiny, and in case you didn't realize, this relationship is over." Petty, I know. But who gives a fuck?

I also slam the door and run away as fast as I can. The streets blur past, not helped by the tears streaming down my face. My only concern right now is to get blinding drunk. I need to get off this shitty carousel of adulting, just for the day. My life has been fucked from the moment I woke up late. Ricky and his power-abusing boss got away from my wrath too easily in my opinion, but revenge is always a dish best served cold. I just had to get out of there.

By the time I manage to escape my insidious thoughts, I take in the boarded-up shops, or ones still clinging onto life, their neon lights broken or flashing half a message. I didn't realize in my haste to get away that I managed to run clear across town, and straight into the dodgier outskirts.

Something shoves hard into my back, sending me sprawling into a puddle. Someone looms over me, and I hold my hand out to them, expecting for them to help me up, but instead, my bag is yanked off my shoulder and the hooded figure sprints down the road with my remaining possessions.

"Stop!" I yell, racing down the road as fast as my battered feet would let me. "Motherfucker!" I continue trying to find any signs of whoever it was, but when I turn a corner, it's just me in the alley. There is no sign of anybody.

It's at this point that I crash painfully onto my knees to the muddy floor, huge sobs making my body shake. My phone and purse have gone. I've lost my apartment and my boyfriend, not to mention my job in one day. Actually, in one fucking morning. I have officially hit rock-bottom.

At least it's stopped raining, I try to placate myself. The sun finally peeks out of the clouds, yet I stay where I am for a while longer, unable to move. No one pays me any attention as they pass the entrance to the alley. They're all used to avoiding the darker aspects of the city. Even though I'm in the more rural side of town, there has been an increase in gang activity with more and more incidents of random attacks. Self-preservation kicks in, so they all like to pretend everything is okay.

Normally I agree with this, doing the same as them. Going to work, striding past all the other commuters, immersed in my music. But now, I would like someone to just stop their day for one second to care. A friendly face, or even a stranger to acknowledge the fact something's happened to me, and I need help.

Dragging myself off this dank floor, I wince as the pins and needles attack my legs, so I give them a stomp to work through the pain. My clothes have mud all over them, contributing to that fucking coffee stain which feels like it happened months ago. Despite my annoyance a moment ago that no one would help, when I slowly make my way down the streets which are getting busier the closer I get to my home, I'm glad no one really pays any attention to the girl covered in mud and coffee, and probably sporting panda eyes from my mascara. I can only imagine how shitty I look right now.

My feet stumble to a halt. Fuck, I can't go home. There is no home left for me. I pay most of the rent, but there is no chance I'm going back to see that asshole in our cum-soaked sheets. No, I'll have to find a diner and call my mom. Being this close to my apartment, I'm not short of cute little coffee shops, nice restaurants and fancy bars. That's what drew Ricky and I to this area. The appeal of going out for a lovely romantic dinner within walking distance, and maybe having a drink after work. Of course, it didn't happen, but it was nice to dream.

Fuck no. There is no way I can go in looking like this. So, I turn around to head back the way I came, back to the outskirts where hopefully I'll stand a better chance at fitting in, and maybe there will be a diner open, or someone to finally take pity on me.

The alleyway mocks me when I eventually reach it again -

that invisible band pulling me back to the gutter where I apparently belong now. Like a child I poke my tongue out, even though there's no one there. Yeah, I have no clue what's going on with me at the moment. I've just cracked.

"Yo sweetheart, what happened to you?" Some guy calls out and I spin around as a car cruises towards me. Instinctively, I go to tighten my bag around me, but there's nothing there.

"Bitch, I'm talking to you," the jerk in the car shouts again when I don't immediately respond, and he rolls to a stop beside me. His face is a picture of shock when I stride over and scream as loudly as possible into his face. The relief at his car speeding off is immense.

Fucker thinking he can take advantage of a woman down on her luck.

When I turn back, my heart stops for a beat. There, behind a dumpster, sits my bag. How did I not see it before? I crouch and with trembling fingers, move the bag to check the inside. Nothing.

A sob escapes at the memories held within that bag. I had images as keyrings on my keys, the contents of my world on my phone. Hidden in the back pocket, I stored a photograph that I held close to my heart. The last one I'd taken with my sister. The edges were worn from stroking it so often, and that absolute scumbag took that away from me. I feel so violated.

With my next sob, I reach out and throw the bag as far as it will go, but something flutters to the dirty floor, which I hadn't noticed on my first sweep.

Hoping this is my photo, I reach it and snatch the cream card off the floor. The same damn one that sliced the skin between my index and middle finger. I turn the card over, a frown creasing my brow. The card is that expensive type, glossy black with crimson swirls curving from the top edge. The red writing is hard to make out straight on; it's almost shimmering and only makes sense when I turn it at a slight angle.

Club Rapture Lock-In

*You're invited to the
exclusive Club Rapture
for a night of decadent
sin and wrathful debauchery.*

*Leave your inhibitions at
the door, and come explore
the darker side of pleasure.*

Well, that's…different. Intriguing, yet not the type of invite you see on a daily basis. I didn't see Ricky receive this, but a plan forms in my mind. I'm already at rock-bottom, and if I can find somewhere to sleep, eat and get some clothes more appropriate, then why shouldn't I go? Leave my inhibitions at the door, and best of all - steal the fun that bastard thought he was going to sneak off and have without me? That sounds like something I can do.

Fuck it. I'm going to go. What's the worst that can happen?

When I said that I had reached a new low, I was lying. This is my all-time low. Despite finding an all-night diner, I couldn't bring myself to call my mom. I know exactly what would happen, and the insane level of judgment she would give me from just a simple hum in her voice. The server was so lovely, offered me food, and turned a blind eye to the fact I dozed off in the corner. In fact, when I woke up, there was a toothbrush in front of me, a clean folded diner uniform, and new flip-flops. I was so grateful that I cried.

The server who I've now dubbed my guardian angel isn't there, so I shuffle on my aching limbs to the restroom and clean up the best I can. My red hair, the shade of a ripe tomato, hangs limply around my face, showcasing my tired eyes which still shine like amber in this dim light, framed by the shadows underneath indicating I'm in desperate need of caffeine.

The diner is strangely empty when I exit the restrooms, and despite calling out, no one seems to answer, so I exit into the cool morning, the sun bathing everything in a soft glow. I've got hours to find Club Rapture, wherever the fuck that is. Honestly, I've never heard of the place, and I like to think that I was knowledgeable about the great places to eat and drink. But with no phone, and looking like a 50's reject, how the hell am I going to find it?

I'm wandering around hours later when I pull out the card again for the dozenth time and turn it over. There, around the edge of the invitation, in tiny print is part of an address. 22 West and 15th Street…Where the fuck is that in comparison to where I am now? A woman strides towards me in fancy designer clothes, pushing an equally expensive baby stroller. I need to pull on my big girl pants and ask someone for help.

"Excuse me," I call politely to the woman. Her shoulders stiffen slightly but then she carries on as if I'm not there. Fuck her. "Excuse me!" I shout louder, moving in the way of her fancy ass stroller so she's forced to stop abruptly.

Her Botox lips curl into a sneer. "Yes? What do you want?"

"Can you tell me if you know where 22 West and 15th Street is please?" I keep it polite despite her hostile attitude. "I've been mugged and don't have my phone. I would be so grateful if you could point me in the right direction." It hurts to keep my tone neutral, but I need this judgy bitch to help.

She gives a loud sigh, digging her shiny phone out. "I suppose I can look for you. Consider this a favor of the day." Her voice grates through me, but I keep my smile on, which is as fake as her perky tits. Sighing in boredom, she shows me the map on her phone and my heart sinks. It's all the way across New York, in the darkest parts, full of depravity and secrets. Stands to reason this sort of invite would come from there. It's across the city and will take me ages to get there, if I make it in time at all.

Nodding my thanks, I suppose I'd better start the walk in these flip-flops from my guardian angel. They roughly fit and allow my blisters to air out, despite the sting. My ankle still hurts from falling on it yesterday, but by nightfall, I eventually pass through the smoothly lined roads before they dip into potholes again, and a build-up of industrial units becomes visible.

My stomach rumbles, and my mouth is so dry that I consider making myself cry just to get some sort of moisture on my tongue. Did I mention the unusual heatwave which decided today was the day for making an appearance has left me delirious? All I can hope for in this club is some cold tap water and maybe some fries to help the stabbing hunger pains. My feet could also do with a rest, but I continue down the main road, certain I am close.

Sure enough, there are a few people in front, dressed a fuck ton nicer than me, in my dusty uniform and dirt-streaked face. On a hunch, I follow them down the long road, until they turn off down a smaller one, and a thrill runs through me at the sight of the signpost. 22 West and 15th Street. I'm here. I'm finally fucking here!

The massive structure in front of me is strangely deceptive. Here I was thinking it would be some run-down piece of shit, but instead, it's a looming building of around nine floors. Smooth, black concrete that lingers between buildings of crumbling brick, set back to make room for a sweeping driveway complete with valet. It's way out of my comfort zone with how I look, but I've come so far that it would be stupid to back out now. I follow a group, shuffling up to a cut-out where a doorman waits for me to approach.

"Invite?" he mutters, not really looking at me, but holding out his hand. I hand it over and wipe my sweaty palms on my dress. He flips it over, holding a scanner to the back which glows green and beeps.

"Ricky Knight?" he asks, his tone bored. Ah, shit. *Shit*. What the fuck do I say? The minute he looks at me, he will see the lie and panic on my face. I know that my eyes give away all emotions, and right now I'm stressed to fuck. When I don't speak, he flicks a glance in my direction anyway and purses the harsh line of his mouth at my outfit.

"Babe, you do realize this isn't a fancy dress party, yeah?" he smirks over at his partner, nudging him to laugh along with his lame joke. His partner looks me over, muttering I can't be presented to the owner looking like *that*.

"Uh, I was mugged actually, and all I have is this outfit and the invite," I reply, too tired to come up with an excuse. Pulling a red bracelet from the various colors hanging out of his pocket, his head jerks back to the double doors of redwood with gold handles. "Head straight through the door to the left, an attendant will see you are properly dressed for your designated floor," he snaps, and I nod, not knowing what's going on. Strapping the red band around my shaky wrist, his eyes assess me with doubt. "Repeat that back to me. Door on the left, put on what the attendant deems suitable for floor Wrath. Got it?" What's crawled up this bastard's ass? I nod again just to appease him, and mumble. "Wrath."

The door is opened, displaying a large lounge with a range of armchairs and sofas, a curved bar beside a small stage set up with a microphone. Ignoring the attendants strolling around with iPads in hand, I duck my way into the left door as instructed. The one labeled locker room. A leggy girl just inside with a smart pantsuit clinging to her stick-thin frame and an earpiece in her ear nods to the instructions I presume are from the doorman, her eyes sweeping over me in understanding. Ushering me further inside, my eyes widen at the plushest locker room I've ever seen.

A luxurious room greets me, full of squashy chairs, and some tables on the right-hand side with a cold buffet and drinks lined up. I practically run over there, inhaling tiny sandwiches, and then pour myself an orange juice, refilling my glass a further three times before my thirst is fully quenched. Luckily, the girl doesn't try to come between me and the buffet, preferring to stand back and witness my savage display.

Through a wide archway lays a lavish row of individual showers, with fluffy towels on hooks, just dying to be used. Placed neatly on a counter, below a huge, lit mirror, is a pile of sports attire I presume the attendant has laid out, complete with hair tie, underwear and stunning sneakers that are conveniently in my size. I don't know what place this is, but I am so fucking happy to see clean clothes.

The shower immediately streams hot water the minute I turn the handle, wasting no time stripping myself out of the dirty clothes and jumping in. I scrub myself until my skin pinkens and then get to work on my hair before I'm happy to step out, feeling a million times better. My scruffy diner uniform has miraculously disappeared, the leggy girl nowhere to be seen. I towel dry my hair and throw it into a messy bun with a hair band so helpfully provided. Forgoing the underwear, I swiftly dress in the soft pair of shorts and a tight tank top with a bra built in, continuously peering back at the door, wondering why I'm still alone. Surely, I'm not the only one here?

Once I'm done, I head back to the buffet and grab an apple, before dropping into an armchair. My feet are throbbing, my eyelids drifting closed as I absentmindedly bite into the fruit. Rolling my head back onto the backrest, my subconscious just about carries me away as the door flies open, and the girl comes swanning in.

"That's much better," she appraises, grabbing my wrist. Hoisting me out of the seat, she pulls me back to the main lounge, rambling it's almost 10 pm and the doors are about to be locked. I don't have the chance to ask what she's talking about as she releases me and disappears in the crowd that's now gathered before the small stage. The lights darken, plunging us into shadow as a spotlight follows the man placing a foot onto the stage. Standing tall in a suit, the man's piercing green eyes peer out in stark contrast to his tanned skin.

"Welcome to a night of sin and debauchery," he speaks into the microphone, his voice carrying around us like a smooth melody, painted with a Grecian accent. "My name is Steffan Lykaios. For those of you who've been a member of my club and delved into our sins previously, this night will truly be different from anything you've partaken in before. For tonight, every single person here will immerse themselves in the darkest depths of their sinful nature and not surface until dawn." Pausing, his head inclines to a few people up front dressed in full tuxedos and glamorous dresses worthy of a runway. Whilst I'm standing here in a sports vest with a draft wafting up my ass. Perfect.

"As most of you will know, you must wait for the lights to flicker to your color, or should I say the one that matches your bracelet, and let your inhibitions fall away as you step inside the waiting elevators, for it's time to embark on your journey of sin and corruption." With a flourishing sweep of his hand to the sphere lights above the bar, he steps off the stage and disappears through the back door, vanishing as the doors audibly bolt shut. The light blooms with a shade of purple, beckoning those with the matching bracelets to the elevators and I...I stand there rubbing my arms like a loner who's completely out of her element.

Eventually, or more specifically - sixth in the range of colors, the sphere turns red, and I direct my attention to a hallway opposite, lined with a spongey carpet I race forward to make my way there before the crowd's flock in behind. When I run my hand along the wall, I'm shocked to feel the soft suede beneath my fingertips, tying in with the expensive decor of the dimmed chandelier overhead. Stepping forward to present myself to the elevators, I fumble my fingers over the button to call one. Just like the owner said, I scan my bracelet once the doors slide closed and begin my ascent. What the fuck have I gotten myself into? Purple mood lighting and sensual music set the tone for whatever seedy club I've entered, pinging to a stop smoothly.

I frown at the door a few feet ahead, not sure what I was expecting but this isn't it. The dark groove of mahogany looms tall, nondescript other than the word *Wrath* stamped in red across the center. Do I knock? Push it open? Why am I being so indecisive?

Before I decide, the door swings open and I'm face to face, or should I say face to bare chest with a whole fucking stack of muscles.

"You lost, doll?" Muscles asks and I have to bite back a growl of irritation. What is it about men who see me as some fragile little thing?

"I'm not your fucking doll," I snap, folding my arms and sticking my chin out in my intimidation pose. It doesn't do shit, apart from make an even wider smile light up his semi-handsome face.

"You gotta name?" He asks, not budging from the door, and I make the split-second decision to go with the lie.

"Name's Ricky," I reply with a raised brow daring him to question it.

"What sort of a name is that for a chick?" he chokes, and I swallow the flush threatening to claim my cheeks. Come on

Harlow, you've got this. I puff myself up and step closer into his space.

"That's the name my mamma gave me, you got a fucking problem with that?" Despite the bravado, I'm shaking inside and desperate for him to buy into my attitude. He takes a step backwards, eyebrow raised.

"Damn. Okay Ricky. Sorry I asked, Fireball."

"Where do I need to go?" I reply, curtly ignoring the way my ego is stroked by the pet name.

"Come on in, little one. We're about to begin." He tips me a wink then performs a ridiculously flourished bow as he steps aside. In the wide foyer, there are only three more doors in front of me, one to the right, one in front, and one to the left. All I need now is a fucking table with a cute glass bottle saying drink me.

"Uh, thanks," I say to the guy as he permits me entry to the central door, and I step in with more than a little trepidation. All I see is red, everywhere. In every wall, furniture, blur of movement and shade. From lustful rose to playful crimson and in all materials, suede to leather, I barely have time to blink when a woman sweeps in to address me.

"Ricky?" She questions, wrapping an arm around my back and encouraging me further inside anyway. "Come on, you're up."

"I'm up where?" I reply stupidly, being dragged along beside her.

"Don't keep them waiting, you're the main event. Although looking at you now, I think it might be over before it begins." Her eyes flick up and down me, the bitchy glare in her narrowed eyes ruffling me the wrong way. She's in a similar pantsuit to the attendant's downstairs, all black and white like penguins in heels.

"What would?" I ask again, not surprised when I don't get a response. Not that'd I'd hear it anyway over the deafening roar assaulting my ears. The club is apparently full now, and it's heaving. A bar displayed across the back wall, various neon signs labeling hallways as *Pleasure* or *Punishment,* and in the center something that has everyone's attention. Holy fuck. It's a boxing ring. The outside is surrounded by mesh, creating a cage for the huge man bouncing around inside. Pumping his fists high, he does well on working the crowd up to a frenzy whilst clearly stalling. For what, fuck knows but I'm eager to find out.

"The fights are usually matched by weight, so I don't know what you've done to piss off the big boss," the attendant stops to yell into my ear. Grabbing my hands, she hovers them in front of me and makes quick work of strapping hand wraps from my fingers to just below my wrist, covering the red band. My stomach flips painfully, as the implications of what's about to happen hits me. He's stalling for...me. Or rather, the 'Ricky' that was supposed to be wearing the band clamped around my wrist. I must fight this guy.

The ring is so much larger close up, complete with a referee who opens the door for me to step in. Stale sweat and the copper tang of blood assault me and my earlier food threatens to make a reappearance. The crowd boos and catcalls as the ref announces my name. *Ricky Knight.*

Mountain man faces me, his lips set into a vicious sneer, and he hops from foot to foot. All I can do is stand there in limp shock, and I miss the part where the ref tells us to begin. The only indication that it has started is a meaty fist flying towards my stomach which knocks the wind out of me, and I fall flat onto my ass with a wheeze.

"At least try," Mountain man says, waiting for me to move. The minute I'm on one knee, he smacks his leg out and kicks the side of my thigh which causes me to fold over with a moan. The crowd's heckling gets louder, bored with the fight already.

They want to see blood and I know it will be mine decorating the space before long.

This time he lets me stand before a punch to my side makes me heave, although I manage to stay upright. But not for long. He prances about, his fist snapping out to connect with the side of my head. A blinding crack sounds in my ears and before I've even hit the ground, darkness overtakes me.

"That one? You can't be serious," Zeke roughly nudges my shoulder. His breathy whisper fans over my exposed neck, reeking of whiskey. He knows better than to drink on a night like this. We're all on call to slink into the shadows without a moment's notice. As fun as a night at Club Rapture seems, we have business to attend to. Shoving him back against those crowded in around us, I give him a brief 'don't-fuck-with-me' glare.

"She can do it, trust me," I growl. Zeke mumbles about how the last one turned out and any curse I had in response is drowned out by the roar of the crowd. 'Ricky,' as she was introduced as, just took a hard blow to the temple, rendering her lifeless on the ground while the ref completes his countdown.

"And she's out!" he cries. Lifting the arm of the douche with more muscle than teeth high in the air, he is labeled as the winner and the crowd goes insane once more. Zeke snorts, plastering a sarcastic smirk on his face as people rush by to greet the victor at the mesh-door exit.

Spinning on my so-called brother, I push against his fitted sports tee and then close the distance to get back in his space. Unlike Zane, Zeke's auburn hair isn't natural, but the pair hold so many other similarities, they encourage the illusion that they're twins. Something to do with connection and belonging, as our childhood therapist once said, but everyone who graced the halls of Warrick Orphanage was unqualified and looking for a fast pay-out. A soft groan sounds, drawing my attention over to the red-headed heap dragging herself up onto her knees. Fuck, I really hope I'm right about this.

"Get the pleasure room ready. I'll take care of the girl," I tell Zeke. He crosses his thick arms over his chest, cocking an eyebrow down at me. Youngest or not, even if by mere months, I've always been the ringleader. These unruly boys needed a mother, which I could never be, but I've got a pussy in between my legs and a cracking pair of tits so I'll have to do.

"Wanna bet on how long it takes for her to fail?" Zeke blocks me from leaving with his smug, open stance. I pause, staring at the girl. Her vibrant red hair has fallen free of its messy bun, blocking my view of her face. Spitting a wad of blood onto the floor, she slowly rises onto shaky feet. Sighing, I grace Zeke with one last look over my shoulder. "If you're so sure she's the one, why not put your money where your mouth is?" he goads me. Beneath a pair of fair eyebrows, his blue eyes twinkle with a challenge I refuse to fail.

"How about *when* she passes, I'll put my fist where your

mouth is." Without waiting for his response, I duck through the crowd and slip into the otherwise empty ring. My Killer-to-be sways on her feet and I swoop in, catching her before she falls back onto her ass. "Hey, stay with me. I'll see that you're okay," I reassure her. Even through the layer of sweat coating her clammy skin, the smell of sulfur rain and pure determination washes over me. With her eyes closed, I take a moment to brush the red hair aside from her face, my fingers lingering on her bruised cheek.

"Who's the..." she babbles, "cheating cock sucker now, Ricky?" Ahh, we can add revenge to the list as well. I smirk, leading her on dragged feet to the exit. No one pays us any attention, its focused on this round's winner. That douche can lap it up all he likes; Zane will be watching from the shadows somewhere, psyching himself up to bring a universe of pain this douche's way. Fuck what the RSVP said, it was clear his opponent wasn't a 200-pound man, and that cunt-muffin should have never laid a finger on the woman draped across my front. Slinking by undetected, I lead her to the ladies locker rooms, my custom sneaker kicking the door wide open.

"Everybody out!" I yell, and luckily for the group of giggling whore-bags reclining across the benches, they obey. Their tiny crop tops and miniscule skirts do nothing for me. No one wants a sandwich with all the filling hanging out. Lowering my shoulder's hitchhiker down in a corner, I dive into my locker for a first aid kit I always keep on hand. I told you - properly motherly and shit. At the same time, I take out my own hand wraps and pull a hair tie onto my wrist for whenever I might need to throw my hair up and fight.

As the Bloodied Skulls seem to be on Club Rapture's black-list, the three of us had to sneak in without an invitation. That also means we're technically ghosts out there and need to rely on our sport's kit to sneak around undetected. As much as my fingers are itching to break some bones, I need to pace myself. We'll get what we came for soon enough.

A soft groan sounds and I drop back to my knees, pushing my waist length, chocolate brown hair back. Judging by the size of the bump swelling on her forehead, I give my companion a little shake in order to keep her from a concussion nap.

"Stay with me now. We're not done with you yet," I soothe, cracking a disposable ice pack. Placing it on her head, she hisses, and I place her hand over the top to keep it there. "You got a name, Killer? Other than the bullshit you said out there?"

"Har-Harlow," she replies, cracking her lids to assess me with suspicion.

"Well, it's nice to meet you, Har-Harlow. Call me Aria, or your majesty. Whatever works." Leaving Harlow to grumble about feeling dizzy, I scan the rest of her with my hands and eyes. Tsking that she went into a bear trap without knowing the most basic of fighting moves, I check her legs, inspecting the growing bruises before moving further up to her torso. Lifting her tank top, Harlow flinches but I bat her hands away to feel her ribs. As I thought, she jolts when I press lightly on her left side, and I curse under my breath. If that asshole out there had any honor, he would have refused to fight when Harlow stepped into the ring. Alas, Rapture isn't the place for honor and equal playing fields. Everyone here is out for blood.

Smoothing my palms around to her back, I shimmy in closer, feeling the length of her spine and assessing her reaction for any pulled muscles. Her amber eyes are fully open now, the dazed sheen having cleared. Blinking her long lashes, she drinks in my every feature while I do the same. Small button nose, youthfully unblemished skin. If it weren't for the fire I can see deep within, I'd question what landed her here. It wasn't to fight, that's for damn sure. But this girl doesn't stay down; no matter what life has thrown at her; she keeps getting back up and that's why she's the perfect choice.

"Nothing seems too badly damaged," I say, fully aware that my hands have stilled on her back. Harlow's breathing grows heavily, her heart hammering in her chest. I smile easily, having played this game many times before. It's always the coy girls who take that tiny bit more convincing, but the reward is oh-so much sweeter. Shifting slightly, my knee edges closer to feel the heat radiating from her core. Her pink tongue snakes out across her bottom lip, subconsciously drawing my attention there.

"I'm not...I don't swing that way," she mutters, and I laugh.

"There is no this way and that way, Killer," I muse. "There's only the feel of fingertips against your skin." Smoothing my hands slowly down her back, I pause to brush my thumbs over her hip bones. "The press of lips on your neck." I don't even have to move far to do just that, sliding my mouth over Harlow's collar bone with a slight scrape of my teeth. "The satisfaction of having your body enraptured by someone who knows exactly how to own it." Harlow's chest hitches, her body frozen but the intrigue is there to spur me on. Tipping my face upwards, my breath fans over Harlow's skin until her lips are before my own. Popping them open like the obediently eager girl I knew she was, I sit back on my ankles and release her waist.

"Alas, the time will come. Right now, we need to get you back on your feet," I smirk. Reaching across the floor, I grab the flyer one of the slut-bags I kicked out had dropped. Scanning the list of names, I see 'Ricky' is partnered with a tank of a steroid head in the next wave. "You've got about two hours until your next fight. That's plenty of time to-"

"My next fight?" Harlow blurts out, her amber eyes wide. "But...but I lost? So, I'm out, right? I'm done?!" I could almost pity her in that moment, if that were an emotion I still indulged in. Yet, the world is too harsh and it's easier to leave empathy at home on a day like this. Instead, I reach out and cup her cheek softly.

"Doesn't work that way I'm afraid. This wristband means you're property of Club Rapture tonight, and a participant of the Wrath floor," I turn over her wrist, revealing the barcode on the red band that owns her for tonight. Other than me now, of course. "It's not clear what the selection process is, because fuck knows me and my guys have been trying to get noticed for one of the prestigious invites that landed you here, but people are chosen for a reason. You're watched and assessed carefully until your night arises. Except, I don't think this is your night after all - is it Harlow? I think you stole some bastard's invite, and it should be him bleeding on the floor right now instead."

Confirming my suspicions, Harlow ducks her head, rubbing uncomfortably at her upper arms. "I wanna go…home," she whimpers, seeming unsure about that last word as tears fill her eyes.

"You're not hearing me. We're all locked in until sunrise. No one leaves - not anyone who's breathing at least. There's a garbage shoot for the bodies. Prevents the smell if you dump them out quick enough." Pure fear settles into her features then and I sigh heavily. How this girl managed to walk in here without a single clue as to what she was getting herself into is beyond me. Yet what my so-called brother is setting up a few rooms away will push her to her very limits. Muscle up buttercup.

Drawing Harlow up to her feet, my hands linger on her hips until I'm sure she isn't going to crumple back into a heap of limbs, before stepping back with an appreciative nod. Not a wobble in sight.

"The seven sins are called deadly for a reason, Killer. People need a place to vent those ugly emotions where there's no repercussions, like a purge that saves the world from falling victim to people like us. We all come here to prove ourselves or die trying." I shrug matter-of-factly, pointing Harlow towards the showers when her small voice asks the one question I always dread.

"And what is it you're trying to prove?"

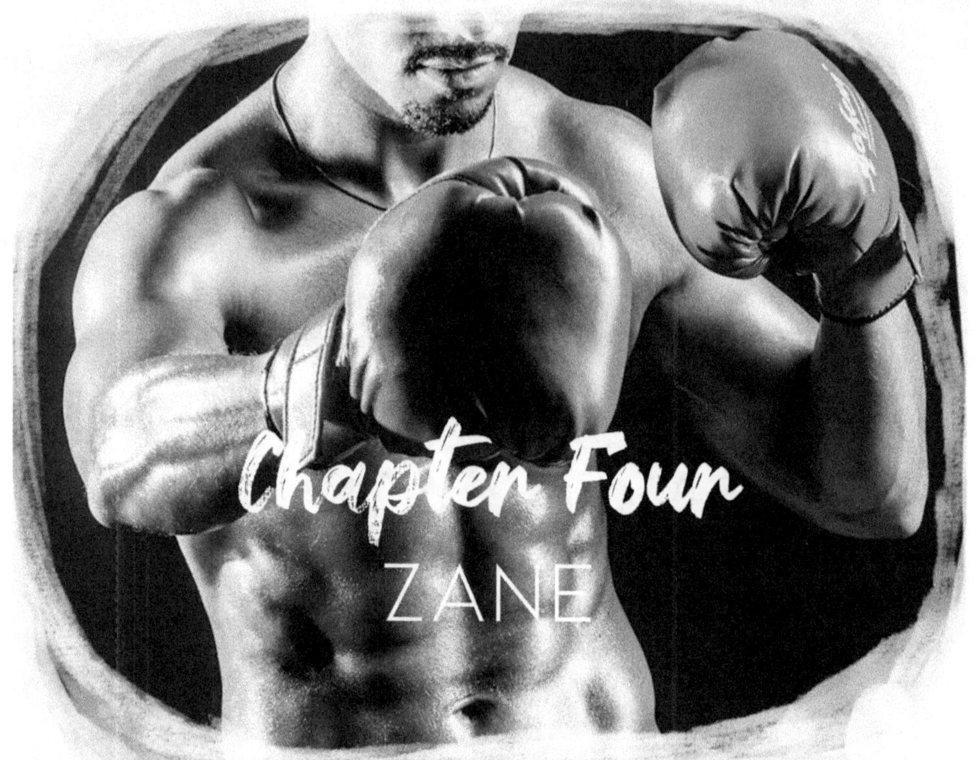

Chapter Four

ZANE

Clenching my teeth together, I pull the door closed behind me and take a moment to exhale my reservations. The noise of the hallway assaults me, after the thickly padded walls inside had quelled the voices in my head. Now they're back, stronger than ever, telling me how terrible this fucking idea is. It's so typical of Aria to make a rash decision without consulting the rest of us. Act now, think later, as always. A hand slams down on my shoulder but I don't flinch. Only one person would dare to approach me in a foul mood, and those who don't know me can generally sense to stay the fuck away.

"Hey," Zeke gives me a small shake. "Don't stress. We'll trial Aria's girl and prove she's not the one. Easy peasy." I huff a bitter laugh, spearing my foster brother with a narrowed look.

"And if she doesn't survive?"

"Then she shouldn't have come here tonight," he replies

gravely, his dyed auburn hair flicking forward. "She made her choice, now we'll show her exactly why it was the wrong one." Resigned, I let Zeke pull me under his arm and wait awkwardly for Aria to arrive with her little…experiment. For many years, Zeke was tall enough to comfort me this way, keeping me tucked into his side as if his flippant attitude could somehow protect me. Now we're fully grown and both over six-foot of pure muscle, his bicep sits heavily over my shoulder, and I have to tilt uncomfortably for our heads to knock together.

At the far end of the Pleasure hallway, the crowd is bustling from the latest fight. Women are throwing themselves at a giant in a lycra one-piece that leaves nothing to the imagination, begging him to drag them into one of the rooms neighboring ours by their hair. A quick flash of appreciation in our direction tells me in an instant their efforts are pointless. Still, an insistent brunette in nothing but a bikini and heels grabs his wrist, uselessly tugging with all her might towards the nearest door. He shrugs her off, striding away on his massive thighs the way he should. This area isn't for some horny chick with a monster fetish, so I'd suggest she finds a way down to Lust on Level Three. This zone is sacred with an extremely specific purpose only the likes of Zeke and I can orchestrate.

Now the crowd has moved on and the circling neon lights are able to permit entry our way, the silhouette of two females appear. I nudge Zeke off me, preferring to stand tall with my arms crossed as Aria approaches, a red head by her side. Her slickened wet hair has been pulled back into a french braid of Aria's doing, a fresh set of gym clothes clinging to her body. At first, my gaze flicks over her with dismissal, a scoff at the ready. But then something catches my attention. A scar trails the length of her thigh, disappearing into a pair of baggy shorts that have no right looking so good pulled up and cinched at her waist. Catching me staring, the redhead is quick to cover the scar with her hand, a flare of anger flashing through her features. Even standing before the judgment of two men that could crush her throat in an instant, she lifts her head higher. Interesting, but we'll be the judges of her inner strength.

"Well, are we just going to stand here staring all night?" Aria tuts, striding through the center of us. "Presuming you've got everything." Twisting the door handle, I scowl after her, grumbling under my breath as I follow. Aria's pet-for-the-evening bumps into me, having thought chivalry would have found us down here in the shadows. I ignore her grunt of irritation, stepping aside to block her way for Zeke to enter first with a knowing smirk. Women ask for equal rights until they realize what they really want are all men enslaved to them. Opening doors, paying for everything, both physically and emotionally, falling at their feet while they walk all over our backs.

"Shut the door," I bark, leaving her bristling with anger behind me. Reuniting with my trio, Zeke shoves Aria's ass off the glass cabinet while I produce the key from my pocket. "Maddox is not going to be happy about this." I huff in one last-ditch attempt to not end up with this girl's blood on my hands tonight. If we were on equal ground in the ring, that would be different, but I'm not typically in the business of disposing of bodies I haven't used as a punching bag first.

"Then don't run off and tell him, errand boy. We need a fourth, that's all there is to it," Aria gives me that bitchy side-eye look I hate.

"Yeah but...her?" Zeke adds in, backing me up. "She looks like she couldn't find her G-spot in a room full of dildos."

"Then I'll just have to find it for her," Aria winks, wandering off as I puff my cheeks out. It kills us Aria is more of a womanizer than both me and Zeke put together, but we've had many drunken nights picking a mark and testing that theory. She uses the sensitive card way too easily, considering I question if Aria even has a heart in that chest of hers. I only need to look at the poor excuse for a fighter she's led in here to have my answer. But if you willingly walk into a lion's cage, you'd better be prepared to be mauled.

"Fine. What level are we starting at?" I peer over my shoulder for my eyes to lock with the stubborn bitch who's foolishly still standing in the open doorway. "She won't last ten minutes above a level two and I'm going to end up more disappointed than if I stayed watching the shit excuse for fighting out there."

"Surely if you're discussing me," the redhead raises an eyebrow, "I should have an input into your conversation." She cocks her head to the side, and I release an annoyed growl. A large hand pats my chest, amusement dancing in Zeke's blue eyes.

"Relax bro, let loose. Have some fun. If she doesn't make it through, we've saved the world another stuck-up cow. Never know, she might surprise us." I huff my disagreement but push the key into the cabinet anyway, the lock popping open with a click. Hovering my fingers over the array of tools and instruments that have one specific purpose, I settle for a thick leather paddle. Level one shit that will have her crying in no time.

"Come on in and join the conversation then," Zeke beckons our guest inside with mockery lacing his tone. Always one to play with his food. Closing the door behind her and stealing the light, he increases the red glow of the overhead bulbs. They've been expertly placed to highlight certain areas of the room which soon steals the redhead's breath with an audible gasp. Shackles on the far wall, ropes hanging from the ceiling, a four-poster bed and my personal favorite, the stretching rack.

"Erm, I don't know what you think I'm going to do in here," she starts in an arrogant tone, and I growl, snatching up another idea before slamming the cabinet closed.

"You'll do as you're damn well told," I bark, spinning on my heels. "Aria has chosen you to learn a lesson in endurance, so when you're screaming, begging for relief, remember you have her to blame for this." Spearing Aria with a death-glare, she simply half shrugs and reaches out for redhead's hands.

"Ignore him," she rolls her eyes. "Zane hates being proven wrong, and even more than that, he hates when I'm right." I grind my teeth, heading straight for the stretching rack. Yep, fuck this shit. I want to get back out there, waiting for my chance to enter the ring, so I'll opt for breaking this girl in an instant. Clicking my fingers for her to obey, the redhead takes Aria's hands and allows my foster sister to guide her over to the bed instead.

My chest heaves with the obvious disrespect, my blood boiling. Yet I remain stock still, watching from the shadows as Aria places a gentle kiss on her victim's neck. Like a siren calling to her prey, Aria whispers false promises into her ear, muttering the magical words that convince her to let Zeke shimmy down her shorts. Breaking away, Aria peels off her pet's vest, revealing her bare chest underneath. Even I'm not stubborn enough to deny she's hot, her rounded breasts casting a shadow over a tattooed stomach. I want to explore the artwork, but I force myself to stay put, tightening my grip on the paddle.

Sitting her on the very end of the bed, Aria catches my eye before tipping up the girl's chin and the pair share a smirk that is clearly there just to rile me. Never missing a trick, Zeke chuckles, lowering to bind the redhead's ankles to each of the bed posts, her legs spread wide and pussy glistening. Fuck.

"What do we call it anyway?" I growl, needing to put a name to the Jane Doe I'm going to toss aside later.

"*She* is called-"

"I'm Harlow," the spitfire interrupts Aria, "and the next time you talk about me like I'm not here, I'll give you a reason to notice me." I scowl right back at her cocky expression, not deterred from my growing hatred of her. It actually makes what we're about to do easier, so I allow the emotion to consume me, filling every inch of my being with unadulterated anger. That is the whole point of a night in Wrath, after all.

Shoving the extra item in my pocket for later, I join Zeke in securing each of *Harlow's* wrists to the bedposts with the slick ties loosely hanging there. I make sure to tighten the knot with extra grip, making her hiss through her teeth, before reaching for the parcel tape. I don't need any more verbal encouragement from her tonight.

"Not so fast," Zeke shoulder barges me aside when I rip a measure of tape from the roll. "I've got plenty of good uses for this sassy mouth yet. While she's still conscious that is." Harlow's eyes widen but I can't deny the flare of intrigue there too.

"You've brought me here for a gangbang?" Harlow asks Aria, curling her lip up at me like the thought repulses her.

"No, absolutely not," Aria chokes on a laugh and Harlow's shoulders temporarily shrug. "The only person getting fucked here tonight, Killer, is you." And there it is. Aria's tone dips, her eyes darkening, and her true colors finally revealed. Taking the paddle from my hand, Aria brings it down on Harlow's exposed pussy, hard and sharp. In shock and from the jolt of pain, Harlow cries out. The glaze of a wounded puppy crosses her face at Aria's betrayal, but in my eyes, it was well-deserved for waltzing in here like top-bitch.

"Oooh, do it again," Zeke hops up and down, growing giddy with excitement and Aria is more than happy to obey. The ruffle of his sports shorts comes next, crumpling around his sneakers as his erect cock springs upwards freely. Grabbing the back of Harlow's head, he silences her protests by shoving his dick in her mouth while Aria gives her the low-down.

"See, these rooms are reserved for people like us." She hands me back the paddle and kneels between Harlow's legs. "The corrupted," she pushes a finger into Harlow's pussy. "The depraved." Another finger. "The sinful." And a third, until

Harlow is crying out around Zeke's shaft. "The three of us had to learn the hard way a valuable lesson I'm offering you so easily."

Leaning up to Harlow's ear, Aria is unfazed by the thrusts of Zeke's groin into her prey's face. "There's pleasure to be found in agony. Beauty in affliction. As soon as you welcome the pain, you'll become numb to anyone ever hurting you again."

And at this, despite all my reservations, Harlow stills. The words tumble around the empty space in between her ears as Aria begins to assault her greedy pussy and she freely accepts Zeke's cock. For the first time, a tiny voice in the back of my mind suggests Aria may have been right. This girl is running from something or someone, possibly even herself, and maybe she might enjoy being broken after all.

Pulling up a stool, I crack my neck on either side, preparing to test that theory. Reaching for the clamps in my pocket, I carefully ease one onto each of Harlow's pert nipples. The clips snap on securely, whilst still attached to the wires that lead to the control in my hand. Meeting Aria's and Zeke's eyes, they both give me a nod in unison as I flick the switch and send the first volt of electricity spiraling into Harlow's body.

uck.

As wave after sharp wave pulses through me, setting all my nerve-endings into a friction fiasco, I realize I've never had a worse idea than to use that stupid invitation for myself. And yet, even as my body jerks around from being fucking *electrocuted* of all things, I can't help but feel a thrill. Does that make me fucked up? Or am I succumbing to a darkness others dare not speak of? The one I've spent years trying to keep hidden, yet Aria saw it in a heartbeat. It's a sensual whisper in the dead of night, the gentle caress of razor-sharp nails on my nape, the need for something *more* which has always been there, waiting for the right incentive to be released. But this - the three of them with haunted eyes and stern jaws drawing reactions from my body I don't understand - this isn't how I imagined I'd find my awakening.

The moan that escapes my lips should embarrass me, but Aria continues playing my pussy, marking me as her new favorite toy. Her fingers brush my G-spot like she knows exactly how I like it, teasing me with fluid strokes and then breaking into quick thrusts. Testing my limits of control. While I've never thought of myself being attracted to the same sex, she's making me feel things none of my exe's ever have. The electric sensation coursing all the way through my body eases, and I can finally breathe a little easier around this guy's cock.

"Suck it," he demands, jerking his hips forward while his hand winds into my hair and pulls me deeper until I gag. As infuriating as it is to not be in control, my pussy clenches, and my last orgasm slides right into the next, my body no longer my own. "Shit, are you sure she's gonna last?" Captain Sea-Monster-Cock asks the room. The only other sounds to be heard are coming from either my choking or the slap of my juices against Aria's slickened hand. I try to pull off the dick, but he keeps me in place as salty tears run down my cheeks, the aggressiveness of this mountain man's cock jamming down my throat becoming too much.

"Zeke, shut the fuck up." Aria snaps as she runs an expert finger over my clit which makes me moan again involuntarily.

"Ooooh, do that again, feisty girl. Moan on my dick," Zeke commands. The other man in the room, the one with shadows looming over him, says nothing. His eyes, though, I can feel them boring into me with murderous intent.

Zeke huffs as if I'm taking too long bringing him to climax and I grit my teeth down along his shaft. Literally doing the best I can here.

"Fuck, Feisty. I want you to suck it, not bite it." I do it again, noting the pleasured hiss that leaves his mouth and how his hand eases the tiniest of pressure on my hair. Of course - this is what they want. They crave pain, thrive off it so if I want to impress them, which the tiny voice in the back of my head tells me I do, I need to change tactics.

Aria joins my breathy groan when my pussy clamps down onto her fingers yet again, the vibrations from my throat seeming to trigger Zeke too. The swell of his dick rolls in time with how I shamelessly gyrate on Aria's palm, seeking every miniscule of friction possible against my clit. But instead, she withdraws completely, and the sharp slap of a paddle comes down hard on my swollen pussy.

"That's it. Take it all, sweet thing," Zeke coaxes, fucking my mouth until I'm seeing stars and I'm forced to choke down every drop of his salty cum.

"Good girl," Aria pats my head as she looms over me, filling my mouth with her fingers the instant Zeke withdraws, forcing me to taste my own arousal. My head lolls on my shoulders, my eyes sweeping over to the silent one. His eyes are unreadable in the low lighting but as he smacks the paddle against his open palm, a cruel smile grows upon his face.

"That was mediocre for starters. Hopefully, the main course proves much more filling," Zane chuckles gleefully as he grabs Aria's fingers to suck the remainder of my evidence off. Untying the restraints holding me ram-road straight between the bedposts, I flop back on an exhausted groan. I should feel embarrassed laid bare before them all, like a prime piece of meat amongst the predators, or trembling, begging for them to let me out, but I can't find an ounce of shame. A modicum of regret. Shit, I really am sick in the head.

Aria finishes untying my ankles and then crawls up the bed, spooning the side of my body to run one of those wicked fingers along my cheek.

"Remember, there is also beauty to be found in pain. You just have to know where to look." I roll my head to the side, wondering for the second time what kind of life such a beautiful woman must have led to end up here. With guys like them. Proving my point, the silent asshole stands with a loud slap against his thighs.

"Well, that was disappointing," he sighs. "You really know how to pick the weak ones Aria." At this, the woman besides me turns her head to growl, a savage look of promised pain passing over her features. I push myself up on my elbows, refusing to be referred to as weak, or spoken about like I'm not even here. The darkened whisper in the shadows comes calling then, filling my voice with steely conviction. *"Game on."*

"Who said I was finished?" I spit, relishing the shared look of shock on the men's faces. "You wanna talk the talk but make no effort to participate - that's on you. But hear me when I say, nothing you can throw my way will defeat me. I might need a partial rest in between, but Aria promised to help me, so bring it the fuck on."

An appreciative smirk rests on Aria's face as the three around me have a silent conversation with each other, the type that shows they have been together for a long time. All I can see from it, is a bunch of eyebrow raises and some lip quirks, so I don't have a clue.

"Alright, Feisty," Zeke grins, using that damn name again. "Let's get you cleaned up and then we'll see what you're really made of. After all, we only have one night here, so better make it worthwhile. Am I right, Zane?" I don't have time to pay the gnawing twisting in my gut any mind as Zeke leans over and whips my feet down the bed. I topple off the mattress, landing hard on the ground as hands then hoist me upright. Pointing towards a closed door, I'm surprised to find Zeke following close behind, leaning over my shoulder to push the door wide. A bathroom sits on the other side, gleaming from floor to ceiling with polished marble walls and a jacuzzi tub to die for. I can't let my elation run away with me though, as Zeke pushes his way in first and digs some travel-sized toiletries out of a drawer beneath the basin.

"What a gent," I sark, letting my inner bitch come out to play. He tosses the toiletries onto the shower floor and straightens to slam the door closed behind me. I manage to just about conceal my flinch, but nothing can hide my widened eyes as he crowds my space against the wood.

"Is that what you think I am, a gent?" Zeke breathes into my ear, eliciting a full body shiver. "Would a gentleman do this?" His hand snakes around my hips, sliding between my ass cheeks for his thumb to rest over my back hole. Applying pressure, I suck in a breath, chewing on my lower lip to hold my nerve. His other hand pinches and twists my nipple, sending my back into a full arch.

"Answer me," he growls.

"N-no."

"No, *what?* I think I'm going to give you a name for me. You can either call me Sir, Master or Daddy. What will it be?"

He pressed against my hole again, his thumb breaching my barrier and I let out an embarrassingly guttural moan. I should be clawing at his eyes to let me free, but I'm curious about this new side to me. I want, no - I *need* to know how far I'll go. How far the three of them can take me.

"Well? I suggest you choose now before I pick one for you. That's how much of a *gent* I am."

"Uh," I reply, not able to form any coherent thought. To be honest I don't want to call him any of them, but the pleasure dawning on me is too intense to care. Zeke chuckles, deep and low in the chest that comes to rest against my cheek. "Daddy it is. Call me anything else and I will deny your orgasm. Not a punishment worth receiving unless that's your kink." Lifting my legs around his waist, his dick already hard again and sliding against the slick folds of my pussy. Teasing my opening, his blue eyes drink in my conflicting expressions. "I want your cunt to milk me dry."

"Yes," I breathe, needing an end to this pleasure/pain he's building in me. I need his dick to ease the pressure building in my back passage and there's no fucks left to give over the fact I met him so recently.

"Yes, what?" he purrs knowing I'm unraveling.

"Please," I reply instead, still not able to call him what he's asked for even though I might go insane if he's not in me in the next five seconds. To my horror, Zeke immediately backs off, leaving me shrouded in a layer of cold rejection.

"Didn't you hear what I said? Pick your punishments wisely. Why suffer more than we're going to make you anyway?" He warns. I run my tongue over my lips and his eyes track the movement with keen interest. This guy wants me. Like, he fucking wants me even though there's a hundred hot girls on the other side of this wall, wishing they could be toyed with by an Adonis tonight. And fuck, I'm one hundred percent in vindictive rebound mode.

In one fluid movement, his arm whips around my waist and he lifts me clean off the floor. The blunt head of his dick knocks against me with each step until I'm lowered in the shower, his eyes darkening. "Let's try that again, shall we?" he purrs, turning the water on. I gasp as icy cold water beats down my head and back, snatching the breath from my lungs.

"Whoops." Zeke sounds anything but fucking sorry as he closes the door behind him, trapping us both between the glass walls. "I forgot to mention that I used all the hot water earlier. So, a cold one it is."

Spinning me, Zeke shoves me forward against the only tiled side, my breasts and stomach pressed against them with his chest at my back. "Remember, if you're ready for me to finish you off, you know what to call me." Without so much as a warning, his rock-hard cock slams into my pussy from behind and a breathy scream rips out of my throat. His pace is relentless as he takes what he wants and I'm just along for the ride.

The tiles squeak with the sound of my body rubbing against them, as well as the slapping of flesh causing my pussy to clench in anticipation. Sensing how close I am, Zeke doesn't even slow before fully pulling out.

"No, please," I gasp, wiggling my ass to get him to continue, but when I glance at him desperately over my shoulder, he's regarding me coolly, stroking his impressive length.

"Say it."

I really don't want to, and I wriggle again with a whimper.

"Say it." he repeats.

Fuck this. I lower my fingers to play with myself, but he grips both my wrists and slams them above my head.

"Say. it."

Fine. Fine. "Please fuck me...*Daddy*," I plead, a piece of my soul dying in that moment. I receive no reply, his dick seeking out my uterus in one, brutal thrust. Holding me up with his punishing grip on my wrists, Zeke takes no prisoners, fucking me senseless in the best hate sex of my life. I am completely lost, overwhelmed by the realization that, for this single moment, he owns me in all the ways I never wanted but has ruined me for all future encounters. My mewls can be heard echoing through the reverberation of the shower, the water not even seeming cold anymore. Not when my skin is burning, my pussy on fire with the impending orgasm he's forcing from me. All the while, Zeke retains his composure, leaning down for his hot breath to flutter in my ear.

"You fucking love this, don't you Feisty?" he mutters between my desperate pants. "I can feel your soaking pussy grabbing for me. That greedy cunt can take all of me, so it's only fair I take *everything* from you."

I didn't think I liked dirty talk, but we can go ahead and

scratch that one from the record. More likely, the key is in finding the right voice. One that creates an artform from vulgar words and ups my temperature with a mere throaty whisper. I also thought I was happy being vanilla, viewing sex as more of a chore on my to-do list. Up until these three sex-craved lunatics decided to show me there's pleasure in being played with. I already know, even now, tonight will change me. I just don't know if it's for better or worse.

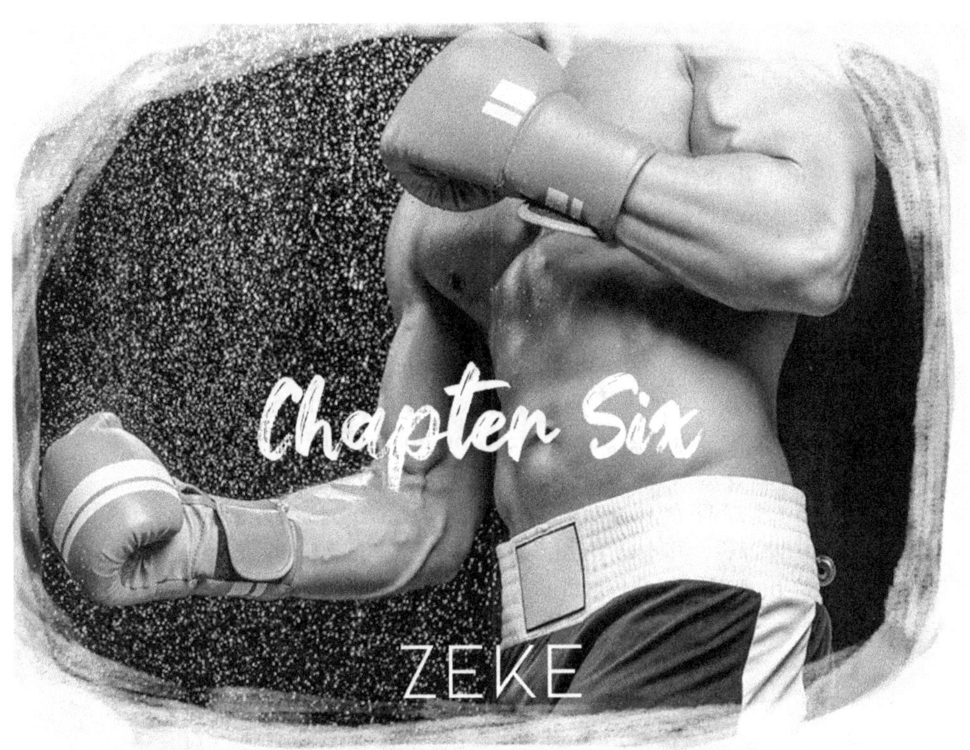

I waltz out of the bathroom with a towel around my neck and nothing else. Aria tries to pretend she finds the thick shaft swinging between my legs disgusting, but I'm not buying it. My best asset is far too plump and long not to sway even the butchest of lesbians. I'm bigger than and veinier than the whole array of dildos she keeps stashed in her bedside table, and why opt for silicone when the real deal is right here? I mean…there is the argument that we're closer than siblings, but I wouldn't turn Zane down if he wanted a reason to wipe that scowl from his face. It's there so often, it might as well be tattooed on. Dropping down on the spanking bench at his side, my damp shoulder bumps him, and he shoves me right back.

"You killed her off yet?" he asks, and I scowl. I'm solidly on Aria's side of this debate - that girl curled up on the shower floor is made of tougher stuff. Zane's just so used to being let down, he's given up on anyone and anything.

"Just limbering her up, *brother*," I say in mockery. Zane studies me closely, then rolls his eyes and pinches the bridge of his nose.

"You made her call you Daddy, didn't you?" My chuckle is my answer, and he groans again. "Maddox isn't going to like any of this." I shrug, whipping the towel out from behind my shoulders to roughly dry off. Aria opens the bottom drawer of the dresser, fishing out a lacey number with the tags still attached. Ooh, a new one. Slipping into the bathroom, a round of protests blares through the crack in the door and I jump up to go witness the cat fight. Zane slaps his hand down on my thigh, pushing me back down and ripping the towel from my hand to cover my cock.

"You should let loose, use her to blow off some steam," I tell him for what must be the hundred-millionth time. No exaggeration. There's a reason I'm labeled the 'fun one,' even if I'm the only one who says that.

"You know I can't. I don't want that blood on my hands." It's my turn to groan at Zane's seriousness. All. The. Damn. Time. Talk about draining the life out of someone. "Besides, we need to press pause on…whatever this is. We came here for a reason, remember?" Zane reaches up and flicks my temple as if that'll spark me back into menacing mode. It's not too far from Lust Avenue so with a disgruntled growl in the back of my throat, I grab the clothes he's collected and folded for me. Holding Zane's eye, I aggressively shove my legs into my black shorts and drag his electric blue sports tee on, leaving my hair a ruffled mess.

"Don't be long boys," Aria singsongs, poking her head around the bathroom door. She smirks widely, the menacing edge betraying the devil living just beneath the surface. "Or Harlow might be all spent by the time you get back." I fight against Zane as he roughly shoves me out of the door.

"How come Aria gets to stay?" I whine, flopping into the

hallway and spinning on Zane as he blocks the doorway. He's giving me that *don't-give-me-shit* stare and I sigh heavily. With a flick of my wrist, I gesture for him to lead the way and follow behind like an abused puppy. We leave the dimmed lights of level six's seedy hallway behind, along with the cries of punishment or moans of immense pleasure. There are many reasons people like us need a place like this to vent under the safety net of an NDA. The shit that goes down here is beyond illegal and most of the time, non-consensual.

Another pair of fighters are announced into the caged fighting ring, the crowd clearly favoring a caveman with more beard than sense. He bashes into the doorway as if he's blind or maybe just blind drunk and I know who my money's on. The much leaner, yet much more sober man opposite with sniper sharp eyes and a nasty scar across his chest. Yeah, that guys like a cockroach - he'll survive anything. Shoving a wad of cash into the bookie's hand on my way past, Zane growls and grabs the back of my shirt.

"Stop fucking around. We came for one reason only, these distractions are -"

"Distracting?" I finish for him, a knowing grin on my face. Zane needs to lighten up and live for once. Not everything is about obeying rules and reporting back to our master. Twisting out of his grip on my collar, I throw an arm over his shoulder and stick my leg out to trip a nearby waitress. Relieving her of the tray of shots in her hand as she falls face-first on the ground, I offer Zane a drink which he rudely shoves away. "You wanna know what I think?"

"Not particularly," Zane grumbles and he's already moving away. I dump the tray into some chick's hands, taking two shots and clinking them together. One I down and the other I tip into her willing mouth. Winking, I race off to catch up with the broody asshole I've spent my entire life with. "I think you need to get laid, and there's a bitch in need of threshold training currently in Aria's arms."

"Threshold training," he grunts under his breath. That's what we used to call it. Punching each other in the nose in turn until one of us gave in and cried. Mind you, we were eight years old, but it was a smooth progression from there into how fast we could recover from a dick-kick and keep fighting. Pain threshold training, what any orphaned boys with no way out do after light's out. Granted, Aria was there in the lower bunk, cursing us out until she joined in and started showing us up ever since.

Moving through the crowd with my shoulders squared, because fuck anyone who doesn't move out of the way, I catch up to Zane's side. Leaving the main fighting area and bar behind, we step into a hallway mirror imaging the one on the far side where we have ventured from. This hallway, however, has a neon sign above the threshold displaying the word 'Punishment' in blood-red. If Harlow thinks her end of the deal is bad, she doesn't want to see what's behind the ten doors splayed out before us. Zane checks his phone, re-reading a text sent from one of his spies on the staffing team. More than likely the same spotty kid who snuck us in here and is definitely losing his job at the end of the night, or worse. I hope the $5K and kilo of weed we handed him was worth it.

"Room seven," Zane says, and I laugh at the irony. What idiot would walk into room seven in a club based on the seven deadly sins? Us apparently, as Zane strolls right up to the door and kicks it in. I step in behind him and twizzle the doorknob to prove it was in fact unlocked and he shoots me a side deathglare. Yet my attention is solely focused on the strangely intriguing sight before us.

A naked red bulb hangs in the center of the room, highlighting the textured wallpaper that looks like crocodile skin. Objects hang from the left wall on large chrome hooks. Where there would have been feathered floggers and leather paddles over in Pleasure, Punishment calls for a more workshop vibe. Chainsaws, grinders, bolt cutters, you name it, we've got it. The floor has been left with a simple coat of shiny resin, a wide drain in the center for easy clean up. Fuck, I'd hate to be the cleaner in here after a lock-in.

Our mark, who is conveniently called Mark, is locked in an upright cage stretching from floor to ceiling and facing the back of the room. His hands are cuffed to either side, his clothes torn with lacerations and a terrified shrill to his voice.

"What's happening?" He doesn't receive an answer from us, or the guy we'd paid to drag him here. Although 'guy' may be simplifying the menace of a man we spotted in the alley outside and knew exactly which floor he had been invited to. Easily 6ft 5, his biceps are bigger than my head, his permanently embedded scowl could make grown adults cry. At our cue, he nods and leaves, not giving one shit that he's wearing a butcher's apron or has an axe clenched in his hand. He's out for death and may the devil hath mercy on whatever mangled soul will be gracing the doorstep of hell tonight.

Zane quickly grabs a pair of masks for us while I give the axe murderer a wave and close the door between us. That's the funny thing about money, it's a universal language and those with it remain invincible. But to have it, we need to put snitches in their place before our entire business goes ka-blooey.

"Hello Weasel," Zane drawls the name only the Bloodied Skulls call him by, his voice distorted by the changer box inside the mask. Rounding the cage, the man inside tenses and a wet patch immediately dampens his crotch.

"Good to know our presence is more terrifying than a human butcher," I chuckle beneath mine, strolling around the other side. Cracking my neck side to side, I take a moment to stare upon the man that had the balls to betray us. I'm equally impressed as pissed to all hell that this rat thought he could fool us.

"N-n-no, fellas, you don't understand," Mark the Weasel stutters but Zane grabs a metal bat and slams it into the bars.

"We understand just fine. You were given a job, and you gave away our position to the Crimson Wolves. I'm beginning to think you were running with them the entire time."

"I wouldn't, I never -." This time Zane slams the bat against the hand draped over the outside of the cage and Mark howls. The crunch of his knuckles sends a shudder through me, straight to my dick. Beneath the black skull mask, I briefly close my eyes and relish the anticipation of an impending death. My blood ignites with the intoxicating darkness I thrive on.

Crossing over to the wall of instruments, I trail my fingers lightly over Zane's shoulder blades as I pass, and he can't hide the resulting shiver. We're the same deep down, two sides of the same tarnished coin, even if he hides it better beneath his macho scowl and bitter outlook on life.

Drumming my fingers over the head of a hammer, my blue eyes catch the glint of a wrench and I smile. A cruel, malicious smile that stretches within the confines of the mask. Heaving it into my hand, I slap the wrench against my palm. Once, twice, then I slam it down on the padlock holding the cage closed, even though the key was hanging beside it. Taunting a tethered dead man with the key so close to the lock was a touch I appreciated enough to make a mental note to tip our butcher.

Zane takes my lead, grabbing a leather belt. I enter the cage, closing the door behind me so my chest is shoved in Weasel's face. Sweat beads from his pasty brow, the very one Zane loops the belt around from behind and leashes his head back and immobile against the bars.

"Whether you're a runner or a big dog, loyalty is every-thing," I lean down slightly to growl beside his ear. "You bit the hand that fed you, now you'll lose every tooth in your traitorous mouth." His scream of fear is quickly replaced by agony as I yank his teeth out one by one, starting with the bottoms. Each one I pluck out goes onto a dish Zane supplies for me, leaning on the outside of the cage like he's bored. He'll get his turn, after I'm done collecting commission for the tooth fairy. That fluttery little bitch has never come for me, but maybe she prefers the pearly whites of a traitor.

At one point, his wails lessen, and I give him a sharp slap to wake him back up. This pussy sold us out to our enemies. He's the reason Maddox is currently standing in the charred remains of the gym we built as our home, hunting for our missing members amongst the ashes. The least Weasel can do is remain awake while we murder him painfully and slowly. His wisdom teeth are stubborn little fuckers and draw out a gurgle of pooled blood, right before Weasel chokes and coughs all over me. Splashes of deep red spray across my front and a moment of shocked tension passes between the three of us.

"Tap out," Zane orders, opening the cage at my back. My chest heaves, the audacity of this fuckface to coat me in his lying blood. A haze covers my vision, blurring the figure through the eye holes of the mask. I'm going to kill him. Right now. A hand lands on my shoulder and I shrug Zane off. Raising the wrench with every intention to bash Weasel's head in, the press of a firm chest crowds against my back.

"Zeke," Zane whispers in my ear. His arm slides around my blooded front and he eases me back out of the cage. I lean into him, ignoring the strained side eyes Weasel is giving us. His toothless mouth is hanging open, oozing streams of crimson that join the tears leaking down his cheeks and drip from his jaw. "Take a breather and let me have a turn. You'll only get frustrated if we end this too quickly." I exhale deeply, taking an extra moment to feel his warmth against me. Not in a sexual way, but as boys who would huddle together on cold nights, the lines became blurred so long ago, they're not even straight anymore. They're zigzagged, warped and do a loop-the-loop every so often.

Taking Zane's advice, I move over to sit on a metal chair in the corner. It has a frame to support the vice overhead and cuffs attached to the arms and legs. Zane's shoulders rise and fall heavily as he steels himself. A man created of hatred and the need for revenge on a world that forgot him. The muscles of his shoulder blades bunch, his tattooed arm rearing back as he slides a knife into Weasel's side as smoothly as butter.

Wrapping a hand around his prisoner's throat, I shift at the dominating display of power and rearrange my crotch. Every well-orchestrated scream pulses through me, each slice of the blade hitching my breath as if it were plunging into me. My fingers trail beneath my tank, brushing over the healed scars lining my torso with a shiver of satisfaction. We didn't lie to Harlow - there is pleasure to be found in pain. You just need to have the balls to try it.

"No. Absolutely fucking not," I hiss at Aria who's holding up a scrap of lace with a shit-eating grin. My venom does nothing to deter her. No, instead the sensual-bitch grins even wider. "I mean it."

"Oh, come on Killer," she drawls, slinking towards me. "This is all part of your training and besides, it's cute you think there is a choice in the matter." She takes another menacing step closer into the bathroom, reaching where my legs are dangling over the counter. I can't deny it is beautiful and unlike anything I've ever seen before, but I have an issue with being dressed up like a pretty doll for someone else's amusement. Especially for an asshole like Zane. To be honest, the issue may lay more with taking orders in general. "After all, you did agree to this the minute you stepped into Wrath," Aria signs sweetly.

Did I though? Did I really agree to this shit? My brain laughs mockingly at me, the darkness chuckling it's far too late to back out now. The minute they feasted on me like I was their favorite meal, I was done for. But somehow, this lacey outfit has my hackles rising, pushing it to another level. I don't care about being fully exposed, but some repressed memories I didn't realize I was holding onto, of my stepfather picking out my outfits, have just been triggered. My stupid moral compass is so off, it's a joke.

Aria steps in between my legs, and my breathing hitches when her fingers trail up the inside of my thigh. I'm still swollen and sore from Zeke taking me, not that I would tell him how much I enjoyed it, but they kindly decided to give me a break and to let my poor pussy recover. Laying the outfit over the marbled countertop at my side, she whips those green eyes on me and tucks the damp hair behind my ear.

"Zeke was right earlier, but I'll kill you if you tell him I said that. We do only have one night here, and then our paths may never meet again. Do you really want to leave in the morning with regrets of what could have been?" Swallowing thickly, I'm surprised to find my head leaning into the feel of her hand. Shit, I'm in too deep and I know it.

"Ugh, fine." I relent, holding my hand out for her to lift and drape the garment over it. The least I can do is retain some degree of control by not playing fetch every time they throw a stick. The lace touches my skin, sending a shudder rolling through me. Aiding me down from the countertop, Aria twirls my hair around her wrist to keep it out of the way while I shimmy into the outfit. Despite the appearance of the material embedded with diamantes, it's not itchy at all. In fact, it smooths over my body like it was made for me, hugging every curve of my figure.

Gliding it up to my neck, Aria releases my hair to ease an invisible zip up over my hip. The gray dress has a high slit all the way to my hip, exposing the lack of underwear beneath. Clinging to my mid-section, the lace opens up in a love heart to reveal my cleavage, although the see-through material highlights my nipples anyway. The back is non-existent from ass crack to nape, and at the front of my neck, the diamonds form a studded collar with a metal ring attached to my throat.

Aria gives a low whistle, turning me to look at myself in the mirror. My chest is flushed, my cheeks pinched and purple bruising is setting in from the fight. Yet I've never seen myself so exposed, so raw, so alive. Repeating the braid in my vibrant red hair, after I took it out to shower, her fingers stroke me every chance she gets. And her eyes, those wells of pure green that feast on me with pleasurable intent, I can't deny the flutters she's making me feel. With her hands on my shoulders, she glides me backwards into the bedroom where a pair of glamorous heels are waiting on the ottoman. Or maybe it's some type of bend-and-fuck horse, I can't be sure.

"Oh man, I really can't walk in heels" I start but Aria places her lips over mine, canceling out my words. Unlike Zeke's roughness, she kisses me gently, bringing my dulled senses to life with a simple sweep of her tongue. It feels naughty, forbidden, to be kissing her back with the same intrigue but damn if it doesn't feel right.

"I want you to look a million dollars for when I parade you through the club," Aria smiles when we part. Wait, what? I swallow my protest, already knowing this is another battle I won't win tonight. Instead, I should relent and enjoy it because like she said - it's one night and then I'll never see them again.

Gently pushing me to sit, she takes care to buckle the heels onto my feet before telling me she'll be right back. I sit there, testing the stability of the ultra-skinny heels when the metal hoop at my neck is tugged on and I find Aria there, gripping the leash now attached to my collar. And just like that, the kind familiarity I'd quickly grown accustomed to has vanished. In its place, she stands tall in a mini dress, those green orbs piercing with me the challenge to fight against her.

"Look, I'm really not comfortable" I start, but her phone ringing cuts me off. She declines the call, until a text comes through which she reads with a furrowed brow. Tucking it back into a concealed pocket, Aria regards me with an icy coolness.

"Comfort is for the feeble. You wanna be a sex goddess with men falling at your feet, or a little old woman in a suede recliner covered in cat hair?" I don't get a second to contemplate an answer to that as Aria tucks on my leash and I rise on wobbly feet. Guiding me towards the door, she doesn't even look back to check I'm okay and I frown at the rigidness of her posture.

The club appears twice as busy as it was when I foolishly stepped into the ring. Just the thought of it makes me cringe, how I was so naïve to think one decent knee to the balls is all that mountain man needed and I might have had the chance at coming out victorious.

Despite the fight taking place in the central cage, it only takes one guy to spot me dressed like a high-class whore on a leash, nudging his friend to look and a ripple effect happens before my eyes. Heads turn, eyebrows raise and tongues lolling from the men's mouths. More interestingly, the women pay me no notice. Where I'd expected their bitchy, judgmental looks, there's a hint of understanding that shows how common such an event like this is on floor Wrath. At least that gives me the slightest bit of ease, but as the men leer, I glue my gaze to the floor. Just putting one heel in front of the other is hard enough, especially with each tug Aria gives the leash, threatening to topple me over.

Leading me through the crowd with confident struts, the sway of glittery material hugging Aria's ass demands my attention. How is it fair for one woman to look so good in a tiny dress, as much as she does in the baggy sports attire, I first saw her in? In just an hour or so, this minx has opened me up to so many possibilities I hadn't even considered before, and apparently staring at her ass is one of them.

The onlookers shift aside, allowing us entry as Aria comes to a stop before a cordoned off area. It's visible to those all around, but no one has passed the ring of red rope surrounding a low, suede booth. Clicking her fingers high in the air, the sharpness of the sound catching the attention of multiple burly guys, they rush forward to remove the red rope, and two even dispose of the central table, carrying it away. That just leaves the red, curved sofa, and me standing with a frown on my face. Aria brought me out here just to sit and be gawked at? But when she tugs me forward again, it's only Aria that sits down and snaps her fingers again.

"Kneel, Killer," she orders. There's a slight smirk on her pretty face, giving it the harshened cruelty, I feel is part of her split-personality disorder. When I don't immediately obey, the crowd begin to heckle me, telling me to do as I'm told *or else.* Making sure Aria gets the full view of my pissed-off expression, I reluctantly lower to my knees. The carpet is surprisingly plush, but it doesn't make the excited mutters of me being a good whore any easier to digest.

Waiting for my next *instruction,* because apparently that's what I abide by - for tonight at least, Aria lazily lets her legs fall wide open. She's completely bare beneath the mini dress, her pussy right there for everyone to see and not a trace of embarrassment to be seen. Damn, I must commend her for her confidence, but the gaze from her half-lidded eyes instantly fills me with dread.

"Come on Puddy Tat, start licking and you might find some cream." My entire body freezes. No, no. Fuck no. Moving to stand, the same dickhead from before slams his hands down on my shoulders, pinning me in place. I wriggle, demanding he release me, but I have no power here. I'm an innocent mouse who's willingly walked into the jaws of a lion and thought I'd survive. The audience picks up a lovely chant from someone, one that has Aria throwing her head back on a wicked laugh.

'Eat. Her. Out.' My skin burns with the flush that coats my chest, my heart beating tenfold in my chest. I didn't ask for this, for any of it. I just wanted…to escape, to prove to Ricky I'm just as deserving of illusive invitations as his cheating ass is. Would he have met a girl here and taken her into one of the pleasure suites. Hell, maybe that was who invited him in the first place and my eyes scan the crowd for a clue of who she might be. Not that I'd have recognized anyone through the masses of face. Some with dried blood coating their noses, some with mascara running the lengths of their chests and no intention to wipe it off.

But if she is out there, I can't have her running back to Ricky and telling her what a pussy I was. Imagining them having a good laugh about it makes my blood boil for a whole different reason than embarrassment and I roughly shrug the guy's meaty hands from my shoulders.

"I don't really know…how," I mutter under the elated roar of the crowd as I scoot closer on my knees. Aria hears me though and sits forward to take my chin in her hand.

"It's easier than you think. Start with what you like, judge my reactions and go from there. But plenty of this will do just fine." Her tongue snakes out, flicking back and forth over the plumpest part of my upper lip and a loud wolf whistle pierces the crowd. Shifting the hand cupping my chin to the top of my head, Aria applies enough pressure for me to take the hint and lower my face between her thighs. Here goes nothing.

The first lick I cringe at, expecting to feel as nauseous as the first time I tried oysters. I say first time, but there was never another. But Aria's perfectly waxed pussy is soft beneath my tongue, the ridges and curves creating a sensation I've never known. And when I flick my tongue over her hooded clit, her sharp intake of breath fills me with the weirdest notion. Acceptance maybe, excitement definitely. Inhibitions forgotten and spurred on by the whooping and cheering, I lick the length of Aria's slit, nudging at her clit with my nose. Again and again, I drag my tongue across her, relishing the soft moans and feminine hand that becomes fisted in my braid. Her juices coat my lips and I pause to savor the taste of her. Of what I'm doing to her. As my confidence grows, my speed increases and soon, her clit is in my mouth. Sucking her bud, the hint of a satisfied smile pulls at my lips at Aria's elongated groan and the crowd goes nuts.

This isn't demeaning, it's exhilarating. Where I thought Aria was forcing my hand, she was giving me control. Of her body, of what I do with it and just like Zeke did to me in the shower, I'm going to make her suffer.

I've always wanted a pet. And watching Harlow thrive on the end of a leash, utterly at my command, is beyond the connection I expected. A dog can lick your face, a cat can mewl in your ear. But it occurs to me, I could have a bitch of my very own to lick wherever and whenever I order her to, and moan on demand. This is quickly escalating beyond an order to find a fourth and into something darker. Need burns deep inside which I yearn to fulfil, yet for once, I don't think bathing in the blood of our enemies will suffice.

Withdrawing myself a few steps from where Harlow is now

reclined in the booth with a large wine glass in hand, I catch Zeke's eye through the crowd and beckon him over. "Here, hold this. I'll be right back." Without waiting for his reply, or question whose blood is coating the side of his neck and disappearing beneath a clean shirt, I weave through Harlow's audience. The fight in the ring has been forgotten, much to some steroid-induced asshole's disapproval. He slams his fists into the cage instead of his opponent, shaking the metal so it rings out over the club's playlist. Billie Eilish is currently streaming from the speakers which grows louder as I descend on the bar and plant my ass on a leather stool.

"Must be a long night for someone like you," the bartender smiles in a way I think is supposed to be genuine. In fact, as he leans his forearms on the polished surface and purposely brushes my hand with his manicured fingers, I reckon it was his attempt at flirting. "Did you come here with anyone, or are you hunting for a big, tough man to take home in the morning?" I plaster on my coyest smile and flutter my eyelashes in a way that makes my stomach roll.

"You know, I was looking for a big, tough man," I slide my hands over the backs of his, feeling not a single callous on his knuckles. I don't care how long the beard on his chin is this dick is just a baby in fighting terms. Lacing his own fingers together, I give no warning in throwing his forearms upwards. His knuckles are instantly bloodied with a nasty crunch from his nose, and I smear the blood over my palms before doing it again. Dude doesn't learn.

"Why are you hitting yourself?" I mock. Pushing up on the bar, I whip my leg around and catch his temple hard, causing him to collapse. Dropping on the server's side of the bar, I cup my mouth and make the caw of a deranged eagle. "Free drink for the first to take it from me!" A waitress returning her empty tray hesitates, her wide eyes looking for backup and finding none.

"Problem?" I ask sweetly, leaning on my hand. The guy at my feet groans and I kick him to shut up. Shaking her pretty little head, the waitress smartly bolts as Wrath's finest thunders over. A true game of survival plays out before me, the dominance of these alpha-holes shoving and beating on each other for the outstretched beer in my hands first proving more comical than expected.

The victor throws himself at the bar, reaching for the glass bottle when I whip it back. With him watching the bob of my throat, I down the entire bottle before smashing it against his head. The others with more muscle than sense wisely back away, catching a glimpse of the crazed look in my green eyes. I shiver as the demon inside I temporarily lost wrapped up in the throes of Harlow's climax resurfaces.

"Huh, maybe I don't need a big, tough man after all," I comment to my friend on the floor. I can't tell if he has fallen unconscious or is just pretending, yet as I see streams of security exit the elevator, I don't wait around to find out. Grabbing another beer, I vault over the bar and slip through the crowd, heading back the way I came. Not even Zeke senses me as I sneak up on him and snatch the leash from his grasp.

"We've got company," I cut off any argument I sense him about to give. Zane is over his shoulder in a second, his head extending to look over the club like a meerkat.

"Time to go," he agrees and steps in to hoist a protesting Harlow into his arms. I snatch a hold of her leash for some reason I can't quite understand, following close as Zeke takes up the rear. Bending low, we round the fighting cage, which is now back in full swing and surprise, surprise, it's the meathead with shards of a beer glass in his temple currently winning. Maybe I didn't give him enough credit but if I want to stay on top, I have to be the victor in my own game at all times.

When looking at the blueprints for this place and working out our best way in, I pointedly decided the layout was similar to a jellyfish. The bar, seating areas and fighting cage sit comfortably in a wide oval, with the Pleasure and Punishment rooms branching off like tendrils. In the middle of those two is the hallway to the elevator shaft and the route we're heading in, to the security hub. Mirrored doors that the security team hide behind - not wanting to interfere in the whole point of Wrath and its lawless allure, but to oversee surveillance just in case of a whole floor massacre or for break ins, like us.

Edging along the wall below the moving camera overhead, darting aside when it suddenly changes direction, Zane leads us to the office through the last door on the right. The one reserved for when the club's owner is around and luckily for us, intel says he's on a different level tonight. Pulling a pin from its safe place, concealed beneath my hair, I duck into Zane's shadow, making quick work of the lock. Zeke's hushed voice is already speaking into the phone between his shoulder and ear as I shove the door open, activating the beep of an impending alarm.

"Alright T, I'm in," Zeke says, his attention centered on the keypad just inside the door. I close us in while his fingers fly over the keys with the number sequences being relayed down the phone. By the time the beeping cuts out, proving the alarm system is successfully disabled, we have another sound to contend with. Harlow's screaming.

"What the fuck are you doing?! Get off me!" I spin and then smirk, watching Zane try to strap her flailing limbs to a bondage chair in the corner. It's the only item out of place in the otherwise deluxe office, although it ties into the color scheme nicely. Stitched with blue leather, the chair has a V which Zeke moves in to buckle Harlow's thighs to. Zane grabs her wrists, fastening them into thick handcuffs and then pulls a metal chain to have her arms shooting up above her head. "When I get out of here, I'm gonna -" Zane shoves the attached ball gag into her mouth, his posture bristling with irritation.

"Aww, I wanted to hear what she was gonna do to us," Zeke pouts, running his knuckles over her cheek. I push my butt up onto the central desk, giving Harlow a fantastic view of my bare pussy to remind her of our wicked fun outside. Following a snap of Zane's fingers, Zeke rolls his eyes and moves to drop in the leather chair behind me. Powering up the laptop sitting on the mahogany wood, Zeke yanks out the phone from his pocket which he didn't hang up, talking our boss through hacking the security system from outside of Rapture. Being our resident tech-genius, it isn't long before Zeke's worked out the password and pushed in a USB to start uploading top-secret files. Just the latest heist in a long line we've been given.

"What were you thinking?" Zane hisses in my general direction and I roll my eyes, wondering how long that'd take. "Showing off, gaining everyone's attention. It only takes one photo or person to relay our descriptions to our rivals and we're fucked."

"Good thing the NDAs at Rapture forbid the use of cell phones or permit any information being spoken about tonight. More fool them if they want their heads caved in," I bob an eyebrow at Harlow. The lack in security present tonight has no relation to the squads of military equivalents that stalk each and every attendee after the night is over. Their phones are hacked, socials watched; not an email is sent, or call made without Rapture knowing about it. Hence, since we're not on their list, we're untraceable. Like a whisper in the night, gone before you fully wake.

Zeke announces he's done with the cell, passing it over to Zane. The screen shows the call is currently muted so Zane exhales and paces while he thinks.

"Wearing a hole into the carpet counts as leaving evidence," I smirk, kicking my legs beneath the desk. I get the response I wanted – the vein in Zane's temple throbs and he glares his auburn eyes my way with murderous intent. I'd like to see him try.

"I'm trying to figure out what we tell Maddox," he slides his gaze towards Harlow. "He doesn't need to know about the fucking mess you've both gotten us into, but we'll need his help to escape without being noticed. Who knows when we might need to come back to hunt down another rat," he shrugs, and I tut loudly.

"Always need your hand held. Maybe stop worrying about kissing ass and start coming up with an escape plan of your own. That'd be a better way to catch his attention. Or you know - you could just suck his dick off and get it over with."

"Oooh, me first!" Zeke shoots around the desk, tugging his shorts down to flop his semi-erection around. Harlow's amber eyes widen, flying to the growing shaft beside her face. I laugh, throwing a hefty paperweight at him. Instead of trying to catch it, Zeke twists out the way and whips Harlow around the face with his dick.

"Behave! Both of you," Zane growls. Rounding to check the laptop's screen, he throws his fists down on the wood either side. "We've been compromised and need to find a way out of here. As always, it's going to be down to me to save our asses." After cleaning the keyboard, riding Rapture of Zeke's prints, he lifts a magazine and smacks me around the head when Harlow makes a noise in her throat. Added to the eye roll and sag of her posture, I'm sure she tried to say similar to 'oh, for fuck's sake.'

"Got something to say there, Leech?" Zane growls, venom biting at his tone. Shadows darken his blue eyes, shifting them to deep navy that spirals with the promise of repercussions. Zeke pulls up his pants, stepping aside for Zane to approach, gripping the chain to pin Harlow's arms in place. With a sharp tug, Harlow's body jostles upwards, her breasts breaking free of the lacey dress' confines.

"Word of warning," Zane growls, getting right into Harlow's face. "You don't want to know me, and more importantly, you don't want to anger me. I can make you sorry you were ever born and pray for death." And just like that, Harlow rolls her eyes at him again and seals her fate. Zeke rushes to join my side of the desk, budging me along and interlinking his fingers tightly with mine. His body is brimming with bubbling excitement and as I meet his gaze, we both share a malicious smile. Fuck yes, this is going to be fun to watch.

My breath hitches at the feral expression on Zane's brutally gorgeous face. The ball gag stopped me from saying anything out loud, but it seems they understood my expressions perfectly. Zane's lip curls as he prowls closer to the chair and ignores Zeke's annoying squeals of excitement as he and Aria watch the proceedings.

I thrash against the restraints when Zane's fingers trail up my leg, achingly slow and pausing only when Aria's throaty laugh interrupts us.

"Do you need a big girl to show you how it's done?" she says huskily. Zane doesn't like that. Snatching the strap of the gag, Zane hoists my face an inch from his, the bite of leather cutting into my skin.

"I am going to teach you the art of accepting punishment. Lesson one, you'll not make a fucking sound. If you so much as breathe too loudly, I'll ensure you regret it." he murmurs in a deadly tone, deftly removing the gag with one hand.

"Why are we hiding in here?" I blurt, instantly defying him. Yet I had to ask what was weighing on my mind since being so unceremoniously dragged into here. My fingers pick at the blue stitching, the lace of the dress rubbing me in all the right ways. I've had fantasies of something similar, and with the right words I might be able to make them all come true. If only my mouth would get the memo.

Zeke clears his throat. "So–"

"Quiet." Zane snaps at his so-called brother. "She doesn't get to know the details. Maddox would–"

"Who's Maddox?" I interrupt, not giving any shits about the pure venom he's shooting my way. "Your owner? Guess I'm not the only one on a leash here," I strain my neck against the collar still wrapped around my neck. Just then, a thought comes to me, the pieces of Aria's words from earlier threading together.

"Wait, you guys aren't even meant to be here, are you? So that's it, you're just criminals?" *Just* criminals, I echo back in my head, as if that's not a hundred times worse. I'm completely at their mercy here and I don't know who they are or what they're capable of.

"You snuck in here too, Feisty. You're no better than us." Zeke gives me a crooked smile, despite the growl easing from Zane's throat as easily as a wild animal.

"I said, quiet," Zane growls, a deep rumble that does more to me than I care to admit. Power radiates from his broad shoulders, making me even more curious as to who this Maddox is. Zane doesn't seem like the kind of guy who would follow orders, but here we are. Once again, he runs his hands up my leg, but this time carries on so that he gently caresses my clit and I'm instantly wet.

"Oh, she wants this," Aria shuffles, flicking off Zeke's grip on her hand to rub herself against the desk.

"No, I don't want this," I lie, despite the evidence between my legs suggesting otherwise. Somehow pretending I'm not consenting makes this hotter, and boy does that mean I'm more fucked up than I realized.

"Yes, you really do," Zane's lip curls in the shadow of a malicious smile. "But I'm on a time restraint, so you'll take it and break for me without delay." Ordering me around like a dog, Zane produces a clit wand from his large shorts pocket. Huh, just carrying that around for when opportunity strikes? Snapping his fingers, Zeke is there in an instant, relieving him of the item. Switching it on, Zeke's blue eyes sparkle as he lowers the rounded head to my clit on a fierce setting.

"Hold it there," Zane demands between my shocked moans. Ripples of pleasure pulsate through me, from the tingling in my toes to the instant dizziness I gain from its intensity. In the brief second my eyes roll back, Zane gropes my breasts sharply in his large hands and I gasp upright. "I said, not a fucking sound," he grunts. Veins pop along his tense shoulders, the restraint hindering him from tearing me to shreds visibly crawling just beneath the surface. Releasing me on a huff, he strides away while I'm left to Zeke's mercy. Yet when he returns, Aria is by his side.

"Light," Zane barks, all three pairs of eyes centered on me. Looming like shadows of lust and longing, a darkened fantasy my mind wasn't able to conjure before tonight comes to life. Aria sparks a lighter in her hand, igniting the wick of a candle in Zane's. His lengthy digits curve around the thick shaft, drifting my thoughts elsewhere with the mix of vibrations owning my being.

Heat sizzles at my collarbone, Zane having dripped the burning wax onto my skin as I fade in and out of the present. Pooling along the bone, he continues to let it drip as the wax rolls down my cleavage. The curl of heated pain caresses me before Aria's knuckles brush over my tightened nipples and I'm lost.

Head dropped back against the chains holding my arms upright, surrendering to the sensations. The stirrings of a climax I wish I could hold off starts to bubble in my core, proving just how weak I am. Furrowing my brow and pressing my lips together, I refuse to give in to them so easily. This is what they promised - a tutorial in enduring pain, turning it into pleasure but that's not where the lesson ends. The real skill to be learnt is biding my time, not giving into them too easily.

"Thought tonight would prove more fruitful than this," I toy with them, claiming back what little power I have left. They can have me, but they can't control my words. They can't force me to surrender as long as my smart mouth has my back.

"Well, you're not even meant to be here, are you, *Ricky?*" Zane spits, bringing the lit wick closer to my ribs. My body arches aside from the burn that graces my tight skin and a shocked gasp of air escapes my mouth. Zane chuckles, releasing me from any more damage, "For someone with a false invite and spunky attitude, I'd expected more."

Blowing out the flame, he steps into the V of the chair, hovering so close to me that I can feel his warmth emanating as he lowers his face and bites down hard on my neck. The sting of my skin snapping beneath his teeth draws a hiss from mine as I buck, struggling to be free. Tears pool in my eyes as I fight against what my head says is wrong and my body is flushed with what is oh-so-right.

Sucking on my neck like a damn vampire, Zane raises his head and seizes my mouth for the first time. Copper floods my tongue, powerful strokes of his laying claim to what I thought was mine. My own mouth, my body, my thoughts and fantasies. His mouth crashes over me like a tsunami, destroying anything in its wake. Without realizing it, my body has leaned into his until Aria is forced to stop her assault on my nipples and withdraw her talented hands. When Zane breaks away from my panting lips, his blue eyes have turned glacial.

"You're going to come around this candle, wishing it was my cock." Before I can question what he's talking about, a solid thrust of the candle enters my slick channel. At the same time, Zeke levels up the vibrator to max speed, jamming it hard against my clit so there's no escape. And worst of all, as Zane lords over me with a knowing tilt to his eyebrow, is that he holds the candle completely still, just out of reach of my G-spot. I roll my hips, bearing down in an effort to stroke that sweet precipice that will make me explode into a thousand pieces. I want it. I need it. Their lessons of endurance, the surprised satisfaction when I pass their tests. And whatever else they might open me up to after the fact.

"Always a tease," Aria comments, the soft chuckle to her tone spiraling into my ear canal. I can't tell where she is in the room now, and without the willpower to open my hooded eyes properly, it doesn't really matter. I can feel the burn of her eyes dragging across my body, watching the pretty show I'm putting on for her.

"No need to hold back," Zeke mutters and through my haze, I realize he's not talking to me. His tattooed, muscled arm is leaning over Zane's shoulders, the two of them like seeing double. "You have free rein to take her, brother. She's signed Rapture's NDA, nothing that happens here can come back to haunt you after sunrise."

"No, I didn't," I whisper through the throes of pleasure raking through me. I didn't even know I said it until the sudden pull of the candle and absence of the vibrator causes me to blink clearly. Blood leaks from the wound in my neck in a red river, mixing with the dried candle wax streaming down the center of my body. Everyone remains frozen, eyes widened like a snapshot of fear.

"When you received the invite," Aria steps forward with a low whisper. "When you RSVP'd, you filled out the questionnaire and NDA, right?" There's a soft plead in her words and despite the answer I wish I could give to finish off this impending orgasm, I slowly shake my head. The three turn so sharply, I flinch. In a three-way huddle, the rest of the candle's wax drips from Zane's grip onto the plush, red carpet.

"She knows our names and faces."

"She could ruin us."

"Sell us out," the hushed whispers come. I tilt my head, jerking against the chains.

"What? No, I wouldn't - I don't really give a shit who you guys are," I inject. But I do, I really do. I want to know everything about them - where they come from, what new experiences they can show me. Three pairs of eyes peer back, a final decision in their blue and green glazes. Without discussion, Zane retrieves the cell phone that was hooked up to the laptop while Zeke releases me from the handcuffs. My arms fall heavily as Aria's dainty hands massage my shoulders, her lips by my ear from behind.

"Very well, come with us. We're getting out of here." Zeke takes a strange amount of care to ease me up on wobbly heels and rearrange the lace dress over my swollen breasts. There's nothing to be done about the blood and wax on me, which holds Zane's gaze as he glides towards the door. A hint of red tinting his hardened lips does something weird to my insides, the knowledge he's still tasting my blood drawing a newfound desire from the depths of my tainted soul. Aria releases me from the leash and hooks her arm through mine as we leak from the room like a virus escaping its confines.

The hallway is just as quiet, set apart from the cries of joy in the main arena. The crowd is the perfect cover, swallows us whole as we make our way to the main door that holds the elevator shaft. All the while, I keep sharing a small smile with Aria at my side.

I know they're not *good* guys, not the type you can take home to mom on a Sunday or even tell your best friend about, but I want to stay with them. I want to know what their day-to-day looks like, and if this rush of exhilaration continues into whatever ordinary life is for them.

Hidden from view by a host of huge guys smeared in blood and bruises that I imagine are waiting for their next fight, the door is up ahead, flanked by a guard with a meaty taser on his hip. Almost in reach, despite the butterflies tussling around in my stomach, warning me once I cross that threshold with these three, nothing will ever be the same. And I'll take it. I'm bored of the mundane life I didn't realize I was trapped in. Zane and Zeke suddenly part then, taking one side each as Aria stands tall and walks me directly to the door. I suppose we're the distraction.

"Excuse me, *sir*," Aria bats her eyelashes sweetly. I smirk at her act, comparing her to a chameleon. "But this girl has been competing without an official invitation, nor has she signed the NDA." As soon as the words leave her mouth, her hip bumps me into the guard and I stagger into his hard chest. An arm bands around me, hoisting me off my feet when I scream, once again gaining the unwanted attention of the crowd. Their eyes assess me, completely ignoring the three smirks that slink into the masses to give me one last mocking smirk. Yeah, I was the distraction alright.

Struggling against the hold, I stomp a heel into the guard's shin and earn myself a taser to the side. The same one with a burn mark singed into the lace and a blister already bubbling at my ribs. The audience boo, shouting 'impostor' at me as I'm dragged through the main door, swallowed by darkness and shame. The door to the right of the elevator presents a row of holding cells and even though I thought it not possible, my humiliation seeps to a new level of rock-bottom.

Reaching around to cover myself as the guard shoves me into a cell and slams the gate closed, I sink onto the hard floor. Everything hurts, yet it's drowned out by the confusion of why I thought for a single second I could mean anything to them. The three devils that warped me into thinking I was something special. That I wasn't just one of many they use and abuse for their own satisfaction.

Yet, despite the numbness claiming my limbs, they have done one thing in my favor. A new burning of hatred seeps through my veins and a promise burns to life in my skull. I can't have been the first girl they've used in more ways than one, but I vow to be the last. They may have taught me to endure punishment, but they've also awakened a dark piece of my soul which refuses to simmer down. Straightening my spine, a cold sternness washes over my face while my lips move of their own accord, pledging to reap revenge on the three assholes I last watched disappearing into the crowd.

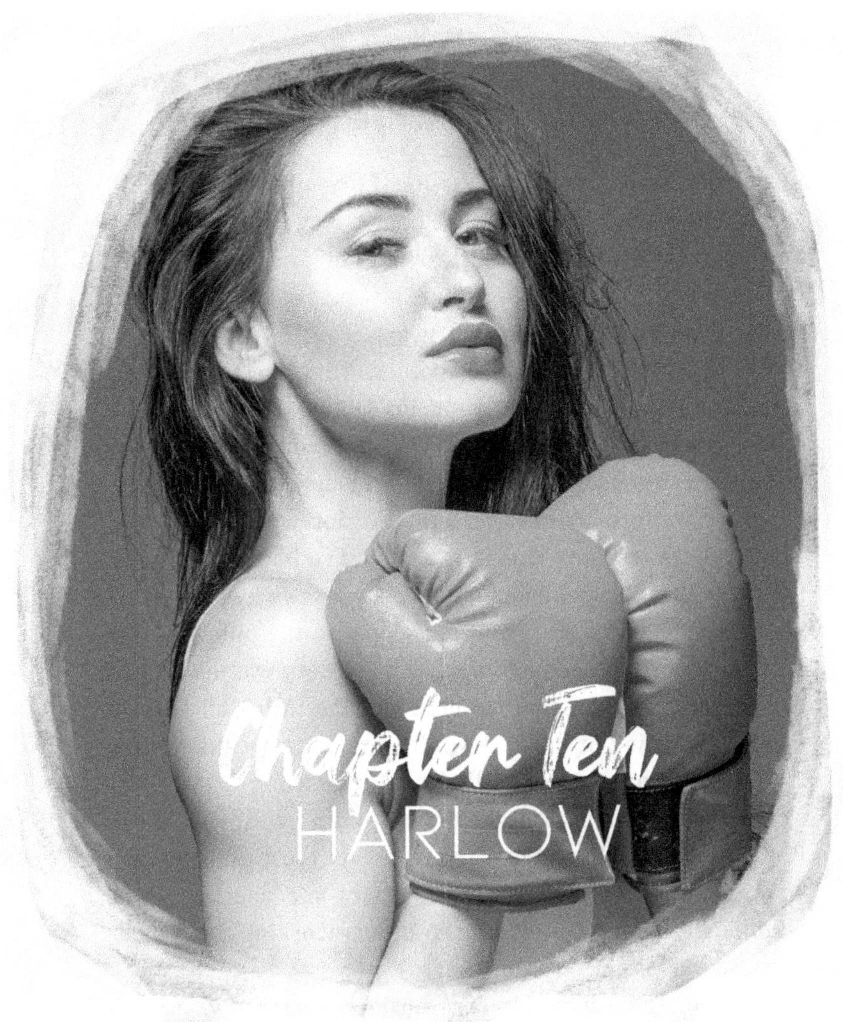

Two Years Later

Sweat clings to my skin. Muscles tremble through the burn of exertion. Red wisps drift from my ponytail, into my eyes. Not a meek rose colored I was satisfied with two years ago. In fact, there's nothing *meek* about me anymore. That girl died when I took a box of vibrant cherry dye to my hair in the motel bathroom. When I fell from the comfortable perch I'd lived life on, I hit the ground hard.

A gloved hand swings towards my face, catching my cheek

as I duck a second too late. Cursing, I tear my own gloves off and spit my mouthguard onto the boxing ring floor.

"For fuck's sake!" I shout, throwing my arms down on the thick, striped ropes. A sigh sounds just before a hand touches my shoulder blade and I shrug it away.

"It's okay, Raven," Freddie soothes, using the fake name I gave him when I took the job at his gym – egotistically also called Freddie's. With a rip of Velcro, Freddie removes the bodyguard pressed against my front. "We all have off days."

"I can't afford to have an off day, not with the fight at RoughRiderz tonight. This is the night I've been waiting for, but my body's decided nah, fuck you." Ever since I woke up this morning and found the blank envelope on the pillow by my face, my mood has been out of whack. I've been waiting for this day for months, but now it's here and I'm losing all faith in myself. Throwing my arms down by my side, I duck out of the ring and snatch my water bottle from the bench.

"There are scouts at all the underground fights, whether in RoughRiderz or elsewhere. You're good. Trust yourself and you'll get sponsored in no time." Giving me one last smile, Freddie strolls away, attending to others working the punch-bags around his gym.

He's young to have his own business, barely twenty-two and definitely too innocent for me, no matter how many times he gives me a lingering look of his sea-green eyes. My tastes have rapidly become more...eclectic since my night at Rapture. I shudder, pushing the memory down deep where it belongs.

Taking my water bottle with me, I slip out the back of the gym. Crisp, fresh air fills my lungs, a well-needed reprieve to the body-heat being generated inside the four-story building. I rest my back against the brick, taking a moment out of view from the main street to calm my nerves. A jog will clear my mind.

Cutting through the alley, I run the length of the street

towards the botanical gardens. A recent addition to the middle-class city I've found myself in. I hadn't intended to stay here for so long. Passing through the bus station for my transfer, state-hopping as far as I could get from my old life, a flyer on the bulletin board caught my eye. Handwritten, asking for an accountant at Freddie's gym, accommodation included. I'm no mathematic, but I assisted with reports at my old firm and organization is key.

The next day, I was employed with a roof over my head and a means to improve on my strength – inside and out. To be fair, I've managed to claim myself quite a comfortable set-up, but settling isn't in my nature anymore. I have a specific goal in mind, and nothing will stop me this time.

The gardens are in full bloom, bursting with color around those who have taken to the grass for their lunchbreaks. Students from the nearby university lay beneath the warm sun, laughing and fooling around. Businessmen and women in sharp suits opt for the wooden benches, juggling the laptops on their knees and coffee-shop baguettes in hand. I smirk, a rush of freedom washing over me as authentic as the wind I create. My legs pump harder, in a bid to put as much distance between me and the life I left behind as possible.

Kitted out in the Freddie's branded gym kit, I cut a path through some tree trunks to the lake hidden beyond. A mile and a half of running track has been carved around the riverbank, a circuit of joggers who want to be seen but remain anti-social following the trail. I join the ranks, although I left my Beats headphones back in my apartment. Pumping my arms, the sound of my ragged breathing fills my ears, the tightness of my chest still as present.

True, scouts do attend all the underground fights that take place on the last Friday of every month. An illicit group who pose as mere gym leaders, but beneath the surface, they train their boxers to fight illegally whilst betting unfathomable amounts on them. Those who win take a cut of the money and the glory, whilst I've seen firsthand what happens to those who lose. Scouts have been known to turn their backs on their own fighters, leaving them to their execution rather than accept the defeat.

I've trained incredibly hard these past two years and have turned down many offers of sponsorship myself. The scout I have in mind rarely looks for new blood and only attends RoughRiderz once in a blue moon, his gym as elusive and difficult to be accepted into as the crew he holds close. But I have it on good authority he will be there tonight.

By the time I return from my run, Freddie is waiting in the back office with a stack of new application forms to be processed. His grin, framed by dimples, is wide. His sandy blonde hair a mess from him clawing his hands through it.

"Our memberships have doubled this month alone," he shakes excitedly. Much like a puppy about to pee themselves. I pat his head, peering at the papers suspiciously.

"Mmm, it sure has. Looks like you're making quite the name for yourself." My tone causes the kid ten years my junior to pause and frown. I shake myself out of it, pushing away my natural instinct to be skeptical of anything that seems too easy. "Your father would be proud," I smile.

His returns it tenfold, sea-green eyes sliding to the mounted frame of the previous owner above the doorway. In direct view from his battered, leather chair, reminding him of the legend who passed when he was a boy. An aunt kept the gym boarded-up, refusing to sell when the rest of this block underwent a huge renovation so that Freddie could take over his father's legacy when he was ready. Not fighting per se but providing a space to those who needed it the most. Teens without an outlet, abused women in need of self-defense training to feel safe again. Raising a hand to his curly hair again, I shake my fingers through the overgrown length this time.

"You're a good kid, Freddie." Sensing the mood shift as his eyes swing my way, filled with longing that I'll never reciprocate, I preempt the conversation we've had many times before and announce I'm going for a shower. I'll work extra over the weekend to get these memberships pushed through if I'm still here that is. If I get my way, I'll have a new home, gym and sense of purpose by morning.

I take far too long showering and preparing myself mentally. By the time I actually arrive to RoughRiderz on my black prized Kawasaki Ninja, exhaustion has raked my limbs and mind. Talk about fucking myself over.

The club is booming with a heavy bass, strobe lights whizzing passed the windows. I throw my keys to the valet with a thinly veiled threat, entering through the middle of two security guards. They tip their heads, unhooking a red rope to permit me to into the club. Taking a sharp left, I follow the hallway towards the bathrooms and stop at a metal door pushed back from sight. Rasping my knuckles, the rectangular slot whips open and a pair of blue eyes grumble for the password.

"Eat shit?" I respond sweetly, tugging the invite out of my side pocket. You'd think I would have learnt my lesson with anonymous invites, but hey, I'm a glutton for punishment it would seem. Satisfied with the calligraphy stating I'm one of tonight's fighters, the door is opened and I look around before entering. No sign of anyone else arriving, despite being exactly the time stated. The music grows softer as I descend the stairs, wondering if I should have taken up Freddie's offer to accompany me. I'd been in big-girl-pants-mode until around thirty seconds ago, but as I step into the hidden underground den, my gut drops.

There's no one here.

A boxing ring stained with aged blood sits empty in the center, the bar and betting station either side concealed with metal shutters. I shudder, a chill seeping into my bones. Rubbing myself, the hand wraps I came in scratch my upper arms. A tight workout vest with ribbing in the sides hugs my slender frame, the straps crisscrossing across my back. Baggy sweats over the shorts on my lower half, also in charcoal gray, covering the laces of my trusty sneakers. Opening my mouth, I turn back when a hand clamps over my eyes. Another covers my mouth, a third grabbing my ponytail and forth closing around my wrists to pin them behind my back.

Oh, fuck no.

I did not find myself thrown into the dirty puddles at the side of the road two years ago, pick up my resolve and carve a new life for myself, just to end up back in the position of a meek, defenseless girl. Let them try to cage me and see what this lioness can do.

Stamping my heel down blind, my sneakers slam into the attacker at my back. Throwing my head back, I connect with his face and twist my hips, jerking back into his crotch hard. Releasing the hold of my hair and wrists, a male groans but I'm not done yet.

Throwing my arm back into his ribs, I use the same arm to swing forward, dislodging the hands on my face. Fisting my vest straps, the male in front brings his head down towards mine before I can get a clear view. Ducking my chin, I let his headbutt go wide, his nose crunching on the top of my head. Bringing my leg up, I slam my knee into his non-existent dick and grip his forearms. Twisting them over each other, I lower my shoulder, using his weakened state to toss him over my shoulder and into the male returning at my back.

Then I get a good look at them. Or as good as the dimmed area around the ring's headlights will allow, but that's all I need. Auburn hair, tangling limbs of equal height, scowling blue eyes. I step back towards the steps when a rope loops around my neck and tugs tight.

"Remember us, sugar?" Aria's voice chuckles beside my ear. "What am I saying? Of course you do." Yanking me sideways, I grip the rope, trying to free some space between the air escaping my lungs and my windpipe. For reasons I can't understand, I don't fight the woman molding herself to my back. My feet skid further from the only exit, the tug on my throat drawing me further into the basement's depths.

Zeke and Zane right themselves, brushing each other off before storming after me. Okay, now I'm ready to fight again. Swinging my elbows backwards, Aria shoves her knee into my back to keep a distance between us, swinging me around in a full circle. I stumble to the floor, the rope falling loose. I gasp in a breath, my hands trembling on the stone floor. Come on Harlow, this is the chance you've been waiting for. To rain down revenge on those who used and discarded me. Pushing myself up on weak legs, I raise my fist and narrow my eyes.

"Seems you have been trying to get my attention," a deeply graveled voice booms from across the room. I still, twisting my head towards the VIP area, reserved for scouts. Unlike the stone ground everyone else must watch from, this section is raised and dripping in red suede. A man sits in an low armchair, a cigar in one hand and glass of whiskey in the other. Sandy blonde hair let loose around his shoulders, and the coating of ink across his neck and hands, are at odds with his sharp suit. Striking hazel eyes, I've seen many times on my laptop screen, peer at me with a lazy drag down the length of my body. *Maddox Caballero.* "Well, Harlow, you have it. Show me what you can do."

Chapter Eleven
MADDOX

She's nothing like what I expected. Nothing like she was described. Raising her chin in defiance, she jerks away from Zane's hold and strides towards the ring. Aria skips behind, holding the ropes open for our guest to enter. When we intercepted her invite to this evening's fight club, taking place right now across town, and detoured her here, the most I was expecting was a brief show of dominance. A speedy end to some half-assed revenge scheme. But now there's a red head with fury blazing in her eyes, stretching out in the ring, color me intrigued.

Shedding her baggy sweatpants, Harlow tosses them aside and Aria sees her chance. Rushing forward, ducking low, Aria's shoulder catches Harlow's side as she spins at the last moment. My prized fighter flops into the ropes, an impressed smirk on her face.

"Someone's a quick learner," Aria raises to stand. Harlow keeps her distance, fists raised whilst bobbing on the balls of her feet. The boys slump into armchairs at my sides, trying to hide the way their attention is drawn back to the ring. I, however, have no qualms with my piqued interest.

Harlow's body is toned in all the right places; her hips wide, ass perfectly bubbled and waist dipped. Her hourglass figure is hugged by a charcoal gray workout vest, her fitted shorts black like the ink spanning the length of her long legs. I can only make out the odd rose and block of scrawled passage between the swirling smoke that curls around the backs of her defined calves.

But none of that has anything on the intense amber eyes which spare a glance my way. Many have said 'eyes are the keys to the soul' whilst falling in the traps of my hazel ones, but Harlow's give no such notion. I can't tell what she's thinking, why a smile hitches at her mouth or when she is about to suddenly lunge.

Sailing through the air, fist raised, Aria squats to avoid the blow and evidently, falls into Harlow's trap. Splaying her hand wide, she grabs Aria's ponytail to hold her in place. Bringing her leg up, Harlow slams Aria's head down to meet her knee halfway. I've trained Aria myself, so I'm not surprised when she quickly regains the upper hand. Twisting and taking out Harlow's legs, the newbie slams onto the ground with an audible 'oomph.'

"Although you are yet to graduate, Killer," Aria mocks, leaning over her prey, hands on her knees.

"You talk too much," Harlow growls, whipping her legs up and locking her thighs around Aria's neck. Instead of jerking her aside, gaining the upper hand, Harlow remains on her back, rearing back to punch Aria's face. Again, and again. Blood sprays from Aria's nose, coating Harlow's face and my breathing stalls. A dangerous craving in my subconscious raises its ugly head, a monster within rousing with the desire to come out and play.

The hand on my whiskey glass tightens, my cigar long forgotten. In my peripheral vision, Zeke and Zane's heads turn in my direction, a question in their raised brows to ask if I'm going to stop the fight. Even if I cared that Aria is getting her ass handed to her by a damn newbie, I can't bring myself to move.

Harlow flips them now, her thighs still around Aria's neck as she sits on her chest and asks how good that pussy smells now. My heart hammers, my dick pressing against the inside of my zipper. Glancing those amber eyes my way, Harlow's chest rises and falls heavily. The moment stands still, a dare igniting in the air between us.

Timid, is how Harlow was portrayed to me. A clueless girl in the wrong place at the wrong time. But the woman before me knows exactly what she's doing. She hasn't had the training and lacks an incredible amount of discipline. But she's feisty. Sees her target and attacks, like a savage primed to kill. Her tongue darts out, licking at the blood coating her pretty lips. Internally, I groan.

Aria taps out on Harlow's thigh, and the moment is broken. Clearing my throat, I rise to stand. If Zeke and Zane spot my hard cock amongst the shadows, creating a tent in my slacks, they don't say anything. They wouldn't dare. I stride across the club's basement, the pounding of a heavy bass hitting the floor above, to the fighter's ring. Harlow has dismounted Aria and risen, folding her arms to resist offering her a hand up. Her amber eyes track my every movement, her jaw tense. Passing her, I stop before Aria, my face devoid of emotion.

"You tapped out, Aria. You know what that means."

"Don't be a grump, Mads," she sits upright, holding her hands out as if I would fall for her charm. I bristle, more so because of the amber eyes watching on in curiosity. I dragged Aria out of the gutter and made her worth my time. Clenching my teeth, I snap my fingers in the air. Zeke and Zane rush to obey, knocking over chairs in their haste to jump the VIP area's railing. Aria's eyes widen and she pushes to her feet. "Serious, Maddox, I was going easy on her. That's all. She's practically a civilian."

"Then there's your weakness. We don't *go easy* on anyone. You know the rules." Turning my back, I pause and look back over my shoulder to Harlow. One last lingering look of her determined face, splattered with blood. Arms crossed and her hip popped to the side. If I weren't in the presence of my crew, there would be no stopping me from taking her right here, right now on the ground like an animal. Alas, if I don't save face now, I'll appear weak.

Heading for the staircase, my foot halts on the bottom step, waiting for the sound of knuckles breaking skin before continuing. Aria knows better than to cry or beg for mercy. Despite being fully aware of the consequences, she made her choice.

Tipping my head to RoughRiderz' owner, tucked back from view in a booth, on the way out, the valet scrambles for my keys. Another figure appears at my side, her sweatpants clutched in her hand. Having used the material to scrub the blood off her face, she faces forward, completely ignoring me. My Camaro is brought around to the roadside, the valet hopping out and leaving the door open for me as he fumbles with another set of keys and runs off.

"Monday morning, Skull Fitness on Southbank. You've got yourself a trial run," I say loudly enough for her to hear over the music spilling from the open door at our back. She doesn't respond. Tendrils of red hair shift in the breeze, my fingers twitching to tuck them behind the safety of her ear. Frowning at myself, I slide into the driver's seat and slam the door closed.

For a man who so recently spoke of weakness, this is not the time to find mine.

Headlights brighten my rearview mirror, the singular shine of a motorbike stopping just behind. Harlow snatches the keys from the valet, jerking her head to make him flinch and squirrel away. Throwing her leg over the leather seat, I watch her pull a helmet over her blood-red hair and speed passed my muscle car, disappearing into the night. My foot twitches, the concerning urge to chase her toying with the code I live by. No women, no drama.

It's not like I don't know where she's going. Zeke has made it his mission to track her every movement and meal for the past two years, and I've left him to it. Zane keeps him on track of business when they have a job to do and I had no time for childish obsessions. But now I've seen her…perhaps his infatuation wasn't so childish after all.

Speaking of the devils, the pair appear in the doorway. Aria is limp in Zane's arms, her head hanging to the side for her hair to cover the damage they'd have inflicted. Spotting me, I grunt and twist the wheel, peeling down the street. They can make their own way back to the house we all share, I have other business to take care of. More specifically, the hard-on threating to burst free of my pants.

Leaving the lights of the city behind, I speed through traffic, my chest tightening with each hindered second that passes. Skidding into a quiet suburb, I pull into the driveway and can't wait long enough for the garage to open. Locking my vehicle, I run into the house I keep for discretion. A simple cottage others would presume is no more than a holiday rental, but it's oh-so much more to me. A retreat which not even the Bloodied Skulls know of.

Slamming the front door closed, I bolt and twist the seven locks before heading straight for the stairs. Taking them two at a time, the railing rattles under my heavy footfall, my breathing increasingly labored. My damn heart is ready to burst out of my chest as I enter the room at the end of the hall with no windows. Flicking the light on, I instantly grab the lube and a nine-inch flesh light from the dressers top-drawer. My cock is sprung free before I've made it to the king-size bed, my fingers trembling to coat myself in lube. Slamming a hand on the wall, I thrust into the flesh light on an elongated groan.

Fuck. It's been too long. I should know better by now. Images assault my mind. Amber eyes beneath long lashes. Pretty, full lips coated in blood. Her small tongue poking out, smearing a path of crimson.

With each visual, I thrust into the fake pussy harder and harder, envisioning her. Bent over in front of me. Cowering beneath me. I'd fuck her tight pussy into submission, completing the job my crew clearly failed in. She wouldn't dream of returning then, but I won't give her the option to escape either. She'd be my plaything. My personal cunt, to fuck frustrations out on after a long day. But I won't let myself do any of those things.

After my initial rush to expel the sudden urge from my system, I slow down with a shaky hand. Pulling all the way out, I keep my eyes closed, playing the scene out in my mind. Pushing back in more steadily this time, I force her to take my entire length. Every rock-hard inch, all the way to her hilt. Curses spill from her, whining that she can't take it. I fist my hand against the wall, as if yanking back on her vibrantly red hair. She will take it without complaint. Like she took no prisoners in the fight.

I'd love to watch her in the underground fights, and I'm more than pissed I denied myself that opportunity by ambushing her. To see her rage and brutality in the ring, only to drag her to the closest bathroom and unleash my own. Punishing her. Branding myself on her.

I hadn't planned to ever see her again after tonight, but I

can't resist. If a few years of mediocre training was enough to have her pinning Aria, I know Harlow already has something others strive for their entire lives. Raw talent. The drive to take what she wants. The passion to win.

Grasping the flesh light tighter, I squeeze firmer around the base of my cock, rocking my hips to delay the inevitable. Every stroke brings me closer. Every groan from my own lips drowns out the lonely room I'm in. My balls tighten, raising in preparation. All that's left to do is imagine her on her knees, amber eyes wide open, just like her greedy mouth.

I sink my teeth into my bottom lip, needing a spike of pain to finish myself off. Bicep pumping, I don't hold back any longer, screwing the flesh light like my life depends on it. In a way, it does – because to give Harlow a hint of control over me means the end of everything I've worked so hard to achieve.

People fear me, tremble at the mere mention of my name. Yet, like everyone, I have a side of me I hide from the world. A man like myself, who exudes power and has built an empire of success, is expected to bed a different woman each night. If only the world knew this piece of ribbed silicone has seen me through many aggravated orgasms.

Punching the wall, I bellow as an explosion rockets through me. Pumping my cum into the fake pussy, oozing from the side as I ride out the waves of pleasure which have me in their grasp. And all the while, in my mind, she stares back. My chest heaves, my forehead leaning on the cool wallpaper. A shiver rolls down the length of my spine. I'm so glad I don't have any mirrors, in this house or any other, because I wouldn't want to see myself in this moment. In any moment.

Dragging the flesh light free of my cock, I dump it in an empty ice bucket to come back to later. Fishing out a hand towel from the dresser, I clean myself and drop back on the bed. Silence falls, my breathing no longer filling the room. And during the darkness and the image of her face that I push aside, a new emotion filters in. One that has my fists clenching by my sides. *Jealousy.*

My entire 'crew' is the trio I took in as teenagers, gave a place to belong. They learnt quickly and work well, giving us a reputation to be feared. Many presume a whole organization works within the walls of Skull Fitness, but it's just us four since… Well, that's a story for another time.

Rolling onto my side, I take the satin cover with me, cocooning myself for a short while before I need to shower and return to the apartment. If I must. Perhaps I'll leave Aria to lick her wounds and keep my distance until the unfamiliar feeling stirring within has passed. My orgasm has done nothing to ease me, and Zeke and Zane's faces will present too much of a temptation. For once, they've had something I haven't. They know something I never will. How good Harlow's skin looks flushed. How hooded her eyes become after her body is wrought of desire. How well she can take torture in the name of her pleasure. I hope they're happy with those memories because they'll never see her that way again. Not while I control their lives and futures.

Pathetic. The word comes to me from nowhere, spoken within my own head in the voice of my father. I grimace, clutching the sheets. Even in death he haunts me. Growling, I whip the covers aside and storm into the bathroom, throwing my fist into the tiles as I go. My knuckles don't instantly split so I do it again, and again, until they do. Blood coats the cracked pearly white tiles and I run my finger through it, painting a H on my chest. Yeah, I'm pathetic alright, but what I do in my own time is no one else's concern. Not even the ghosts of my past.

The shower is switched on, the spray set to freezing before I step underneath. Forcing my head beneath the jet, I freeze out all toxic thoughts. One woman can't be allowed to affect me so much, from barely twenty minutes in her presence. I can't let her have that power. Although, a few more rounds of jacking off may be in order. Come Monday, I'll have to contend with seeing her every day, wondering what the hell I was thinking giving her a trial run to join my crew. Naturally, I can't let her pass. No matter how much I hope she proves me wrong.

I haven't slept in the slightest. My mind raced all night, the break of dawn a welcome reprieve from my thoughts. At least this is a semi-acceptable hour to be active, even for a Saturday. Dressing in the closest lycra to hand, I'm downstairs in the gym without need for breakfast. I don't think I could stomach food and manage to keep it down anyway.

Out of all the events of last night, one stands out, and it's accompanied by the cringeworthy crunch of a rib breaking. Zeke and Zane didn't show any remorse, laying into Aria as she merely stood and accepted it. The little I saw was enough to have me grabbing my sweatpants and running the hell out of there. I wanted nothing to do with them in that moment, two years of revenge plotting going out the window. But then… Maddox invited me for a trial. I shudder to think what that would include, and if I have the balls to go through with this anymore.

Typical, I scoff at myself, strapping on the first boxing glove. The other, I have to use my teeth to secure the strap in place. I've spat my fair share of blood, grown detached from the damage my fists cause in the underground fights and received my fair share in return. It's what we go for. Yet one hint of violence from the gang I've built up in my mind to mean more than they really are, and I'm questioning my life choices. Straight back to the woman I left behind, second guessing my worth and if I have what it takes to face them again.

Come Monday, I don't have much of a choice. This is the time to buck up and shut up, see my plan through. Stage one is complete – I have my in. Now I've got the weekend to hide away and pretend I don't exist one last time before the spotlight is on my every move.

Throwing my gloved hands into the body of a freestanding rubber dummy named Bob, I work myself into a state of exhaustion. Punching, kicking, an unhealthy dose of screaming. The burn of exercise mixes with fatigue until my arms are floppy and my legs are on fire. I drag myself over to the bench, laying back across the wood. The gym isn't due to open for hours and as uncomfortable as it is, the solid plank beneath me will do wonders for straightening out the kinks in my back and neck.

The lights overhead blink on and I hiss, throwing my arm over my eyes. Unaware that I'm lurking in the dark like a vampire, Freddie sets about powering up the vending machines and checking the water dispenser. I squint out the corner of my eye, noting his casual t-shirt and cotton shorts, his curly hair damp from a shower. Damn him and his youth. I swear the nights he's opened the gym up for his friends to come 'hang out,' i.e., smoke and drink themselves into a coma, he wakes the next morning, as rejuvenated as ever.

Turning with arms-filled with freshly cleaned and rolled hand towels, he spots me and flinches. The towels tumble all over the ground, unraveling as they go. Forcing myself off the bench and onto my knees, I help to scoop them up.

"What the hell are you doing down here? I gave you the apartment upstairs for a reason," Freddie scolds. I raise a brow at his authoritative tone, giving my usual morning response.

"Coffee first. Talk later." But this time, Freddie doesn't let me go so easily. His hand shoots out, cupping my cheek. I still, allowing him to inspect the tenderness lingering on my cheek. One of my eyes feels like it's not opening as far as the other, and by the curse beneath Freddie's breath, I can tell it's worse than I expected.

"I won't let you continue down this route, Raven," he sighs and I wince at both his thumb stroking my cheek and the use of the fake name. I really shouldn't still be lying to him, and it's not a trust issue. I'm just in too deep now to admit I came here for a reason he won't understand. "I won't let you put yourself in danger for the sake of some illegal fights. What's the point of chasing a thrill if this is the cost?" I pull my face away from his touch and lower my chin. There's a question I don't have the answer to.

Standing, I take the towels to a utility room out back, needing to put them through the wash again. Freddie remains close, taking my wrist in his hand to turn me once I close the washing machine. His hold is loose, too soft and I retract from it instantly.

"Raven, seriously. I care about you. Let me." He reaches for me again and my ass bumps into the washing machine in an effort to escape. Dropping his arms, Freddie's sea-green eyes hunt for the right thing to say. He doesn't make me uncomfortable, but the atmosphere between us does. I want to be the kind of woman that can enjoy a decent man's company. I wish I could pretend his sweet nature would be enough for me. But there's no use lying to either of us.

The Bloodied Skulls did many things during the lock-in at club Rapture, including awaken me to new possibilities. I must see this through. I need to know what I'm capable of handling, test my hard and soft limits, understand who the fuck I am now and where I belong in this world.

Resignation filters through his features but from somewhere, Freddie manages to produce a smile. "You haven't even given me a chance. Let's go to dinner tonight. It can be casual; it can be more. At least you can say you gave it a shot, and then I won't bother you about it ever again." One eyebrow raises, disappearing beneath his mop of curled hair. I assess him in a way I haven't been able to before.

Standing around a foot above me, his body is lean, his muscles are defined. The expanse of his creamy skin is begging to be inked and I reckon a neck tattoo would do wonders for his appeal. If I was able to get over the feeling he's like a kid-brother to me, maybe it could have worked. But he won't stop until I prove to him it never will.

"Fine. Dinner. I could bring some of the revised contracts to go over-"

"No," Freddie cuts me off, his lop-sided smile in place beneath his eye roll. "Just food and natural conversation. You remember how to have one of those, right?" He chuckles and walks away while my face falls, unsure if I actually do.

"This is a nice place," I comment, looking at anything except the man before me. I managed to spot the hint of his white collar and tie through the keyhole of my apartment, giving me barely a few minutes to run and change. Somehow, I don't think Freddie would have appreciated my jeans and hoodie approach when he's gone through so much trouble. The guy that took me in when I had no experience or references, essentially saved me from homelessness, deserves me to give him as much as he's put in for me.

Smoothing my hands down the only dress I own, I shift uncomfortably. The strapless bust is in the shape of petals, in black and gold netting that cover the black fitted garment underneath. Whereas the skirt finishes on my thighs, the leaf-imprinted netting swirls to the ground where my black heels shake uncontrollably. It's the only fancy outfit I own, bought on a whim in the sales. I felt like a new woman the first time I tried it on, but the more muscley my body became, the more I've shied away from wearing it.

I may love my figure, but the side-glances and hushed whispers I'm receiving from those seated around us were exactly what I was worried about. Freddie doesn't seem to notice, and if he does, the appreciative glint in his eyes hasn't waned.

"So," he regains my attention for the first time since asking if I'd like to order first. Even the waiter looked uneasy, frowning at me in a 'what are you doing with this kid' kind of way. "You've never told me where you're from originally." I nod, agreeing that I've never told him. He didn't seem to mind my past being a secret before now. Freddie grins, laughing under his breath. "Let me rephrase that as a question – where does Raven hail from originally?" I smirk, seeing an out.

"Raven is from right here, born and bred." Not a complete lie since I made her up upon arriving at the bus station in this city. Freddie's brows raise, his forearms leaning forward on the tablecloth.

"Oh really? Which school did you go to? After my father died, I was sent to stay with a cousin since the schooling was supposed to be better in that area. Aside from that, I've lived in this neighborhood my entire life."

"Was it not?" I ask, lifting a glass of wine to my painted lips. Makeup was a given when I looked like I'd been mugged. Freddie's head tilts in confusion. "You said the school was *supposed* to be better. Was it not?" He grins, taking a swig of his beer.

"You're very deflective, but fine, I'll bite. I don't know a single person who has positive memories from school. It's a prison for children, except the wardens miss more than they catch and the concept of learning amongst hormonal teens is ludicrous. I've taught myself more since leaving, in the comfort of my boxers." I laugh into my glass, covering my mouth with the back of my hand.

"I've never heard you speak so freely," I say as our starters are placed before us. A tiny portion of salmon tartare that fits the opulent surrounding perfectly. Sprinkled with caviar and two blades of lemongrass, the smell is divine. Mimicking the woman with a pearl necklace to my right, I flick out the cotton napkin and lay it over my lap. Freddie waits for the waiter to retreat before answering.

"We rarely speak about anything except work." I take my time cutting off tiny pieces of my food, wanting to make the serving last until the mains are ready. Sea-green eyes watch me as I make the appropriate noises and point my fork at the plate. Tension lingers in the air, thickening with each moment I don't have a response. Crossing one leg over the other, my foot starts to shake again.

"Why are you so nervous?" Freddie asks casually, finishing the last of his food and placing his knife and fork down on the plate. "We literally see each other every day. I know you blast

Lady Gaga in the shower and prefer to eat finger food. Don't let the setting change what you know to be true. Next time, I reckon I should opt for chicken wings at a bar, hoodies and jeans. How's that sound?"

"You're presuming there will be a next time," I quirk a brow. Forcing my foot to still, my heart squeezes. Finishing my starter, I lower my cutlery and sigh. "Look, Freddie-"

"I meant next time, just as friends. I'm not too young and naïve to read the room. It's cool. Why don't you talk business with me if that'll put you at ease?" This time, I grin for real and slump back in my seat. Like a weight being lifted, I begin to relax, even if I'm sure someone nearby just commented on the red-headed man in a dress.

"I'll do you one better. Takeout and a movie back at mine? I'm sure this," I raise my voice, "man in a dress," I look around at the rich couple glaring at the back of my head, "has pajamas to fit you. Baggy is my niche."

"Really? I hadn't noticed," Freddie chuckles, offering me his hand to stand. "But then again, I didn't realize I was gay either because I happen to think you are the hottest chick in this place." I down my wine glass and take the rest of the bottle, holding it high above my head. Leaving only our laughter behind, we move between the tables. Freddie pays the bill at the waiter's station and then we're outside the extravagant glass doors, looking to hail a cab. Typically, there are none when you need one, so we walk arm in arm down the street. Now Freddie has let go of pining for me, it's as if our friendship can finally bleed through the cracks of the walls I put in place.

Reaching the corner, I go to step off the sidewalk to cross the road when Freddie yanks me back. A black sedan skids to a stop in front of us, a pair of twins jumping out of the driver's and passenger doors. No, not twins but Zane and Zeke. Their auburn hair gleaming in the glow of a streetlamp. Zeke, who's closer to me, headbutts me in the temple without warning. My legs give out, only Freddie's arm linked in mine keeping me from hitting the pavement hard. Zane grabs my boss and friend, tugging him away. I hear the struggle as I drop to my knees, Zeke's grip yanking my chin up to face him.

"Not so tough now, are you Feisty?" he mocks. Dragging me into the back seat, I notice Zane slamming the trunk closed through the rear window, no sign of Freddie anywhere. It doesn't take a genius to figure out where he is, but it's the lack of yelling and banging coming from within the trunk that worries me. The door slams closed, my heart juddering as I rush to act.

Trying the door handles, neither side works. Zeke slides back in the driver's seat, Zane taking the passenger's and the sedan peels down the road. As if to mock me, Zane lowers his window and hangs his arm outside, moving his hand in waves through the night air. Taking a tight corner with an ear-piercing tire skid, I'm thrown to the side and scramble to right myself. Fine, they want to play. Let's play.

Launching myself into the central space between their two seats, I angle my body to face Zane's. Lashing a hand out, I claw at his icy blue eyes. Zane growls like an animal, grabbing my hair and yanking me further into the front of the vehicle. My hips get stuck halfway, making me wish I'd come up with a better plan. Too late now. Twisting, I grasp the steering wheel and tug. We swerve into the center of the road, a truck horn instantly blaring. Zeke curses, pushing on the top of my head to shove me into the backseat again and this time, I stay there.

Arms crossed, lips pursed, I glare at the assholes eyeing me in the review mirror. Let them take me wherever we're going. As soon as I've made sure Freddie is okay, I'll find a way to make them regret messing with me this evening. I'm practically their bitch from Monday anyway. Tonight, is fair game.

Chapter Thirteen

ARIA

Tires skid to a stop, disturbing the sleep I'd been trying to cling onto. Rest is the best and quickest way to heal. Holding a hand over the tight bandages around my middle, I ease myself from laying to standing without trying to move too much. My head pounds. My lip throbs.

After letting Zeke injure me enough so Maddox wouldn't force them to do it again, Zane did me the curtesy of knocking me out with a single fist to the center of my forehead. Lights out for Aria, but also completing the punishment she was owed. We all know the rules. If we throw a fight, we must be beaten unconscious by the others. It teaches us all a lesson in never showing weakness and so it was crucial Zeke and Zane didn't go easy on me for being the only female in the group.

Making my way over to the window, I peer through the blinds. Zane pops to the back of the sedan, and a nymph in a ballgown dives at him. Clawing and scratching his head while smushing his face into her cleavage. Zeke strolls passed, popping the trunk. Dragging out a limp body, Zeke tosses the male over his shoulder and the four of them disappear, entering the house below. I curse, panic surging through me.

Here? They brought them here when Maddox can return at any minute? I rush as quickly as my body will allow to the door, uncaring if I'm only in a pair of tiny shorts and a crop top. Gripping the handrail, I navigate the stairs, swearing to all fuckery that my adoptive brothers are idiots. Catching sight of Zeke, I hiss at him for his attention.

"What are you doing asshole! Neither of you thought to take this shit to the warehouse next door?"

"The warehouse doesn't have central heating," Zeke shrugs, despite the weight of the man across his shoulder. Striding away, I'm forced to follow, wincing every step of the way. Zane leads the way, a familiar voice screaming obscenities at him the entire way through the building. Out the back door, he takes the path to an outbuilding which poses as an office. Nondescript walls, basic furniture, all covered in plastic sheeting. Not that there's any other houses for a good mile but in case anyone comes sniffing around. Maddox has a few properties in different suburbs but this old fisherman's home on a pier is the only one we're permitted to stay in.

Leaving the door open for us, I hear the struggle before I step inside, spotting Harlow's wrists bound in chains. Zane heaves her up, hooking the chains over a hook hanging from the ceiling. She takes the opportunity to kick out wildly, swishing around the netting of her dress before Zane yanks on the hook. It zips across the room, creating enough speed for him to release his hold and Harlow flies into the far wall. Her entire body takes the impact, an audible 'oomph' leaving her lips. She's going to have to work on that.

Closing the door, I pull a plastic chair in front of it and lower myself down. My bros may be absolute twats, but I won't miss what's happening for the sake of a little more rest. Zeke works on tying up his victim, a young guy with curly sandy-blond hair. His suit is a little much, the collar and cuffs buttoned beneath a black jacket. His tie is still smartly in place, despite the growing lump on his head. He begins to rouse as Zeke finishes tying his hands and legs to an X-shaped wooden stand.

The walls, floor and ceiling are covered in white plastic for an easy clean up. The building is intended for whatever is about to take place, but only on Maddox's orders. Beat the truth from a snitch, kill a rival. The usual. Zane lifts an ankle bar from a pair of hooks high up, grabbing Harlow's legs in turn to fasten the cuffs tight. She struggles, causing her body to rock back and forth on the hook.

"Wakey, wakey, Sunshine," Zeke slaps the guy's cheek. His eyes snap open and he grimaces, working on a feeble attempt at breaking the binds at his wrists and ankles. It's pointless. We know what we're doing and it's best to just give us what we want, even if it's your life.

"Who the fuck are you people?! What do you want with us?" he yells, his eyes connecting with Harlow's. She's stopped struggling, a look of resignation on her face. I smirk when our gazes connect, ignoring my pain long enough to raise a hand and wriggle my fingers.

"Good to see you again so soon, Killer," I wink. No weakness, remember? The only stranger in this room grunts, cutting his wrists something fierce with all that useless straining.

"Raven, what's going on?" he asks and as if planned, the

three of us burst out laughing. Zeke, Zane and I. Holding my ribs, I wheeze, breathing deeply to calm myself down. Zeke skips across the room, stroking a finger down Harlow's flushed cheeks.

"Yeah, *Raven*, what is going on? Why don't you tell your date exactly who we are, and what kind of predicament you've dragged him into?" She spits in Zeke's face, fury blazing from her amber eyes. He laughs again, scooping up her saliva and flicks it to the floor. This time when he touches her, he grabs her chin harshly and jerks her face down to his. "Save it for my cock." Jerking her face away, he turns away.

"They're no one. A bunch of rejects that didn't get enough hugs through their childhood. The only compassion they're shown is forced and fake."

Zeke looks at me for the briefest moment, a smile playing about his lips. Yeah, she really shouldn't have brought our upbringing into this. Returning his attention to Harlow, he yanks down the top half of her dress. She's bare underneath, but that's not enough humiliation for Zeke's mean streak. Reaching beneath her double skirt, he yanks on Harlow's panties, dragging them down her legs. Using two hands, he tears them clean in half, and brings them up to his nose to inhale deeply.

"Not exactly the type of underwear you should wear for a date, but that's okay. Save the lacey lingerie for ours."

"In your fucking dreams," Harlow bites back. The flush from her cheeks has lowered to cover her chest, her eyes firmly avoiding the male across the room. He, in turn, doesn't look her way. Something Zeke and Zane have already spotted. "And it wasn't a date. Freddie is my boss. It was a business meeting is all. Just let him go," she sighs. Zeke's head tilts and I don't need to see him to know he's smiling.

"It's a long walk back to the city. What's the offer you're putting forward to get Aria to drive him back?" I roll my eyes, knowing I'd manage to get the short end of the stick. They beat me up and I'm the chauffeur. But that's the price I pay for letting Harlow pin me yesterday, and for believing she'd be the same, inexperienced woman I met at Rapture. She stills now, her mind working over Zeke's question.

"What...what do you want?" her voice comes out small. I ease myself to sit forward, also curious in the answer. Zane has stepped back, leaning against the wall with his foot raised and arms crossed. He's always preferred to wait, see how things play out, whereas Zeke is an instigator.

"I want you to prove to this naïve prick you're not who you're pretending to be. I want him to watch how I can take ownership of your body at the snap of my fingers, when he's been struggling to so much as hold your attention for the past two years." Zane catches my eye, his head downcast in a frown. I share his confusion, until it all clicks into place.

Oh, that's right. Zeke's been stalking her. He knows far more than he lets on, keeping his cards held close to his chest. For what reason he has been unable to let this girl go, I'm not sure. It's definitely not the 'I just want to make sure she doesn't sell us out' bullshit he originally told Maddox.

Silence passes, my spunky attitude sorely missing from this dynamic. I'm taking a day off, seeing how the situation plays out without my input. Zeke kicks the ankle bar, forcing Harlow's body to wobble and tits to jiggle. The hint of a tattoo pokes out from her sternum where the dress is doubled over on itself.

"I'll make you a deal," Zeke threads his fingers over his groin, planting his feet wide. "If you cum for us twenty-four times within the next twenty-four hours, we'll hand deliver the pair of you back to the shithole you call a gym with a fruit basket to top up the vitamin C your body has lost. I'll even let you decide who brings you to each orgasm, between the five of us – yourself included."

"Zeke," Zane mutters, nudging his head aside to signal he wants a word. I don't need to hear the hushed whispers to know what will be said. Something along the lines of us not being in Rapture now, there's no NDA's or anonymity out here. Ever the rational one, Zane's faith in this kidnapping scheme is quickly fading. I doubt there even was a plan but rather, a pair of men looking to restore my honor and took their opportunity.

Both sets of cold blue eyes slide to mine, searching for my input in the situation. I shrug, gesturing with the hand not holding my ribs for them to go ahead. Even when we venture off script, even when Maddox has us turn on each other, nothing comes between the bond we've forged with the tears of three, unloved orphans. Being abandoned is nothing new to us, so we vowed to never do it to each other.

Satisfied he has our approval, Zeke moves towards the only piece of furniture in the room, aside from the garden chair beneath my ass. A wooden box covered in so much varnish, any blood spilt rolls straight off. Spinning the numbers on the combination lock to pop it open, Zeke lifts the lid upwards. Pulling out a machete first, he pretends to inspect it, causing both bound prisoners to jerk against their restraints. Placing it down, Zeke whips out a length of stained, tattered cloth which Zane steps forward to take from him and proceeds to wrap it around Freddie's mouth. He shouts around it, louder now than when he was able to speak.

Next time he reaches inside the box, Zeke removes a long piece of scrap leather which he whips out, smacking it against the ground. The only person that flinches is Freddie, his tiny yelp making Zeke chuckle. Turning his back on the man readying to wet himself, he faces Harlow whilst wrapping the leather around his hand.

"I'm not hearing a decision there, Feisty. So, I suppose I-"

"Zane," Harlow suddenly shouts. Zeke smiles, while Zane

freezes. His eyes meet mine, an emotion I can't read within their blue depths. Which is a feat because I can usually read Zane incredibly well. Whatever it is, he's hiding it well, whereas my emotions are all over my face. I'm pissed she didn't choose me, considering how I played her body like an instrument in need of a good fiddling in the Pleasure rooms. Perhaps my obvious injury had something to do with her decision but still – I could have powered through.

Relaxing back in my chair, I watch Zane's shoulders tighten as he turns to face Harlow. Now I wish I'd grabbed some popcorn on the way through the house, because I'm about to witness one hell of a show. He wastes no time and doesn't for one second act like he's enjoying himself either. Zane reaches up the inside of Harlow's skirt. I watch her face flitter between hatred and horny and see the exact moment Zane's fingers thrust into her. A soft gasp, followed by the clink of chains as she struggles. His arm pumps, her mouth open in a perfect 'O.' Sparing himself from looking at her, Zane lowers his head to take her nipple in his mouth.

"She can't tell which one of us it is with this on," Zeke holds up the leather, bringing it closer to Harlow's eyes. She writhes, glaring at him with so much malice, her jaw might break under the strain of it.

"You're not touching me. I do *not* consent to you." Harlow spits at him again, and this time, Zeke doesn't take it so lightly. Closing a hand around her neck, Zane continues, ignoring the confrontation happening above him.

"If you don't want to be treated like a dirty whore, then don't act like one." Shoving her away, Zeke paces back to the chest, dropping the leather inside with a sigh. Then his attention turns to Freddie. The kid hanging from the X with his eyes scrunched shut and one ear pressed into his shoulder. Apparently, he doesn't enjoy the mewls from Harlow as much as I do. Pulling my legs up to cross them, my hands drift south to graze my inner thighs. The shorts have risen, my core dampening with the sight of Harlow's head being thrown back, her hands flexing into fists. She bucks against the chains but I reckon she no longer cares to be free.

There she is.

The woman I noticed as soon as I saw her step into the fighting cage at Rapture. I knew she had a dark side to her, waiting to be unleashed. It takes some persuading, but when she submits to the pleasure taking over her body, she's a fucking goddess. Rubbing myself through my panties with my bruised knuckles, I suddenly regret nothing about last night. I can take a beating better than most, and if that's what it takes to see her so enthralled once more, it was worth it.

Zane's arm works faster, pumping into her slickened pussy with vigor. Like a machine programmed with only one setting. His mouth moves over to her other breast, leaving a trail of teeth marks visible on the one he's just released. Harlow's nipple is stretched, her areola deep red. He did not go easy on her, and judging by the screams now filling the outbuilding, he still isn't.

Slamming his forearm into Freddie's dick, Zeke forces him to watch via the hand beneath Freddie's chin holding his gaze up. "The best part is about to happen," Zeke affirms. "Miss it and we'll have to get creative with how to pry your eyes open for the next one."

My head whips side to side, drinking in the two ends of the spectrum from hate to desire. Harlow's thighs clench tight, trying to slow Zane's fingers. Fuck knows how many he's plunging inside of her, so I use my imagination, rubbing my clit in time with his arm thrusts. Stamping his foot down on the ankle bar, Zane forces Harlow's legs to straighten. In doing so, he permits himself full access and she's putty in his hands. Screaming and mewling in pleasure, Harlow breaks for us all to witness. A display of flushed skin, heavy pants and trembling limbs. Her nails dig so hard into her palms, bloodied marks are left when Harlow falls slack.

Zeke crosses the room, muttering in Zane's ear. On a stiff nod, Zane complies with the request. Removing his hand in one, swift motion that makes her gasp, tense and then collapse against her restraints again, Zane swaps places with where Zeke was. Lifting his fingers, soaked with Harlow's cum, he smears them over each of Freddie's cheek.

"Smell that, pretty boy. That's the scent of a woman thoroughly pleasured. Commit it to memory because it's the closest you'll come to Harlow's cunt." I shiver beneath the amount of testosterone battering around this compact room, until the chains at Harlow's wrists rattle. Zeke proceeds to release her from her binds and whether she likes it or not, Harlow collapses into his arm. Giving her barely a moment to recover, Zeke places Harlow on the ground with her ankle bar in place and shifts away, turning his back as she falls on her ass.

"Go on, get out. Like I said, it's a hell of a long walk," he mutters without looking her way. Zane unties Freddie too, jerking at him with his shoulders bunched, just in case the kid got any ideas.

"But I thought?" Harlow asks in a small voice, working on the buckles at her ankles. Zeke heads for the door, touching the handle when he scowls down at her.

"You thought what, Feisty? That I actually want to watch you cum twenty-three more times? Nah, I just wanted you to admit in front of your little boyfriend that you'd choose one of us to do it over him. Call that one last pity-fuck, but we've got better things to do than you." As if remembering I'm even in the room, Zeke pushes the door wide and bends to scoop me up. I smack his chest, not some damsel that can't walk her own two feet back to the house, but he doesn't pay me any attention so I give up.

"Hey, what's going on with you tonight?" I ask. The coldness of Zeke's attitude is unnerving. I've reckoned many times, without his jokey spirit, our group would spiral into despair. And tonight, has proved my point, going to a place we haven't ventured before. Where our emotions took over and the result…well, it was messy as fuck and not in a good way.

"Nothing," Zeke shrugs so I slap him instead. Zeke rolls his eyes, keeping his voice low for my ears only as we enter the house, Harlow and Freddie being shoved along behind. "The basement of RoughRiderz," he scowls, looking back at Harlow. "That was the last time my fists will ever touch you. We've come too far to back down because of some pretty pussy. I won't let her come between us." Placing me on a bench that conceals a shoe rack underneath, Zeke kneels in front of me.

"I know you threw that fight. But the thing is, Zane and I would have done the exact same. She's a weakness to us as much as we are to her, so I'm giving her a reason to stay the fuck away. We'll never see her again after this, I'm sure of it."

From across the hallways, Harlow bursts into laughter. Our heads snap her way, watching her ease her tits back into the dress. Once covered, as much as the garment allows, she drops to her haunches and nudges Zeke aside. He drops on his hip, more stunned than annoyed as Harlow helps herself to a pair of my sneakers.

"Don't be shy, Feisty. I like a joke as much as the next asshole," Zeke drags Harlow up by her arms. A lazy humor dances in her hooded eyes, her smile aggravating him more than anything else could.

"You'll see," she shrugs him off. Taking my coat from the hook above my head, Harlow drops onto my lap and bends over to adjust her shoes. Hot damn, she's screwing with all of us.

"I don't fucking think so, Leech," Zane growls this time, crossing his arms, using that pet name even Zeke and I hate for her. Harlow's many things, but a leech is not one of them.

Freddie shifts uncomfortably on the spot in the hallway. "What's so damn funny?"

"I've just realized, you guys don't know," she laughs again, leaving my lap to pull her coat on. I instantly miss her heat, but her laugh makes me smile too. Zeke glares daggers at us both but what can I say. I love me a feisty woman. So instead, Zeke grabs her collar and yanks her back a step to face us all.

"If you don't spit it out, I'll drag you back into that building by your hair and make good on my threat," he dares. I can't tell if he's serious, but the yawn pulling at my mouth doesn't help the situation. Adrenaline waning, I need to get back to the comfort of my bed. Harlow juts her chin out, more defiant than I've ever seen.

"Maddox invited me to a trial run in your little gang," she belittles us with a bitchy up and down look at Zane. Jerking out of Zeke's stunned hold, she grabs Freddie's hand and flees out the front door with a final dash of salt to the wound. "See you Monday, crewmates."

The three of us remain still, the carnage of Zeke's plan crumbling down all around us. His face is the picture of horror, his lips spilling muttering of lies and deceit. Maybe he's right, but something in my gut doesn't agree. Harlow spoke true, her eyes twinkling with pay-back. An engine roars to life, headlights spearing the front of the building.

"The fuck?" Zane rushes to the doorway while all I can do is say 'oh.' Half smirking, half wincing, I push myself to stand and edge my way to the stairs.

"Um, oops. My keys may have been in my coat pocket," I shrug and climb the stairs as quickly as I'm able, my name being hollered behind me. I should be cursing like those throwing their fists around on the floor below but as I close myself into my bedroom, spotting the sedan rushing away in the distance, all I can do is smile. I do like my women feisty, indeed.

Chapter Fourteen
HARLOW

I hate them. With everything I am, I hate them so much. My hand balls into a fist as I raise it and pound on the door of Skull Fitness, wondering what the hell I'm doing with my life. Yesterday was spent hiding, the doors to my apartment, bedroom and en-suite bathroom all locked. Curled up in the bath, avoiding looking at myself.

At some point in the last couple of years, I've lost everything that made me, me. To the point where my own reflection is a stranger. I picked Zane to pleasure me because I'd be damned if I gave Zeke the satisfaction. Aria was injured, I don't think I'll ever be able to look Freddie in the eye again and I sure as hell wasn't doing it. Zane gave me exactly what I was expecting, a one-way ticket to Orgasm Town on the speedy express. Those bastards have taken what they desire from me one last time.

Yet here I am, my heart thundering as I wait impatiently for the door to swing open. I picked the back one because I wasn't standing outside the main shutter. Locks unbolt from the inside, my breathing quickening as I steel myself. And who should it be coming to my aid, but Zeke the fucking asshole.

"Oh, hey Feisty. Didn't realize you were stopping by," he smirks. His blue eyes ignore me, shooting to the Sedan parked in the empty lot across the road. I toss the keys, uncaring if he caught them and barge inside. Might as well get on with this 'trial'. Zeke closes the door and walks away, leaving me to inspect the inside of the gym I've spent years planning to infiltrate. The plan is simple, yet after last night, I reckon it will be even more effective than I'd hoped.

The main, elongated room is shadowed by a shutter over the glass entrance, strips of sunlight highlighting the boxing ring in the center. White brick walls, which have been artfully graffitied, accommodate punching bag stands, sparring dummies and weight benches around the outside of the ring. They must get a majority of fighters in here, because the extension out back isn't half as big. Brand new treadmills, rowing machines and the likes can be seen through an open archway, the changing rooms labeled just beyond. Pushed against the side of this area, a metal staircase winds to a platform up above, a series of closed doors piquing my curiosity.

"Little under-dressed, don't you think?" Zane appears on the top balcony. I frown at my gym attire, fitted and red, all branded with Freddie's logo. The vest top sits beneath an unzipped hoodie with an incredibly soft inner lining, the leggings cover all traces of me scrubbing my skin raw in the six-hour bath to rid myself of their touch. My hair is tossed up into a messy bun, and my hand wraps and gum shield are in my pocket. Not under-dressed or under-prepared in the slightest.

Making his way down the spiral staircase, Zane approaches me with the lingering slowness of a lion stalking his prey. He sucks all the air from the room, making my throat too dry to swallow. Walking all the way into my personal space, the scent of bodywash drifts from him, alluding to a recent shower. Have the Skull already had a full work out this morning? Zane grimaces, apparently unhappy with my appearance.

"Everything you need to know is on this piece of paper," he pulls a folded sheet from the back pocket of his jeans. I ignore his bare feet poking out the bottom, or else I might give into the overwhelming urge to stamp on them and break all his toes. "Make sure you stick to the schedule. One delay and you're out. Welcome to your trial, Leech."

Tucking the paper into my cleavage when I make no move to take it, he strolls the way Zeke exited. My jaw tenses so hard, it might just crack. Between all the pet names they each give me; Princess is the one I hate the most. Snatching the paper from my sports bra, I unfold it with the distinct sensation I'm being watched.

9am — Bennie's Café. 2x mochas, brown sugar in one, 1x caramel latte with soy milk. Nothing for you.

9:30am — Be back to receive a delivery. Stack boxes in storage area.

11–1pm — There's a bag of papers in need of shredding in the office. General tidy, fix the wobbly handle on the desk.

1pm — Meet with Maddox in his office. The rest is on you.

I snort to myself. Eyes drag over my body, watching from either the shadows or the surveillance cams for my reaction. They mean to rile me, but I made myself a promise this morning. No matter the cost, do not give them what they want. Shoving the paper into my hoodie pocket, I give the cameras a big wave and make my way to the back door. Exiting, I dump the list in the nearest trash can and almost skip down the street. Looks like I'm free until 1pm.

The promise of another warm day brightens the sidewalk, the sun warming me through, even at this early hour. We've been blessed with an extra-long summer this year, although we're sure to pay for it when rain season hits. Without a destination in mind, I meander along the sidewalk, smiling at passers-by. Funny how one's outlook can change with a mere glimpse of sunlight and the knowledge at the end of all this turmoil, she will come out on top. All I must do is stick to the plan, and not let those three slimy fuckers...well, fuck me. I wish that was as easy as it sounds.

Turning a corner, I happen upon Bennie's café. The coffee hut is infamous for some specially infused beans they use, only made more of a sensation by TikTok. The caffeine-deprived travel for miles, evident by the line of people out the door. Passing without the desire to peer inside, an overly charming voice chases my ear amongst the muttering.

"No, you have a fantastic day," he praises the barista, a girl in her twenties with fluttery, fake lashes. Through the window of hanging plants and an overly large logo vinyl, I scowl at Zeke. He carries a tray of mugs to a table in the back corner, bending to place a kiss on top of Aria's head. She bats him away, her smile wide as she accepts her drink. Pushing my way through those blocking the doorway, I storm across the small café and stomp my feet to a halt.

Then, no words come out. I just stand there, unsure what I was thinking even coming inside. I should have kept walking, left them to their tea party. Ignoring me, Zeke hands out small plates and dishes a croissant and caramel shortcake slices onto each. It's Zane who drops their jolly act first, sliding his blue eyes to me.

"What's wrong, Princess? Did your stubbornness fool you into thinking you were in control, *again*? How…cute," Zane narrows his eyes and tilts his head to the side. Zeke laughs over the gentle jazz playing from invisible speakers.

"You still don't get this whole 'keep Harlow out of the picture' thing, do you? We reversed your reverse-psychology. As if I'd trust you to sugar my coffee," he scoffs, sipping from a cup he needs two hands to hold. Aria doesn't spare me a glance, her cold shoulder as much of a blow as any insult she could have thrown my way. Out of the trio, I thought she might have a pinch of compassion. But that's a ridiculous thought, she's one of *them* after all.

Their combined laughter at my stunned silence fills my limbs like dread. I grow heavy under the weight of their deceit. I'm not the type to cry easily, but when they constantly mock me at every turn, my resolve is disappearing at an alarming rate.

Watching Zane lift the handle of his cup in delicate, lengthy fingers, his pinky raised, I feel the blush creeping up my cheeks as I remember what he did to me. How Freddie twisted his body towards the passenger window the entire ride back, not wanting to be anywhere near me. I disgusted him, myself, everything I stood for. And it all has to be for something.

"You know what," I say, tapping a finger in the air. A smile grows across my face and I turn away, leaving them guessing. Then I fly from the café, almost knocking over several people with coffees like bowling pins and race back to the gym.

I know what to do. I'm going to complete their bullshit list, slam it in front of Maddox and let him see how his crew are toying with the rookie. Sure, this plan hangs on the boss giving a shit about his recruits, but I'll make him give a shit. He'll shit all the shits for me. I'll prove I'm worth more than this pathetic attempt to haze me. Everyone loves a bit of determination.

Ten minutes past two, I'm still sitting here with my feet tapping. No one has returned to the gym all day, and if they've been watching me on their live feed, I'm sure they would have. The longer I was left to my own devices, the bolder I became. Except now I'm sat on the edge of the boxing ring, my chin in my hand, the nerves I struggle to hold at bay have broken through the dam. What if it was all for nothing? A trick Maddox and his crew formulated just to waste my time. At some point, I need to decide if they're messing with me because I'm an easy target, or if there's more to it than that.

A whirring sounds as the main shutters begin to rise in front of the windowed wall. Sunlight bleeds through, the street outside busy with clients waiting to enter. Maddox is revealed in slow mo, from his smart dress shoes to navy slacks, casual white tee with a V neckline. His face comes in view, hazel eyes zeroing in on me. A flash of confusion beats across his stern brow before he unlocks the main door. The crowd all flock inside, switching on lights and treating the place like a second home. Shit, I didn't know there would be other people here…

"Zane!" Maddox shouts so loud, I flinch and all customers

fall silent. They usher each other into the locker room in a rushed huddle, shutting themselves away as Zane storms into the building via the front entrance. He, too, stops to stare at me as Zeke and Aria follow quickly after. Their mouths drop and Aria winces, stepping behind Zane to avoid Maddox's wrath. "Care to explain why the *fuck* our sign has been altered to say Bloodied Trolls?"

Oh no.

The paint is still dripping, cascading down the wall. I dare say, I had appreciated the graffiti artwork that displayed the crew's name. But the longer I spent alone, the more mischievous my ideas became and when I found the can of red spray paint laying around at the hardware store down the street, I thought it could use an extra touch.

Now, the skull, which held a tilted crown, has the shaggy beard and bulbous nose of a troll. I took the liberty of adding a stubby body, complete with a tiny hairy cock. Didn't even bother to put the step ladder away, but feeling the waves of fury leaking from Maddox, I'm quickly deciding I went a step too far. I shiver, fighting against the urge to turn my shoulders inward and drop to my knees, begging for forgiveness. If there was ever a time for the ground to open and swallow me whole, this was it.

"All of you, my office – now." Maddox marches in the direction of the office I found the trash bag of paperwork in to shred. There wasn't anything of use, only a thousand receipts for the same coffee order as if they'd stashed them just in case a new recruit needed to be kept busy. So, I got creative. My gut flips. Any smirk I may have wanted to let loose dies and I fasten my pace, getting to the office door just before Maddox.

"Um, you know what – out here seems much roomier," I barricade the entrance with my body. Hazel eyes darken, a twitch of irritation in Maddox's five o'clock shadow. Dark circles suggest he hasn't slept in a while. One meaty hand shoves me aside like yesterday's trash, Maddox storms his office with an enraged roar. Yeah okay, I see where the boundary line is now – and I sailed across that bitch in a self-powered rowboat.

Peering around his muscular frame, even with his shoulders bunched, I spot the glass frame hanging on the wall. Empty. Discoloring on the cardboard backdrop shows where a garment used to hang until very recently, the outline of a gym vest imprinted inside the case for all to see. I briefly wonder what I was thinking but acting coy now is pointless. I was thinking to royally screw up the tasks given by those gasping at my back so Maddox would see I'm no one's little bitch. Pretty sure it's about to backfire. Slowing rounding the desk in the center, the boss of the Bloodied Skulls grapples with the last inch of his patience.

"Someone had better speak, fast," Maddox growls like a freaky mountain bear. No man should be able to make that noise, but alongside the heaving of his broad chest, it seems only natural Maddox can. Swallowing, I nod and step forward, deciding my chances of joining this crew are screwed. I wanted revenge, and I suppose I got it. Just not the complete soul-destroying, gut-wrenching agony I was hoping for.

"You know what, Maddox," I address him with an even tone I certainly don't feel resonates with my inside. But hey, I'm going down with this ship. "Fuck you."

"Fuck me?" his brows raise, that hardened jaw falling slack for a millisecond. Slamming his fists down on the mahogany desk between us, that growl comes again from deep within. "I offered you the chance you wanted. The chance others have died trying to get, and you've thrown it back in my face, ruined my gym and now you're cussing me out? What makes you think you're walking out of here alive?"

A silent message is passed through his words, the trio at my back stepping closer to box me in. Ignoring their company, the way they do to me, I glare Maddox in his stunning eyes and lean my hands on his desk.

"You can do whatever you like to me, but you'd better make it swift. Unless you want me to start screaming about the contents you've stashed beneath the false compartment in your bottom drawer. You really shouldn't use locks that are so easily picked." A beat passes and for a spilt second, I see Maddox's Adam's apple bob beneath his stubble. It's brief, but a surge of thrill explodes within me. For one milliest of milli-seconds, I have this infamous monster scared.

"Resorting to blackmail already? I thought you'd have at least put up a fight," he stretches his neck. I purse my lips, stirring up the last of the badass bitch who seems to have answered my calling. Maddox tries to hide the way his eyes drop to my mouth, a shudder clawing down my back wondering just what he's thinking about doing with them.

"I work smarter, not harder. Now are we doing this trial bullshit or shall I find another scout who looks like he wants to drag me over his desk and screw the life out of me?" Zane curses under his breath and Aria bumps me, her eyes wide and head shaking slightly. A warning, I suppose.

"Get out," Maddox barks sharply. I turn on an exhale, scampering after the others when a hand clamps down on my shoulder and the door is kicked closed. Locking Zane, Zeke and Aria outside, with Maddox and myself remaining behind.

"I don't play games," a hot slither of a whisper caresses my neck. "I create them, the rules only known to me. I like to watch those beneath me squirm, battling for my praise. And when they have beaten all foes, ready to receive it," fingers shift under my hair, brushing my nape. Tightening his hold around my bun, Maddox rips my head back and looms over me. "I flip the script and force everyone to play again." His mouth drops within an inch of my own.

"There are no winners here, Harlow. Only me, and I will not let you think otherwise." My name spoken in his rumbling octave does wicked things to my body, the spike on my hair calling to a feral side of me I struggle to contain these days. "From now on, you will do as you are told. Exactly as you're told. By me, or my crew. If they take advantage, it's my job to see them punished – not yours. Do you understand?"

Poking my tongue out to lick my lips, I accidently graze his. Desire bleeds into Maddox's eyes, a groan filtering through his chest. My brows raise in shock, but I make no move to jerk away. Especially not as his hand on my hair tightens and a battle of control takes place across his features. Yanking again, a gasp escapes me and I remember he asked a question.

"I understand," I attempt to nod. The grip on my head loosens, Maddox's body stepping away. The sudden loss of his heat is all encompassing, dragging the very air from my lungs. "However," I rush to say. Maddox spins with the stealth of a feline, grabbing my nape and slamming me into the door. A cold panel smushes the side of my face, shadows looming outside the frosted glass.

"You don't get freedom of speech," Maddox pushes harder. The length of his torso shifts, caging me between the lower panel of wood on the door and his own. "If you want to be part of my crew, you will obey simple rules. Showing weakness requires punishment and stay the fuck out of my way."

Dragging me back a step, Maddox shoves me onto the balcony. I stumble against the railing, my death-like grip holding me upright. Zeke leans against it, his forearms pressing on the metal.

"Well, what did he say?" he asks in a bored tone, but I see the shift of his eyes, intently watching me from the corner. Regaining my footing and composure, I steady my breathing for a moment. Aria is nowhere to be seen, but Zane is pacing around the boxing ring below, dragging his own hands through his hair as he stares down. From up here, the penis shape I carved into the leather flooring is much better than expected. This time, I let the grin I've been concealing wrap around my face as I turn to face Zeke, the image of confidence.

"He said, he's going to freaking love me."

My head drops from Zane's shoulder and I jerk awake. Artificial lighting continues to glare, the smell of paint invading my nostrils. It's a wonder if I fell asleep or simply passed out from the fumes. Discarded pizza boxes lay across the floor at our feet, my ass so numb, it's probably not attached anymore. When I stand, it'll drop right off and there goes my best quality.

Across the gym from where Zane, Aria and I decided we'd have the best view, Harlow stands at the top of the ladder, her roller gliding over the last patch of brick. Maddox's orders – as the fresh white paint would stand out too much against the different coats, she had to repaint the entire wall. I'd have made her do the entire gym to be honest, but then I'd also have to sit on the damn floor and wait until she's finished so, small wins. Using Zane's shoulder, I push myself up and stretch. Cracks filter down my spine in quick succession, several butt flexes bringing the feeling back to my behind.

Hopping down the bottom step of the ladder, Harlow wipes the back of her hand over her forehead, smearing a splodge of paint into her hair. Her arms are shaking and her feet drag as she heaves the paint cans to the storage room out back. I help Aria to stand, angered by her hiss of pain. Not just because she's been forced to sit on the hard ground for hours with an injury, but because I was the one forced to give it to her. Pulling her t-shirt up, I check her ribs with deft fingers, no matter how much she bats me away.

"The last fucking time," I mutter the promise again, shaking my head. Aria shoves me away this time, having enough of being pandered. She did always prefer to be the momma bear that screams at her kids to shut the fuck up and eat their greens. Zane winds his arm around her waist and for some reason, she lets him aid her to the back door. It's almost as if she doesn't trust me or something. Harlow reappears then, grabbing her jacket from a nearby bench.

"Where do you think you're going?" I step into her way, crowding her beside the boxing ring. Irritation claws at my insides, so many thoughts barging around my mind and I'm looking directly at the source of all of them. "Your training is just about to begin." Harlow rolls her amber eyes, attempting to push passed me. I don't think so somehow.

Bending, I toss Harlow over my shoulder and climb the ropes of the boxing ring, King Kong style. Torn or not, I dump her on the leather flooring and shove her onto her back with my sneaker.

"You want to be one of us so bad? You need to learn how to defend yourself." That's fair warning for me to bring my foot down in her gut. Not as hard as it should have been, but enough for Harlow to grunt and wind her arms around her middle. I'm fully aware Maddox is in his office, possibly watching through the surveillance cams, although the 'showing weakness' rule doesn't apply here. It's not a do-or-die fight, but some light sparring at best.

"You're the only asshole attacking me," Harlow glowers, standing with more ease than I expected. A smile grows upon my face at the opportunity I've presented myself. Testing Harlow's weaknesses under the guise of training; I couldn't have planned it better if I'd actually planned it.

"I'm teaching you. Pay attention." Widening my stance, slightly bending my knees, I urge Harlow to raise her fists. We're doing this. She sighs but follows suit, keeping her face defended. Jabbing from afar, I bounce lightly in a circle, careful of the ripped leather beneath my feet. Harlow is impatient, lunging forward to kick my side. I block her shin, knocking her with enough force to make her stumble.

"Please tell me you're better than that," I snort. Like *please*, tell me, because that weak shit won't see her through tomorrow.

"I'm tired?!" she hisses, barreling her body into me. Her fists throw wild punches, lacking any finesse and those that do land, barely tap me. Grabbing those flailing forearms, I whip Harlow around, crossing her arms over her front, pinning her back against my chest.

"Powering through when you're at your most exhausted is a skill that will save your life. You'll never be able to see through three rounds with a real fighter, but you can wear them down. Trick them into losing their energy while you reserve yours."

Nudging her away, Harlow's limbs fall heavily by her side. She turns to face me, her eyes unfocused. Exhaustion settles in the dark circles lining her eyes, a yawn stretching her mouth. She's given up, standing there undefended, accepting the inevitable. Very well.

"Duck," is all the warning I give, swinging hard. She doesn't. My fist slams into her chest. Flying backwards, Harlow trips on the torn base and hits the ground. All of the air is forced from her lungs. Attempting to curl into a ball and cough, I drop down on Harlow's waist, pinning her legs with my feet. Grabbing her wrists, I slam them above her head, shoving my face into hers.

"You're fooling yourself if you think you're cut out for this," I growl, no longer sure who I'm talking to. My dick thickens in my shorts, confusing me more than what my point was straddling her like this. "Just leave. No one wants you here."

"I do," the blunt reply comes from above. I crane my neck towards Maddox standing on the balcony outside his office, hands resting on the railing. Complete disbelief washes over my features.

Not once has Maddox ever said he wants any of us around. We're just the kids he picked up from the streets and let hang out in his gym. Then the self-defense training started and we just…stayed. His orders gave us a purpose, his reputation provides a sense of belonging. But does he actually want us to still be piggy backing off his name and fortune. Probably not. But he wants her.

Dragging myself off Harlow, I begrudgingly yank her up by the hold on her wrists. Making a show of dusting her down, I bow to Maddox like the King he thinks he is and head for the back door. Zane and Aria left ages ago but they'll be waiting in the car. They have to, I've got the keys. I make it all the way twisting the handle open when Maddox simply clears his throat and I still. I know better than to keep my back to him, or place one foot on the pavement outside.

"Forgetting something?" he asks. I turn, one brow raised, running through a mental list in my mind. All other doors are locked, the gym is closed until further notice. The calendar on my phone is synced to Zane's so I know we didn't have a meeting tonight. I shake my head and his hazel eyes narrow.

"Harlow is training to become one of you. And as you well know, Bloodied Skulls-"

"Stick together," I grit out the rest. Hanging my head, I grip the handle. Are we being punished – is that it? Maddox wasn't impressed with our display at Rapture and the sloppy way we handled a relatively simple task, so he's forcing us to accept Harlow into our ranks. Nothing has been noted about our performance, and Maddox is usually content with us handling shit our way, but it's the only explanation I can come up with.

"See that she's fed, clothed and rested. Above all else, make sure your new roomie has a proper introduction to the rules," Maddox orders, his voice fading as he retreats into his office. "Tomorrow, you lot have business to attend to."

As far as first days go, that was nothing like I was expecting. I was almost glad when Zeke pulled me into the ring to fight, because the hatred between us is something recognizable. A culture I've grown to understand. But sitting in the back of the Sedan, speeding down the freeway with the boys in front ignoring my existence, is not territory I thought I'd be in so soon.

I do my best to keep my mind occupied. Streetlamps blur past the window, the remnants of my free-will trailing behind. Roads bend, civilization falls away. I'm catapulted between my thoughts, the crescent moon lingering high overhead, my nails digging into my palm and the warehouses creeping closer. An overriding scent of fish filters through the vents, yet no one else seems to notice. Covering my nose with the back of my hand, we pull to a stop before a darkened structure. I recognize it as the one I fled in this very car, with Freddie traumatized in the passenger seat. And here I am again, back for more.

Climbing out of the car, I take a moment to look over the pier. A long walkway of wooden slats that lead to a small hut at the end. The moon glistens over the gentle lap of water, spreading tranquility across the horizon. When I turn around, however, it's all derelict warehouses, sandy mounds and forgotten, rusted machinery. Amongst it all, Zane and Zeke head for the crocked two-story house they call home.

"Shit," Aria hisses through her teeth, leaning on the sedan's hood. I make my way over to her, placing my hands on her hips from behind.

"What's wrong? And no bullshit you may have fed the others." Aria peers back to smirk at me, even if it doesn't translate to her green eyes.

"Bruised ribs, that's all. I sat in a weird position on the gym floor. Just aches a bit more than usual." Leaning her weight back into me, Aria sighs and for a moment, we stand there. The weight of the world lays heavily on our shoulders and for once, I let my guard down. I can't keep up this fight constantly, especially when Aria is hurt because of it. I'll reserve my hatred for Zeke, Zane and Maddox.

"You need a warm bath," I say when I've given Aria time to rest against me. She laughs, turning her head on my shoulder.

"Now there's an offer," she grins. I roll my eyes, sliding her arm over my shoulder. We walk to the house, entering through the door which has been left ajar. Up the stairs directly in front, Aria leads us to the third door down the hall. There's only one more, right at the end of the peeling wallpaper and tacky carpet. Entering Aria's room, I ease her onto the bed and busy myself in an en-suite bathroom.

Setting the hot water running and pouring in a heavy dose of muscle relaxing bubble bath, I leave the tub to fill and return to Aria. She's trying to peel her t-shirt over her head, but can barely raise her left arm.

"Hey," she tries to laugh softly. I'm not buying it. "Wanna help a girl out?" I stand in the doorway of her bathroom, tilting on eyebrow. Not so long ago, she was trying to beat the shit out of me. Now she thinks I'm going to strip her? Aria hangs her head, her voice so small, I need to lean forward to hear her.

"No tricks, I promise. My range of movement is limited and there's just some stuff I don't want the two knuckle-heads trying to help me with," she peers up through her brown hair, trying to push a smile through the pain. "Don't get me wrong, they'd give it a go. But that's a cringe fest none of us need." Chewing on the inside of my cheek, I sigh and relent. Fine.

Striding to her bed, I aid her in peeling the tight material over her right arm and head, then peel it down her left. White bandages are wrapped tightly around her midsection, disappearing beneath a sports bra. I shake my head and purse my lips, before giving her a lecture on bandaging too tightly. Restricting her lungs isn't going to help, neither's sitting in the same position for too long. Unwrapping them, I can't withhold my gasp. It's bad. Blue and purple, swollen and tender, bad.

"Aria, these need checking out," I try but she holds a finger up to my lips. That same hand moves, her fingers softly stroking my cheek and easing into my hairline.

"I like it when you care," she smiles. I don't return it, pulling away from her instead.

"Well maybe I would have if you'd given me the chance," I turn my head away. A new emotion I can't quite grasp churns within my chest. Regret? Or plain annoyance that the dynamics of our…relationship were determined without my knowledge.

An index finger stretches out to curl around mine, not realizing I'd left my hand on Aria's thigh. Full lips tilt, emerald eyes sparkle. I receive the same mask Aria shows the world, but I want more. I deserve more.

"Why did you choose me?" I ask, allowing her fingers to remain linked. My breath stalls, the answer to everything I've been through and become hanging in the balance. Aria started all of this. She chose me, and nothing had been the same since. Parting her lips, an audible exhale seeps from her. This is it.

"The bath must be ready to overflow by now," she says, replacing that perfectly practiced smile. I nod, standing to leave. As I turn off the faucet and leave her room completely, Aria's hand catches mine, using me to pull herself up. "There's room for another," she winks. "Besides, I'll need help washing my hair."

"Hair washing I can do from outside the tub," I tell her.

"You're no fun," Aria laughs and a smile grows on my face. Me? No fun – yeah right. My entire life right now is a fucking joke. A sigh of defeat slumps my shoulders. Didn't I just decide outside to let this bullshit angst go in her company? It's hard enough keeping up with Zeke's bipolar mood swings. I need somewhere, one place in my life and mind to release the angst. To find the person I once was, who could down wine and laugh with girlfriends over cheese and bad experiences.

Following Aria into the bathroom, she rests against the counter while I test the water. Without being asked, I peel off the rest of her clothes. Starting with her sports bra, then her baggy shorts and the nude colored thong underneath. Aria stands there, allowing my eyes to explore her. The first and only woman I've ever been with, and she hasn't changed in the slightest. Aside from the bruising I now feel somewhat guilty for. She went easy on me, knowing she'd be punished for it.

Taking her hand, I help to ease her into the tub and grab a stool from her room to perch on. Aria slides beneath the bubbles, resurfacing like a shampoo ad. She's stunning, not a single natural blemish. I won't comment on the scars as I don't want to delve into that rabbit hole. With her eyes fluttered closed and her soft moans filling the room, I swallow and clear my throat.

"So you've seriously never…you know, with the boys?" I ask, curiosity burning in my mind. There's so much I still don't know or understand, but I need to. Aria jolts and splutters, as if the very idea offends her.

"Hell no. I think it was sharing a room with Zeke and Zane at the orphanage that put me off men for life," she eyes me seriously. For some reason, that settles something erratic in my chest I hadn't realized was there. But then again, a whole new range of questions have opened up.

"I didn't think they'd allow gender mixing in group homes."

"Maybe not at the richer ones," Aria shrugs, the water rippling around her. "We're gutter rats who had learned to land on their feet, that's all." I look at the bathroom around us, noting the stain of scrubbed mold between the tiles and the draft seeping in from the small, top window. I wouldn't call them 'landing on their feet' myself. Aria notes my looks of concern, flicking some bubbles my way. "Don't be sad for us. We make our own happiness." Her look lingers on my face and I sit up straighter.

Does she mean me? Or am I reading into her gaze too much, before she sinks below the water once again. You know – I'm taking it. She totally insinuated I made at least Aria happy, for a very short period of time. When she resurfaces, I reach for the shampoo and set about squeezing a dollop on her hair.

"Speaking of happiness, or lack of, I swear Zeke didn't hate me so much before," I ponder out loud. Aria chuckles to herself between groaning at my fingers massaging her scalp.

"You drive him crazy, literally. I don't think he's had a

straight thought in the past two years. He couldn't let you go, you know? Needing to know where you were, what you were doing, like an obsession. It's just his way of dealing with unwanted emotions. Give him time, he'll come around." My hands fall still. My mind reels, unsure how to compute what I've just heard but while Aria is being so open, I push on.

"And Zane?" I ask, drinking in every drop of information. Aria lets me ease her head into the water to wash out the shampoo.

"Oh, you can forget about Zane. That stubborn asshole will take his grudges to his grave." I scoff to myself, because Aria can't hear me. Figures. After rising to sit upright, I use a jug to pour water over Aria's hair, washing away the rest of the bubbles.

"I wish I could forget about all of you," I whisper the truth. Aria pulls out of my hold, spinning her body. Reaching for my cheek, I lower to kneel by the bathtub and let her pull me close.

"No, you don't. Or you'd have never understood how this," she lashes out her other hand to twist my nipple, "can become this," her lips plant on mine. Water droplets drip over my t-shirt, her mouth opening to push her tongue into my mouth. Within a second, by the time it takes me to gasp and reciprocate, the last two years wash away. As if no time has passed at all, I'm right back with Aria and the familiar lust I've bottled up uncorks itself.

Tremors of forbidden lust trickle through me and I scoot forward, giving her more access to my breast. She massages me through the t-shirt, and it's not enough. I catch myself on the edge of a precipice, ready to dive into the bath and let her take me in any way she deems fit. Aria is lust and destruction. An enigma who rewrites all the traits I thought I knew about myself, and opens me up to new opportunities. Ones I grew up thinking were wrong, but she feels oh-so right.

"Let's," I pull back, catching my breath, "not." Dragging

myself back onto the stool, I ignore the rigidness of my nipples pushing against my crop top and t-shirt. One breast is soaked, the other dry and Aria stares at them hungrily. Oh yeah, she would have ruined me, and injured herself in the process. Not that I care. Only that…fuck, I kinda do.

"Can I ask you a question?" I decide to change the subject. Aria reins herself back into the tub, using her feet on the T-shaped faucet to keep herself reclined.

"Anything. I'm done playing these cat and mouse games – you deserve better," she goes back to playing with the bubbles and misses my frown. I want to believe that, but time will tell. I know better than to trust openly where I have no proof to validate it.

"Um, okay. Why do you guys live here? Maddox and his Skulls are notorious among street talk, speaking of the heists and the riches you guys manage to bring in. Yet…this place is hardly the Ritz." I look around, hoping I haven't offended her. But the smell of fish has yet to leave my nostrils and I'm sure I hear the scurrying of rats within the walls.

"Maddox is all about power plays. He needs control to soothe his damaged soul," Aria replies easily. Too easily. How many times has she asked herself the same question?

"Like sitting on the floor at the gym instead of on a chair?" I continue. Aria nods. "So that's what Maddox needs – but what about you guys? What possesses you to live a life like this?" I coax, knowing I'm going too far. Perhaps being too obvious in my digging, but I have to know.

"And us," Aria peers back to frown at me. Her brows knit together as she runs out of rehearsed answers to give. "Well, we simply don't know any different. I reckon one week of living in some sky-high penthouse, Zane would have some incurable STD and Zeke would have either overdosed on cocaine or dived off the roof."

"Jesus Christ," I gasp, my eyes flying wide. This causes Aria to smirk, falling back into the tub.

"It's the truth. We can't handle that lifestyle. Trust me, we've tried. Didn't work out."

"So you prefer to live like this?" I raise a hand towards the mildew thriving at her basin.

"United? Together, in a bubble of trust, separate from the toxicity of the world? Yeah, we do," she nods. I drop my hand loudly against my thigh on a bitter laugh. It's hilarious, because that's all they bring. Toxicity. Corruption. If what Aria is telling me is true, the remaining Bloodied Skulls believe they deserve a shitty life, yet they do nothing to prove otherwise. They may be fed. They may have a sense of purpose thanks to Maddox's rules, but all I see is a possessive overlord and his three minions. Suddenly, the hatred I've been clinging onto slides into pity.

The silence weighs on me, my mind spinning. Between the heat radiating from the steaming bath, the lavender scent washing over me and the long, shitty day I've had, I push up to my feet and stride out of the room. With one focus in mind, I ignore all other people, sounds and sights. Right now, my muscles ache, my head is beginning to pound and all that matters is the bottle of wine I locate like a blood hound. Returning to Aria's bathroom, I slam the door closed with my boot, chug an unhealthy dose of wine from the bottle, strip and slide into the tub.

Who knows what tomorrow will bring, and I suppose Aria is right. The crap-hole they've chosen to reside in is nothing if not an oasis from the real world. Perhaps when I'm recovering from heists and illegal fights, this will be the only place I want to be too. In the brief time I'm here, at least, before I burn it all to the ground.

Chapter Seventeen

ZANE

The ping on my phone informs me a new morning has arrived. Not that I would have known otherwise. Sleep evades me. I merely lie each night, completely straight on my back with my head tilted towards the ceiling. I like to think at some point my body enters rest mode, giving me enough momentum to see through another day. But the truth is clear for all to see. I'm not living this life; I'm simply coasting through it. A drone following orders because that's all there is to do.

Sitting upright, I peer at the lock screen, noting the message from Maddox. It wouldn't have been anyone else, because the only other people who have this number are snoring in the rooms either side of mine. I don't waste my time on social media either, preferring my dull existence wasn't broadcasted to all.

"Dining room in ten," I holler, leaping from the bed. Pulling on a pair of sweats I left folded on the dresser, my fist beats on Zeke and Aria's doors on the way passed. I pause at Harlow's, the last closed door at the end of the hallway. There's no doubt in my mind she'll fuck up any simple tasks I delegate her way, but Maddox's message was clear. We *all* must work together today. Thundering my fist on her door twice as hard, a startled scream is lost to my shouting. "You too, Princess! Dining room, ten minutes!"

Flying down the stairs, I switch on the coffee machine and set up a laptop on the varnished oak tabletop. Retrieving a sketch pad and floral pencil case from Aria's backpack, I lay this out and get on with breakfast. Zeke swoops in by my side, attending to the coffees. No need for cheery shows of affection. Zeke knows, regardless of sleeping or not, I've never been a morning person. By the time Aria and Harlow appear in the archway of the dining room/open kitchenette, *twelve minutes later*, I'm placing a plate stacked with toast down amongst an arrangement of butter, honey, jams, and bowl of mashed avocado for Aria.

"Sit," I order Harlow, tugging out a chair at the top of the table. "Remain quiet and commit everything you hear to memory. I'm not a fan of repeating myself." She complies, narrowing her amber eyes on me as I move away, forcing myself to ignore the red tousle of her hair. Curled, slightly matted and the perfect bedhead if I've ever seen one. Trickling over her shoulders in a cream vest that does nothing to hide her nipples, I clear my throat when Aria catches me looking. Preferring to stand, I lean on the table to relay Maddox's message.

"We need to intercept an item for a Mr. Callahan at 17:00 hours today. Here's the coordinates," I skid my phone to Zeke. His fingers fly over his laptop, researching where exactly we need to go. Aria opens her sketch pad, more of a physical strategist.

"It's the southside of a delivery depot, about a three hour drive from here. I'd imagine we're intercepting a departing truck to relieve Mr. Callahan of his impending arrival," Zeke ponders out loud. I nod in agreement.

"It's been a while since one of our jobs have had a personal attack involved," Aria adds in. We're all wondering what this Mr. Callahan did to piss off Maddox, but no one will voice it. No questions asked, we follow the orders we're given.

"Hijacking a moving truck is too messy," Zeke scratches his stubbled chin. "We should head in half an hour earlier, catch the package before it even leaves the depot." Shimmying his chair closer to Aria's, he turns his laptop so she can start sketching in what she likes to call a 'brain dump.' Entry and exit points, the keypad system on the electronic gate, the rear shutter of the depot, a rough drawing of the uniform one would be expected to wear. Along the side in colored pens and highlighters, Aria makes a list of calculations, weighing up variables and times.

Taking my phone back, I scroll through the contacts while Harlow reaches over and slides the plate of toast her way. The ceramic screeches on the tabletop, but she isn't fazed. Standing, her breasts hover a millimeter over the toast stack, her arms outstretched to wrap around the other jars and plates, gliding them over the varnished wood to the top end of the table. My eye twitches. Relaxing in her seat, Harlow proceeds to butter her breakfast while I huff, refocusing on the Bloodied Skulls who actually earned their right to be here.

"I have a contact who can arrange uniforms and ID badges," I inform, my thumb tapping on the call button. He answers after a beat, accustomed to incoming calls from blocked numbers.

"Slimy Lenny at your service," the voice comes at the same time Harlow bites into her toast. *Crunch.* I glare at her.

"It's Zane. I'm sending you an order. We need to be ready

by," I lean over Aria's pad. She taps her pen on a time, circled numerous times in purple. "Noon."

Crunch.

"Yeesh, that's a tight timeframe, my man," Slimy Lenny makes a series of noises. "I don't know if I'd be able to swing it this time."

Crunch.

"Name your price. We'll be there soon, and Len – we have a tag along." I look to Harlow who flips me off, a second piece of toast in between her teeth. "I'll send you her measurements."

"Ohhh, you finally found a replaceme-" I hang up the phone and grip it tight in my hand. The next time Harlow crunches, my arm swings out, swiping the toast stack all over the floor.

"Are you so fucking obtuse, you can't sense the atmosphere in the room right now?!" I yell, slamming my fists into the dining table. Aria's pen is jolted aside, her green eyes widening in time with a gasp.

"Dude!" Aria throws her pen and it bounces off my chest, leaving an ink splodge on the white cotton. "Go take a fucking chill pill. Stressing before a job never bodes well." I growl, pushing myself away. Stalking through the kitchen, I snatch a wooden box out the back of the top cupboard and exit through the back door. Dropping into a plastic garden chair, I make quick work of rolling a joint and light it just as the door opens and closes again. Fucking Zeke, never leaves me alone, I think to myself, as a redhead pops into view.

"I'm sensing some tension here," Harlow singsongs, rocking back and forth on her heels. She doesn't look at me, her face angled to the outhouse where we strapped her and her wannabe boyfriend up. Without her amber eyes searching mine, I spare myself a glance at her bubbled ass in tight leggings, making sure my first toke on the joint is a big one.

"What the fuck do you want from me?" I rasp, holding the smoke in the back of my throat as long as I can. The immediate effect filters into my mind, equally clearing and fogging it. Breathing out one puff of smoke, I immediately go in for another toke. I don't have the time to waste fucking about here, especially with her.

"I figured it would be a good idea to settle any hostility before going any further with this 'job,'" she air quotes. I bristle.

"See, that's your problem. You think this is all a game. Act as if you're untouchable. The moment we leave this house, everyone's safety is on my shoulders. Except yours; I don't give a shit what happens to you." Harlow laughs. A whimsical sound I wish I could hear in better circumstances, but that would entail actually spending time with her. It's much easier to keep her at a distance so when she ultimately gets bored and leaves, it makes no difference to me whatsoever.

"I know you don't like me," Harlow starts and this time, it's my turn to laugh.

"I fucking hate you."

"Trust me – the feeling is mutual," she rolls her eyes dramatically. Her pocket vibrates then, as Harlow peeks at the message on her phone and swiftly pushes in back out of view. See, it's shady shit like that which makes me not trust her.

Plucking the joint from between my lips, she lifts it to hers. Inhaling, holding, exhaling. I watch her chest rise and fall, trailing my gaze over the body which hasn't lost its curvaceous figure, despite the addition of defined muscle. Passing the joint back, Harlow rounds my chair, leaning over to grip the arm rests either side.

"But at least I have viable reasons for my opinions. Yours are completely unwarranted. You hate me because…well, I don't even know. Because Aria picked me? Because I exist? Or maybe…because you just don't want anyone else to look out for. Whatever it is," Harlow's eyes hold my stare, the grimace at what she sees there making her top lip hitch up on one side.

"Sort it the fuck out, because the problem we have here, is completely on your end."

Shoving herself upright, Harlow strides inside, leaving me to my thoughts. The fuck? My skin crawls as if I've just been flayed, stripped bare for the entire world to peek through my impenetrable exterior. I face every day with an impassive outlook and blank stare. I'd even convinced myself that's all it was. But now, emotions begin to war in my chest, my breathing growing shallow, and I don't like it one bit.

Gripping my joint tight enough to crush it, the cherry fizzles out in my hand. Dusting away the remains, I grip my thigh through the sweatpants. There's no time to think on all of the valuable points she just made. We'll save those feelings of self-doubt for a drunken bender after this job is done. Standing and lifting the chair high above my head, I throw it on an enraged roar. It splashes into a small fishpond Zeke started as a side project and never finished, sinking from view. Excessive, but needed.

"We all good, bro?" Zeke asks as I storm through the house. I don't respond, vowing to never lie to those I love. But no, we're not all good. As Maddox's second in command, the weight of introducing in a new recruit is all on me. Today of all days, I can't be caught losing my shit.

By the time Slimy Lenny's camera flashes in my face, my mood has soured to the point of dangerous. My fingers twitch, ready to lash out at the nearest object or person. Unfortunately, Harlow is nowhere to be seen. Her and Aria wandered off to change into their uniforms around twenty minutes ago. Every second in which they don't return makes my jaw tense harder, wondering exactly what they're doing. Not mentally prepping for the job ahead, that's for sure.

The printer whirs, spitting out my fake ID card. Standing from the stool, Slimy Lenny pushes the card into a lanyard and hands it to me, completing my disguise. A white polo shirt, navy chino shorts, black trainers with the socks pulled up to my shins. Pulling on a flat cap displaying 'DPS' to cover my auburn hair, I find Zeke strutting around, his shorts pulled up passed his navel.

"Kinda suits me, don't you think?" he grins, posing with his knee-high socks and severe lack of t-shirt in a full-length mirror. The warehouse Slimy Lenny operates from doesn't have much – just enough that he can pack up and be gone within five minutes. I force a grin at Zeke's reflection, my eyes traveling to his butt.

"Looks like you have a permanent wedgie," I comment, dragging his belt loops higher to make it worse. He howls, yanking down the shorts by the cuffed hems on his thighs. Aria and Harlow appear, giggling at the display.

"Thank fuck for that," Aria's arm is linked in Harlow's. "The world doesn't need any more Zeke's walking around." Harlow's red-painted lips smile wide, her eyes lingering on Zeke's bare torso. The grin on my mouth, that wasn't so forced for a millisecond, drops. Turning my back, I block off Slimy Lenny's wolf whistle.

"Damn Zane," his hand slaps my back. True to his nick-name, a slimy coating covers his stained teeth. Limp greasy hair on his head needs a serious wash and with the amount we pay him, I don't know why he's not having a blow-dry at a salon daily. But it's the way he's eye-fucking Harlow that's repulsing me the most. He wouldn't get within a foot of her while I'm around. She may be temporary, but for today at least, she's a Bloodied Skull. I protect my own.

"Either you're shit at sizing up women, or you're a fucking genius," he grins those disgusting teeth my way. I don't need to look to know he's referring to Harlow's chest in the open neck polo, unbuttoned to her cleavage and tucked into the shorts cinched tight at her waist. She even makes the long socks look good, her tattoos poking out in all the right places.

Shrugging him off, I grab the keys for the Sedan and order everyone to get in. I take the driver's seat, needing something to focus on for the next three hours aside from the erection throbbing into my waistband. I had to fasten the fucker in there and leave my shirt loose over the top, not wanting to give anyone the satisfaction of ridiculing me. My mind needs to be on the job. Not on all the ways I'd gag and restrain Harlow, and lash her with a whip for ruining the perfect dynamic we had going before she showed up.

Zeke slides in the passenger seat, finally with a shirt on. Placing his laptop bag in the footwell, he leans across me, pushing the central locking button on my door before the girls have entered.

"What's going on?" he asks, not moving far enough away out of my face. I roll my eyes, trying to shove him away. Quick as a flash, Zeke slaps me around the face and grips my collar in his fist. "Snap the fuck out of it. This is just like any other job," he glowers. Gripping his wrist, I twist sharply, pinning him back in his chair with a chicken wing.

"Except it's nothing like any other job. She shouldn't be here," I hiss. Zeke winces and I release him, needing his hands intact to hack the security gate when we get there.

"Well, she is. Maddox ordered it. He calls the shots and we obey because that's what lackies do. Unless you want to live a menial life, working as a postie for real?" Zeke punches my bicep. I let this one slide, sighing and bracing my hands on the wheel. "Exactly. You like our set-up just as much as I do. We thrive on adrenaline, and don't need to boast about being better than everyone else. We just know it, and we have each other."

"I just...don't want anything to jeopardize us," I grunt, leaving out the word 'again.' We both know it should be there, but neither want to voice it.

"She won't. Trust Maddox. And if she does, we'll fucking

kill her," Zeke shrugs as if we're discussing something as casual as ordering at a drive through.

Unlocking the doors, Aria and Harlow slide into the back. I watch closely in the rearview mirror. Harlow reaches across, buckling Aria in while her range of movement is still hindered by her injuries. She won't complain, nor will she sit out on a job so I don't bother suggesting it. Retreating, Aria places a quick kiss on Harlow's lips, catching both her, and us watching from the front, unaware. Zeke's hand drops to my arm, squeezing me in a way that I'm sure was supposed to calm me, but it doesn't.

Revving the engine, Slimy Lenny pushes the warehouse shutter upwards and I fly us forwards, throwing Harlow back into the middle seat. Zeke doesn't withdraw his hold. As if I'm not a fragile fucking flower what might wilt at the sight of Aria being a played like a fool. This girl is no good for us. She won't last, and she certainly won't be around long enough to be initiated. Only question is, who is going to get hurt in the process? Not me, that's for sure.

Taking a corner too harshly, I gun onto the highway, leaving all signs of civilization far behind. The girls in the back play hand games, laughing and generally messing about. I shake my head, sensing all of Aria's keen rational plummeting.

"Stop giggling and get your fucking heads in the game. Harlow," I snap, spearing her with a glare in the rearview mirror. "Repeat the plan back to me." She rolls her fucking eyes and my hands shake on the wheel, almost steering us into on oncoming tree just to see her fly through the windscreen.

"Do it, or I will leave you on the side of the road looking like every postie's wet dream. If we're lucky, some serial killing bastard is roaming the highways today, looking for his next victim." Aria nudges her shoulder, encouraging her to do it so Harlow parts those red lips and sighs.

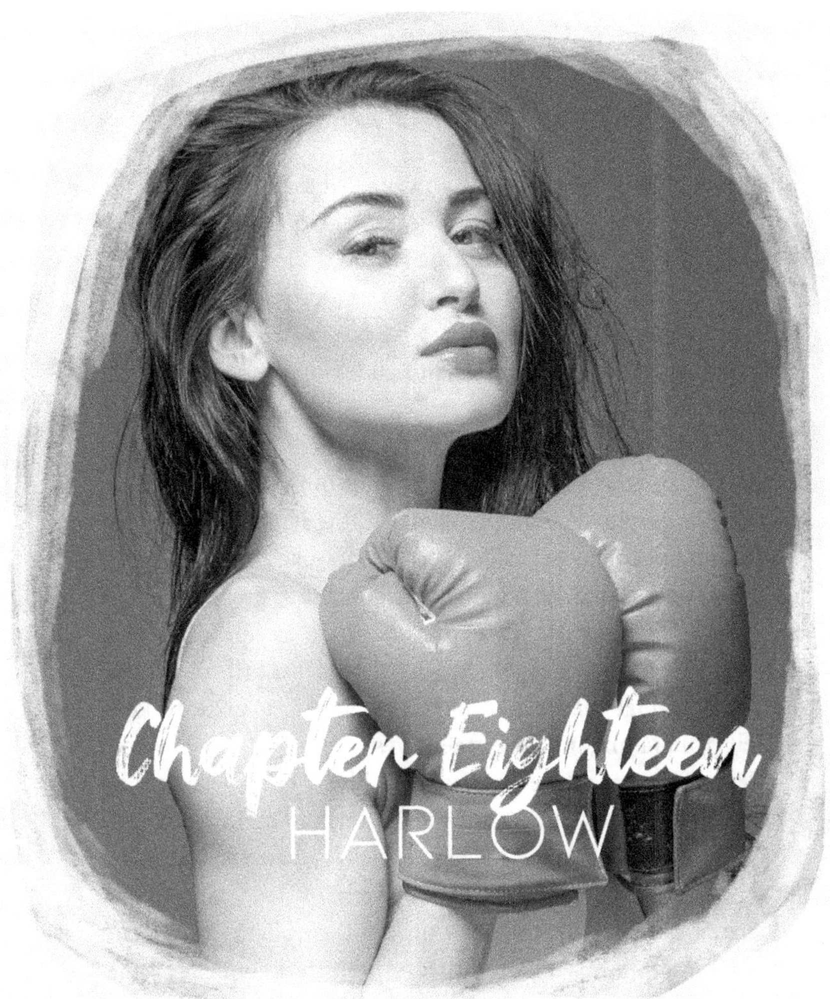

"We're currently driving to the depot," I drawl in a bland tone and Zane barks at me once again.

"Wrong! We're driving to the delivery van we have stashed to swap out vehicles halfway," he takes great pleasure in correcting me. Aria's hand links with mine, sending me strength when diving forward to strangle Zane seems too tempting.

"Sir, yes sir," I salute. Zane physically relaxes while my mind boggles – is he seriously that much of an egotistical asshole?! Apparently so, as he turns up the music and we all melt into our thoughts. Somewhere between Shawn Mendes and Connor Price singing of heartache, my thoughts trail to Freddie. I wonder if he's looked for me since I disappeared from his gym apartment, or figured I just didn't want to see him again. I hate how things were left, but I reckon I couldn't face him again to correct them. Aria's hand slides over my bare thigh, her palm warm and inviting.

Turning away from my thoughts, I focus on her. The mysterious woman who's drawing out feelings in me I didn't expect. She truly is gorgeous – model worthy if life had been kinder to her. Long chocolate hair floats past her waist, beautiful green eyes blink up at me through her lashes. Sure, everyone has a girl-crush. But you never expect them to reciprocate your outlandish lesbian jokes. Fuck, I need to get a grip of myself. Remember what they did to me if that's what it takes to keep myself from falling into her green eyes.

"What does it matter anyway?" I blurt, figuring angering Zane is my best solution for the butterflies taking over my body. Pursing my lips, his icy blue eyes in the mirror watch me closer than the road. "I haven't been given a role to play. I'll just be sitting here in the car, waiting for the valiant soldiers to return." Slumping back, I reflect on the bitterness in my tone. Do I secretly want to feel the thrill of a heist, or am I just pissed at always being the outcast? Either way, Zeke chuckles and turns to face me.

"Everyone in this vehicle has a role, Feisty. I'm the tech guy, Zane's the muscle, Aria's the brains."

"Dare I ask what I am?" I withhold a shudder at the cruel smile that grows across Zeke's face.

"Your role is what you've already proven to be best at," he winks and my heart sinks. He can't possibly mean….My head begins to shake, a look of hurt twisting to explore Aria's face. The lipstick, the outfit, it suddenly makes so much sense. *I'm the distraction.*

"Oh, no, no. I won't, I'm not doing that again," I wriggle away from Aria but her hand grips tighter, reassuring me it's going to be better this time. I'm already visualizing the cell, only this time it won't be a dimmed room with a cushioned bench like Rapture's. It'll be cold, hard and framed by metal bars with no one coming to save me. I was supposed to be putting my own plan in action but look at me now. My first official job and they're hanging me out to dry – again.

"Harlow, breathe," Aria grips my arm and gives me a rough shake. I hadn't realized I was hyperventilating but now I do, a blush claims my cheeks. Zeke is staring, Zane's eyes flicking to the rearview mirror every other second. "I promise it's going to be okay this time. You're one of us now, we don't leave each other behind."

"Well, that's debatable," I vaguely hear grumbled from the front, although I'm not sure who it came from. My ears pound with the drum of my heart, blocking out Aria's bid to soothe me. Shoving my hands beneath my butt, I squeeze my eyes shut, counting the seconds I can in and exhale. A pair of headphones are slapped over my head, Airhead by Wes Patrick playing at a volume I'd usually consider too high. Right now though, I welcome the beat. The rhythm, and sometime during the fourth or fifth repeat, my shoulders have eased back down to an acceptable level. Peeking to see the boys are no longer interested in my panic attack, I slump down to rest my head on Aria's shoulder.

Remember the plan, I tell myself. Remember the reason you sought them out. I'm here to seek revenge, and to do that, I need to cling on like a freaking koala. They won't ditch me today, because I will not let them. The music in the headphones cuts mid-song, a slap on my thigh making me flinch upright.

"We're here for the vehicle swap," Zeke announces. There's far too much joy in his smile considering the episode I had, but that's fine. All the more to pay for later. Shuffling along the backseat after Aria, I don't miss her hiss of pain at the jerky movement. Her arms are wrapped around her middle, holding the bruising on her side that I'm sure the guys don't realize is so severe. Bad enough that I had to help her change back in the warehouse, urging her to see a doctor soon. I may still consider her part of the rival team, but she's more than begun to thaw on me. If only her choice in kin was as good as her ability to put me at ease with one smile.

Placing a foot on the grassy trail Zane has taken us down, hidden from view of the main highway, he appears the second Aria separates to head to the delivery van.

"Not a single scratch," he grunts, pushing the Sedan's keys into my hand. I frown, trying to give them back but Zane steps into my body, leaving no space between us and the open doorway at my back. If he so much as leans in, I'll fall back into the car on my ass.

"You have a five minute head start. Continue driving south, the depot is twenty-five miles away on the left. It's your first day on the job. All you have to do is get in, find us a way in and not get caught. Think you can manage that?" A hint of dare and disbelief are reflected in Zane's tone, a mocking smile hidden within the shadows of his cheeks.

"Come on then," I jut my chin upwards, mustering every ounce of willpower I have to not let Zane see me crumble. "Let's get this shit over with so we can go back to the house on the fishing dock none of you seem to notice the smell of anymore. Once Maddox has swung by to pick up the package, I've got a new season of The Circle on Netflix to binge with ice cream and wine."

I shove Zane back a step, catching him off-guard with my newfound confidence. Slamming the rear door closed, I round to the driver's side. Aria hangs back from the van's cab, offering me a reassuring smile. I reciprocate it, dropping into the seat.

Honestly, I'd expected this 'job' to be a tiny bit more exciting. If it wasn't Maddox's instruction we all had to attend, I'd be fast-tracking to the evening I have planned in an attempt to salvage my day. All that's keeping me going is Aria's light-hearted company and the decision I made upon waking up to Zane's hammering on my door this morning to not let his orders affect me. *Easy peasy,* I chuckle to myself. What was it Zane said – make a scratch?

Throwing the Sedan into reverse, I race backwards on the bumpy trail and fly back onto the highway. A truck blares its horn, a few meters from colliding with me if I wasn't quick enough to wheelspin out of the way. Shoving the stick into drive, I skid down the highway with the scent of burning rubber and Zane's hollers from the van dragging behind me. Five minutes my ass. Hanging my arm out the open window, I bounce my middle finger around, deciding this job isn't so boring after all.

I don't slow until the depot is in view. Leaning across the car, I search the glove compartment. For what – I'm not entirely sure. A weapon perhaps. A means to defend myself. But all that comes to hand is a microfiber cloth and a stick of chewing gum. The defense of fresh breath it is. Pushing the stick into my mouth and veering left, I'm presented with a security booth and closed barrier. A man around his fifties holds up a hand to signal I should stop, his mustache invading my side of the car to peer at the ID badge around my neck.

"I don't recognize you," he leers a little too long to be professional. I smile sweetly around chewing the gum, thanking all fuck I'm not actually looking at a future of employment with this creep.

"New transfer," I bat my eyelashes and chew seductively. If that's a thing.. "First day at this depot. I hope you're my personal tour guide." *Vom.* The bodyguard chuckles, his next words interrupted by a horn beeping behind.

"What's taking so long?!" Zeke screams out of the passenger

window. "Some of us have jobs to do and families waiting at home!" Zane beeps the horn another few times and the body-guard groans. Bidding me a lovely afternoon, he slinks back to his booth and releases the barrier. I make a show of waving and giving him a wink before leisurely rolling forward. Thankfully, the split roads ahead are signposted so I take a right towards the employee parking lot. The van behind goes left while I assess the size of the building, trying to keep my bearings as to which side I'd need to give the Skulls access to.

Parking up, I exhale, telling myself over and over I can do this. My trainers hit the gravel, my knee-high socks pulled all the way up. In the reflection of the car's windows, my red hair glints in the sunlight. Pulling out my phone, I quickly search up other DPS depots as I make my way to the main entrance. A bubbly assistant welcomes me from behind her desk, a sheet of Perspex separating us.

"Hey, I'm Vicky," I blurt out the fake name on my ID, counting the cameras in each corner of the lobby. Holding up my badge, the assistant leans into the plastic sheet to peer closer. "I was sent over from Vancouver for a spot-check." Her eyes widen and I smile, falling into this role is easier than expected.

"Oh, okay. We weren't expecting any more visitors today," she fumbles, looking through papers on her desk. I lean an arm on the counter, chuckling lightly.

"That's why they call it a spot-check. It's not supposed to be planned. The bosses want to make sure we're all following the same system and that operations are running smoothly on a day-to-day basis."

"Of course," she returns my smile and lifts a phone to her ear. "I will call down the manager to greet you. Please wait by those double doors." Following her instruction, I try not to twitch my thumbs. I've just escalated from asking a security guard for a tour to having a manager on his way to interrogate me in the span of five minutes. Smart move, Harlow. The entrance lobby is white, everywhere. A blind man would miraculously be able to see with the sheen from the tiled floor. A stack of magazines sit on the table in a small waiting area, but I couldn't sit still if I tried. The double doors buzz and release, revealing a man in a business suit.

"Ahh, Miss…" he offers out his hand, avoiding staring at the tag positioned over my chest.

"Winters," I shake his hand. "Vicky Winters." Welcoming me, Mr. suited and booted tells me to call him Nick and leads me through the doors. The warehouse beyond shocks me with its sheer size, machines lined along the floor below. Packages fly along conveyor belts, being checked by an assistant before being tossed into mailing bags. As far as I can see, the bags are heaved into crates and wheeled up ramps to the trucks waiting, rear doors open. I swallow hard. How the fuck are we supposed to intercept a parcel amongst this chaos? Nick leads the way along a metal platform, railings either side.

"We're the largest DPS depot in the country. Nine hundred thousand parcels pass through these walls every day, that's a record amount for any postal service in the world. Usually, it's only head office that perform these checks but I'm not surprised others are interested in our swift turnaround policy. Which branch did you say you were from?"

"Vancouver," I stutter, still overwhelmed by the sheer size of the warehouse I need to somehow navigate. High in the air, a large digital clock displays the time as 16:35. Only twenty-five minutes before Mr. Callahan's parcel is due to go out on one of the delivery vans before me. Has it already been loaded? Is this entire operation pointless because we're going to miss our window of opportunity anyway?

"Of course," Nick stops beside a staircase leading down to the ground floor. I quickly peek over my shoulder at a fire escape door on the west side, deciding that's my best bet.

Hopefully it's not alarmed, but creating a distraction is my whole purpose, right? Nick continues to watch me closely, his dark eyes hiding all his secrets. "Follow me this way. You've caught us on a very exciting day," he walks past the staircase and I hang back. When he looks to me, a question in his brows, I force my feet to move further from the doorway I need to somehow get to undetected.

A few steps lead us up to a closed door, out of place in the industrial setting. Dark brown, silver handle. Beyond, a hallway of offices is presented, Nick guiding me all the way to the end. Without knocking, he enters a suite labeled as 'occupied,' introducing me to a table full of men and women all dressed in the same business attire as him. "Please join us," Nick encourages and I take a step backwards."

"You know, I was much more comfortable on the delivery floor. Learning your ways of operating will be hugely beneficial," I try, failing to come up with any more words. My tongue grows thick in my mouth, the exposed patches of my thighs and breasts suddenly feeling overly naked. Nick places his hand on the small of my back and gently urges me to enter the room, despite all of the judgmental stares that know I don't belong here.

"Oh…okay, sure," I nod, putting on a smile as Nick guides me into a chair and tucks it in from behind.

"Would you like some coffee? Doughnuts? They've just been delivered," he gestures to the plate of confectionaries in the center of the oval table.

"Through DPS I hope," I joke and multiple people around the table laugh. I relax a smidgen, joining their laughter. See, absolutely nothing to worry about. I'm winning them all over here, and within a few minutes, I'll miraculously need to pee and excuse myself. No biggie. Nick takes a spot at the top of the table, shaking his papers back into a neat pile.

"Excuse the interruption everyone. Before we dive back

into the presentation, I'd like to introduce you all to Vicky Winters. She's been sent to perform a spot-check on our systems today, and I trust she will be pleasantly surprised by our efficiency. Vicky, around this table are members of the board, trustees and such. And this man to my left is Chris Danvers, the head coordinator for Vancouver's depot." My breath locks in my lungs.

Screwed. I'm so fucking screwed.

The same internal spasms of an oncoming anxiety attack rise back within me. Chris gives me a brief nod, his mouth fixed into a permanent scowl. But as Nick begins to spiel some numbers and facts I don't understand, Chris doesn't say anything. Sure, his stare is burning me alive with the flames of my own lies, but no words pass his lips. Perhaps he's on Maddox's payroll? Whatever is about to happen, it's going to be okay. All I need to do is actually breathe before I pass out and keep repeating that mantra.

This is fine. Everything's going to be just fine…

"Still convinced she'll come through?" Zane growls at me, his thumb knocking against the steering wheel. If I had full range of motion, I'd smack him one for just being a general twat waffle. From the front bench of the van we're all crammed on, I stare intently at the fire exit door, willing it to open.

"Fuck's sake," Zeke grits out through clenched teeth. "I knew giving her such an important job was a stupid fucking idea."

"All the more reason for Maddox to kick her aside before

she learns too much," Zane nods. Removing my sneaker, I find enough strength to twist side to side and slam it into each of their faces before returning it to my foot. My side screams in pain, the swelling beneath Harlow's bandaging pulsing. Leaving my laces untied, I fold my arms around my middle, looking casual as fuck. It won't do the guys any good to know the pain I'm in; their guilt will only distract them from the job at hand.

Zane curses under his breath, muttering about a guard coming our way. The same one from the booth at the front barrier. Without hesitating, Zeke reaches behind his seat, grabbing his bag and tugs it onto his lap. Pulling out his laptop, he taps his fingers over the keys, bringing up a black screen of coding. Aside from Zeke's clickety clicking, the silence grows louder, penetrated by my deep breathing.

"Hurry it up," Zane leans over me to nudge Zeke, not helping in the slightest. The guard comes around the driver's side window so I nudge forward as Zeke twists his laptop out of sight. Plastering on a relaxed smile, Zane opens the window, doused in charisma. "Is there something the matter?"

"I didn't check your ID's at the gate," the man is a serious case of moustachivitis grunts, out of breath from his mini jog. The gray hair on his lip is heavy enough to cover the top row of his teeth, yet there's not a lick of stubble on the rest of his chin. Creases frame his aged eyes, a desperate attempt of a thinning combover on top of his head. He looks me up and down, eyes hovering over my tits a moment too long. Zane leans in the way.

"Of course, our mistake." Offering the guard his ID badge, I check over Zeke's shoulder to see how he's doing.

"Thirty more seconds," Zeke hisses and my heart picks up a beat. We might not have that long, as the guard speaks into his walkie-talkie, checking our permitted clearance. Static follows as another in the booth searches for us in the database. The one we are definitely not in, unless Zeke works his magic pronto. This time, I nudge him too eager for the streams of numbers filling his screen to mean something. Finally, he slams the laptop closed and announces it's done.

"That's affirmative, Sir. They have full clearance," the static reply comes through the walkie-talkie. I withhold my relieved exhale until Mustache has apologized and walked away. In my peripheral, Zeke's shit-eating grin has tripled. I ignore him as usual, my gaze snagging on the fire exit door which has now popped free from its lock. A slim shadow frames our entry point and finally, I feel like this gig won't be a complete shitshow.

"Oh – the door is open," Zeke touches a hand to his chest, feigning shock. "How on earth did that happen? Wait, that's right – that would be me." Sticking a thumb towards his own chest, he laughs and slides out of the cab. Zane mirrors him, twisting back to tell me to stay in the van. Fuck that. Hopping down to ground level, the slap of my sneakers on tarmac covers the hiss that escapes my mouth. Zane cuts me off two steps around from the van, his narrowed eyes having zero effect.

"Save your breath. I'm the brains, remember? You need me in there." Pushing passed Zane, Zeke doesn't bother trying to speak any sense, holding the door open so I can enter first. Rows of machinery are laid out before us, all manned by assistants. I watch piles of mailing bags be carted into numerous delivery trucks, any of which carrying the parcel we may be looking for. But this is why the boys need me to accompany them.

"Zeke," I grab his arm and walk casually. "Empty computer two o'clock, get me an address for Mr. Callahan." He diverts, leaving me to walk with Zane at my back. I veer around a few trollies of packages, approaching a large map on the wall. A metal walkway stretches overhead, leaving this part of the depot almost unseen. A strip of light filters down onto the map, showing this state split into sections. Each is labeled with the corresponding area code and truck number. My eyes fly over the details, absorbing as much as I can when Zane bumps my shoulder.

"What do you need from me?" he asks quietly. I smile to myself. Zane likes to give everyone the opinion he's some sort of leader between the three of us, but when no one else is looking, he's the first to seek my advice. I pat the back of his hand like a mother would to her child, keeping my face forward.

"Go find Harlow." The hand beneath mine tightens into a fist just before he huffs and storms away. I watch Zane go in his postie outfit. He's not fooling anyone when his muscles are bunched so tight in the white polo and chino shorts. I wish I had time to take a photo and mock him with the length of his socks forever more, but alas, I'm a woman on a mission. Luckily, everyone pacing around are too invested in their headphones or oblivious to this warehouse draining them of their souls to pay me any mind.

"Got it," Zeke appears at my side. Pushing a torn scrap of paper into my hand, I compare his jottings to the map in front of me.

"Truck 47 is our target," I state. Spinning around too fast, I wobble and clench my side. Zeke's hands linger around my arms, the frown in his brows starting to understand I'm not healing as rapidly as I may have said earlier. I push him away, pointing to a bay across the warehouse labeled with the number we need. The back of the van is already full, a delivery guy checking over a clipboard in his hand.

"We need to move," I whisper shout, weaving through those milling about in my way. Zeke is quicker; his long strides eating up the distance in half the time. A woman misjudges his pace, stepping out from behind a machine with a stack of papers in her arms. They go flying at the same time she does,

Zeke's quick reactions catching her just before she hits the concrete floor.

"Well," Zeke barks at the delivery guy we need to stop. He's just slammed one rear door closed, his hand hovering over the other. "Don't just stand there. Come lend a hand!" Zeke's malicious tone has the guy dropping to his knees, scooping up papers while my so-called brother ensures his damsel is okay. It has nothing to do with her pretty, young face, or the stark red hair that'll remind him of Harlow, I'm sure. Side stepping around the mess, I catch Zeke's gaze once I've made it to the back of the van. He gives me a small shake of his head but he should know me better by now. I never admit defeat on a job.

Sliding into the van, I scoot between mailing bags, filled to the top and bulging at the seams. Fuck, where do I even begin? Spotting the driver's clipboard on the ground outside, I hesitate, but decide I won't be able to creep unseen into this van twice. So, I only have one other option. Tear the mailing bags apart with my hands and rummage through the addresses myself.

Rip. One after the other, I destroy someone's hard work in a matter of seconds. I don't have long to locate the package I'm after. Neither do I have any details on its shape and size.

"Nope. Nope. Nope." I toss parcels over my shoulder one by one. The addresses aren't even close to the location Zeke gave, but I know he won't be wrong. I don't say this often, but when it comes to hacking, I trust Zeke's ability 100%. I don't have time to wonder if Zane has found Harlow yet, and if he'll return her safely when he does.

"Aria," Zeke's voice leaks through the anarchy happening outside. I pop my head out to see Zeke piling the delivery guy with a stack of paper, ducking aside to growl at me. "There's no time."

"Make time," I scowl back. He rolls his pretty boy blue eyes, and promptly fakes a sneeze, knocking the paper stack aside once more. Slipping back into my own world of chaos, I huff at the packages and continue to rifle through. Diving to my knees, I hunt like a rabid animal looking for meat. None of them are right, and none of this makes sense.

Bang.

The back door of the van slams closed, the reverberations knocking me on my bad side. Stars burst behind my eyes, stealing my vision. Like an explosion has detonated inside, every ounce of anguish I've been suppressing, by medicine or sheer stubbornness, bursts back to into existence. I groan, curling up like a fetus as the engine roars to life. Pain explodes through me when we jolt forward, the van's horn canceling out my scream of agony.

Stretching for the back door, the vehicle moves again – this time, smoothly gliding up the ramp and exiting the depot. The glow of undying sunlight streams through a mesh divider, separating me from the driver's seats. Unlike the van we stole, this one must be an upgrade. Vaguely, I hear Zeke shouting, although I can't make out his words. Not when I'm struggling to breathe and every stop and start forces my body to slide around the floor against the packages. Forcing myself onto my back, I struggle to inhale, my hand clutching my ribs to stop them from jostling too much. We turn sharply, slamming me into a series of mailing bags I hadn't opened yet, and fly down the highway. Well, there's no time like the present.

"Hey sweetie," the man up front says and I freeze, my hands gripping the seams of a bag in preparation to tear it open. "I'm going to be home late. They've changed our routes again at last minute, sending me to a suburb I've never even heard of." A female voice replies through the speaker, telling him to be safe. I sink back onto the floor. So that's it then. Not only am I trapped and in an unbelievable amount of pain, I'm in the wrong damn truck.

My eyelids droop, only the powdered sugar on my lips keeping me awake. Who knew a head director could make something as simple as delivering parcels so in-depth? Bar charts, proposal models and graphs fill the flipchart positioned at the front of the room. An assistant dragged it in, bulking under the weight of paper loaded on top. I lick my lips, eyeing up the last doughnut in a bid to stay awake. To be fair, it's only me that's eaten all the rest.

Turns out my toilet break idea didn't work, since I was

accompanied to the stall and back. I haven't been able to breathe without someone's eyes watching me intently, everyone thinking the same thing. What the fuck is she doing here? In my defense, I had the best intentions, but somewhere along the way I've found myself stuck in the character I created. At least when I need to restart after the Bloodied Skulls have had their way with me, I'll have a new career ahead of me. Because fuck knows, I know enough about DPS's future scalability to last me a lifetime.

"And that brings us to the end of the first portion," Nick finally stops talking, resting his palms on the table. "Before we go for a break, does anyone have any questions?" I glare around the table, daring anyone to open their mouths. One woman jerks her arm as if to rise it, and promptly changes her mind at my nostril flare. Message received, loud and clear. "Very well then. Let's resume in thirty minutes. There's a kitchen at the end of the hall for teas and coffees," Nick nods. Chairs scrape and I fight against myself to appear too eager. Waiting for a few others to go first, I move with the crowd. Out the office door, down the hallway towards the main depot. I hope I'm not too late.

An arm wraps around my waist, yanking me away from the others. My mouth is covered with a cloth, and amongst the excited chatter about going for a vape, no one bothers to look back. Dragged into a side room, darkness falls over my vision. Aside from a slip of light through the blinds, my captor is cast into shadow. The hand around my waist dips beneath my polo shirt, rapidly skating upwards to my bra.

"Now then," a voice I don't recognize growls. "I kept your secret, you have thirty minutes to pay up what you owe." My eyes widen and it suddenly occurs to me to struggle. When your everyday life becomes a game of being kidnapped and pulled from pillar to post, my subconscious had forgotten of the real monsters in this world. The assholes that sit across business meetings watching you closely, only to order you to pay up for a favor you didn't ask for.

Throwing an elbow back into his ribs, I grab the hand covering my mouth. Twisting into his body, his arm is forced to follow until my head ducks and a swift snap on the bent angle of his wrist is enough to break it. I take the cloth he used to silence me, stuffing it in his own mouth when he screams. The door behind me opens and I turn, swinging my fist wildly. The silhouette of a very pissed-off Zane doesn't flinch, catching my hand and spinning me into his body. Unlike the asshole screaming around his handkerchief, Zane's hold is light. Almost tender, his back a solid and soothing presence at my back. Switching on the light to another meeting room, Zane peers around at my disheveled polo top and, what I imagine, smeared lipstick. His jaw ticks.

"Wait outside," Zane growls, trying to move me aside. I refuse to let him.

"I've got this handled, thanks," I step away from the hold I was far too comfortable in. Zane kicks the door closed behind him.

"Suit yourself. Stay right where you are." Zane moves with the grace of a gazelle, and the speed of a cheetah. The dick-weasel is on his back on the table within seconds, crying through the vice-like grip Zane has on his neck.

"Like taking what's not yours, do you?" he lifts the guy's head and slams it back down on the wood. From shock and morbid curiosity, I remain still, content to watch. Is Zane defending my honor or does he just seriously hate rapists? I'm happy with only the latter being true, because anything else causes too much confusion to wade through.

"Fortunately, so do I," Zane continues, oblivious to my internal monologue. Flicking out a switch blade from his pocket, a blood-curdling scream follows. Zane doesn't hesitate. Doesn't relent, until he's holding the asshole's finger high for me to see, wedding ring still attached. A married rapist asshole, even worse. Outside, fists begin to hammer on the door, voices calling out.

"Zane, come on," I beg him. Up to this point, we'd kept our hands clean and could only be arrested for breaking and entering at most. Now we're down for full on manslaughter. Rushing closer, I place a hand on his bicep, trying to tug him away. The asshole spits out his cloth, yelling for help, only to have his own finger swiftly shoved down his throat. Zane leans in close, his voice barely audible beside the choking guy's ear.

"Do you really think someone like her wouldn't have a man who would come looking?" My mouth pops open but Zane sweeps me from the room, concealing his bloodied knife and hand in his pocket. The group that have gathered outside the door are shoved aside and we don't hang around long enough for me to see their faces. Somewhere along the way, Zane's hand shifts from my forearm, down into my palm. I clench his, questioning all my life choices up to this point.

But all thoughts are forgotten when we breach the main depot to see Zeke outside the row of open shutters, chasing after a delivery van. The large clock in the middle of the warehouse displays 17:01, and all trucks are rolling out of here for the nightly round of deliveries. I know all about it, thanks to Nick's in-depth presentation. A new system with monthly employee incentives from Christmas bonuses to a pay rise and a bonus scheme, doubling their productivity for this quarter. Yeah – I listened.

"Zane," I yank him towards the staircase but whatever man came to my rescue is long gone. Ripping his hand from mine, he flies down the steps, mostly using his grips on the railings to propel his legs forward. I race behind as an alarm rings out. A blaring sound that brings the entire warehouse to a halt. Several security guards respond, popping up from hidden crevices to take chase. Jumping the rest of the steps, I dive out the way of a depot assistant feeling brave, sprinting for the fire exit door Zane disappears through.

"What the fuck happened?!" he shouts at Zeke as the pair of them jump into the van they drove here. Skidding forward, I throw myself in the way, arms raised. There was no guarantee they wouldn't just flatten me, but for some reason Zane skids to a stop with barely inches to spare. Rounding the passenger side, I open Zeke's door and use the step to lift myself to their height.

"Aria is in that truck," Zeke points in one direction with a shaky hand, his cheeks pink and breathing shallow. "But the one we need just left that way," his hand swings in the opposite direction. *Shit.* I peer over at the conveyor of vans leaving through the open barrier, opportunity slipping through our fingers.

"You guys get the package. I'll get Aria." I decide, lowering myself back to the ground. Zeke snaps out of his exhaustion, grabbing my polo by the collar.

"That's not how this works. Aria's a big girl, she can sort herself out. Completing the job comes before everything, even us." Trying to wriggle out of Zeke's hold, I manage to claw his hand open, only for it to latch back down on my hair. Tilting my head upwards, he has me exactly where he wants me. At his mercy.

"Aria's wounded!" I hiss through the pain in my scalp. "She won't be able to do anything that requires an excess of physical activity. Not to mention – it's all your fucking fault she's injured in the first place." Guards burst free of the depot while the mustache-inclined guard jogs over as quickly as his pot belly will allow. Zeke's blue eyes darken.

"It's your fault she has a soft spot for you. If she'd just given you what you deserve at RoughRiderz, none of this would be happening," he yanks on my hair and I throw a fist into his side.

"Well if you hadn't-"

"Enough!" Zane shouts, revving the engine. "Both of you! Harlow, just go, for fuck's sake. Rescue Aria and I might not regard you as total scum of the earth. We'll get the package." The security guards raise their batons, creating an arc to close in on us. Zane skids the van forward and thankfully, the grip on my hair is released. Aiding Zeke to slam the door shut, I remain alongside the van, using it as cover whilst the four wheels jolt in sharp bursts, keeping the guards at bay. Once level with the turning for the parking lot, I pull out the Sedan's keys and make a run for it.

My ass hits the driver's seat, my hand clutched on the stick as I reverse without looking, peeling out of the barrier behind the last van to leave. Zane and Zeke's. The mustached guard yells at his partner in the booth to lower the barrier but it's too late. I skid left, the smell of burning rubber filling the car and push the pedal to the floor. For what reason exactly, I'm not sure – but I'm coming for you, Aria.

With the DPS vans ahead going a normal speed, it doesn't take long to close the gap between us. I swing out onto the wrong side of the road, counting four in total and swerve back into my lane. Do I play eenie meanie miney mo? The highway stretches on, my hands becoming jittery on the steering wheel. My pocket begins to vibrate and I gasp, digging it out. The number is blocked but I hit the answer button, putting my cell on speaker and drop it in the cup holder.

"License plate, BHG-" Zeke begins to reel off and I interrupt him with a panicked half-screech.

"How the fuck did you get my number?" I start with, because that seemed like the most relevant. Sure, he's saving mine and Aria's bacon, but I can't overlook a breach of security. Whether I'd expected an answer or not, I don't get one.

"585. I'll set up your maps with a location once we've shaken our tail." At the sound of police sirens in the background, the call dies and I grumble to myself. We're going to address my personal privacy settings for life later. Twisting the wheel hard, I take the dirt trail alongside the road, speeding past one van after the other. My entire body judders until I come level with the driver I've been aiming for. The one who's license plate corresponds with Zeke's tracking skills. Catching his attention, although I'm sure his mouth just moved in perfect sync to call me a 'crazy bitch', I hold up the ID badge on my lanyard.

"Pull over," I shout, waving my arm. He frowns but indicates to veer onto the dirt track. I pull back and slow to a stop, my heart hammering in my chest. Shaking out my sweaty palms and exiting the car, the driver of the van hops out of his, looking me up and down.

"Is this some kind of joke? It isn't my birthday for two weeks yet," he twists his lips. I look down at my cleavage and short shorts, my mouth opening on a silent 'wow.' Does he really think I'm some kind of DPS Strip-o-Gram, stopping him on the side of the road for a show? Hiding my shock, I smile sweetly, walking forward slowly.

"You forgot something," I say coyly, fluttering my lashes. The driver crosses his arms, asking me what it is. Rearing back my fist, I swing directly for his nose. "This." He crumples to the ground and I step over him, not feeling the least bit remorseful. I was going to apologize, but dude basically called me a whore because I'm comfortable in my body. Why shouldn't I show it off?

Tugging on the two handles at the rear of the van, I swing them wide and feast my eyes on the mess inside. Packages tumble out, littering the ground around my feet. Luckily, the other vans have long since passed and there's no other witnesses to watch me scramble through the boxes, scooping them out into the dirt. Off to one side, beneath a torn mailing bag, Aria groans. Her chocolate hair spills across the plastic flooring, her eyes completely closed.

"Psst," I try to get her attention. Hopping into the van, I clear all the bags and boxes from her, assessing the damage. Her bandages are intact, one hand resting over her ribs in protection. Blinking her green eyes open, Aria smiles like she's drunk, reaching out for me. When my hand links with hers though, and she realizes I'm very much real, she gasps herself back to reality.

"Harlow?!" Aria asks, appearing more terrified than relieved. "What the fuck are you doing here? Maddox will have both our heads if he finds out." I roll my eyes, lifting her good arm around my neck.

"I'm not leaving you. I could, trust me - it's the karma you deserve. But I'm not you. So get the fuck up, lean your weight on me and let's get out of here." Dragging her back to the Sedan, the driver just starts to rouse as I wheelspin a shit ton of mud his way and hightail it back the way we came. Aria holds my phone, directing me back towards the depot. An abundance of police cars and an ambulance fill the parking lot, the security booth abandoned. I duck my head anyway, passing at normal speed as to not attract any unwanted attention.

"You...shouldn't have come back for me," Aria says, her voice quiet. I spare her a quick glance, noting her arm is yet to move from around her middle to hold her ribs. "Maddox will punish me for it."

"Like fuck he will," I growl. My hands tighten on the wheel, my foot pressing harder on the accelerator. "What kind of conflicting message is he sending? Punishing you for showing weakness but raves about the Bloodied Skulls sticking together. It's all bullshit."

"We've been through a lot; Maddox especially," Aria sighs, slumping further into her chair. Bringing her legs up, she tries to curl in on herself but it causes her too much pain. "He loves us really. He just…struggles to show it." I shake my head, clenching my jaw. There's nothing Aria could tell me to redeem their so-called leader in my eyes. He's a fear-mongering asshole who needs a reality check. But as long as his minions abide by his inconsistent rules, he won't get the message.

"Next left," she says instead. I follow her directions, taking a back-route tour around a collection of small towns. Eventually, we pull into a McDonalds and park in the furthest bay. There's no need for a signal since Zeke is apparently tracking my every move now. The pair appear around the back of the building, wearing a matching set of black hoodies and sweatpants. Zeke hitches his backpack up on his shoulder, Zane carries a paper bag of food. Striding to the driver door, he pops the door and orders me to move. I glare at Zane's tone, snatching the paper bag before scooting through the middle of the seats. Zeke scoots in by my side, snatching a burger box to hand to Aria, who remains in the passenger seat.

"Well?" I ask as Zane pulls out of the parking lot and sets up on a path home. "What was in the package?" Aria snorts, beginning to tell me we wouldn't be allowed to look when Zane's grave tone cuts her off.

"We didn't get it."

"What?!" Aria shoots forward, groaning at herself. Zeke sits forward on the edge of his seat, trying to pander her but she won't let him. "Then where's the truck? Let's go get the damn thing before-"

"It's too late," Zeke replies, settling for stroking her brunette hair. "The parcel has been delivered. We took too long shaking the police entourage we gained. If Maddox wants us to break into the house to retrieve it back, he'll let us know. For now, we'd best return home and regroup until the inevitable."

Sliding his blue eyes to me, Zeke does something that freaks me out more than if he'd just slapped the burger from my mouth and smeared my face in ketchup. His hand slides over my thigh, stroking the bare patch of skin before giving a reassuring squeeze.

"Enjoy your last meal, Feisty. Maddox will have us all drinking our meals through a straw once word gets out we failed."

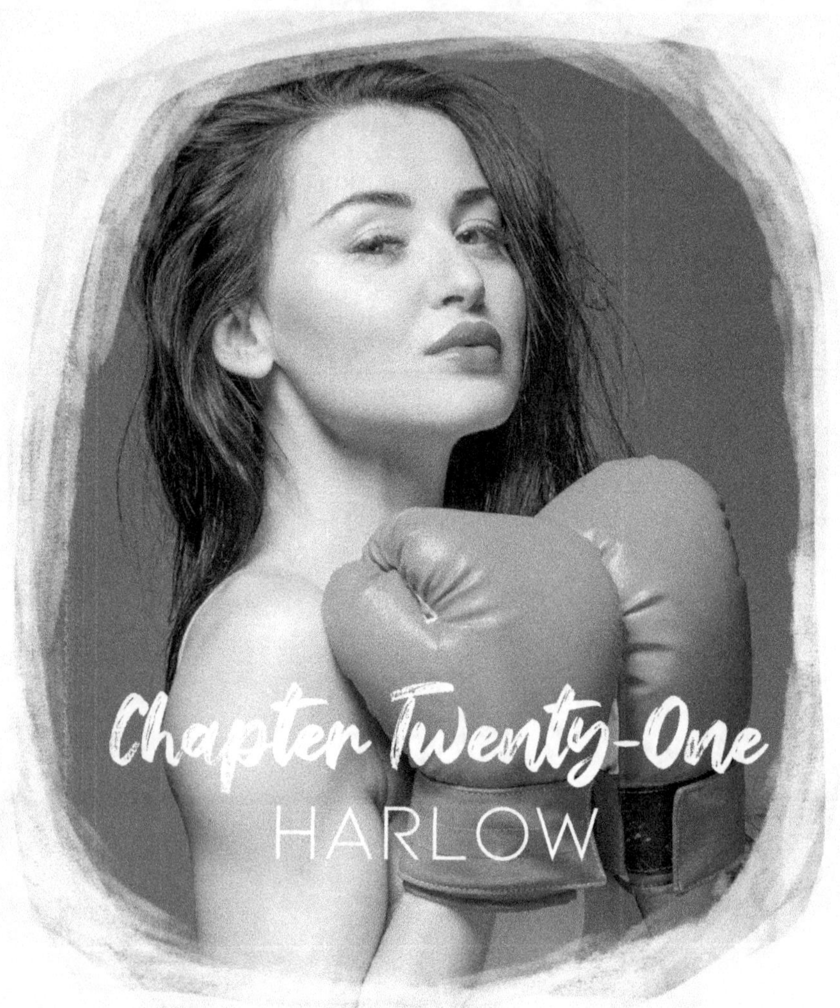

Chapter Twenty-One
HARLOW

It's a little after midnight when my head sinks into my pillow. Everyone retreated to their rooms almost instantly after getting back to the fisherman's house. The atmosphere was solemn, as if a tsunami is due to land any minute and there's nothing we can do to outrun it. My damp hair has begun to curl around my cheeks, the promise of an epic lion's mane in the morning lingering like the scent of Aria's raspberry shampoo.

I scrubbed myself clean of makeup, and the whore-ish persona I've had to put on all day. I wouldn't mind so much if I were able to look Maddox in the face the next time I see him and let him see I was willing to do what it took. But I'd failed. I need his trust. His complete belief in me, or my entire plan to bring the Bloodied Skulls to their knees will fail. As if conjured by my thoughts, my phone buzzes on the bedside table. I wince at the brightness of the screen, groaning and throwing it back down again after reading the message.

> Unknown Number: Nicely done today. Keep up the good work.

Easier said than done. With each twist on my heart, the idea of revenge is beginning to look much less bloody and a little more submissive. All four of them, on their knees, begging for me to allow their release. Wicked images flash behind my eyes. Ones I dare not even imagine as the dampness between my legs grows and I clench my thighs together tight.

Yet they continue to play out. Scenarios, both individually and all together. The pain I would inflict, the pleasure I would take. And all the while, they'd beg for more. To give them the punishment they deserve.

My mind turns to Zeke. His palm on my thigh has left an imprint the shower couldn't touch. Yet, for the sake of a brief moment's intimacy, he's been the cruelest to me. Unlike Zane, Aria, and even Maddox, who haven't felt the need to pretend, Zeke is a master of emotions. Putting me at ease only to turn on me like a rabid dog. He would tear my heart out just to watch it beat, and sew it back in my chest to act like nothing had happened. For that reason, his torture will take the longest.

I jerk, not realizing I'd drifted off into a world of bondage and screams of mercy. They'd filled my head with happy sounds, but the beads of sweat now coating my skin are the sudden reminder I'm a long way from reaping any sort of revenge yet. And now my heart's racing, my throat is dry and there's no chance I'm going back to sleep. Rolling out of bed, I ignore the stupidly early hour that mocks me from my phone and head downstairs.

It takes longer than it should to grab a glass of water. Mainly because I don't know where shit is, and even if I did – my limbs are sluggish, my movements are clumsy. Turning, I rest my lower back against the counter and sip the water. Darkness covers each surface, glooming around the archway into the dining area. Less than twenty-four hours ago, I was eating toast at that table, wondering how I could screw with the Skulls. Turns out, I didn't need to, because I've let Aria's injured-self creep into a soft place in my psyche.

Placing down the glass, I sigh and rub my eyes. I need to sleep. My arm drops heavily and when I look back up, the shadows have moved. I freeze. In the archway, a ghost stands tall. I don't even think to run when it steps forward, jumping my ass up onto the countertop with a high-pitched shriek. The shadow rushes forward on silent feet, stopping directly before me. In the back of my mind, my subconscious is screaming one name. I know who it is. Who it must be, before his hand grips my jaw and a rumbling voice penetrates the air.

"What. Happened?" I flinch, unable to calm my nerves. Maddox's grip tightens. He shoves his way between my legs and slams something down on the countertop beside me. I twist my head aside, only because Maddox permits it. Using the flashlight on his phone, I'm given a whole five seconds to glance upon a squashed box, Mr. Callahan's name printed on the side.

"You got it back?" I whisper, my chin being jerked back to the darkened face.

"No." That's the only answer I receive. Placing down his phone, Maddox's second hand skates up to wrap around my neck. Although, he doesn't close his grip, just yet. "I loathe physical contact, but you're giving me no other choice. Tell me what went wrong. Now."

Scattering around my brain for a response, I feel his grasp closing in on me. The truth lingers on the end of my tongue, yet no words pass my lips. Aria fucked up, but she's already injured. Zeke and Zane failed too, and I don't owe them anything. Although a tiny voice that has no business being in my head speaks up. Maddox will be far harsher on them than he would me. I'm new and inexperienced. Surely he'll take into account his crew hasn't had the chance to train me. Right?

"Well?" Maddox's hand releases my neck to skate into my hair, fisting tightly. I force my tongue out to wet my lips, unsure of what will come out until it's finally said.

"It's my fault. I messed up." For the longest while, I didn't think he heard my small, defeated muttering. The outline of a shadow far bigger than any man I've been this close to remains statue still. Barely even breathing.

"You're taking the full blame? Be warned, in doing so means you will receive the entirety of the punishment." A shiver rolls through me, from his hand clutching my throat to the center of my open legs. Anticipation skates over my skin like a thousand tiny bugs writhing around my shorts/vest pajama combo.

"It was all me."

"I see," Maddox replies and my entire body sags. If only for his acknowledgment cutting through the tension. Then he moves. I yelp as my arm is tossed over his shoulder and legs are lifted. He carries me through the hallway, my eyes peering over his shoulder to the mysterious box left on the counter. It seems so small and insignificant now, yet has caused so much trouble.

Entering a room I've yet to explore, Maddox kicks the door closed and halts. Still surrounded by the shadows he wears like a mask, his head dips into my neck. He inhales me, lapping up the scent of my shampoo and fear. I shiver, only to be dropped the next second. Switching on a tall lamp that provides a dim glow, I assess the office I've found myself in. Four desks are pushed against the walls, two facing out of a bay window over the pier. Blank computer screens and a stack of sketchpads sprawl the white surfaces, shelves of books sitting high above.

Click.

Maddox locks the door at my back, slowing prowling the office space. Reaching for one of the highbacked leather chairs, he spins the seat around five feet from me and lowers himself onto it. I peer up, forgetting how to breathe.

His sandy blonde hair is loose again, trickling over the edge of his shoulders. His straight nose and rigid jaw are a photographer's dream, although he hasn't been far from my dreams either. Patterned ink covers his skin, from collar to jaw line and along the backs of his hands. Those thick fingers are threaded. His elbows on his knees cause him to hunch forward. Licking a full set of lips, Maddox speaks, frying all good sense I had to get up and run.

"You've taken full responsibility for the downfalls of my Bloodied Skulls. There's honor to be found in loyalty, but also stupidity. Tonight you will discover how fine a thread you've decided to walk, Harlow." My name on his lips is a sin. I fight a groan, wishing I could record him saying it to play on repeat for next time I use my vibrator. His Adam's apple bobs, my mouth waters. "Until I permit you to leave, you're now my pet. You will kneel and wait patiently until I call for you."

I snort, looking for the leash and collar he must have on hand. If he does, Maddox makes no move to use them.

"And what would possess me to do that?" I cock a brow, remaining on my hip with my legs stretched out to the side. It's uncomfortable as fuck but I'm not kneeling for this man.

"Because you want to," Maddox replies. His hazel eyes watch me intensely, pinning me to the spot. When I don't move, he does. His boots eat the space between us in two steps and he's suddenly hunching before me. This time when he touches me, it's gentle. Tipping my chin up, Maddox stares directly into my eyes, consuming my vision.

"You want to know what lengths you can be pushed to, just how responsive you can be in the right circumstances. And do you know what you want the most?" He presses his thumb to my chin and nods my head for me. "You want a life without regret. Even after everything my crew did to you, look where you are. Right here, ready for more."

Maddox stands, leaving me breathless. His presence sucks the air from my lungs, his graveled words leave me hanging on each syllable. Maddox slowly moves towards the chair, while the rational part of my brain packs its bags and fucks off beneath the gap around the locked door. With it, my knees drawl up beneath me.

"There's really no…chains or whips?" I ask, trying not to let the disappointment leak into my tone. Maddox resumes his seated position, elbows on knees, fingers threaded, a smirk pulling at the corner of his mouth.

"Would that make you feel like less of a submissive? If I were to bind and punish you? Would it give you some sense of self-esteem to be forced, so in the dead of night, you can tell yourself you didn't have a choice?" His throaty chuckle fills the entire office, but there's no humor in it. Just the harsh bark of a man who radiates power and has played this game many times before.

"I have no need for chains and whips. You'll do as you're told, Harlow, simply because you wish to please me." Holding his intense stare, I drag my hands off the floor and skate them over my thighs, settling my palms on my knees. Maddox releases a full smile, spreading a warmth through my chest. Every instinct I've spent thirty plus years honing screams at me to get up, but damn if his simply cruel smile doesn't make it worth ignoring them. This man can and will ruin me, and I ache for him to do it.

True to his word, he makes me wait. My knees press into the hard floor, my nipples pushing through the silk of my cami vest. Goosebumps prickle my skin, doubt clouds my thoughts. Am I doing it right, kneeling here like this? Or is this all a test to see how long I'll follow his orders? Perhaps he wants me to disobey.

"Come here," Maddox finally beckons. I move to stand until he holds up a hand, halting my movements. "Crawl to me." Pressing my lips tightly together, I exhale loudly. He may mistake it for an annoyed sigh, but either way, Maddox doesn't say anything else. Pushing my palms into the wooden floor, my knees scream in protest as I move on all fours, crawling to Maddox's ankles.

"Closer." I scoot my shins across the floor and sit tall, my face level with his crotch.

"Free me." Maddox jerks his waist, as if my attention wasn't already on the thick erection in his jeans. The zipper is strained. I wet my lips. Reaching for his belt buckle, Maddox pushes his heels against the wood and scoots the chair backwards on its wheels.

"Without your hands," he demands. My brows raise, my mind going blank. Like a puppet on his strings, I shuffle forward and hold my hands up before me. Maddox's eyes track them as I slowly press down on his thighs and lean forward. Drawing the leather free of its buckle with my teeth, as instructed, I fumble and nudge with a mixture of my lips and nose. It can't look sexy, but Maddox's cock only jolts with each brush of my chin along his solid erection.

Managing to pop his button, I use my tongue to draw the zipper into my mouth and peel it downwards, able to look up and lock eyes with my so-called boss. Somehow, I don't think he's used this style of punishment on the others, but they aren't secretly plotting against him either. One night of blazing hot pleasure won't change my reason for being here. Maddox may think I'm being his sub, and I can't wait for the day he realizes I've been playing him all along.

Reaching the base of the zipper, it becomes apparent Maddox went commando this evening. Amongst a patch of dark hair, his cock bursts free of its confines. I don't withdraw, my eyes crossing to take in his thick, veiny shaft. On the underside, a piercing of two small balls glints in the lamplight. Maddox waits. I wait. There's a dare in my tilted brow, showing him I'll play the role he's given me to perfection.

"Take it," is the only instruction I receive. More of a croaked plea, and right there – is my power. Keeping one hand on Maddox's thigh, I reach beneath the chair and push the lever that lowers him barely more than a foot from the floor. I lean forward and wait for the next jolt of his dick to take it into my mouth.

Straight to the back, where I hold him still. Waiting. Toying. A muttered curse escapes Maddox and every drop of adrenaline in my body surges forward. Releasing him with a pop, I smile and do it again. Drawing out of Maddox the stifled moans he didn't want to give me. Two can play a game of patience, and the performance I give is as skilled as a trained actress. Batting my lashes innocently, I keep my gaze on Maddox's face, sliding my tongue along his shaft until he can't take the teasing anymore.

"Suck," he barks harshly. I obey, like a good girl. My suction is automatic, despite the new element of a piercing. I'm nowhere near experienced enough to know what to do with it, but I've been told my blowjobs are one of my best traits by a bunch of frat boys I used to hang with in college. Drawing Maddox's plump head all the way back, I work my throat muscles. He groans, relaxing back in the chair. My hands skate over his thighs while his hands raise to grip the back of his own neck. Whatever it takes not to touch me, I muse. A bead of salty precum flavors the back of my throat.

"Faster," he orders. His eyes are closed so he misses the salute I give. Bopping my head up and down, I will my mouth to relax around the metal bar and dual balls, all the while imaging how'd they feel inside me. My own need grows as my breasts bounce, the material of my cami slipping over my nipples deliciously. My shorts cum soaked. Maddox is at my mercy, his body both limp and rigid. Fuck it, I'm going for it.

Grasping his cock in both hands, I work his shaft while I suck. He jerks forward, his arms raising as if he's about to tear me away from him, but then he relaxes again. Whatever this guy has against being touched will have to wait. I'm in the zone. Nudging his jeans lower with my forearms, one hand dives inside to massage and scratch at his balls. Maddox tries to hold back his moans of pleasure, despite trying not to give me any type of praise, but he's as enthralled in the moment as I am.

Working him harder, faster, deeper, his hand suddenly fists my hair and shoves me all the way to the base of his shaft. His cock fills my throat, pumping salty cum directly into me. I jerk, my airways completely blocked but he holds me still. Tears stream from my eyes, my lungs burning. Scratching at his jeans, Maddox finally releases me, throwing my head back so I topple and fall onto my ass. I glower at him, but he misses it. Running a hand down his face, he groans, a sated sound with a trace of anger. Throwing his own fist into his leg, he hastily tucks himself away. I watch on, propped up on my elbows. Maddox doesn't look my way, stepping over me and heading for the door. I snigger to myself. A 'thank you' might suffice.

"Something funny?" he growls, halting short of flicking the lock open. I lay back, my red hair all around as I arch my back and peer at him upside down.

"For some unintelligible reason, I didn't think you would be the type to leave a girl unsatisfied," I play with my breasts through the silk. Lifting my legs, I rest the backs of my calves on the leather chair. "But I suppose assholes like you are why vibrators were invited." Shooing him away with my hand, the other skates down the center of my torso, slipping beneath my waistband. My wrist is grabbed in a punishing grip, a gasp escaping my mouth. I hadn't heard him move, but Maddox's grimace hovers over me.

Chucking my arm aside, he roughly parts my thighs, dropping a leg into each hole beneath the arm rests. The lower half of my body is forced to raise to relieve the discomfort at the back of my knees. Planting himself back in the seat, Maddox's hips pin my legs in their awkward position, so I'm trapped. I wriggle, trying to free myself but it's no use, and Maddox knows it.

"Pets remain on the floor." Two large, fisted hands rip my shorts directly down the middle. The material falls aside, still clinging to the tops of my thighs while a wash of cold air settles over my pussy. Cold, hazel eyes lower, committing the sight of my shaved and glistening pussy to memory. I try not to shift, holding on to any small power I might still have. His dick in my mouth was liberating, but now I'm exposed. I'm vulnerable. And Maddox's cunning smile does nothing to calm the erratic beat my heart has fallen into.

He didn't want to touch me. That much is clear in the way he flexes his fingers back and forth. Almost touching my thighs, then doesn't. But ultimately, he calls one of us a stupid cunt and grips my ass to jerk me higher. Two fingers spear me, no teasing involved. Gliding through my wetness, Maddox pushes a thumb against my clit, applying a heady amount of pressure. I groan, my head twisting to push my cheek against the wooden floor. I hike my hips up higher, figuring he's in there now – I might as well set him up to make it as enjoyable as possible.

His free arm wraps around my lower abdomen, holding me in place. His fingers curl inside me. Anticipation wraps around us, an icy chill from the floor to Maddox's persona. His breath fans my clit and I still, not daring to breathe. Is he...smelling me? Just then, he moves. A surprised scream is torn from my throat. Maddox doesn't go easy, and considering all the time he wasted before, he sure makes up for it now.

Fingers plunder in and out of me at a furious pace. More are added, a twisting motion is worked into his rushed rhythm. I grab Maddox's shins, needing something to stop myself from sliding all over the place. There's an element of skill as his fingers fuck me, even if Maddox classes this as my punishment. Twisting his fingers again, I groan. His palm pushes against my clit, an animalistic growl emanating from his chest.

My entire body shudders, a flush racing over my chest. I'm hot and cold, shivering and sweating, climbing towards the tip of the most violent orgasm of my life. He pumps faster and faster, drawing me higher and higher. In the back of my mind, I have a very real fear he might just stop and in there, lies my punishment, but he doesn't. Maddox is giving me everything I want.

Arching my back higher, I greedily search for more. More fingers, more sensations. More, more, more, is all I can think. The only words that are whispered past my lips in heavy pants. One at a time, my legs are freed and I slump back onto the ground, Maddox dropping on top of me. His body runs the length of mine, his mouth brushing mine.

"You want me to fill you?" he groans and my heart near about stops. Oh fuck, I want it all.

"Yes," I breathe. His fingers, still inside of me, pump fiercely. His knees spread mine wide. Just the thought of his full, veiny and pierced erection entering me pushes me over the edge. Spots burst behind my eyes, ecstasy ripples through my body and resonates in my cunt. I explode, messily, noisily and shamelessly. Squeezing Maddox's fingers tight, he refuses to slow, pushing through the barrier my body tries to create. Wringing each ounce of cum my body can produce, coating his fingers and knuckles. Only once I'm spent and limp beneath him, does Maddox slow and withdraw all together. I jerk, groaning at the loss of contact.

"You want my cock," he rumbles into my ear. "Then you'd best not fuck up the simple job I give you next time. And trust me, Harlow, if you bring my crew down, this punishment will seem like child's play to what you'll receive." I turn my head, my lips scraping his five o'clock shadow. If I kissed him, would he return it or shove me away? I don't risk it, but my mind doesn't get the memo to back off.

"When you threaten me like that, it reallllllly makes me want to see just how far this type of punishment can go," I breathe. In the dimmed light, Maddox's eyes ignite with desire. I see his face contort with raw lust before he's able to hide it. He wants me to fail just as much as I do, if only to have the excuse to do this to me. For whatever reason, Maddox lives by his own strict rules, believing in rewards and consequences. And for the time being, that's just fine by me.

Fumbling with the keys to my office, I drop my phone and watch it bounce through the slats on the platform, to smash on the gym floor below. I brace myself for an eruption of fury that I can't be fucked to release. So instead, I sigh, push my key in the lock and twist. Everything is wrong.

From the second I realized I'd overslept, and that it had been the best sleep I'd had in years, anger has clung to my back like a shadow. My hand subconsciously brushes over my abdomen where I spilt my morning coffee, where a sensitive reddened patch of skin now sits beneath my thick navy hoodie. My other hand on the door handles shakes, from the subsequent five more cups of coffee I had to calm my irritation, and push the door open wide.

"Late to work?" a feminine voice says from behind my desk. Oh no. "And wearing sweats?" Fuck, no, no, no. "You really have fallen Maddox. Although, I suppose losing me will do that to a person."

Trina pushes herself up from my chair, scooting her hip onto the desk to reveal a thigh-high slit in her crimson skirt. Her blouse is black, like her soul, with some fabric tie hanging loose over her low-dipped cleavage. Pale eyes, a shade lighter than my own, blink at me from a face perfectly made up. Just enough cosmetics to show she's wearing them, but not enough to hide the natural beauty she uses as a weapon. And boy, did she cut me deep.

"You've got some fucking nerve coming back here," I snarl, slamming the door closed in case the Skulls should turn up. I haven't told them to come in, but they tend to end up here every day anyway. Running the gym and sparring with the clients fill their days between whatever I may need them for.

Trina makes no move to leave, not even when I shove her ass aside to pull my laptop out of the top-drawer. I sink into my chair, pretending she's not in my personal space. Especially when her fingers toy with the edge of my hood, and I have to refrain from snapping her fingers. Why today, of all days?

"It doesn't have to be like this, you know?" she lies through lips painted the same color as her skirt. I smack her hand away when she tries to touch my face. No one touches me anymore.

"Oh yes, it does," I take the bait and scowl at her. "You made sure of that." Trina folds her arms, drumming her fingers for the large diamond on her ring finger to catch the sunlight from the window behind us.

"You hold a grudge better than Aliyah," she raises a brow. Moving my hands out of view beneath the table, I ball them into tight fists. My patience is too thin on any given day, but after a night of my dreams replaying Harlow's lust-filled moans and stunning pussy clamping around my fingers, I'm particularly fried. Trina leans in, the perfume I used to crave wafting around me with the opposite effect. Now, I just feel nauseous. "You've never asked me."

I don't need context. My body begins to shake with the desire to grab her by the neck, to snap every bone in her betraying body, to watch the life fade from her eyes. But I can't do any of that, and she knows it. Her lips brush my ear.

"Ask me." And then I snap. Yanking my laptop screen back with too much force, it cracks away from the keyboard and with an extra tug, I'm hurling the damn thing across the room. Next, my arm sweeps out, sending everything across the other side of the desk flying into the nearest wall. Trina doesn't even flinch. "Nice to see your temper is still intact."

"Hear me, Trina, because I will only say this once. I don't give a fuck who's sprog you've spawn, because she's being raised by the one you chose over me. Now, get the fuck out of my office and don't show your face again, because next time, I won't be so polite."

"But you haven't even heard my proposal yet," she blinks at me innocently, refusing to budge. I scoff at the word 'proposal,' because that's exactly what I was doing when Theodore walked into the restaurant to laugh at me. To tell me Trina had been playing me the entire time and she was pregnant. Fuck knows who by, because I can't believe she was only screwing the pair of us.

"Theo is reevaluating. There's to be a fight next week, for *everyone*," Trina continues, oblivious to the pure disgust I feel towards her. Or she's just a heartless bitch who never felt a scrap of compassion towards me. That's more like it. "Every crew must show they're still in peak fitness, including your most recent member." My jaw ticks and a cruel smile grows across Trina's lips.

"You seriously thought you could take on a new recruit without him knowing, didn't you? Theodore doesn't miss a trick, and she has to be initiated, just like everyone else. Prove herself a worthy fighter if she's to remain in your pathetic excuse for a gang. Besides, Theodore is *dying* to meet her." Every instinct inside of me bristles as I put a reasonable amount of steps between us to calm myself. Theo isn't setting his eyes on Harlow, not after how he tore my crew to pieces last time.

I trusted the old man. Viewed him as a father figure when I was a teen myself. Theodore took in rejects, gave us all a purpose and then sent us out to do the same. Now, he hands out heists and orchestrates underground fight clubs, moving the crews around like pieces on his personal chess board.

His system is simple, yet brilliant. Each crew is hidden behind the guise of a gym, giving us the perfect cover to remain in peak physical fitness while we await our next mission. We're all formed of one boss and four crew members. The brains, the brawn, the techie and the distraction. That last one is essential, needing to be a chameleon who can play any role, slip into character at a moment's notice. Trina was ours, and she played her part to perfection. More specifically, she played me to perfection.

"So you've come all the way from your fancy penthouse suite to mingle with the commoners, just to relay a message I'll receive by fax?" I grit out, trying to rush to the part where she leaves. Theodore is old school, not believing in the advancements of technology. I own two fax machines, one here and one in the hidden suburb retreat I've claimed for myself.

"My *husband*," Trina slides off the desk and makes her way over to me, "wants to raise the stakes this time. Whichever members of your crew win their fights, can remain a Bloodied Skull. However, those who fail, become exiled. Including you." She toys with the laces attached to the neckline of my hoodie.

"What would he gain from that? We bring in more than all his other crews put together." I know this for a fact, because I have Zeke keeping tabs on the others. They're probably doing the same to us, but we have nothing to hide. If there was an official Theodore Collective's leaderboard, then the art gallery heist we did last month would secure us in the top spot. Trina leans in close, the lips that once enticed me now far too close for comfort.

"He wants the twins," Trina whispers and I exhale harshly through my nose. Trina, thankfully, moves away, falling back into my chair and crossing her long legs.

It would seem Theo has had his eye on more members of my crew than I realized. Biological or not, Zeke and Zane have raised themselves as mirror images of one another. They live and fight in complete sync, making the pair of them lethal weapons and indispensable, but only to the right boss. They need keeping tight in line, or they'd fall victim to the luxuries of this world and destroy everything we've worked so hard to achieve.

"Besides," Trina laughs to herself, "It's about time you were knocked from your pedestal. Just because you found three misfits that remain loyal to you, doesn't make you worthy of the reputation you hold. Let everyone see just how weak the boss of Bloodied Skulls really is, and once cast aside, you'll get the time to do some soul searching. You might discover exactly who Maddox is, and why he can't allow himself to touch or fuck a real woman anymore."

Red bleeds into my vision. None of that last part came from Theodore, and I'm beginning to think this whole win all or lose all situation was whispered into his ear from his much younger wife. Don't ask me what I did for Trina to loathe and betray me, but what I hate the most is that she's right. How does she know I don't desire to touch another woman again, barring last night? Or that the thought of slender fingers and painted nails touching my skin makes my stomach roll? Somehow she does, and it's just another reason I need her out of my office.

"You already know the answer to that. Leave. Now." Trina

smiles at my dangerously low tone, always being the one to push me to a place I don't wish to visit. The darkest corner of my soul. Standing slowly, Trina passes around the far side of the desk and slinks her way towards the door.

"Come now, Maddox. It's been four years. A little heartache is so easy to bypass if you find the right rebound. Unless…you already have?" In the morning rays, she peers back at me and laughs. I barely see her through hazy eyes, my lungs struggling to expand. I withhold my breath, force down all emotion until she's out of my sight. But I can't let her leave whilst having the last laugh.

"You were a misfit too once, but loyalty was never your strong suit." I bite out as Trina opens the door and hovers in the threshold. Long, painted lashes blink up at me, a tiny shrug pulling up her delicate shoulders.

"I was the distraction; I can't help being too good at my given role." She leaves, whilst her voice trickles through my head on repeat. There's something in her words I'm missing. For a woman who vocalized her lies so easily, she never once mentioned she wanted to play a different part in our dynamic. If being leader was her goal, she wasn't ready back then. Now though, she'd suit being the callous boss bitch of a crew who would equally hate and want to fuck her in the same breath.

It doesn't take more than a few minutes of me standing, rooted to the spot and contemplating all the ways I could react, but don't, before two pairs of sneakers run up the metal stairs.

"What the fuck was she doing here?!" Zane bursts into my office first. Zeke is over his shoulder, his eyes immediately lowering to my crotch. A full, throbbing hard-on tents my sweatpants.

"Oh, boss, tell me you didn't," he begins and I stride to stand behind my chair.

"Of course I fucking didn't," I growl, hating that Zeke could believe I would dare sink my dick into Trina again. I've learnt my lesson, and I got more than fucking burned for it. But I can't help that some deprived part of me loves the fight. I literally get hard for it, my body yearning for hatred to seethe my cock, yank on my hair and tell me how disgusting I am. Fury gets me off, and while my fingers dig into the back of the chair and my mind races for a way to shake off the rage consuming me, a gentle laugh floats into my office from down below. I clench my hands tighter, ripping the leather.

"Car, now. All of you." My bark is rough and when Zeke and Zane don't move right away, I hurl a paper weight at them. The air is filled with an onslaught of 'yes boss,' 'right away boss' and similar as the pair fly down the stairs, shooing along Aria and Harlow as they go. By the time I exit and drop into the driver's seat of my Ford Mustang, everyone is seated and buckled in.

"Where are we going?" Harlow leans forward to ask when the others wouldn't dare. Her amber eyes hold mine in the rearview mirror a beat too long, and I rev the engine.

"Sit back and shut the fuck up," I growl, pushing the pedal all the way to the floor.

The Mustang pulls to a halt outside a non-descript warehouse. My mouth opens and snaps back shut again before any words come out. There's no point asking questions that will go unanswered, and the thread of anticipation trickling through me prefers the mystery. Maddox, seeming to be the only one familiar with this place, exits first. We follow behind, to the rusted metal door which is at odds with a speaker system. A voice asks for the codeword and Maddox taps a few times on his phone to generate one, replying with a clipped bark.

"Pilot." A buzzer releases the door and Maddox extends his arm to grab my wrist, yanking me through the center of the others and tosses me inside. My heart leaps in my chest, the overriding panic flaring to life in my mind that I'm going to be trapped in here alone. Turning, I slam into Maddox's chest. He grunts, nudging me backwards with the expanse of his torso. Well, at least I'm not alone.

A moan penetrates the air. I still, taking in the small room. The rusted metal only appears on the exterior side, the rest of the compact area created with plasterboard to provide an entrance. Beside a slidable grate, a rectangular cut-out in the wall allows a skinny tattooed guy to leer through, a cigarette pushed between his lips.

"Welcome to the Reverse Glory Hole. Which one is the sub?" he mutters, the unfocused eyes moving from me to Aria. Maddox nudges my back, forcing me a step forward. The tattooed guy chuckles, directing me to a single door on the right and tells me to take bay three, whatever that is supposed to mean. Another moan comes from the gated area Maddox and the others are given entry to.

"Um, I really…don't think," I stammer, taking a few steps back. A hand slips into mine and it's Aria who moves into my side with a reassuring smile.

"I go where she goes," she announces, and then urges me towards the door. I wish I could say that settles my nerves, but my heart is currently trying to jump into my throat and choke me. Our joined hands reach for the handle, twisting the brass together. The second it swings open, that moan comes again, and again. Louder, faster and all too sexual.

Before us, the 'bays' are clearly labeled, separated with sheets of wood and nothing else. Nothing to hide the woman splayed across a leather bench, her pierced nipples exposed in lacy lingerie which her heavy breasts hang over. Although, I can only see her top half, as a third sheet of wood boxes her in and conceals the other side of the large room. A semi-circle cut-out gives enough room for her hips to slot through, and a screen mounted above provides a view of her legs. Legs which are strapped upwards in a V while multiple men plunge fingers, toys and their own dicks in and out of her, fist bumping each other in between.

"Nope," I announce, turning to leave. Aria grips my hand, tugging me back, despite the pain it causes her. "Aria, let me go," I hiss, pleading her with my eyes. "I'm not ready for this. I...can't just..." The girl on the table moans again, this one too close to a whimper and I point in her direction. "I can't do that."

"And no one is forcing you to," Aria soothes. I give her an incredulous look with my brows. Drawing me slowly down the walkway to bay three, she stops to stroke a hand over my cheek. "You asked me the other day, why you. I didn't have an answer then, but I do now." Aria eases me onto the leather table. I see what she's doing, but I hang on her every word anyway. Desperate to know the reason my life was thrown into a tornado and splintered in a million pieces I couldn't ever fix.

"You're a paradox, Harlow. Someone who can venture out of their lane and thrive in any scenario. You can navigate the mundane, manage the odd curve ball, but with the correct set-up, you could be so much more."

"So...," I blink away from her green eyes, noting a camera positioned to her left. Fuck, I hope it's not on. "You ruined my life...because you thought you could mold me into a better version of myself? Did you ever think I was perfectly content as I was?" Aria's fingers lift my chin, drawing my attention back to her small smile.

"There was nothing contended about the girl I saw having her head beaten in, during a cage fight she had no reason being in. You were hunting for something. Be it adrenaline, a sense of purpose or perhaps just a swift end to the bitter past you left behind. One way or another, you were never going to leave Rapture as the same woman you entered as. And that's what you really wanted."

I swallow, noting my fingers together in my lap. I wanted answers, but now I don't know if I was ready to hear them. Did I really do all of this to myself, in search for a new life? Because if so, then I have no one to blame for any rejection I feel but myself. And if I'm not being driven by revenge, then what the fuck am I doing here?

"I still...don't think I can do this," my voice lowers to a whisper. "I'm not...good enough. For all of you." There it is. The truth I'd been hiding, especially from myself. A shudder of self-doubt rolls down my spine. Aria lowers to a crouch, removing my sneakers and socks. Her hands trail up my shaven legs, to the hem of my sports shorts.

"You had no business being at Rapture, but you were. You never should have entered the ring with someone out of your weight class, if at all, but you did. And after we used you as our distraction, you could of retreated to your ex with your tail between your legs, but look where you are. How far you've come. You have drive, fight, and a thirst for the unknown."

Her hands shift to my waistband and I lift, allowing her to pull my shorts and panties down together. I showered barely an hour ago, as evident by Aria placing soft kisses along my thighs and inhaling my vanilla and raspberry body wash. When she peers back up, her green eyes are glistening with some unknown emotion. Or maybe one I don't want to consider, because falling for Aria means letting go of the whole purpose of infiltrating the Bloodied Skulls. But then she speaks, and I feel the entirety of my inhibitions floating away.

"I didn't choose you because I wanted to ruin your life. I chose you because I wanted to enlighten it. Now strip, get on your back, and let us show you an entire world of pleasure you never knew existed." Aria unzips my hoodie, with painful slowness, and peels my t-shirt over my head. Distracted by my sternum tattoo, a mandala starting between my breasts that fans out to my ribs in a mix of black and red delicate artistry. Her fingers graze the small burn mark on my ribs, an expression I can't read filtering over her face. It's the mark Zane gave me at Club Rapture, and the longer she stares, the more uncomfortable I grow. Wriggling, Aria's attention is brought back to the present. She locates a black box from beneath the leather bench and inside finds a range of outfits, lingerie and such, all clothing tags intact.

Leaving my fate in Aria's hands, I lean back on the bench to steady my breathing. No sound comes from the other side of the barricade and I dare not look. Only the rushed moans of the woman in bay one fill the air, her hurtling towards a groundbreaking climax by the sounds of it.

Lifting my ankle, Aria pushes a heel onto my foot and delicately winds the straps around my lower calf to buckle halfway to my knee. I raise my leg in the air while she does the other. Assessing the black platforms I could never stand in, the back heel impossibly slender, I grin at the chrome studs coating the back. At least if the guys get out of hand, I have a weapon to stab them with.

When the pair are secured in place, I tentatively push them through the gap in the wood before me. The mounted screen is turned off and I doubt anyone is even there, until hands grip my ankles and yank me the rest of the way through. Managing to withhold my scream, a blush floods my cheeks. Thank fuck they can't see me. Until the little red flashing light of the camera catches my eyes and I groan, covering my face with my hands. Aria drags them back down to my side, securing my wrists in handcuffs that are apparently attached to the bench.

On the other side of the wood, my legs are lifted in turn and strapped to the board, much like the woman in bay one. Cold air fans my pussy, leaving me completely open and exposed.

The worst part is, I can't see them, but I don't know if I would want to. Fingers lazily track my clit, down my pussy and scrape my ass. Then again, although the touch this time is different. More calloused, pausing to splay me open. Withdrawing, I exhale, telling myself that wasn't so bad when a sharp slap connects with my cunt. I scream out in shock, tugging against the binds that hold me.

Aria smiles down, her chocolate hair tickling my breasts. Holding a pair of purple, silicone suckers in her hand, she licks the rim of each one and places them over my areolas. Releasing the bulb at the top, they tighten, causing my back to arch. A sting of pressure tugs at my nipples and when I shake my head, telling her I can't handle it, she tugs on them to make my tits bounce. Somewhere amongst my protests, a moan escapes me. A twinge of pleasure leaks through and fingers press against my clit, I settle back into the bench.

Multiple digits open me up, one hand tilting my ass to angle my pussy higher in the air. Wetness strikes. Once, twice, three times, each echoed by the sound of Maddox, Zeke and Zane spitting on me. There's no time to wonder why that didn't feel as degrading as it should have. Fingers push inside my pussy while the others continue to hold me open. Positioning me exactly as desired for one of them to finger fuck me with the ferocity that Maddox did. But I can't believe it's him. He's more of a 'I'll finish her off last' kind of guy.

I groan, twisting myself into the bench. I must shift too far because the spank I receive has me jerking back into place. Digits spear me, while a hand soothes the sore spot on my ass, only to do it again. I hiss, cursing colorfully. Aria pushes a soft bar of suede between my teeth to bite down on, and shut me up, as another finger enters me. More circle my ass, coated in lube before easing an anal bead inside. Working in time with each other, the men fall into a rhythm. I can't tell where one ends and the other begins, and I no longer care. Each added anal bead stretches me, each joining finger widening me. They're prepping me for something.

Closing my eyes, I submit. Give over control of my rigid body, playing out the scene in my mind. Maddox will be standing back, watching his men work first. Probably close enough to spank me each time he deems it fit, but a bystander otherwise. Zeke's fingers are in me – of that I have no doubt. His speed, his aggression. It's telltale Zeke and whatever vendetta he has against me today. But as long as he keeps taking out his anger on me like this, I'm game.

And then there's Zane. The one who clearly doesn't want to touch me, so uses the anal beads as his way out. He's probably looking away the entire time, forcing himself not to enjoy it. Not to enjoy me, because heaven forbid he's a lifeless drone for once. Either way, once they're in, the large head of a vibration wand is pushed against my clit and my groans around the gag turn guttural. It pulses, increasing in strength and then cuts out to start again. Each sequence drives me to the point of breaking, and stops before I manage to get there. I cry through my gag, begging for the setting to be changed. But it's not.

"My, you are a noisy one," Aria comments in the background. Tearing the gag from between my clenched teeth, I crack an eye to see her fully naked. Ignoring the bruising at her ribs, I crane my head to look at her in full. She truly is stunning, full-bodied, yet toned in all the right places. Her hips dip above her waist, her full breasts the perfect size. Climbing up onto the bench, her knees straddle either side of my head. My eyes widen and mouth opens in a protest that never makes it out. Aria lowers and my mouth opens wider, the muscle memory of last time I ate her out snapping back into effect. Her sweet taste automatically skates over my tongue as I locate her clit.

"You're a natural, Killer," Aria praises me. With the suction cups on my nipples tugging to the point of pain, and the onslaught happening to my pussy almost too much to bare, I pour every sensation into Aria. Sucking hard. Licking harshly. Twisting my head into her thigh, I bite down just as a climax rockets through me, the tainted copper of her blood seeping into my mouth. I pull back, worried I went too far, but Aria doesn't move. Easing her fingers into my hair, she strokes and nudges my face back into her cunt. "Such a fucking good girl."

Chapter Twenty-Four

ZEKE

Watching Harlow come for Maddox has my cock aching more than ever before. We've never done this. Never shared a pussy with him before. The excitement is getting the better of me, but I don't want to explode before I've had my chance to make her scream.

Zane stands at my side, trying to hide his reaction, but what's the point? We're here for a reason, and I'm not passing it up for the sake of acting nonchalant.

Harlow's juices cover Maddox's fingers, spilling down to the anal beads he inserted. Now, with the wand jammed against her clit, he shoves down the band of his sweatpants to free his pierced dick and slams home inside her. I bite down on my bottom lip, bouncing on my heels. Aside from the initial touch, spreading and spitting on Harlow as ordered, we've been told to back off.

Maddox has something he needs to work out of his system,

and I reckon it has everything to do with the surprise visit from his former lover. Bracing himself on the chain holding Harlow's leg upright, he slams into her, jostling the bench beyond the wood. Anger contorts his shadowed expression, the make-shift reverse glory hole threatening to collapse. *Fuck this.*

Zane grabs for me but I shrug him off, swooping into Maddox's side. Taking the wand from his hand, he doesn't look my way or protest. He's lost to his own thoughts, drowning in a void where his control has gone to die. Now both hands are freed, Maddox braces them on each of Harlow's ankles and screws her like a man possessed. Almost twice our age or not, he fucks as good as a guy on spring-break, his abs flexing with each violent thrust.

Splaying a hand on Harlow's lower abdomen, I locate her hidden bud, ramp up the vibration speed and press it down hard. She jerks, unable to move while her cries come out muffled. My eyebrows knit together and I cast a glance over to the monitor that is holding Zane's full attention. His hand inside his pants, working his shaft in measured strokes.

On the screen, Aria is sitting on Harlow's face, the camera repositioned to give us a perfect view of Harlow's pink tongue flicking back and forth over Aria's clit. Smart move, Aria, but nothing will stop me from drawing every ounce of pleasure, cum and noise from Harlow before we're done here.

I notice the descent on Maddox's hands before he does. Sliding down Harlow's toned legs, his thumbs caress her skin. Pressing his forehead against the wood, his thrusts ease. Slowing to a pace which would be enjoyable for both, if he maintained it. But I know Maddox, and he doesn't do pleasure. He thrives on pain, is driven by hatred. And above all, he despises physical contact. Hazel eyes snap open as he throws his arms down in sudden realization.

"Fuck's sake!" his roar comes as he jerks out of Harlow and paces in a full circle. Crack. His palm comes down on her ass, leaving an instant red mark. Then again on her upper thigh. The scream that comes from the other side of the wood is full of shock and confusion. My chest squeezes, my heart stuttering as if I was struck myself. Harlow doesn't know Maddox, she won't understand his temperament or the demons he battles on a daily basis. I share a look with Zane and on the screen beyond, Aria slides off Harlow. I think we're done here.

Easing back the wand, Maddox's fury-filled eyes swing to mine, his jaw barely moving as he grinds words through his teeth. "Don't you dare. Keep going. Fucking give her everything she's worth," he snarls. My brows hit my hairline and for a moment, I'm unsure how to take that. Luckily, Zane steps in to block me from asking any questions, whipping out his cock. Sliding it into Harlow's soaking wet cunt, he drops his head back on a groan. Nonchalant my ballsack.

Switching off the wand, I have a better idea. This side of the room is shared between all of the bays. Five cut-outs along the wall, and aside from ours, only one other is occupied. Seven guys at the far end, all butt naked and fully focused on the woman they're sharing. I ignore them too, heading to the back of the room where a metal shelving unit holds all toys and sex aids imaginable. I've had my eye on a particular toy since arriving, because let's be honest – Maddox is a hard act to follow. I'd only seen his dick in the gym showers once and it was instantly imprinted on the inside of my mind. Not in a gay way…in a 'I had nightmares of my dick shrinking in shame for months' kind of way.

Pushing the toy into my sweats pocket, I grab a cock ring for now. Attached to the top, a small bullet vibrator is sheathed in a silicone holder. Returning to Zane, I wiggle it at him and he rolls his eyes. Pulling back from the steady rhythm he'd built up, no doubt hitting Harlow's g-spot with ease each time, I run my fingers through her cum. Scooping up enough to lubricate the inside of the cock ring, I grab a hold of Zane's dick. It jerks and my eyes fly to his.

"Is this weird?" I ask, standing within a breath of his face. "I feel like this just got weird."

"Just get it over with asshole," Zane throws his head forward into mine. It's no more than a knock but the rejection cuts deeper. Wow, first time I've ever touched his cock, even when we only had enough hot water and shower gel to share a shower, and he headbutts me. Fucking rude is what that is. "Zeke!" Zane snaps me back to the moment at hand. And speaking of hands, Zane's dick is still fisted in mine.

Oh right, yeah. Pushing the cock ring over the length of his shaft, all the way down to his groin, I switch on the bullet and leave him to do the rest. I've got to get myself ready, because last always has to be best. Pushing himself back into Harlow, I relish her cries. Her toes scrunch tight in the sexiest fucking heels I've ever seen. A smile crosses my face, because regarding of whose dick is in her – I did that. I orchestrated her pleasure, and why that fills me with the warm fuzzies, I have no clue.

Beside Zane, Maddox pumps his shaft aggressively. His eyes downcast, glued to Harlow's pussy. I don't blame him. Glistening, tight, ripe for claiming. Her pretty pink lips cling onto Zane's cock like a lifeboat, wholly prepared to go down with this ship. Zane's hands splay over Harlow's ass, one cheek angry and red. He tilts her upwards, picking up his pace while his grunts fill our side of the barrier. He's close, his head dropping back again.

"Not yet," Maddox growls, nudging Zane's foot with his. "We do this together." Zane stills, as do I. Say what? But Maddox ignores us, refusing to look away from Harlow. After a beat, Zane nods and withdraws, twisting the cock ring around to vibrate against his balls instead. Looking to me expectantly, I jerk into action.

"Picasso style. I like it," I grin, stepping into Zane's spot for my turn. The one that will break her. The one that will stand out as the single best fuck of her life, and she'll never even know it was me. Withdrawing the toy from my pocket, I wave it at Zane before tugging down my sweatpants. My cock springs free, and I push the ring over my shaft. Similar to the one I gave Zane with a bullet on top, except mine has a second silicone cock attached underneath. Double penetration at its best.

I bend first, drawing my tongue over Harlow's pussy as I remove the anal beads and toss them aside. Sweet cum fills my senses, and I repeat the action, pausing to gently soothe her over-sensitive clit with my tongue. She moans, the jostle of handcuffs sounding beyond the wood. I bet she wishes she could claw her hands into my hair, to hold me in place and force me to continue soothing her. But this isn't her fantasy. It's mine.

Standing, a cold spurt of lube sprays over my dick and I gasp. Zane narrows his eyes at me before stepping back out of view. Spreading the lube over my dick, and the additional one beneath, I glide both into Harlow's opening. Her legs tremble, her hips jerking upright. I stroke her thighs, going slow at first. As desperate as I am to take her, causing her damage isn't going to help anyone. Especially not Maddox, next time his frustra-tion gets the better of him. Brushing my thumbs in small circles around her pretty pink lips, Harlow relaxes, her hips lowering and her pussy opening for me.

I'd planned to take her hard and rough. To imprint myself inside her; to leave her sore with a void only I could fill. But as my hands travel her smooth legs, her soft moans speak to me like a bird's song, Harlow unknowingly rewrites what I know to be true. That I'm not a sociopath like Maddox, or a creature of indifference like Zane. I yearn for more. Ache to prove I can be better than my past should permit. Gliding into Harlow's tight, yet accepting, cunt, I find that's exactly what I needed yet couldn't quite grasp. Acceptance.

With the assistance of the silicone cock alongside mine, I fill her. Slowly, completely. All the way to the hilt, branding myself in a place no other man will be able to. She groans, muttering inaudibly because she doesn't know whose name to call out. Anonymity drives my movements, providing the perfect scenario to drop my macho bullshit and just *feel*. Let her know me, the real me. The man who craves to fulfill a woman's sexual desires and base needs. 'Give her everything she's worth,' is what Maddox said. And that's exactly what I'm going to do.

Screwing her, steadily and deeply. Listening out intently for what makes her groan. How her contented screams shift to guttural cries when I seat myself and rock my hips a certain way. Ironically, despite the divider between us, I have never felt so in tune with the woman I happen to be fucking. I see pussies as objects, women as toys.

Yet Harlow…well I don't fucking know how to describe what she's doing to us, but we're enthralled. Captivated by the woman who was meant to be a one-night stand. Maddox and Zane jerk off at my side while Aria sucks on Harlow's nipples via the monitor, driving me to give them a full show. To draw more ammunition from Harlow's hoarse throat for us all to enjoy. Tenderly winding my hands around her thighs, I hit home, deep and hard.

Come for me Feisty, I repeat in my mind. As if spurred by my will, her pussy clamps down, driving me crazy with need. My balls shoot upwards and it's only by Maddox's command am I able to refrain from exploding. I can't disappoint him, not if I desire to do this again – and oh, I fucking do. Screams fill the air as I drive through her tightness, enhancing her climax, milking her of every ounce of cum she's able to give. A hand slams down on my shoulder, tugging me back a step and then it's game on.

As a trio, more united than we've ever been, Maddox, Zane and I pump our cocks in iron fists. Cum spurts from us all, covering Harlow like the prettiest damn painting I've ever seen. She's a piece of art, dripping in the evidence of our barriers crumbling down. Nothing will be the same after this, and I'm not prepared to pretend otherwise. Maddox's free hand slams down on my shoulder, using me for stability while the shifting of Zane's bicep brushes mine.

Emptying my sack entirely, I tug off the second cock with a sharp hiss and use it to smear our cum over Harlow's ass. Pushing it into her back passage, she gasps, struggling against her restraints. I don't stop until I'm sure a mixture of us all has entered her, oozing cum from both holes.

"Clean her up," Maddox orders, his voice lacking its usual harsh edge. He leaves us via a door labeled 'shower room' and an idea sparks in my mind. We've already teetered on the edge of our boundaries – might as well go the entire mile.

Untying Harlow's ankles, I ease them down slowly. Gently rolling her ankles in my palms, I ease her legs through the hole as Harlow shimmies back. Her stifled groans are music to my ears, each movement a mark on her memory. We own her. We've claimed her and I'm not backing down. A new lease of life flourishes within my chest, possibilities flashing before my eyes. Could Harlow be the uniting factor between us and Maddox? I'm sure hoping so, as I tuck myself into my sweats and pass through the doors to end up on Harlow's side of the bays.

She flinches, covering herself as if she expected us all to leave and never speak of this again. *Cute*, I smile to myself. Lifting Harlow into my arms, Aria starts shooting questions at my back. I ignore every one, carrying Harlow to the shower room. I avoid the stall Maddox is in, not going to push him anymore today, and enter a cubicle triple the regular size. Zane and Aria follow, taking my lead as I lower Harlow and begin to strip.

"What…is going on here?" Harlow pops her hip out, trying to take back what little control she can. The smile biting at my cheeks deepens. Slamming my palm on the button fixed in the tile, the shower head bursts to life, dousing Harlow in a warm spray. Grabbing her by the waist, I drag her into me, repeating back what Maddox said in the car. He's full of wise words today.

"Shut the fuck up," I chuckle, lowering my mouth over hers.

Holding the boxing gloves in front of my face, I tiptoe around the ring. The flooring has been replaced, but with this bulky foam and leather helmet over my head, it's impossible to see where I'm going. Especially as my eyes are trained on my opponent, anticipating his next move. Completing a full circle, I grow bored of waiting. Lunging forward, I throw a fist at his gloves, providing enough of a distraction to stamp my foot into his hard stomach. Lowering his hands to knock my foot aside, I quickly twist the heel still on the floor to angle myself and strike his head with a full force kick.

"What the fuck was that?!" Zane muffles through his mouth guard, dropping his guard to hold his arms out. His mistake. Punching his face in rapid succession, I use my foot to shove him a few steps back via his stomach again and spin myself into a roundhouse kick. My heel slams into his head, and if it wasn't for the helmet, it would have been a knockout for sure. Zane stumbles, regaining his balance while Zeke cheers on from the ropes.

"Since when can you actually fight, Feisty?" I pay him no attention. Mostly because, I don't know what to say. How to act. It's been two days since we left the Reverse Glory Hole; showered, sated and our dynamics utterly screwed. I'm unsure of where I stand, or why I'm even still here. My phone has been going crazy with unanswered messages, my heart being twisted in all directions. I should have left already. Yet here I still am. Training for some fight that's supposed to initiate me as a Bloodied Skull. Hiding in my room hasn't helped to regain any sense of clarity on the situation, or why Zeke washed and caressed me in the shower as if he actually cares.

Regaining his footing, Zane tackles me low, slamming me onto the ground. He mounts my hips, knocking my head aside with gentle taps. Through my mouth guard, I laugh, bucking my hips to throw him over my head. Bracing himself on his gloves before he topples, I jolt myself upwards and headbutt him straight in the dick. Jokes on me though – he's wearing a cup.

"Stop fucking around," Maddox slams his palms on the edge of the ring, bringing me back to the present. With him, I know exactly where I stand. At the bottom of his shit list, in the 'do not talk to or even look at me too long' zone. Even since he told us about the stakes of this weekend's fight, he's been extra pissy. Dragging at the tie knotted too tightly at his neck, his hazel eyes blaze. "Go again!"

"I can't see in this damn thing," I sit up and shake my head, trying to push the helmet off with my gloved hands. It's no use, but I struggle anyway. Suddenly, the spongey helmet is torn from my head and a very angry Maddox is standing above me.

"You will practice in the helmet. You will train until you can no longer stand, and you will learn to obey me. Theodore's fight will determine if our crew still exists after this weekend, and I won't have some pre-existing head trauma fuck it up for everyone." Beyond the glare he levels on me, I spot Aria sitting on the balcony outside his office. So much for pre-existing conditions. She's unable to train, giving herself as much time as possible for her ribs to heal. I grit my teeth at Maddox, the fucking asshole who did that to her. His bullshit rules and caveman persona don't fly with me.

Dragging back the Velcro at my wrists with my teeth, I use my feet to yank the gloves off. Once free, I stand and lob them at Maddox's retreating back in quick succession. I feel the air tighten before I hear the trio of shocked gasps. The leather whacks him in the back of the head and Maddox stills. I swallow, taking a step back but a chest is there to stop my retreat. Looking back, none other than fucking Zeke is there, creeping in for a front row seat to my impending punishment.

"What shall we do with her, Boss?" I can hear the excitement in his voice. Feel the thump of his heart at my back. Fingers wrap around my middle, dipping beneath my t-shirt to soothe over my sweat-coated skin. I wriggle, trying to shake him off as Maddox retraces his steps. Leather loafers chew up the space between us, placing himself as the other slice in this Harlow sandwich.

"If we don't win our fights on Friday, we lose everything we've worked so hard to protect," Maddox sighs, but his words aren't for me. Peering up at the strong definition of his jaw, he stares directly at Zeke and lowers his voice. "But…maybe that isn't so bad."

"What do you mean?" Zane immediately steps into my side and I groan. Not wanting to be privy to the conversation happening over my head, I try to slide away. Zeke's fingers dig into my flesh, and a shudder runs the length of my spine. When I stop trying to escape, his touch eases. Lengthy, skilled fingers stroke my waist in small circles, working a path towards my abdomen.

"I'm torn, boys. I haven't slept, I can't," Maddox runs a hand through his hair and then settles his arm over my shoulders. "I don't know what's best anymore." Crushing me into his chest, Maddox's next deep sigh rattles through my ear. He smells divine, like a walking cologne ad. The soft fabric of his shirt brushes my cheek and I force myself not to melt into him further. Zeke's hands trail south of my abdomen, running the length of my waistband before dipping underneath. Is he for real right now?

I dare not move. To not draw attention to Zeke pushing his digits into my panties and finding my clit straight away. Clamping my lips together, a blush claims my cheeks. Zane blocks my view of the rest of the gym, and considering its currently open to clients, I'm thankful for that. Raising a hand, Zane's thumb pries my bottom lip free of my teeth and that's when I'm made aware – they know exactly what's going on. That same thumb pushes into my mouth, stifling my gasp as Zeke's fingers also enter me. A solid erection presses against my ass, whilst another grows against my stomach.

Thrusting into me with steady, powerful strokes, I'm instantly wet. I'd feel ashamed, if Zeke didn't lower his mouth to brush against my ear and whisper.

"Good girl, Feisty. Take what we're offering." Sucking on Zane's thumb, I try to steady my breathing from my nose. Try and fail to calm the heavy pounding of my heart. Maddox's hand dips into my hair, dragging my head back and I release Zane with a pop. Heat flames my cheeks further as hazel eyes consume me. This is the first time I've felt so close to Maddox, which is insane considering what we've done together. The hunger in his gaze makes my legs weak but Zeke ensures I remain standing. One hand holding me flush against his dick, the other working me to a frenzy within minutes. I'm a slave to his touch. To their desires.

"I can't lose again," he whispers, releasing my hair. It tumbles down my back until Zane collects every red strand to wrap around his hand, keeping my head tilted upwards. Maddox's hand hovers over the side of my neck, his arm on my shoulders being to tremble as if he really wants to touch me. His jaw clenches tight. Whatever he wanted to do, doesn't come to fruition so he resigns to staring at me instead. Zeke's fingers curl, rapidly drawing me closer to a speedy climax.

"Um, is the ring taken?" a voice comes from behind Maddox. I freeze, although Zeke quickens his pace, releasing a laugh.

"Give me about…" he jams the heel of his palm into my clit and I rock against him, "twenty eight seconds." Oh my fuck. Let the ground open up and swallow me whole. Maddox doesn't react, too enthralled by the sinking pleasure on my face. The sighs spilling from my parted lips, the conflicted pinch of my brows, the sheer panic in my eyes. That's probably the bit he's enjoying the most.

And in turn, my body gives him exactly what he wants. My orgasm is just as Zeke intended; swift and all consuming. My vision blacks out and thankfully Zane releases my hair so my face can crash into Maddox's chest. I moan softly into his shirt, taking his tie in between my teeth to bite down on. Zeke fingers me speedily all the way to the end, once my body slumps lazily between the three of them. Withdrawing his digits, he wipes my cum on my inner thigh and then sucks off the rest as he leaves, as if he's found his favorite flavor of ice cream. Zane disappears too.

Clearing my throat, I replace Maddox's tie, trying to straighten out the teeth marks I've left. He holds up his hands, telling me to back the fuck off without needing to say it. His next words, though, are just as harsh a rejection, if not worse.

"You're never going to be ready for this fight," Maddox announces to the entire gym, turns on his heel and strides away. Never has someone been so quick to enjoy my pleasure and insult me in the same breath. Not even Ricky, and he was a lying, cheating scumbag. Ducking my head, I ignore the multiple eyes facing my way. Climbing out from between the ropes, I spy Aria on the balcony, exchanging words with Maddox before he slams his office doors closed. Climbing the stairs, I drop down next to her, swinging my legs over the edge.

"What the fuck is my life?" I huff, leaning my arms over a railing at chest level. Aria repositions her body, her green eyes as wide as her mouth. "What?!" I ask when I can't take it anymore.

"Do you realize what just happened?" Aria gapes, dramatically pretending to pick her jaw up from the floor.

"Yeah, I was used as a human stress reliever," I roll my eyes and rest my head on my forearms.

"No, not that," Aria shakes me back to sit upright. Below, Zeke and Zane are spotting each other in turn on a weight bench. Even on his back, Zane pointedly ignores looking anywhere near my direction. Whiplash – that's what these guys are giving me. "They were all drawn to you without even noticing. You soothed them, simply by being there. That's never happened," Aria turns my shoulders to face her. I blow a raspberry through my lips, shrugging her off.

"Yeah right. I bet you all go clubbing every weekend and end up sharing a woman." A twinge of jealousy rears its ugly head and I shove it back down into a box labeled 'do not open.'

"No, Killer. The four of us have never shared a woman. Especially Maddox," Aria's eyes shoot to the office door. Tugging me closer, she whispers beside my ear. "Zeke reckons Maddox hasn't actually been with anyone in the last four years. Some kind of pact with himself after Trina, but he broke it for you." Hunting for Aria's gaze, my breath mingles with hers. We remain there for a beat, too many emotions being passed between us.

I break away first, shaking my head. I'm becoming too involved. It shouldn't matter if Maddox broke his sex ban for me. Or that he's allowed his crew to join in his exploits for the first time. It's just sex. Nothing more. Spiraling into my thoughts, Aria's hand cups my cheek. She eases my head down onto her shoulder, stroking her thumb back and forth.

"Relax," she coaxes. "I've never heard such a loud thinker." I close my eyes, sinking into Aria's good side, I heed her advice. Nothing from yesterday, or even last week has changed. I need to remember I hold the cards here. *I'm playing them.* Not the other way around. Before long, my body has fallen still. I hadn't realized I was so jittery until it stopped, but that could be due to being fingered in public. Another tick on the bucket list I didn't write.

People on the level below have resumed their usual activities. Zane and Zeke have swapped places. The veins along Zeke's arms protrude from his tattoos as he lifts the heavy weight bar. I wish to explore the mix of roses and tribal linework, but that would require getting close to him for a lengthy amount of time. From this distance, without his cocky smile or confusing actions throwing me into a tornado of confusion, I can appreciate his beauty. Thick biceps and wide shoulders. Traps frame his neck where an Adam's apple bops in time with his counting. Like Zane, his vest is tight, clinging the valley of cum gutters I know to be underneath.

Our four-way shower was *very* revealing, in more ways

than one. As if they'd all left their egos at the door, we were able to explore each other's bodies, lost to the spray of water.

"Our trust has been betrayed before," Aria says out of nowhere. I tilt my head, hanging on her words. "Naturally, my brain isn't in my balls, so I've adapted better. But the guys are coming around. Just give them a little more time."

"Time?" I echo back. Time for what? The door at our back is whipped open, and the storm that is Maddox breaks through any sense of calm Aria and I had managed to find. Aria starts to drag herself up, but Maddox barks at her to stay where she is. After shoving a scrunched piece of paper in her hand, the platform shakes with each of Maddox's stomps, leading him down the stairs towards Zeke and Zane. They are by his side without needing to be told, exiting via the main door.

"Should we go with them?" I ask but Aria's grave expression gives me all the answer I need. Instead, she passes me the paper, the text faint and grainy like that of an old fax machine.

Urgent meeting – Club 66. Men only.

Chapter Twenty-Six

Stepping over the club's threshold, the heavy bass hits me like a thump to the chest. The glittery flooring is tacky beneath my shiny dress shoes, the bar to the left heaving with more bodies than the four bartenders can serve. Maddox leads the way, cutting a path through the women in tiny dresses who throw themselves at him. Then me, then Zeke at my back. All three of us ignore their efforts, veering for the VIP staircase. A bouncer takes in our matching suits which Maddox stopped to purchase on the way here, getting Zeke and I to change in the back of his Mustang. Nodding, he unhooks the red rope, permitting our entry away from the overcrowded dance floor below.

The balcony gives a clear view of the empty stage, tonight's entertainment being provided by a DJ high in his booth. Hands pumping, head banging with a thick set of over-ear headphones – he's having just as much fun as the crowd jumping in unison at his feet. A mosh pit has formed just before the stage, rowdy shirtless men diving high and piling on top of each other. Usually Zeke would have diverted away by now, sneaking his way into the chaos. The fact he's still at my back, facing forward when I check over my shoulder, is a miracle.

"What?" he asks and I half-shrug, mumbling to myself. The VIP area is made up of rounded booths on various platforms, the seating surrounded by thick curtains for privacy.

Maddox heads directly for Theodore's, always the most central with the largest entourage. Through a crack in the curtain, the OG bosses from all of Theo's crews can be seen huddled around the table, awaiting the main man himself, and nursing drinks in their hands so there's no chance of being poisoned. Theo's a shady bastard at the best of times. If he no longer has a use for you, you're gone. Men from those subsequent crews fill a majority of the other booths, most being entertained by a woman dancing on their table.

"Let's grab a drink, brother," Zeke calls over the music, grabbing my collar. Yanking me in the direction of the much emptier bar on this level, I toss Maddox a look. He nods, straightening his jacket before lowering on a suede seat at the far side of the table. A waitress unhooks the curtain, drawing it closed for privacy until Theo decides to show up. Typical of him to call a meeting and then be late for it.

"Two vodka and cokes," Zeke leans on the resin surface, holding up two fingers to a waitress who immediately complies. "Make them doubles and charge to Theo's tab."

Taking one of the many stools, I slide into Zeke's side, my eyes continuously returning to the strange look on his face. Calmness fills his piercing blue eyes, his jaw relaxed and fingers drumming a steady beat on the bar. I wouldn't go as far as to call it happiness, but contentment, perhaps? Whatever it is, he's no longer looking for his next high. Seeking out the nearest adrenaline hit to fill his life with some kind of meaning.

"For fuck's sake. Just say whatever it is or stop staring at me. You're giving me a complex here," Zeke whips his head my way. I hold his stare before exhaling and holding up my hands.

"You don't normally come up here, that's all. I'm just…not used to having company at these things." Zeke pulls at his tie, loosening the knot and unbuttoning his top button.

"Well if I knew you were going to be a big girl's blouse about it," he strides over to the railing, watching the dancers below. The bartender returns with our drinks, placing them down with a napkin with her number scrawled on. I take the glasses, leave the napkin and carry them to Zeke. Nudging his shoulder, I put my best effort into a smile, until his blue eyes travel over my shoulder. A frown pulls at his mouth.

Placing the drinks onto the wide railing, I turn to see a man reach the top of the stairs. Lean, with a mess of curls on top of his head. A baggy basketball jersey and wide, red shorts make him look scrawnier, the pathetic excuse of muscle on his biceps enough to make a nun ask 'what the fuck?'. Hardly nightclub attire, but if his aim was to promote his own brand, the giant 'Freddie's' logo across his chest does just that. Zeke falls into step with me, barricading his way towards the booth Maddox is in.

"What the fuck are you doing here?" I snarl. Freddie halts, scowling right back.

"I was invited to meet with Theo," his eyes slide past us to the closed curtains. I raise one brow, releasing the smile I can no longer hold back.

"Turn around and walk away kid. You have no business fucking with Theo." I nudge his shoulder with the heel of my palm, knocking him back a step. He slaps my arm away.

"Last time I checked, I can do whatever the fuck I want with my life. And once I'm a part of this," Freddie gestures to Zeke and I, "I'll be able to protect Ra- I mean, Harlow from the likes of you."

"Oh, this is precious," Zeke laughs. I, however, don't waste any more time on small talk. Rearing my arm back, I slam my fist straight into Freddie's cocky face. He stumbles back and, to his credit, recovers quickly. Throwing his shoulder into my gut, I swiftly raise my knee, making contact with his nose. Wetness splatters over my slacks and I curse. Maddox's going to lose his shit. Winding my forearm around Freddie's neck, I hold his head in my armpit to rain punches down on his kidneys. Zeke taps my shoulder, telling me it's his turn.

Releasing Freddie with a shove, I step aside, grappling for a hold on the strange emotions warring inside. My chest heaves, my fists clenching with the notion to kill this fucker for even mentioning Harlow's name. The idea of him protecting her *from us* riles me no end. I'll break his jaw in so many places, he won't ever be able to mutter those words again. Zeke lifts his arm and Freddie flinches. I grin maliciously.

"It's okay, I just wanna talk," Zeke says and my grin instantly slips. Wait, what? Freddie narrows his eyes, and for some stupid reason, tries to duck around Zeke to get a step closer to the booth. My brother twists with ease, grabbing Freddie by the scruff of his jersey. "Look dude, I'm doing you a favor. Leave while you're still able to."

Freddie struggles against Zeke's grip, throwing his elbows into Zeke's ribs. I see red, stepping forward to teach this kid a life lesson he won't forget but Zeke holds up a hand. Lowering his voice, I have to step in and mostly lip-read to catch onto his words.

"If it's Harlow you're worried about, there's no need. I'd never let any harm come to her that she wouldn't enjoy." Zeke smirks with a knowing look in my direction. Funnily enough, Freddie isn't reassured.

"What's that supposed to mean? If you're trying to get me to back off, I'm only more certain now she needs my help. I will hunt her down and –" Zeke sighs and throws a fist into Freddie's gut. Chucking him to the floor, Zeke stomps a dress shoe onto Freddie's chest and shrugs.

"Seriously kid, take a hint. She's one of us now, and that's what she wants. She chose us, but I'll be sure to pass on your concerns. If Harlow wants to reach out to you, she's free to do so." Without giving Freddie another chance to argue, Zeke drags him up by his jersey, headbutts him in his already bloodied nose and drags him to the staircase. Wiping the blood from his forehead over Freddie's jersey, Zeke gives a cheery 'bye now' before tossing Freddie down the stairs.

"Now, where's my drink?" Zeke smiles, returning to the railing where we previously stood. I slowly join his side, unable to rid myself of the bitter anger churning in my chest.

"You're going soft," I grind out through my teeth. "The ruthless asshole I knew would have killed that guy and stuffed his body beneath a table for someone else to find."

"Our dynamic is changing, brother," Zeke muses, lifting his glass to down the vodka coke in one gulp. Whatever angered him before Freddie's appearance is now a distant memory. I sigh, feeling the ache of self-induced misery in the depths of my soul.

"I like things the way they are," I reply hollowly and Zeke barks a laugh.

"That's the biggest crock of shit I've ever heard. What about when we went to Vegas and shared those triplets with Aria? You were blind drunk, high as a fucking moth, and you said-" Zeke shoves his empty glass into my hand to air quote, "*I wish we could have this all the time.*"

"And you continue to take those words out of context. I was referring to the booze and strippers, that's all." Zeke chuckles at me, his blue eyes sparkling with the truth I refuse to acknowledge.

Leaning my forearms on the railing, I pick a dancer below to concentrate on. It's that, or throw myself over the railing to avoid this conversation. Unfortunately for me, she happens to have vibrant red hair and a body men would kill over. Lifting her arms above her head, she sways her hips completely out of time with the heavy rock music. Her face turns to the ceiling, the simple smile across her face highlighted by strobe lights. It would seem she's having a concert of her very own inside her head, much like another free spirit I know would.

I throw back my vodka and coke, immediately signaling to a passing waitress to take our glasses and refill them. At least if I were at home, I could work out in my room and pretend the world doesn't exist. But here, there's no chance. The world is very much real and the only way to evade it is to drink myself oblivion.

"You're wrong," I point at Zeke, deciding if he's not going to dance the night away, I'll do it for him. One of us has to play the role of shithead party boy, and when Zeke veers out of his designated lane, it sends my mind spiraling into chaos. His brow raises, an entertained smirk upon his face.

Spinning, I bump into the waitress. Her tray hits my chest but I manage to save the drinks, downing each one in quick succession before swerving around her. My feet hit the stairs as I race back down them, too impatient to wait for the red rope to be moved for me. If given the chance, I'll talk myself out of being reckless and maybe for once, it'll do me good to act out. Hopefully this will also put things into perspective for Zeke, and prove why we can't dream of running off into the sunset.

Working my way through the crowd, I aim for the red head. Those filling the dancefloor are jumping, fists pumping and hair swinging in all directions. Mostly in my face as I near the girl in my sights, my hands coming to rest on her waist. Her head spins to look upon me with dark eyes. Too dark, compared to the endless pools of honey I'm used to, but I tell myself that's for the best. I didn't pick her because she reminds me of Harlow, but because of her spirit. She smiles, approving my silent request to join her personal concert.

Easing back against my shirt, her head tips back onto my shoulder and together, we move. Rolling our waists to a beat all of our own, my crotch against the ass of her tight shimmering dress. Sequins adorn her from chest to upper thigh, bound tight to her hourglass figure. A leather strap runs across her cleavage to the clutch bag she reaches into, producing a pair of glass tubes. Vibrant liquid sloshes around inside as she passes me one, and uncorks the other with her teeth. Throwing back the liquid, she shudders and grins, continuing to dance to the song in her head.

I look at the test tube, dubious to drink something gifted to me by a perfect stranger. But then I look up to Zeke, who's watching me intently. Waiting for me to fail in whatever I'm trying to prove. If our positions were truly switched, he'd down the drink without a second thought, so out of spite that's exactly what I do. How's that for changing up the dynamics?

The taste hits me in the back of the throat, making me gag. Whatever the fuck I just drank, it was too akin to petrol for my liking and without a doubt, homemade. Yet within minutes, I'm reaching into her bag for another. Anything to rid me of the thoughts that plague my mind. The rigid rules I've forced myself to live by, the sense of purpose I'm always struggling to achieve. For one evening, one brief moment, I'm going to let it all go.

Before long, I begin to hear music of my own creation too. A mix between various 90's R&B songs, drawing me from one to the next as my limbs grow lighter. The girl's ass swaying over my dick pulls me into a pretty fantasy I throw myself into. Winding my arms around her waist, my cheek leans on her head and my eyes drawn closed. It doesn't matter who this girl is, only who I believe her to be.

Amber eyes blink up at me, sparkling with longing. Filled with purity which crash through my barriers and peer inside. Would she like what she finds? Or just realize there's nothing there worth knowing. My mind slips between reality and the fiction I wish I could achieve. No one needs to know. It won't even continue after tonight, but I hold this girl tighter and dream on.

"Hey," a hand taps on my arm. Forcing my eyes open, I find the redhead twisting, trying to escape the tightness of my grip. "I need the bathroom." Releasing her, my head swims. The heavy beat of rock music crashes down on me with the weight of a thousand bricks, my head both weightless and assaulted by the thumping. She hands me another test tube drink, her parting gift, before disappearing into the crowd as if she never existed. Did she even – or was I just hugging myself?

Bodies bump into my back, shoving me around. Dragging the cork from the tube with my teeth, I spit it aside and maneuver back towards VIP. Taking the shot, it hits just as hard, making me choke as I hand the tube to the security guard at the bottom of the steps. Returning to Zeke, I try to remember if I've eaten today, or if I'm just willing my legs to turn to jelly with each step.

"See," I throw my hand into his chest. "Fuck your dynamics." Zeke throws an arm around my shoulders, leading me towards an abandoned booth in the corner.

"Wow. You sure showed me," he agrees, lowering me down. Leaving the curtains open, we have a clear view of the dance floor below. More specifically, of the redhead who has returned in the center, looking around for me. Ha. She wanted this D. Zeke disappears briefly, returning with a bottle of vodka and two glasses of coke. I take the bottle, chugging directly from the rim.

"Please enlighten me Zane," Zeke grins, shimmying into my

side. "Do you enjoy living in denial or are you trapped there? Like purgatory for your own stupidness?"

"What the fuck are you talking about?!" I balk, shoving him away. He doesn't budge, which is good because in the next second, my head goes light again and I have to lean on him to stay upright.

"Seriously? Choosing to grind against a Harlow-lookalike is classic denial. You won't accept you want her but head directly for the next best thing?"

"That's not what I was…No, it's not like. Ugh, just go fuck yourself, okay?!" I sink further down in the leather seat so that the table in front blocks my view of the redhead below. She'd found someone else quick enough, sharing her moonshine concoction with him instead. Just whoring that shit out now, apparently.

"I want to show you something," Zeke announces after a while of drinking and shimmering in our own thoughts. Shifting, he pulls his phone from his pants pocket. The screen brightens as he loads his emails and clicks on an attachment. I hear it before I see it, the volume turned right up for a desire-filled moan to penetrate the air. I roll my eyes.

"This isn't the time or place for another one of your jack-off races," I groan, wondering why I even like Zeke. Sure, he's my brother and I'd take a bullet for him any day, but he's basically an asshole through and through. Zeke chuckles, pushing the phone into my hands for when the image finally catches up with the audio.

Harlow's face fills the screen, flushed and contorted with pleasure. Her back arches, pushing her perfect nipples into view. Her chest is coated in red, a sign I've come to know that she's had a mind-blowing orgasm. Laying across a bench, sporadic tears rolling from the amber eyes I've been picturing, her body jerks from the onslaught of pleasure.

"What…where," I breathe, suddenly too enthralled to talk.

Just seeing her so exposed and vulnerable, the deprived part of me awakens with the rising of my dick.

"I got the Reverse Glory Hole to send me the footage from the cameras. I've got this one too," Zeke exits the video and I force myself not to elbow him in the face. My jaw ticks with the loss of Harlow's unhindered moans, until he opens the footage from our side of the divider. Maddox, Zeke and I, all furiously pumping our shafts to explode all over her pussy. Three men, completely enthralled and utterly captivated.

"You see that?" Zeke pauses the screen as Maddox's hand grips his shoulder and I subconsciously shuffle into his side. The three of us. Seeking pleasure together. United by desire. Connected by her. "We've got somebody at home who won't divide us. We no longer need petty fucks or brief thrills. Harlow completes us, and the sooner you realize that and accept it, the quicker we can make her feel like she belongs. I'm not running the risk of her slipping through our fingers. Not when this is what we have to lose," Zeke's hand cups mine to raise the screen closer to my face. My vision is blurring so I press play, relishing the guttural moans as Maddox steps into view in from across the table.

"Is this a jack-off race?" he raises a brow, taking a step back. All of us are used to Zeke's idea of brotherly bonding and me not having anything better to do, usually go along with it. Zeke laughs, taking back his phone to show Maddox the screen. Our boss' brows raise further, sliding into the booth."

"Forward that to me, and pour me a fucking drink," he orders. I lift the vodka bottle over a glass of coke, trying to keep my hand steady but end up spilling it all over the table anyway. I slide the glass towards Maddox anyway, keeping the bottle for myself.

"How'd it go?" Zeke asks, and I jolt upright. Shit, I'd forgotten we were here for business.

"I'm not sure," Maddox frowns, watching the dancefloor.

The lights shine from the crevices in his face. He's only ten years older than us, but carries the weight of his burdens like a man who's seen too much. Been forced to fight too often, and not just physically. "Theo didn't show."

"Maybe he got caught up," I shrug.

"Or maybe someone wanted all of the crews pre-occupied," Maddox swerves the contents of the glass without it surpassing the rim. Drumming his fingers on the table, I can practically see the wheels turning in his mind. "Although I did discover it's not just us who has everything riding on this fight. All of the crews have been told the same – the winners will remain part of Theo's set up, being clumped together as he sees fit, and the losers are to become outcasts."

"But you don't believe that," Zeke leans his arms on a dry part of the table. I know it was my big idea to trade places for the night, or perhaps that was an excuse to get utterly shit-faced, but seeing Zeke as logical and sober is plain unnerving. Maddox shakes his head, angling his body in our direction.

"Theo wouldn't let us simply walk away. There's a reason none of the OG's have fought in years – he doesn't want to admit some of us might have slipped. To do it now seems... odd. Rushed. And not something we're likely to walk away from." Maddox is careful to keep his voice low. There's still entire gangs hanging around who would gladly snitch to Theo for brownie points.

"We all know what we know," I raise my bottle, a grin spreading across my face. Fuck, that was like... some Lewis Carroll riddle shit right there. Snatching the vodka bottle from me, Maddox grabs my hair to yank my head back. He cooly assesses my face, from my glazed eyes to my wide smile. I don't know what his grimace is about, I feel fan-fucking-tastic.

"How much has he had to drink?" Maddox directs the question to Zeke.

"Not enough," I reply anyway, stealing back the vodka bottle. *My* vodka bottle.

"He's dealing with some things," Zeke pitches in. Maddox releases my hair and I slump back against Zeke, who's fingers dive into the auburn strands to massage my head better.

"Aren't we all," Maddox grunts. "Whatever it is, sort it out. We all need to be on our A-game until this bullshit has blown over." Grabbing my wrist, Maddox begins to pull me from the booth like a rag doll. I will my limbs to obey, pushing up to stand at the end of the seat. Maddox rounds on me, gripping my arms tight with intensity burning in his hazel eyes. "And Zane? Just give the fucking girl a chance already." My smile slips, the barely rational part of my brain computing we're not talking about the redhead downstairs. "You won't be able to move past your own stubbornness if you don't. Give her a chance, you might surprise yourself."

"Maybe you," I weakly shove at his chest, "should take your own advice." My stomach rolls and I fight aside covering my mouth, not wanting to lose face. Maddox stares at me for a long moment, before giving a swift nod.

"Maybe I will."

ollecting up the empty pizza boxes, I tear them to fit in the trash can as my phone buzzes. Peering at the message from a blocked number, I slide it back into my pocket and set about clearing the dining table. Taking the cardboard to the trash can outside, I spot the small package on the back door step, as the message instructed. Scooping it up, I shove it into my hoodie pocket and return to the house, casual as all fuck.

Aria left a while ago to soak her ribs in the bathtub, trying to recover in the few short days before the weekend. There's no way she'll be able to fight, but her stubbornness wouldn't admit that either. Washing some left-over dishes from breakfast, I dry my hands as headlights flash across the other end of the hallway. A mixture of elation and nerves bubble inside my gut until I shove it all down and lean against the counter. Act cool, Harlow.

The door flies open and a pair of nearly identical men stumble inside. White shirts and dislodged ties hang over their shoulders, their black slacks hanging low. Zane's missing a shoe, but I bet when they were fully put together, they'd have been a stunning sight. Unable to walk in a straight line, Zeke attempts to hook his suit jacket on the coat rack and fails. Zane isn't in much better shape, a vodka bottle clutched in his hand as he tackles the stairs.

Thud.

Zeke laughs, all rushed and high-pitched like a hyena. Making his way towards me, he uses his hands on the walls for stability and soon finds a dining chair to drop into.

"Good night?" I ask, replacing the hand towel over the oven handle. Zeke's reply is a slur of sounds I can't quite make out. Something about a mosh pit and too many girls. Oh the horrors, I roll my eyes to myself. Switching on the coffee machine, I grab two cups from the overhead cupboard. These boys need sobering up before they say or do something that, in the morning, I'll have to admit I thoroughly enjoyed.

"You've really..." Zeke trails off and I look over my shoulder. He's slumped over the table now, moving his hand around in my direction. "Got a perfect ass." I roll my eyes, returning to the coffees. Mixing in two brown sugars, I carry Zeke's into the dining area, pausing to blow on the steaming liquid. Can't add third degree burns to the list of ailments the Skulls need to recover from. Then I return for Zane's.

"He'll be on the roof," Zeke mumbles, laying his head on his arms. "It's his go-to."

"The roof? What do you mean, the roof?!" I ask but a rumbling snore is the only response I get. Zane could barely walk up the stairs; now I need to worry about him teetering on the edge of the fucking roof?! Coffee forgotten, I shoot upstairs. Aria's singing can be heard through the open doors to her bathroom. Probably hoping I'd join, but I've got to make sure Maddox isn't about to lose a member of his crew to a drunken misstep.

Avoiding all of the bedroom doors, I try others, finding an office, a second lounge area and a staircase. Taking those stairs two at a time, I find myself in an old attic while a large circular window sits at the far end. A breeze guides me forward, my arms prickling from the chill. Grabbing a folded blanket from on top of a cardboard box, I shake the dust out and wrap it around myself before slipping through the window's small opening.

The part of the roof is flat, framed by a short, stone wall. A heater glows, providing warmth over the hunched figure sitting on the ledge. I exhale, calming myself as I approach. Zane tips the vodka bottle upright, taking a long chug without issue. I move to sit by his side, not speaking. I'm merely here for suicide control.

Across the bay, the moon hangs low, reflected in the still water. A briny scent washes over me, but not as strongly as the first time I arrived. For once, everything is still. Including me. Not a bird in the sky, not a ripple of the lake. I'm beginning to see the appeal of living somewhere so derelict, because out here, the world doesn't exist. Nothing matters, but those who reside in this building and the bond which unites them. What I wouldn't give to have someone feel that strongly about me. But as it stands, I'm completely alone. No family, no friends. Only the bitter grasp of revenge slipping through my fingers.

"Trina was with us," Zane says into the silence. I flinch. He'd been so still, I forgot the entire reason I'm up on this roof, lost to my thoughts and the view. Passing me the vodka bottle, I place it down on the ground behind me. "At the orphanage. It wasn't just the three of us. There was four. There's always been four."

I don't reply. Mostly out of fear he'll stop talking, and I want to hear everything Zane is willing to offer. I might not get the chance again.

"She was one of us," he repeats, mumbling to himself. Drawing my knees up, I wrap the blanket around my pajamas. "But she was ambitious too. Felt like she deserved more from life than what we had. So she did whatever it took to get it."

"This is the brunette I saw at the gym, right?" I play dumb. I know exactly who Trina is. Zane grunts, reaching out for his vodka. His hand tugs at my blanket, unraveling me and I roll into his side like a burrito filling spilling free. Suddenly his arm is around my back, pulling me against him. I freeze and swallow hard.

"Every heist we pulled, Trina was at the forefront. A true chameleon, as Maddox would say. She could don a wig and an accent and have the entire world eating out the palm of her hand. But none as much as Maddox. He loved her, gave her every piece of himself. Even proposed to her." I brave a look up at the harsh contours of Zane's shadowed face. I didn't know that part. "And she destroyed him. Was working with Theodore the entire time to 'weed out the weak,'" Zane finger quotes around me. He scoffs and I'm inclined to agree.

There's nothing weak about Maddox. I can't even imagine him loving someone, but I've only seen the man shrouded in hatred who hates to be touched. I imagine once upon a time, he was the type to give his woman the entire world. To worship the very ground she walked on, and he paid the price for it.

"Not just Maddox," I murmur, desperate to continue this conversation, despite sensing Zane on the verge of shutting down again. I need to know what happened, to understand the dynamics. The fate of my plan and conscience rests on it. "Trina betrayed you, Zeke and Aria too. You guys are tighter than siblings. Have you ever…spoke to them about it?"

Zane's blue eyes drop to my face, his fingers trailing my jaw. The mask he hides behind slips. Raw emotion bleeds from his eyes. Misery, disloyalty, pain he's never tried to deal with. Tugging the blanket around me tighter, his head lowers.

"Be real," he whispers. His breath fans my face, tainted by vodka. "Please, be real." Zane's lips seize mine, stealing the air from my lungs. My chest expands, my senses drawing on everything that is Zane. The tip of his tongue licks along my bottom lip before permitting himself entry, raising my brows into my hair line. Zane pours an unfathomable about of passion into his movements, whereas less than five minutes ago, I was sure he hated me.

Our mouths crash, our bodies twisting of their own accord to get closer. I fist his shirt as he claws at my hair and nape. Precariously sitting on the ledge, danger dances with the tangling of our tongues. He is a Bloodied Skull after all; the world would fall off its axis if Zane did anything without figuratively living on the edge. I smirk to myself, downing in the taste of Zane and vodka as I allow him to eat my face. But just then, like a dam breaking, a flood of memories bursts through the void.

"Excuse me, Miss?" a female voice wakes me. Covering my eyes against the harsh, midday sun, her brunette hair tumbles around me like a curtain. Aria? I push myself upright, hating how easily my heart lifts at the thought of seeing her again. But the woman who kneels down and hands me a carrier bag isn't her. Dragging up the large sleeves that swamp my arms, I dive into the bag, finding a bottle of water amongst a range of lunch items. My tongue thickens, my

throat too raw to speak. Fuck knows I've cried enough in the last twelve hours to render myself completely dehydrated. Unscrewing the cap, I down the entire contents, resting back against the brick wall. A few streets over from Club Rapture, this is as far as my bare feet would carry me before I collapsed. Wearing some security guard's jacket over the lingerie I was cast aside in, I look like a hooker sleeping amongst the trash cans. My hair is tatted beyond repair and as the woman offers a wet wipe, I scrub my face free of the makeup smeared everywhere.

"I hope you don't mind me waking you," the woman smiles and I take in her appearance for the first time. She's stunning, like straight out of a magazine. A white blouse and black skirt tie in with her cow-print heels and matching handbag. She smells like money, and certainly doesn't belong in an alley hand delivering food to the homeless. Holy fuck, I'm actually homeless.

"Do I know you?" I squint against the headache rousing in my mind. Her laughter makes it pound and I hold a hand against my temple.

"Not yet, but you will. I was in the crowd last night. I saw what happened to you." I groan, turning my head into my shoulder. I was hoping to forget last night and pretend it never happened. But I should have known, karma has ways of keeping tabs on you. Don't ask me what I've done to deserve this fate. Maybe something in a past life. The woman's smile doesn't falter as she offers out her hand for me to reluctantly shake.

"I'm Trina, and I'm here to help."

"Why would you care to help someone like me?" I avoid her gaze, withdrawing my hand to curl into a little ball against a dumpster. This is my life now, discarded and forgotten.

"Because the Bloodied Skulls need to learn a lesson in loyalty, and you're going to help me teach it to them. Besides, hell hath no fury like a woman humiliated, right?"

A hand glides beneath my hair, cupping my nape. The roughness of Zane's fingers calls to every inch of my body, wanting to feel the extent of his touch. To see how far his drunken haze will allow him to venture. His tongue dips into my mouth, lazily and unhurried. Seeking for the truth I'm unable to give, because it's not only Zane who's been hiding behind a mask.

I'm the one who is currently betraying him.

"I-I have to go," I push at his chest and grasp for what's left of my self-respect to high-tail it out of there. Leaving the blanket and Zane's look of confusion behind, I scramble through the attic. Zeke is still passed out on the dining table as I grab the sedan's keys from the kitchen side. Stuffing my feet into discarded sneakers and grabbing my hoodie, I'm out the door and in the driver's seat before I can breathe. Whacking the car into drive, I don't know what's worse. The fact Aria stands in her bedroom window, or Zane sitting on the ledge above. Neither call for me to stay, but both watch me go.

Fuck.

Tears sting my eyes, my movements erratic. The sedan swings side to side along the bumpy track through the warehouses, until I breach the main gates and manage to get a hold of myself.

It's okay, it's not too late. I can still fix this.

Only taking four wrong turnings, I manage to remember my way back to the gym. I swing the sedan into the back alley, my heart hammering in my chest. Taking barely a moment to clutch the steering wheel, I lower my head. Zane's kiss still lingers on my lips, a reminder of how close I came to knowing the real him. By morning, he'll have sobered up and shut me out, but I still need to do this. For all of their sakes, I need to correct my mistake. Punching in the code, I access the gym via the back door and my eyes are instantly drawn to the dim light in Maddox's office. Here goes nothing.

Climbing the stairs, I knock tentatively on the door. No answer. Twisting the handle, I permit myself entry, peering inside. Maddox breathes softly, eyes closed, reclined in his chair. Entering fully, I push the door closed with a click. His hazel eyes crack, taking one glance in my direction and close again. He doesn't consider me a threat, which was the whole point. Padding across his office, my eyes are drawn to the desk. An open bottle of whiskey sits beside a discarded flesh light. Around nine inches in length and seeping cum over the polished wood. Rounding to Maddox's side, he kicks against the wheels of his chair, angling his open fly towards me.

"Come to finish the job?" he asks, head lolled to the side. "Well, you're too late." I shake my head, despite knowing he can't see me.

"Maddox, I need to tell you something." Somehow, my voice is even, not resembling the bag of nerves I feel inside. The chances of me walking out of this room unscathed are slim-to-none, but I'm here now. I've made my decision and even if I don't have a family to call my own, I can withdraw my part in screwing up theirs. "I've been playing you."

"Touch me." Maddox's fingers trail to his shirt buttons. Unhooking them one at a time, the fabric falls away from his hard chest. I stammer over my words, forcing my feet to remain in the same place.

"Are you listening to me? Trina hired me, told me how to gain your attention. What I can do to destroy your crew from the inside out."

"I know," Maddox replies softly. Eyes still closed, he spreads his shirt wide and waits on bated breath. I shuffle forward and his brows pinch, his abs tightening in anticipation. It seems Zane isn't the only one feeling some alcohol-induced bravery tonight. But I refuse to give in this time.

"You know?" I ask, leaning on the armrests. Maddox tilts his head my way, a smile sliding across his lips as those hazel eyes finally settle on me.

"Since the start. And I'm not going to lie to you, Harlow. You're really shit at it." A bubble of laughter spills from us both, meeting in the middle and churning in full blown hysterics. I came in here fearing for my life, but now, it all seems so stupid. Maddox holds out his hands for me. Pressing my palms into his, I kick off my sneakers and mount him in his chair. Licking my lips, I sigh, dipping my hand into my hoodie pocket. Maddox tracks my movements in the dim lighting of his lamp, eyeing the small bag of powder I place on his desk.

"I'm supposed to put this in your water bottle before your fight this weekend," I offer up the last of my secrets. Now I'm stripped back, holding no more cards and the woman Maddox is now looking upon is the real me. No secret vendettas. Just me.

"Touch me," he orders again, unzipping my hoodie and pushing it over my shoulders. "I want to feel your hands on my skin. To remember what it's like." Careful to keep his fingers to the cotton, Maddox pulls my t-shirt over my head. My breasts heave in a simple black bra, but Maddox's eyes darken as if it was the sexiest of lace. Taking my hand, he lowers it onto his chest and groans deep.

Here goes nothing.

Sliding my fingers over the hardened panes, I pause at a scar. Lengthy and neat, like those the Skulls bare on their backs. Tracing the line down to Maddox's abs and back up the other side, he clenches his teeth, moving his head to the side. Using a single finger, I draw his chin back in my direction.

"Watch me," I command. He obeys. This time, I use two hands. Starting at the sides of his neck, my featherlight touch outlines his traps to shoulders and I push at the shirt to rid him of it completely. His tattooed biceps flex beneath my exploration, a swirling mix of Viking runes and imagery leading all the way to the arrows individually inked onto each one of his fingers. Returning to Maddox's chest, my pace quickens, lowering to carve lines around each of his individual abs.

"I can't fight this weekend, Maddox. I won't win," I breathe. A strangled noise comes from his throat as I make it to his unhooked belt buckle. Trailing his own hands up my arms, a millimeter from actually touching me, deft fingers unhook the straps at my shoulders.

"I know that too. Which is why we're not going to be here." I tilt my head, causing my red hair to skate over his hand. He teases the strands, inhaling deeply. The question in my eyes doesn't go unanswered for long, even if Maddox's gaze continues to return to the bra in front of his face. "The entire fight will be sabotaged. Not only by you. I knew it from the moment I heard the invite from Trina's treacherous lips. The Bloodied Skulls aren't supposed to survive this weekend; I just didn't realize the extent she was willing to go, in order to make it happen."

"Where are you going to go?" I breathe.

"You say that as if you're not coming with us." Maddox tugs my hair behind my ear. I still, relishing the tiny scrape of fingertips against my skin. If it were anyone else, the touch could be considered a mistake, but not with Maddox. Any contact is carefully planned, his intentions intricately thought out ahead of time. Reaching for the whiskey, Maddox lifts the bottle to his lips, watching me as he takes a swig.

"Well, honestly, I figured after I came clean, I'd have to find a new venture in life. Decide what the fuck I'm actually going to do with myself," I shrug. That same strand of hair pings back out from behind my ear and I use it to cover my vulner-ability. Placing down the bottle, Maddox takes my chin between his thumb and forefinger. Easing me towards his mouth, he tugs my lips apart and places his on top. Cool liquid pools into my mouth, the drips I miss splashing onto my breasts. I linger, withstanding the burning working its way down my throat just to remain close to him for a beat longer.

"Regardless of your original intentions, *Harlow*," he growls my name and short circuits my pussy into overdrive, "you've managed to unite us again. Remind us what it's like to be whole. I'd fallen into a routine, not knowing what else to do with myself. But this," Maddox gestures a hand around his office, "is no longer the life I want to lead."

"So what do you want, Maddox?" I relay his own name back, just as huskily. My hands are still resting at his belt buckle, the hair sprouting from underneath suggesting he's not wearing boxers. Again.

"I want to disappear." Maddox moves to stand, taking me with him. Planting my ass on his desk, there's no embarrassment on his part about the used flesh light not so far away. His chest presses against my face, his voice rumbling though my entire body. "Me, my crew, in some remote corner of the world. A woman I can trust at my side."

"That's clearly not me," I mutter, ducking my head. Stepping back, Maddox leans on the desk, bringing him eye-level with me.

"Did you not just come here to confess everything? Did you barely last one week in our company before deciding you couldn't hold onto your anger? Trina held onto her grudges for years, slowly planning our demise."

"I don't want to talk about her," I shake my head, my nose skimming over his.

"Neither do I," Maddox breathes. I bite down on my lower lip. This close, I can look upon the darker flecks in his hazel eyes without reservation. Appreciate the five o'clock shadow he keeps trimmed to look like he hasn't spent years perfecting the style. His expensive cologne mixes with the whiskey, making my mind spin. All these light touches and near kisses are driving me crazy with need.

Deciding I can't take it anymore, I reach around the back of Maddox's head. Not gently this time, but hard, with my nails dragging through his long hair. He moans. A shudder moves between his shoulder, his mouth tilting ever closer near mine.

"Make no mistake, Princess, initiated or not, you're one of us. Where we go, you're coming with us," Maddox assures, closing the last inch to cement his promise with a fevered, passionate kiss.

Buzz, buzz, buzz.

I frown in my sleep, rousing to a continuous pulsating. Fuck, did I roll onto my vibrator? Scrambling around, I find my phone beneath my pillow and slump back. Maddox is blowing up my screen like no man's business.

Maddox: Meeting in the kitchen.

Maddox: ETA twenty minutes.

Maddox: Aria, get the fuck up.

Maddox: Everyone must attend.

More messages come through and I groan, tossing my phone away. The voice control on his Mustang needs disabling. Rolling out of bed, I head into my bathroom to sort myself out. Brush my teeth, do damage control on the nest of brown hair on my head. I passed out in my towel last night, and not drying my hair is a big no-no. It'll be a specific mix of greasy in the roots and dry on the ends with various kinks throughout until I wash it again.

Dragging my hairbrush through the tatted ends does nothing to ease my already unstable mood. I hate being left behind. All this 'men only' bullshit never ceases to stop pissing me off, and the only remedy I've found to work – sinking in the tub with a bottle of red.

Padding back into my room, my phone is still flashing with notifications on the floor as I make my way to my dresser. Figuring Maddox wants us so desperately and we have a fight to prepare for, I don a black sports bra and leggings, lowering a fuchsia pink vest over the top. The arm holes gape low enough to reveal the bruising at my ribs, while the back is longer to cover my ass. A car door slams outside and I exit my room the same time Zane does.

"Woah, dude. You look like shit," I shout, praising myself for his following wince. Grabbing the sides of his head, Zane bumps from wall to wall, possibly still drunk. His auburn hair is a mess, worse than mine but he's not able to hide his in a braid. Still wearing low-hanging slacks and an unbuttoned shirt he didn't manage to shed, Zane reeks of alcohol and shame as I follow him down the stairs. Suddenly, my morning just got a hundred times better.

Maddox slams the front door open as we breach the lower

level, making Zane groan again. Raising a brow, he allows Zane to head towards the kitchen first. I hang back, crossing my arms.

"Enjoy your sexist evening?" I ask boldly.

"You didn't miss anything." Maddox half-smirks and winks at my attitude and I almost topple over in shock. In fact, now I'm not focused on the state I'll probably never see Zane in again, I notice the casual jeans and t-shirt Maddox has arrived in. His wavy hair is still damp from a recent shower, his cologne drifting through the smell of coffee and bacon Zeke is working on. But that's not what strikes me as the most surprising. On his neck, a ripe hickey is splayed like a medal of honor. Who did he let close enough to do that, and just how fucked up did these boys get last night?

"Is Harlow up?" he asks, taking a particular interest in the stairs. I look around with wide eyes, rendered speechless. Maddox grunts, heading towards the kitchen. I'm hot on his heels, taking a door through the living area to access the dining room first. Sliding in a chair, I rest my chin on my fist, thoroughly intrigued by what's happening beyond the archway.

Maddox pats Zeke on the back, wishing him a good morning. Zeke hands our boss and Zane a coffee mug each, his own smile wide. Somehow, Zeke also looks refreshed, the smile on his face revealing his dimples. He hums a tune to himself, finishing a round of five bacon sandwiches to carry into the dining area.

"And good morning to you, dear sister," Zeke places a tea in front of my face.

"Okay seriously, did you guys switch skins or just go on a magic mushroom bender? Not saying I don't like it…but I'm tripping out here." Blowing on my tea, Zane drops down on the chair beside me and slumps into my good side. I hold still, allowing his head to roll around to find a comfortable spot on my shoulder. Lowering my voice, I keep one eye on Zeke and

Maddox conversing in the kitchen. "Seriously, Zane. You okay buddy? I've never seen you so hungover."

"I had some shit to sort through," he groans, hiding his eyes from the light. I'm taken back to a time when we were younger. Hiding out by the dumpsters to smoke weed when the four of us were meant to be in class. Sneaking out of the orphanage to go clubbing underage. Zane couldn't handle his drink back then, needing carrying home on many occasions.

That's what happens when you hold all your thoughts and feelings on the inside; as soon as they have an outlet, it's hard to pull back. It's why he's usually so careful. But things are different now. I feel it down to my bones. Everything has changed, and I can only think of one reason for it.

"Where is Harlow?" I ask, realizing I left my phone upstairs. Zeke strolls in, pulling up a seat on Zane's other side to transfer his head onto his own shoulder. Maddox sits opposite, linking his fingers on the table.

"She's probably sleeping," he hides another smirk. Yeah, I'm never going to be able to adjust to that. Even with Trina, Maddox reserved his emotions for behind closed doors. "And it's probably best we get some time to talk before she comes down."

I sit up straighter, as does Zeke. Zane forces himself upright, his head swaying slightly. Definitely still drunk. Whatever happened last night, Zane must have felt the need to drink until morning. The three of us give Maddox the time to find the words, his expression finally falling back into familiar territory. Business.

"We're leaving," he states, flexing his fingers out and back into their linked position. "I can't tell you where, but everything is arranged. I'm giving you twenty minutes to pack, just grab the essentials. We'll sort the rest."

"Wait, what?" I answer first, my heart picking up a beat. "What about Theo's fight?"

"It's rigged. The entire thing. One way or another, Theo was going to ensure we all lose our fights. And believe me, there wouldn't be any walking away or outcast shit. We know too much. It'd be an escort to the back alley and a bullet to the head." Maddox grimaces at the thought.

"And you know this, how?" Zeke asks, casually sipping his coffee as if our lives aren't about to be upended. Everything we've done has been for a simple, quiet existence. We keep the right people happy and fuck the rest. But not anymore, apparently. Maddox leans forward, inhaling deeply to choose his next words carefully.

"Harlow came to me last night. She was hired by Trina to sabotage us. But, before any of you blow your lids," he holds up a hand at the same time Zane's head snaps upright. It causes him to hiss through his teeth, but he strains his blue eyes against the light to glare at Maddox anyway. "We all knew she was up to something, and she came clean. That's what's important."

The calmness of his tone should soothe me, if it wasn't like watching Michael Myres at a meeting for recovering psychopaths. I'm weirded out, okay?

"None of you will mention any of this, or hold it against her," Maddox continues this rehearsed speech. Might as well hear out the end now. "We all found our own paths into this life, none of which were pretty. Cut Harlow some slack, because you all know as well as I do, we're better with her."

"She could have been anyone. Aria could have…picked anyone," Zane babbles but there's no conviction in his words. Tension radiates from his bunched shoulders, his hands fisting his sweatpants beneath the table. I reach out to take one, reminding him to breathe. Once he's sober, he'll be able to process, but at the moment, he's whining something about Harlow leaving him.

"Dude," I whisper in his ear, not wanting to unsettle the

peaceful aura around Maddox right now. "Listen to what's being said. She's not going anywhere, we're taking her with us." But he won't listen. Grabbing his coffee cup, Zane launches it across Zeke for the porcelain to smash into the wall. I grab his hand harder, expecting the dam of Maddox's patience bursting but it never comes.

"Level with me, Zane," Maddox sighs. "Do you know why I chose the four of you as my recruits?" No one responds, but Zeke sits forward, hanging on every word. "Because you were already a family. You had a bond of trust that would take years to establish otherwise. And I thought, at some point, I could have been a part of that too. To feel like people cared for me like I do them. So I tried…being the nice guy, protecting you from Theo by taking your lashings, then with Trina, but nothing worked. It was easier to be the boss you hated than the friend you rejected."

Maddox looks away and suddenly, I see him. Not for the ruthless man I knew. But the guy who's never had anyone. Someone who's only relationships stemmed from power and control. No wonder Maddox struggles to bond with us, but I can't say we've opened up enough to let him. After Trina, we turned in on ourselves. An impenetrable trio, even to the man who gave us a home and a purpose.

Flattening his hands on the table, Maddox's chest rise and falls heavily. Then, out of nowhere, he begins to smile. "The four of us have never shared anything until two days ago. Harlow provided us with the chance to be more than what we currently are, and we needed it. I've never felt like so much of a team as that moment. We don't need this manufactured life of heists and fights. Let's go carve our own."

"Wow," I raise my brows. "The power of pussy." Chuckling to myself, I push upright and my chair squeaks. Two sets of auburn eyes swing to me. Zeke, trying to hide his eagerness behind a wall of distrust. And Zane, with the aura of a wounded puppy. He'd rather save himself the heart ache that might arise, than dive down the rabbit hole and hope for the best. But that's the difference with me; I refuse to leave this life with regrets. "Come on boys. It's an adventure. Roll with it and you might just enjoy yourselves."

Leaving the dining area, a mixture of chairs scraping and cups being placed down follows. Zeke announces he'll wrap the sandwiches for the car, while Zane mumbles about painkillers. Footsteps pound behind me and halfway up the stairs, Maddox pushes past to take the lead.

"I'll get Harlow. Twenty-four minutes!" he calls, taking two at a time. I laugh, holding my ribs.

"Someone's an eager beaver." Returning to my room, there's still a smile stretched over my face. I don't know how she did it, but Harlow's managed something no one else has. She's cracked Maddox. Picked his lock and opened the safe within, giving him something none of us are familiar with. Hope.

I head for my bathroom first, gathering up toiletries I barely use yet suddenly feel the need to take. Pausing in the mirror, I stretch back as far as I can to pat myself on the back. Good fucking job Aria. Am I taking full credit for choosing her? Fuck yeah I am. The boys have been mocking me for two years, saying my gay-dar was off. Well, look at Maddox now, rasping on Harlow's door asking if she's decent. Back in my room and grabbing a backpack, I stuff my comfiest clothes in first, and whatever space I have left goes on underwear and one pair of ripped jeans.

"Aria?!" Maddox calls, flying through my door like a battering ram. "Where is Harlow?"

"What do you mean, where is she? You said she was with you last night," I frown. His hazel eyes are wild, his chest moving too fast. Oh Jesus Christ, how many men-stral moments am I going to have to deal with today?

"She was, until she left to come back here. We didn't…It wasn't like-"

"Dude, please spare the details," I hold up a hand, dumping my bag on the unmade bed. "I'm happy you're happy and all that shit, but I still get jealous when we're discussing the woman I'm crushing on." Sidestepping closer to my window, I view the skidded marks in the dirt where I saw Harlow tear off into the night. At least now I know where she was going. "Hmmm, the sedan hasn't returned. You don't think she…"

"No." Maddox scares me from directly behind. His chest bumps my back as he peers over me and shakes his head. "She wouldn't have left. Not after last night. Not after I let her… touch me. She wouldn't do that to me."

"I mean…Maddox, we don't really know her that well," I say in a small voice. Two large hands grab my biceps and whip me around, jolting my bruised ribs.

"Don't. Just don't say it. I-" he trails off, returning to stare out of the window. His mouth pulls down at the sides and his hands jerk back, as if just realizing he's touching me. Hazel eyes dim, losing the twinkle of excitement to shut right back down. "She's genuine. I'd bet my life on it."

"You're right," I nod, moving away from the window, bringing Maddox's attention with me. "She's the real deal. So let's be logical about this." Pausing in my doorway, I shout for Zeke and Zane to get in here. Footsteps hammer down the hall, adhering to the note of unease in my voice. As they spill inside, Maddox frowns and pulls his cell phone from his pocket.

"What-" Zeke starts until Maddox raises a finger to his lips. Beckoning us to follow, he walks into my bathroom, places his cell on the countertop and proceeds to turn my shower on full blast. I'm last in, closing the door before joining Zeke and Zane to read the open message.

Trina: Real deal? Give me a break.

My eyes fly wide as Maddox returns, his hands fisted at his sides. It's Zane who snatches the phone first, squinting to type 'where is she?' The reply comes instantly.

Trina: Change of plans.

Waiting on tenterhooks, the room begins filling with steam. Huddled together to view the screen, the next string of messages come one at a time.

Trina: Maddox, alone, must complete his fight.

Trina: If he wins, you can have your precious whore back.

Trina: If he loses…

We all wait in anticipation for the next message being typed, although I could have guessed what it'd say before it comes through.

Trina: She dies.

And there it is. The sudden death of any happiness we may have briefly felt. Not to say Maddox wouldn't win his fight, if it was fair. But this is only the start of the traps. Theo is a connected man with too much money and time, and a vengeful bitch sitting on his lap, whispering ideas in his ear. We were fools to think we could have opted out and started over. But now the notion has been suggested, staying here under Theo's rule doesn't appeal anymore.

With the phone still clutched in his hand, Zane begins typing using one index finger whilst trying not to sway.

> Maddox: Who has the same phone number for four years?

He chuckles until Zeke snatches the phone and Maddox slaps the back of his head. Considering the 'brawn' of our group is inebriated, it's almost lucky we have three days to come up with a plan – if Harlow manages to hold on that long. Leaning forward, I write through the steam which has collected on my mirror.

What are we gonna do?

Maddox pushes the three of us out the way, his hand steady as he writes out an answer he doesn't even have to think about.

Save our girl.

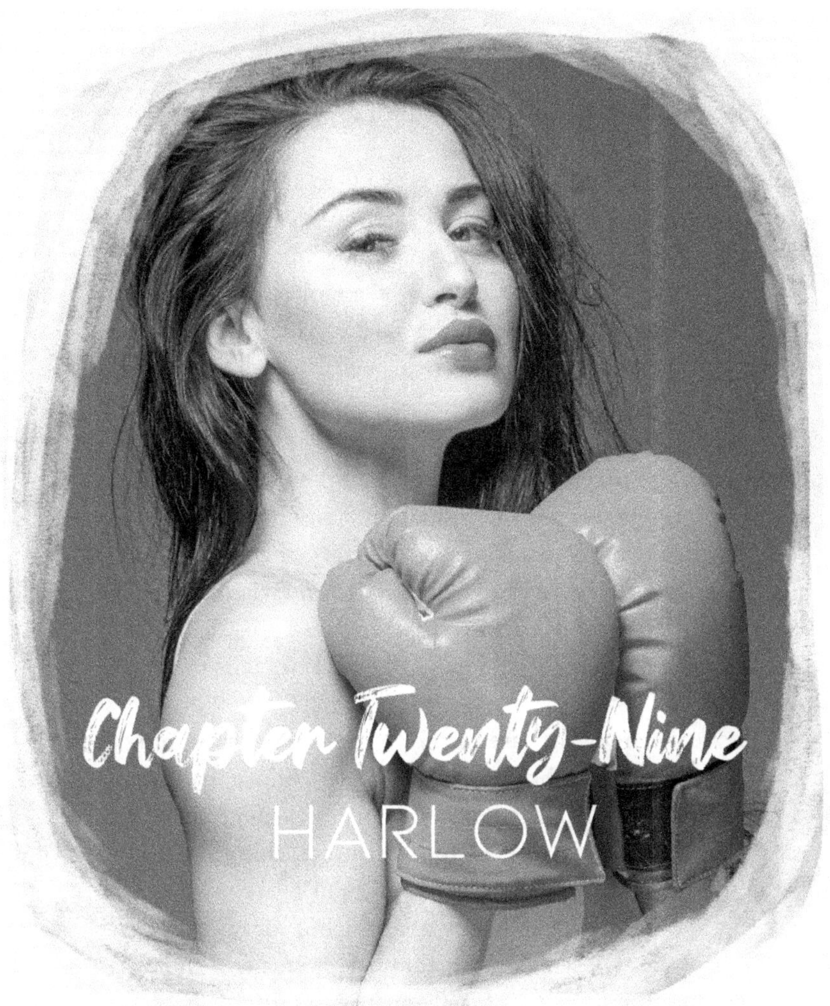

Chapter Twenty-Nine
HARLOW

ry. How is my throat this dry? Fighting against a swallow that makes me heave, I force my eyelids open. A cluttered room stares back, the type one hordes all their shit in and closes the door, pretending it doesn't exist. Except for the wide circle around me, pushing clear of anything I may have been able to use as leverage.

Where the fuck am I? More than that…how did I get here? Dropping my head back, I swing. As in, my entire body sways back and forth and the sudden slice of pain from my wrists makes me groan. The lack of feeling in my shoulders concerns me more, as I hang like a pig waiting to be carved up and served on a platter of apples. I've been in this position before, at the outbuilding on the fishing pier. But I managed to ignore the pain then, in favor of the way Zeke looked at me. Like his favorite appetizer and I would have let his teeth sink into my flesh just to see how good it could feel. If only I had such a distraction now, but I'm all alone.

Like the rope cutting into my wrists, my ankles are bound. Fastened together in the same leggings I wore to Maddox's office. I wriggle, testing the rest of my body beneath the vest, cringing at the damp, stickiness I feel everywhere. Full disclosure, I have no doubts I've peed myself somewhere along the way, and the throbbing aching all over speaks of lacerations I can't see. I've bled at some point and a part of me is thankful I wasn't awake for it.

Above me, my wrists are bound to a metal bar fixed into the ceiling which curves like a hook. I've seen similar before, for holding up punching bags. The loop cutting through the carpet at my feet would make sense too, as the punching bag would need to be tied down by a chain to prohibit movement. At this present moment, it is being used as an anchor for my ankles.

Getting my bearings now the fog over my vision has cleared, I search the room for clues. It won't do much good if this becomes my final resting place, but I have nothing else to focus on. Boxes are stacked on the retro, dusty carpet. Those bursting open at the edges are stuffed with random shit; maps, trophies, photo albums. As if someone's entire life was packed up and thrown in here.

Fuck, is that what they'll do with me? The saddest part is, I don't even have enough belongings to fill an entire box. Whatever small savings I had, I wasted on drink, takeout and anything that took my mind off the shithole my life was spiraling into.

The door across the room rattles, a key being jimmied into

the lock. I straighten, yanking on the bar above my head. Maybe if I had woken earlier and had more time by myself, I could have worked on wearing down the ropes. But as the door swings open, all thoughts of escape temporarily evade me.

"Ahh, you're awake," Trina beams through a pair of perfectly painted lips. She's dressed down, or what I'd imagined 'dressed down' means to her. A sweater hangs over her slender shoulders, cinched at the waist in a vivid, pea green. Tight, dark jeans hug her legs, disappearing into knee-high black boots. A huge handbag sways in the crook of her arm. Strutting towards me, the intensity of her smile doesn't ease, giving her an iconic crazy-ass stare.

"Wha-" I try, rasping out an inaudible croak. Trina pulls a sports bottle of water from her handbag, popping the cap and holding it out before me. I lean all the way forward, bowing my body to draw the teat into my mouth like a baby bottle, sucking as much as she'll allow. When the bottle is withdrawn, I slump back into my restraints. My stomach flips, too empty to handle the onslaught of water intake.

"You were about to ask me what's going on," Trina fills in for me. I shake myself back to the present. Yes, exactly that.

"What the fuck is going on?!" I'm now able to shout. The accompanying scream still scratches my throat, but I throw myself against my binds to prove a point.

"You were preparing to back out of our deal and run into the sunset," Trina assesses her nails, seemingly bored. "I thought we had a good thing going, Harlow. Everybody was going to get what they wanted. But you had to do something stupid like grow a conscience."

"What?!" I gasp, my mind shouting *'shit, shit, shit'* on repeat. Every fiber of my being rouses from my comatose state, my awareness now passing over my skin like a thousand vaults of electricity. "Y-You've got it all wrong. I was just...I went a different route. To get Maddox to trust me, that's all," I force out. Trina narrows her eyes, pursing her lips and produces a lengthy 'mmhmm' sound. My mind is thrown back to Maddox's office, trying to remember exactly what I said. I know I gave him the drugs Trina had left on the back doorstep, but then my memory laps to his kiss. How his body leaned over mine, crushing me into his desk. How all of my senses were filled with his passion, the floodgates well and truly open for his desire to pour freely.

"Wait," I frown, refusing to sink back into the pounding of my skull. "How do you even know about that? You," I breathe, shaking myself to remain awake. My eyelids are heavy, my vision beginning to swim again. An image bleeds to life in my skull, of being ambushed in the alleyway outside Skull Fitness, a rag soaked in fumes held tightly over my mouth and nose. It could be a figment on my imagination, but I really don't think it is. "You've got his office bugged," I groan. Of course she does. I hate myself for being so naïve, but I know better than anyone how closely Trina has been watching the Skulls.

The woman in question doesn't respond, shifting to place her handbag on a table pushed against the edge of the room. Beyond her, Trina has left the door wide open. I stare at the hideous floral wallpaper as if I can will myself closer to the hallway. The edges of painted portraits are just about visible if I crane my head to the side, the frames flourished with gold. Either she's wholly confident I can't escape, or likes her chances of stopping me if I do. Whatever has her feeling so confident, it will be her downfall because I'm not as meek as I appear. As soon as I'm alone again, I'll start working on these ropes and a solid plan.

Lifting a cell phone from her bag, Trina's pale brown eyes spear mine as the call tone echoes from her loud speaker. The call is answered by a simple grunt.

"Hello to you too, darling," she smiles that crazed smile again. Like a Cheshire cat who has all the milk to herself. "The invitations to tomorrow's fight are going out as we speak, but I thought I'd personally ensure you received yours. Theo's home in the hills, commencing at sunset." No response comes from the receiver and I have to wonder if anyone is even listening. But Trina seems to know, because the longer the silence continues, the more humored she becomes.

"Don't forget, Maddox. If you lose your fight, she dies." Trina lifts her chin higher. I still, my entire body freezing in place.

"Unless you'd prefer I just kill her now," Trina nudges. Reaching into her bag once more, she pulls out a length of rope. Black in color with a sturdy handle. No, not a rope – a whip. I should probably shout, or start yelling what I can see of my location in hopes they might come to my rescue, but deep down, I know it's pointless. I was a stranger to them the week before last. None of the Skulls will risk breaking a single fingernail trying to save me. The traitor in their midst. More silence follows, confirming my suspicions.

Releasing the length of the whip, Trina slithers it across the ground like a snake moving cross the ugly carpet. I trace its movements, almost lost to the trance until Trina lashes out, her movements too quick for my sluggish mind to catch. Searing agony slices across my thigh, drawing a strangled cry from my throat. I scream through the burn, heated tears spilling from my eyes as I give Trina exactly what she wants. Slithering the whip across my shoulder and through my cleavage, I sniffle and twist as much as my restraints will allow, anticipating her next blow.

"I'll do you one better," Maddox finally replies, distracting Trina. For now. But it's not the intrigue in her cocked eyebrow that unnerves me. It's the fact Maddox has been listening in the whole time, and despite what we shared in his office, his voice is completely avoid of emotion. "How about you kill yourself and save us all the trouble?" Trina cackles, snapping the whip again on my stomach. Not as hard this time, and since I was preparing myself for it, I manage to control myself. Tightening my abdomen, a hiss of pain leaks through my teeth.

"And miss watching the life leave your eyes? Not a chance," Trina chuckles. Ending the call, she drops the phone back into her bag. I shudder, now eyeing the leather as if it's an arsenal filled with weapons.

For all I know, she could have a grenade in there, planning to blow me to pieces. Although, now I've been given insight into her plan, I have the small peace of mind I'm not being killed straight away. That doesn't mean she can't torture me in the meanwhile and make me beg for it. Trina wants to dangle me in front of Maddox like the carrot on the end of a stick. If I mean enough to him for the incentive to work.

The whip lands several more times, slashing me in various places. At some point, like my screams, the pain all blends into one giant ache and when Trina pulls out a syringe, I sigh in relief. Nearing me close enough for her overpoweringly expensive perfume to invade my nostrils and make me choke, I force myself to look her dead in the eye.

"Why are you doing all of this?" I rasp out. Trina lifts the syringe to my neck.

"You double crossed me," she shrugs, the point of the needle pressing against my skin.

"No," I'm careful not to shake my head and impale myself any sooner than necessary. "Why are you doing all of this to Maddox? You rejected him, right?" At some point, I grow a slither of bravery. I'm about to be knocked out cold anyway, I might as well know the reasoning behind it. Trina's elbow comes to rest on my shoulder, a low rumble of irritation sounding in the back of her throat.

"Oh no, Harlow. Maddox rejected me first. I should have been the leader of the Bloodied Skulls. I was always the one in charge of heists. I was ruthless enough to make the decisions

Maddox could not. And when his own weakness for a family became apparent, I proved to him exactly why that wasn't his place. Men like Maddox need a tragic backstory. A reason to be an asshole, so I gave him one."

The needle presses into my neck and any response I had quickly evaporates from my tongue. My head rolls back, the tingle of a kiss being placed on my cheek. Vaguely, I hear the shuffling of her retreat, the door closing and being locked. But that, nor the fact I'm slipping back into an unwelcome sleep, matter at the moment. Not when all I can think is...Damn, poor Maddox.

Chapter Thirty
MADDOX

"You guys all set?" I ask, hanging around in the entrance of their fisherman's lodge. I feel like such a fucking idiot now, making them live here all this time. Forcing them to believe it's all they were worth when in truth, they're the closest thing to a family I've ever had. Aria hops down the last of the stairs, dumping her bag at my feet.

"Yeah we're ready, but I still don't like the thought of leaving you." Eyebrows dip over emerald green eyes, a pout in her bottom lip. I withhold my sigh, refusing to show any weakness in the final moments we have together.

"I've made my choice," I stand tall, acting as if there wasn't any other option. I whistle for the pair of boys hanging back in the kitchen to join us. They're not happy with my decision either, but I'm the boss around here. My word is final.

"Maddox, please let us help you," Zeke tries one last time. Looking down at the pair of duffel bags I arrived with, I nudge one towards him with my sneaker, desperate to get this interaction over with.

"The best thing you can do now is just go. Whether I survive this fight or not, and regardless of what happens to Harlow, I need to know you three are safe. I brought you guys into this mess. Let me die knowing I managed to help you get out."

Zane barrels down the hallway taking the other duffel bag. He doesn't look at me and he refuses to speak. Whatever happened that night after the club, he hasn't opened up about it. Not that I expected him to. The hard knock of his shoulder hitting mine on the way past is as much of a goodbye as I'm going to get from Zane.

Also taking his leave, Zeke follows, giving me a quick fist pump on the way out. That just leaves Aria who, for the first time ever, dives into my arms for a hug. I freeze, not reciprocating at first, but the longer she clings to me like a little bear cub, the more awkward it becomes. *Screw it.*

Enveloping her in my arms, I give Aria the justification she's secretly always wanted from me. A father figure to pat her on the head and tell her she's done a good job. Placing her down, I reluctantly pick up her backpack, navigate it onto her good shoulder and show her out the door.

The trio slip into their replacement sedan, bags on laps and gazes avoiding mine. Aria throws the car into reverse, disguising her wince at the movement, and peels down the dirt track. I stand in the doorway watching them go, warring emotions beating inside my deadened chest. I hadn't been prepared for the end of an era so soon, and damn if I hadn't become comfortable with the dynamics we fell into.

Were they healthy? Fuck no. But what relationships are these days? None that I've ever seen.

Pulling the door closed behind me, I drop the keys onto the front step. No doubt the mysterious buyer who snapped up this property in three days is Trina. She already has the place bugged, she might as well own it too. Scuffing my sneakers through the dirt, I make my way to my Mustang and drop into the driver's seat and sigh heavily.

The first two days of not knowing what danger Harlow was in were the worst. Despite only being at the house briefly, the gaping hole now in our lives was too much to ignore. Until Trina's call came, and then we knew exactly what we're dealing with. A bitter ex and her jealousy over the one who could unite us.

Refusing to let any form of doubt creep in, I follow in the tracks Aria left, not once looking back in my rearview mirror. The pocket of my gym shorts vibrates but I dare not look yet, not until I'm miles down the abandoned highway and pulled over in a lay-by. Slipping the burner phone into my hand, I note the text from another with a simple grunt.

Unknown Number: Two tails. Navy Blue Audi's.

Maddox: You know what to do.

With Trina listening in at the house, we gave her the story she wanted to hear. I'm to be the complacent fighter, following orders and putting on a good show for all the wealthy guests who don't realize the extent of blackmail I'm under. Meanwhile, my crew is supposed to have a one-way ticket out of this hell I've subjected us all to, but we knew Theo wouldn't let them go. It's not the way he works, yet the old bastard has never been able to turn down an old-fashioned chase and execution. Only now, his lackeys in blue Audi's are doing it for him.

Removing the battery from the back of the phone, I snap it, winding down my window to throw the entire handheld out into the grass. Zeke will have done the same, as per the plan he's come up with. We can't take any chances. From here on out, there will be no more contact and we'll only know if we've succeeded if everyone makes it to the rendezvous point on time. With or without Harlow, I'm determined at least some of us are making it out of today alive.

Returning to the highway, I follow the route I've memorized by heart. Two cities over, nestled between the likes of millionaires and celebrities, Theo will be waiting. I settle in for the long drive, unusually airy in my red sports shorts and black fitness t-shirt. It's been years since I've left the comfort of my gym in such attire. Doing so takes me back to the seventeen-year-old boy who left an abusive father behind and set his sights on a new type of life. One where using my fists gained praise and using my smarts brought in more money than I had sensed at the time. Shaking myself out of that train of thought, I turn the radio on. Shawn Mendez has a new song out, singing of love and despair, which instantly floods the mustang. I raise my hand to the touchscreen, intent on changing it. But I don't.

Dropping my hand back on the wheel, lost to the solace of a couple of hours of the ride ahead, I give myself time to process. To try and understand how I allowed myself to fall for this feisty young woman so quickly. How I could permit her to touch me, to kiss years of unresolved heartache away, right after telling me she was a traitor? But I did all of those things, and I'd do them again in a heartbeat.

In any other circumstance, Harlow wouldn't look at me twice. A bitter man, ten years her senior with a sense of hatred for the world. But she entered my gym, caught my attention and now, I can't imagine life without her. I actually woke up the other morning excited about new prospects. Ones I'm going to see through because even though Harlow wouldn't have picked me in the real world, I'm not going to give her that choice.

The sedan remains silent. Not a single sound coming from the radio or any of us. From the back seat, Zane and I watch our tails via the wing mirrors, our fingers toying with the zippers of the duffel bags. They sit heavily on our laps, waiting for the exact moment our plan comes together.

The plan I alone am responsible for. Maddox used to roll his eyes at my stalkerish side hobby. But I knew keeping tabs on everyone we know would come in handy one day. As soon as Trina announced the fight would be at Theo's very own house, my fingers were flying over my keyboard, securing my server. Theo owns two other properties. Both of which I've kindly been surveying for years. Trina isn't the only one with fingers in many pies.

I've always been underestimated, labelled the party boy, when in reality I take my job as the brains of this crew seriously. The façade is just a helpful disguise. It's what caused Trina to misjudge me and not think I would have my drones fly over all three of Theo's properties, looking for heat signatures.

Naturally, the last time I checked where the fight is going to be held, there was an abundance of bodies in each room preparing themselves for tonight's entertainment. That's where Trina and Theo will be. Neither would miss out on the chance to see Maddox fight for his life. Harlow could be there too, but that's down to Maddox to find out. Between Zane and I, we have two more buildings to scout out, both with limited personnel.

The snapping of Aria's fingers brings my attention back to the road. Entering the city, our timing has to be perfect. Zane begins to peel back the zip on his duffel bag, sliding out the weighted mannequin inside. We've used these dummies many times in Skull Fitness for training, but today, the hoodie already placed over the silicone torso mimics Zane's.

Aria pulls to a stop at the traffic lights, while Zane waits for the Audi to pull up along his side and get a good look at the camo print hood he pulls up to cover his face. The light turns green and Aria jolts forward, turning at the last minute to cut into the next lane over. Several cars skid to a halt, each having a knock-on effect with the next and amongst the blaring of horns and angry drivers, Zane makes his switch. The half-bodied dummy shoots up right in his place, while the real Zane folds himself in half to jam his head against my thigh.

"Whilst you're down there," I jerk my thigh against his auburn hair. Zane reaches under the duffel bag on my lap, but before I can get too excited, he punches me in the dick, reminding me I'm not supposed to be talking. Aria swerves this way and that, and at some point I have to wonder if she's putting on an act or if she really just can't drive.

Working her way through the city, the sidewalks become narrower and the streets become busier. We enter downtown, taking a tour of everything the locals have to offer. Bars are beginning to fill with their usual punters, while food trucks are brimming with customers on their way home from work. I sigh to myself, pressing my face against the window. I reckon, had I chosen a different path, I could have found contentment leading a simple life. Own a bar maybe, host salsa evenings to bring in the sexy Latinos and poker nights to rob the rich blind. Spoiler alert, the house always wins.

Absentmindedly, I stroke my fingers through Zane's hair no matter how many times he tries to shove me off. Aria snaps her fingers again, readying us for the moment she turns violently into an alleyway. With barely enough room to pop the door open, I lean over Zane, making sure to grind my crotch in his face. This may possibly be our last interaction so it's best he has something to remember me by. As I shove him out of the moving vehicle, he rolls and hides from view behind a dumpster. Right on cue, I slam the door closed and a navy blue Audi turns into the alley behind us. Buckling my mannequin friend into the seat, I settle back and tap the duffel bag on my knee.

To his credit, Theo has cleverly positioned his three main properties in the complete opposite directions. One is right here in the city, with a gigantic attic if the blueprints are still relevant. Another is the house Maddox is currently on his way to for his fight, which leaves the third to me. All the way across state in some abandoned farmhouse. I know where I would personally take a captive, but when it comes to Theo and Trina, there's no telling what they would do.

Aria shoots her way across town, handling the sedan with much more grace now. I guess her terrible driving was all for show. The other Audi approaches from the left, putting both of them back in our viewpoint. My foot begins to tap, my eyes returning to the clock on the dashboard between checking the mannequin at my side is still in place. The distraction for Aria to keep these goons busy while we divide and conquer. Like the dummy decoy, Zane and I went full military today; dark hoodies, cargo pants and heavy boots. Beneath my black hoodie, a gun is tucked into my waistband. We only have a set amount of time to track down Harlow whilst Trina is distracted by Maddox's fight, if Harlow is even in one of these houses. Trina's always been a step ahead of us before, I don't see why it would be any different now.

We skid across corners and fly across lanes without indication, leaving a trail of accidents happening behind us. It's Aria's job to hinder those following us by any means necessary. Once we're far enough away from the bright lights, I begin to ready my silicone stunt double. Checking there's no one around, we trade places as I cram myself into the footwell and buckle him in. A hand stretches back Aria squeezes my shoulder. We've barely spoken in the last few days, aware that every word could be listened into, but I don't need Aria to tell me what I already know.

Blood or otherwise, this girl is my sister and the mother I never had wrapped into one. Not to mention, aside from Zane, my best friend. We don't need to exchange words to know what's true in our hearts. That our bond could never be broken and if I don't make it out of tonight alive, I'll be forever grateful I had someone like her in my corner.

Taking her hand in mine I turn it over and kiss the back, giving her a silent goodbye as she veers into the tree line and I promptly throw myself onto the rocky ground. I'm on my own now, with only my wits, the map I've memorized and the idea of a happily ever after spurring me onwards.

Have we all elevated Harlow onto a pedestal, out of our own desperation to know true love? Probably, but it's a pretty fantasy I'm willing to risk everything to achieve. Besides, it truly is our fault she's been dragged into this mess and it's my guilt that's caused me to stalk her for the last two years. I hoped she'd move on or return back to the mundane life she had before, but with each mile she grew closer to us, my excitement grew. I didn't tell the others. I couldn't let them know of the dreams I'd been having, or how I was plagued with the image of her beautiful face every time I took a woman thereafter. That was my secret.

Yet now it doesn't have to be. She could be our salvation, our uniting factor to a future we never thought possible. All we have to do is save her from the world's most malicious bitch, manage to escape unscathed and disappear without anyone ever finding a trace of us. Simple.

Heading east, I cut through a forest and navigate a field of wheat on the other side. Ducking low within the overgrown cover of beige, I'm constantly looking around to make sure I'm not being followed as I continue my trek. The distance seemed much shorter on my laptop and as the sun sets lower in the sky, I pick up my pace. A layer of sweat clings to me, the air too balmy for a run through fields. Coming to a small, wooden fence hidden within the wheat, I'm finally at the property's boundary.

The farmhouse peeks at the orange sunset, smoke billowing from its chimney beyond a large shed and abandoned tractor. I use the monstrous machine as cover, slipping behind a large wheel to steady my breathing. If my last look at the heat signatures is still correct, there's only three people inside the rotting walls of this property, and I'm seriously hoping one of them is Harlow.

Pulling out my pistol, I confirm the magazine is full, despite checking twice back home. Shit…not home anymore, just the house that smelt like fish I used to reside in. Holding the pistol close to my thigh, I check the coast is clear before running to duck behind the barn. Bit by bit, I edge closer to the house, noting the dim lighting and occasional flashes coming from within smeared glass windows. Sneaking up the porch steps, I duck beneath a window just as a shadow walks past, holding my position to see if I've triggered any alarms.

"Yo Benny!" a gruff voice shouts. "Grab some beers, the game is about to start!"

"I'm coming I'm coming," the other voice – Benny – replies. Crawling around the porch on my knees, I pick the window closest to the blaring noise of a packed stadium, peering up to see the back of a TV screen. Two men lounge on the sofa, the TV loud enough to cover my movements without the need to sneak anymore. I do anyway – because that's what James Bond would do. Only one more body to find, I think morbidly and then shake my head at myself. Not body – person.

Continuing to creep around the edge of the building, I come to a back door and let myself in. The gun remains plastered to my side as I edge around the kitchen, noting the refrigerator door has been left ajar. It's only polite of my naïve hosts to offer me a beer, and I gracefully accept. Waiting for the next outburst of cheering, I take a bottle and pop the cap before slumping against a dining table in the middle of the room. Tipping up the bottle the crisp fruity liquid skates over my tongue and trickles down the back of my throat. After my evening jog, it's well and truly deserved, but my mission isn't complete yet. Finding the farmhouse was only phase one, investigating it top to bottom is phase two.

Quietly placing the empty bottle on the floor, I crawl gorilla style to a darkened hallway. Every door is closed, the tacky use of floral wallpaper coating every inch of the space. Once I've proved myself her knight in shining armor and escaped with my girl, I'll do Theo the favor of returning to blow this place up someday. God knows there's no decorator in the world who could fix this mess without fully demolishing it and starting again.

Doors number one and two are a bust, used for nothing but storage of old boxes and knick-knacks you wouldn't want to burden the landfill with. I'd figured as much, considering the amount of dust on the door handles but if I'm being truly honest with myself, I'm trying to delay the inevitable. The small voice in the back of my head warns me against the last three doors in fear of what I might find.

I've seen enough dead bodies for it not to affect me anymore, but deep down I know I've started to care for Harlow and there are some images my mind wouldn't let me forget. The sense of guilt would rid me from living out the rest of my life in peace. We forced ourselves to hate her. We dragged her into a lifestyle she never belonged in, and now there's a beautiful girl awaiting our help, and I just hope one of us happens to get there in time.

Steeling myself, I wait for the next round of arguing from the two on the sofa before attempting to open the next door. The handle rattles but the door doesn't budge. I brace my shoulder, preparing to ram it inwards when a glint of metal catches my eye in the dimmed hallway lighting. Hanging from a string beside the doorway, a rusted metal key presents itself. My heart hammers in my chest.

If I was going to kidnap a woman and hide her away, it would definitely be in a locked room - not that I've had too much experience with such. Just tying them up in clubs and giving them the most intense pleasure of their life. Untying the knot, I slip the key from the rope and ease it into the lock. Twisting slowly, a click sounds just before I am able to turn the handle and ease the door open.

"I wondered what took you so long," a voice bleeds out of the darkness, but not one of the woman I've come to know. The gruff male's voice is quickly followed by the mountain man who jumps to his feet from a chair in the center of the room and runs for me. I jump back into the hallway and spin out of his path, directly into the chest of another. The two men are no longer watching their game, but standing in my exit, glaring at me with wicked smiles.

It was a trap, but as I stagger back and press myself against the wall, I can't help the relaxed smile that spreads across my face. I expel a sigh of relief, or at least that's what I hope it is. Either these three men are the only ones here or Harlow's body is already too cold for my drone to have picked up on. It's a niggling feeling I've had this entire time, and one I refuse to acknowledge - especially out loud. Either way I'm not leaving here till I've inspected every inch of this place. Only then can I justify making my way to the rendezvous point, knowing I did everything I could. How I'm getting there is a problem for later, but we're all under strict instruction. Either arrive by sunrise, or we're to go without one another.

Without thinking as much as I should, I raise the gun, shooting a bullet through the window at the end of the hall. The glass shatters like the cry of an alarm as I run for it and throw myself through the empty hole onto the wooden porch. I've scrambled up onto my feet and made a run for it before the guys can follow, bullets flying in all directions. Except the gunfire is aimed towards the field they expected me to run to, whereas I'm already around the back of the house and reentering in the kitchen.

With them distracted, trying to muscle their way out of the window one by one, I race for the staircase across the other side of the farmhouse. Vaulting up the stairs, my heavy footfalls have no doubt given me away so I don't bother trying to be quiet any longer. I check each bedroom by throwing the doors wide, hastily searching for what I already know in my heart is true.

Harlow isn't here, and my cover is well and truly blown.

Permitting myself entry through the door I've entered many times before, I barge through the crowd already accumulated in the entrance lobby. I'm here for one reason and one reason only, and it's not to fight as everybody assumes. Hands pat my back, men I've never met wishing me luck and telling me they've bet on me winning my fight. The one I'm not planning on participating in, but at some point I will no longer be able to avoid. Trina's made sure of that.

Theo's main home is a manor house in an upper class area. The neighbors probably think wild parties happen here every night, and that he's some sort of Hugh Hefner with the wife, a third his age, trotting around on heels tall enough to break her neck. Although I'm not that lucky. In actual fact, the crews who enter his home are all affiliated with the crime boss himself. The master organizer who learned early on delegating his work to others while he sat back and reaped the profits was the kind of life he wanted to lead.

The lower level of the manor wraps around a grand staircase, from lounge areas to games rooms and a theatre which meet at the back of the house in an open plan kitchen. The 'home help' live in some of the fourteen bedrooms upstairs, all of which conveniently don't speak any English and are happy to oblige with any of Theo's requests for the promise that they can remain in the United States.

Three of those employees are in the kitchen now, continually preparing snacks and serving drinks to those who huddle around them. A fourth is in the bar outside, taking bets by the poolside. A freestanding chalkboard at his side shows what order the matches will take place in and between who. I poke my head out of the sliding French doors, just enough to see which opponent I've been paired up with. Road rage Jack. A massive fucker, riddles with scars with a hobby for drink driving. He's cost Theo more in fines than he's brought in, but when it comes to fighting, he never loses.

Returning to the kitchen, I reach for a glass of whiskey until I remember my pledge to myself. I will not consume any food or drink while I'm here, knowing that I'm being watched. Now my eyes have been opened to the lengths Trina will go to, to throw my fight, I cannot let myself be sabotaged.

Keeping within the masses of men, I fall in with the crowd on their way towards the basement door. It's been left open, hordes of muscle trying to shove their way down the staircase for a better view at the fight currently taking place in the professional boxing ring Theo had installed. The same fight is being streamed onto the monitors in each room, but there's nothing like seeing the real thing. Like sensing the atmosphere of rage and smelling the copper of spilt blood.

Although it's not the fight I'm trying to get a closer look at. Hidden within the massive bodies, I scout for security guards, noting two by the front door where I entered and a few more prowling around in the kitchen. Machine guns strapped to their front make sure this amount of randy men are kept in line.

I push my way towards the front before making it known obscenely loudly that I need to take a piss. Diverting away, I storm through a games room, rapping my knuckles on a billiard table and generally making myself as well known as possible. There's a queue outside the guest bathroom on the lower level but when they see me coming, the men flinch back a step. The one at the front quickly bangs on the door to let the occupant know I'm coming.

"Dude, hurry up! Maddox is on his way," he calls through the door and his friend appears almost instantly. Eye wide, he dives aside and proceeds to linger, as if waiting for a thank you or some shit. Those who frequent Theo's underground fights know my face, but usually only as the man powerful enough to keep Zeke and Zane under control. They are the fighters, and Aria is the secret weapon. While I'm the boss who looks on with a glass of whiskey in hand. The fact I, myself, might be fighting today is a huge deal to them.

I push my way into the bathroom without any grunt of thanks, slamming the door closed and locking it tight. Now that everyone, and especially - the security guards, know where I am, I race to the window and slide it open. The crux of my plan rests on the exterior surveillance not being monitored in favor of the fights happening downstairs. My Nike's hit the manicured grass and without a moment to lose, I scramble up the terrace towards the second story window.

The first one I try is locked, so I use an outcrop of brick to swing myself towards a patch of sloped tile. My feet skid out but luckily I'm able to grab a ledge and shove the window above open in the same movement. Dragging myself inside, I lower my sneakers into the guest bedroom without a single sound. Stealthily, I work my way across the upper level, listening intently against each door before peering inside. The more I check, the more disappointment flares within me. Harlow's safety is paramount, but the selfish asshole in me wants to be the one to save her. For once, I want to prove myself worthy. To be forever gazed upon with loving eyes and knowing, that at least to one person in this goddamn world, I was a hero. It's a foolish dream for a crook, but it's the first dream I've had my entire life.

Creeping along the hallway, I avoid meeting the eyes of every ostentatious portrait painting hanging along the wall. The head of each crew dons the walkway to Theo's master bedroom, in a series of tacky golden frames. My own is the one I hate the most. Strokes of oil paint forcing a smile onto my face and cementing me in Theo's personal hall of fame, forever brandishing me as one of his lackeys and nothing more. A few weeks ago, I could have lied to myself believing this is the best kind of life I could hope for. But I've been shown a light now, and I'll do whatever it takes to stoke that flame.

The door before Theo's bedroom is his office. A room I know to be cluttered, like that of a madman who can't organize his thoughts. It's the one place in this entire house which is untouched by staff and unseen by members, unless they are summoned. That never bodes well, and quickly results in an ambush by the guards to tie you up and let all bosses of subsequent crews beat you senseless.

Pressing my ear against the wood, I flatten my palms on the disgusting floral wallpaper either side. A faint shuffle and a whimper catches my ear just as I'm about to pull away and my chest squeezes tight. A key pokes out of the lock, so with deft fingers I twist it for a solid click to sound before I slowly permit myself entry.

It's dark inside, the night sky streaming through the large bay window behind a mess of boxes. In the center of the room, the outline of a female silhouette increases my heavy breathing as I reach around and flick on the light switch.

"Well, well, well. Look what we have here boys," Trina's shrill voice leaks into my ears before my eyes have had time to adjust. Four bulky men shuffle out from behind the boxes, each with a gun in their hand aimed at my head. Men I've essentially known half my life. Those I've trained and learned with, who now look upon me as if I'm a stranger. That's what Trina does – she manipulates and toys with people, turning us against one another. To anger Trina, is to sign your death warrant with Theo, and we've all come too far to risk that now. Aside from me. What was once my singular goal to become Theo's right-hand man, I couldn't give less of a fuck about anymore.

Placing one heel in front of the other, Trina closes the distance between us. The men around the room move in time with her, until I'm staring into the devious eyes of my ex with four guns pressing against my head. The black dress clinging to her carefully sculpted curves dips low, her cleavage on full show. A side slit reaches the top of her thigh, flaunting her creamy skin for all to see. The things I used to love about her now repulse me. She uses her body as a weapon, but it's her ever-plotting mind people should be aware of. Her long brown hair has been curled and pinned into an updo, two tendrils framing either side of the bitchy glare on her face.

"I thought I made it clear, darling," she strokes her index finger down my jaw. I fist my hands, the urge to knock her hand away and strangle her until she's stopped jerking riding me hard. "The only way you'd save your precious Harlow, is to fight."

A sigh lifts her breasts higher, allowing them to fall and relay the depths of her disappointment. I don't move. Hiding behind the mask I've perfected, I refuse to give her what she wants. The knowledge that she's winning this game she's created, despite only one of us knowing the rules. Running her finger along the length of my jaw again, Trina twists her wrist and peers at her diamond studded watch.

"Alas, your fight has already begun, and your lack of appearance is an immediate forfeit."

"Have these men lower their guns and I'll give you the fight you're so eager for," I grumble. Trina's red lips widen, her smile stretching her cheeks tight. Pulling her cell phone from a concealed pocket, I make a move to grab it. All four guns surrounding my skull click, the release of their safety vibrating through my ears. Grinding my teeth together, I watch the twinkle of her lifeless eyes intensify as she holds the cell phone to her ear.

"Go ahead," a man says through the receiver. Trina pauses a moment, as if waiting for something.

"Maddox lost his fight. Kill the girl." Ending the call as swiftly as it began, Trina juts out her chin. "Walk. We have business to attend to," she prods a talon into my chest. I huff, hiding the dread settling within my soul. I've just signed Harlow's death warrant. Had I fought – who knows what the outcome would have been, but there's no doubt in my mind Trina wouldn't have let Harlow walk out of this situation alive.

Turning on my heel, I stride from the room and enter the hallway. A single gun pushes against the back of my head. One man who thinks he's going to stand between me and what I should have done years ago. Jolting aside, the crack of a shot bursts beside my ear. Grabbing the gun, I twist hard enough to break the wrist of the man holding it, and shoot him directly in the face. Ducking low, his body falls over my shoulder, becoming riddled with bullets from those inside the office. Around my human shield, I pick them off one by one, pulling the trigger until the barrel is empty.

Stillness comes from within, but I dare not hope. Peeking around the dead body, Trina steps into view. Long legs, narrowed eyes and her cell pressed back against her ear. Fuck.

A few guys, I can handle alone, but if the entire army of trained security guards make it up here, I'm royally screwed. I shove the body in Trina's direction and dive into Theo's bedroom, making it halfway across the room before a repetitive beeping meets my ears.

Machines surround Theo's bed, the old man himself laid beneath a thick duvet with his eyes closed. Tubes disappear beneath the covers, a suction pad placed over his heart. Trina follows in behind, quickly closing the door behind her. A member of the home help strolls out of the bathroom then, holding a metal tray of medication until Trina barks at her to leave. Flinching, the pills fly over the Persian rug and the woman rushes to obey, leaving me and Trina alone with Theo's sleeping form.

"What the hell is going on in here?" I demand, keeping to the opposite side of the bed. When Trina starts to walk towards me, I rush to grab a handful of wires, clenching them in my fist. "I'm already not getting out of here alive. There's nothing stopping me from taking your *beloved* with me," I growl. Adrenaline thrums through my veins, twinged with the bitter loss of a love I didn't get to know. Harlow was going to be my salvation, if only my past would allow it. Trina laughs, continuing to stride closer.

"What does it look like I've been waiting for this entire time?" My hand tightens around the tubes, blocking whatever fluid was running through. Theo's heart machine picks up a beat, his body sporadically jerking. Whether Trina is bluffing or not, I'm about to lose my only leverage. She makes it to me, her fingers curling around mine to open my grip. "Can't have any foul play involved. Don't worry, it won't be long now."

Releasing the tubes, my arm drops to my side. I take a step back. She follows. It's comical really. A fully grown man who remains calm facing the barrel of a gun, yet the prospect of Trina being too close makes my stomach roll. Her perfume clogs my senses, clouds my judgement. Soon enough, I'm boxed in beside a stained glass window, specifically made to stream colored light into Theo's room.

"I heard you," Trina whispers, as if divulging a precious secret. "In your office. You asked her to touch you. You moaned and muttered her name between kisses. We never had passion like that."

"Correction – you never had passion like that," I lean back when her lips try to find my ear. "I'd have given you the world. You wanted to dominate it."

"You can't blame me for being ambitious," Trina winks, standing tall so that only her chest brushes mine. She smiles and sighs contently. I know better than to fall for her act. "At one point, you told me that's what you loved about me." She's goading me. Craving the man who no longer exists. The one who gave her a power trip by submitting to her whip, but once she had that first taste of dominating confident men, she couldn't get enough.

"Ambition," I nod, sliding my gaze back to the man dying in the bed and understanding dawns. This is what it's all been about. Trina wasn't satisfied with going for my post alone; she wants to rule everything Theo has created. And above all, she's wanted to make me pay for not aiding her in doing it. It makes sense now – the desperation to see me lose a fight, the drive to take away everyone I've ever loved. Trina wanted to belittle me, humiliate me. To break me.

Her pink tongue pokes out to wet her lips, hanging on our exchange like a leech. To that end, I refuse to engage anymore. Not when it's all playing directly into her fantasy. Trina's hands skate up my arms, raising goosebumps from my flesh for all the wrong reasons. But I let her. Even worse, I play along. Tilting my head to the side, my eyes dip to Trina's lips. I step into her personal space, hovering my hands over the small of her back.

"I couldn't resist you once," I mutter, blocking out the

painful memories of her hatred. The way she tore my soul from my body, crushed it beneath her heel and had the audacity to laugh about it. Easing my hands onto her bare skin, I pull her into me, pressing her against my body. Heat sears everywhere, the taste of betrayal crawling up the back of my throat. Harlow's body isn't even cold, and I'm here cradling the woman responsible. But she won't have died in vain. If the only reason I have left to live is avenging Harlow, then that's all I have left to live for. Trina will pay in kind for the crimes she's committed against mine for the last time. And with that final thought, I tighten my hold and throw us both through the nearest window.

Chapter Thirty-Three

Hands in the pockets of my hoodie, I walk with casual slowness. The hood is pulled over my hair, shielding the top half of my face while I observe everything. Reaching the end of the street, I wait against a tree trunk for ten minutes before turning and walking the length of the sidewalk again. Each time, I keep the house in my eyeline. A three story building sandwiched between ones that look exactly the same. According to Zeke's digging, almost all houses on this block have been converted into separate apartments. But not Theo's. His remains three full levels of criminal activity.

Whitewashed walls have turned a shade of dull grey. Potted plants along the windowsills have died, the windows themselves coated in grime. A Toyota sits outside, the license plate too dirty to read and the wheels almost unroadworthy. On first look, anyone would assume the property is abandoned or rarely used, but I've been watching. Despite the advantage of Zeke's heat cams pre-warning me there's five people inside, the figures lurking inside have brought my body count up to four. All men, all large in build.

The front door opens and I drop to the ground, unlacing my boot so I can spend precious moments retying it. One of the men, blonde with dark sunglasses, pulls the door closed, locks it and jogs down the stone steps. He turns right in a pair of sweatpants and sneakers that are at odds with the black trench coat reaching his calves. I've done recon on the entire block, noting the row of houses adjoining at the back which make it impossible to sneak into the house undetected by neighbors. My best shot is to walk straight through the front door.

For now however, I follow Trench Coat to the local burger van. His order is ready to go, three large bags of food. I grind my teeth. If Harlow is in the town house, I could bet my balls none of this food is for her. Trench Coat makes small talk with the vendor while I retrace my steps. There's an alleyway at the end of the street, which I step into.

Leaning against the wall, I peer up at the dark blue sky above. Night has truly fallen, the window of Trina and Theo's distraction closing. On a mission where timing is everything, I don't hesitate to strike as Trench Coat steps into view. Grabbing him from behind, I drag him back into the alley by his shoulders and throw him into the brick wall. He stumbles back in a daze, recovering quicker than I'd anticipated.

Spinning on me, we fall into an evenly matched fight of fists. I uppercut him, raising my leg for a powerful kick to his side. Only, before it's able to land, he's lunged at me and a spike of pain spears my side. I don't look, forcing myself to react on pure instinct. Whereas Trench Coat thought I'd back down, my fist cracks his jaw hard enough to turn him around. My palm flattens against the back of his head to slam it into the wall over and over, and once more for good measure. He crumples to the ground, where I promptly remove his trench coat and pull it onto myself.

My hand touches my side, wrapping around the handle of a small blade slicing through my hoodie and into the flesh above my hip. Stepping into the glow of a streetlamp, whilst still out of view of the main street, I get a clearer view. The handle is plastic, slightly wobbly against the serrated blade which is about two fingers in thickness. A classic kitchen knife. This dick was actually carrying a kitchen knife in his coat pocket. With a grimace, I quickly weigh up my options. I don't have time to waste, yet removing the blade without any medical supplies isn't an option either. I will bleed out before I make it to Theo's front door.

There's only one thing for it – snapping off the handle and leaving the rest in there. A car horn covers my grunt of pain, my back hitting the brick as I take a few precious moments to collect myself. My hoodie covers the blade, and for the most part I can stand upright and pretend it's not in there – for now.

After covering the asshole with some trash bags, I collect up the food order and stride from the alley, directly towards the house. I find the keys in the hidden pocket by my chest, and quickly assess the shape and size of the lock to get the key right first time. The hallway beyond is a mix-match of patterns, from a tiled checked flooring to the revolting floral wallpaper leading up the staircase at the end of the hall.

"Leave it in the kitchen, Pete. We'll be done in a second," a voice calls out. A door to my left presents an open living/dining area with a kitchenette against the four walls. The trash can is piled high with takeout bags and pizza boxes, flies hovering around. I cringe at the smell, wondering when the last time the majority of these men have left this house. My mind races ahead of me, jumping to the conclusion they're guarding something, or someone.

Dumping what's left of the takeout order on the kitchen side, I unlock the backdoor and make my way around the windows to do the same. In such a cramped building, escaping is going to be tricky. Finding no one on the lower level, I re-enter the hallway and peer up the stairs. A shadow passes over the top of the landing before a male steps into view. Spotting a door in the side of the staircase, I whip it open as heavy footfalls stomp down the steps. A cloakroom presents itself, and since hiding inside would seem shadier, I pull up the trench coat's collar and slowly start to take it off. Drawing one arm out of the sleeve, I wrap my hand around the gun in my hoodie pocket.

"Better get up there, Pete," a heavy hand slaps me on the back. "You're missing all the action." He moves away, being fooled by my size and bulk as resembling his friend's. Once he's entered the lounge area, I throw the coat on the cloakroom floor, shut the door and race up the stairs on my tiptoes. Both this hallway, and the one above, are coated in the same, floral wallpaper. Golden framed portraits line the walls between open doors, the eyes seeming to follow me as I quickly check each one. Deducing there's no one here, I travel up the next flight of stairs.

According to Zeke's blueprints, this is the top level aside from a vast attic. I eye the ceiling hatch as I pass under it, mentally logging every detail. A pair of dents in the carpet suggest there's a ladder held within the hatch, and the hooked bar mounted on the wall must be how to pry it open. Just then, a sound akin to vibrating catches my ear, quickly followed by a female scream. A man's snigger can be heard underneath, drawing me towards the third door on the left. It's slightly ajar, but I don't risk trying to get a better look. Dipping in the bedroom next door, I hide behind a beast of a wardrobe and press my ear to the wall.

"She's out cold again," a gruff voice states once the screams have sizzled into silence. My heart picks up in my chest. She's here. I've actually found her. "Come on, let's go eat." Another crackle of vibrations sounds before metal hits metal just on the other side of the wall.

"To be fair, I wouldn't bother staying awake for that kind of torture either. You've really taken electric play to an entirely different level with that one." A thud precedes their joint chuckling before one announces it's time to eat. Leaving the room, I sneak a look at the pair, noting who I need to make suffer before leaving. Two men, one taller but both with a military style-buzz cut. They're wearing black from the neck down, guns holstered at their sides.

"Trina said to entertain myself until her call comes through," I see the back of the taller one shrug. "Just following orders." The short one laughs bitterly.

"And the amount of cash you've been offered for each lasting scar has nothing to do with it?" They round the staircase, laughing on the way down like they haven't just been brutalizing the love of my – what? Pushing my back against the wall, I hit myself in the temple with the butt of my own gun. I won't do any of us any good getting wrapped up in some sense of nobility. This isn't a fairytale. Like the rest of my life, it's a fucking nightmare.

Once the coast is clear, I move. The sting above my hip tugs uncomfortably as I come to the door. It's now closed and as I try the handle, it doesn't budge. Fuck. Looking around for a key, I come up empty and my breathing begins to speed up. My body is going into overdrive, trying to fight the foreign object in my side. Returning to look over the railing, I just have to hope those tasked with torturing Harlow are far enough away to miss the sound of me ramming my shoulder into the door. It takes two tries before the wood splinters and bursts inwards to a fully lit room, and that's when my gut drops.

Hanging before me, Harlow's wrists are bound tightly

above her head. Blood seeps from the restraints, her hands a worrying shade of blue. With her ankles also bound to a metal hoop amongst the carpet, she is stretched taunt with no escape from whatever those men have inflicted on her. On the table, pushed against the wall I was recently behind, a girthy taser has been tossed onto a metal tray. Beside it, empty syringes lay around a rogue scalpel with crimson coating its tip.

Oh, Harlow. What have they done to you?

Pushing the door closed for a few moments of extra privacy, I take the scalpel and quickly cut the binds at her feet first. Her left ankle is swollen, bulging from her jeans cuff and twisted at an unnatural angle. I can only imagine one of those bastards kicked her. I'm going to kill them all. With excruciating slowness, I will make them beg for mercy before calling Harlow in to provide the final blow. It's the least she's owed.

Once her feet are free, I rise too slowly, inspecting her body without touching it. Blood seeps from open slits in the denim, her vest no much more than a piece of slashed material hanging from bruised shoulders. I see where the taser has been used the most – on her neck. Red hair has fallen in front of her face, which I brush back just to see her. I can't help myself, tipping her head back to press of a brief kiss on her lips. Not just for me, but for all of us hunting for her.

Wrapping my arm around her waist, I work to cut the rope at her wrists free. Harlow slumps onto me, held up by my arm. Her head lolls back, eyes still closed. Lowering my head onto her chest, I pick up on the faint beat of her heart. I need to get her out of her. Now. But that doesn't force my feet to move. Rather, my other arm rounds her body and I simply hug her. A sob locks in my throat, the truth of what she's had to endure slamming into me like a blow to the gut. She isn't even a Bloodied Skull. She hasn't been accustomed to handling pain. If anything it should have been one of us, and I'm finally ready to admit to myself what I've been ignoring. I'd have taken her place in a heartbeat.

Her pretty amber eyes deserve to be filled with light, her full lips to be curved into a permanent smile. Harlow deserves to be worshipped, and once we're clear of here, I won't hold back from doing just that. When the fragility of life presents itself, there's no use denying what my head is currently screaming. I've fallen for her hard.

Emotions war in my chest, but nothing is clearer than the woman cuddled against my body. She's managed what no other could – to find a shortcut through my barriers and bury herself inside my psyche. I'm no longer saving her because Maddox ordered it. This rescue is all me, out of love.

"That was the call we've been waiting for, boys!" a man shouts from the ground level. I freeze, my head whipping to the doorway. Footsteps storm through the lower floors, dread warping around the heart I was just about to pledge to Harlow. "It's time to die little one!"

Rousing between headaches, certain I no longer want to wake up at all, my brows twitch. Someone is…hugging me? My arms are heavy as lead, but they're hanging freely at the sides of my cuddler. I can't feel my limbs for the most part, aside from one of my ankles. That one throbs like a bitch and sends a shot of acid-like pain up my calf should I put any weight on it. Forcing my eyelids open, a tuft of auburn hair pokes out of a hood, shimmering blue eyes captivating me. Like the mirage of a tropical oasis, I dare not believe it's true. More than that, the hardness to his jaw tells me it's not Zeke, and that's when I'm fully sure my senses are deceiving me.

"Zane?" I ask, although it comes out slurred. The hold tightens around my waist and I choke out a pained cough. I don't let him retract though, not when the warmth of his arms is the closest thing to comfort I've felt in days. Weeks? I don't know how long I've been here, only that I'd given up hope. Until now. Burying my face into his neck, he lifts me as gently as he can, despite his own groan of pain. He's injured. Somewhere, somehow. I'd protest to walk if I thought I could make it more than one step without collapsing.

Carrying me from the room, my vision blacks in and out. Portraits glare at me with faces I never want to see again. My legs sway uselessly, the never-ending pain seizing me in a clutch I can't escape. Whatever happened to me while I was unconscious, I've decided I don't want to know. I doubt I'd be able to comprehend the knowledge with what I've already concluded. I might never walk again.

A shout comes from within the house, an alert being made that I'm missing. Further men answer and I shudder, pushing my face further into Zane's neck. My eyes are scrunched closed, my lips beginning to tremble. Now that he's here, presenting me with the slither of hope I previously cast aside, I can't let him go. Tears fall from my closed eyes, pooling in his collarbone where my lips are currently pressed.

We turn sharply, Zane's hand snaking up to place a delicate finger on my lips. "I need to put you down Harlow," he whispers, already lowering me to the floor. Shaking my head, I dislodge his finger and fist his hoodie. Blue eyes pierce mine, a promise held in his stare. "I'll be right back."

"No, wait," I whisper, reaching out. Zane slips through my weak grip, standing tall to peer around the doorway. I grab his cargos, dragging myself up his calf. I really don't want to be this kind of woman, who begs and whines, but turns out when in danger, that's exactly who I am. "Please don't leave me."

"I'm coming back," Zane quickly crouches to run a hand over my hair. "I promise." Every fiber of my body clenches with dread, the tears yet to stop spilling from my eyes. Through sheer willpower, I release Zane and shuffle back from view. I force myself to remember the man who came for me in the DPS depot. He defended me then, no questions asked. I may not know where we stand, or even know him that well, but I trust him. I have to, if I want to survive this hell house. Zane watches me for a beat too long and I curl into myself, knowing I'm a complete mess and not just physically.

"Okay," I nod. Pulling out a gun, Zane checks the hallway again before darting out with less grace than I'm used to. As soon as he gets back, I'm going to find out where and how he's injured – because he is coming back. I have to believe that. Huddled in the corner, I wrap my arms around my filthy, blood smeared arms, wholly avoiding looking at or touching my legs. I wait there with bated breath, listening out for when the subsequent gunfire rings out.

Clamping a hand over my mouth, my heart jackhammers in my chest. It's not just my safety I'm worried for now, but Zane's. He came to rescue me but at the risk of something happening to him, I wish he hadn't. Not when he has those who love him waiting for his safe return. I have no one to mourn for me, as my mind has reminded me of every second since I woke up restrained.

The gun fire continues, growing loud. It takes a bullet flying through the wall a few feet above my head to spur me into action. I can't just sit here and wait for death to find me. Sliding out from behind the door, I let my legs straighten just enough to stretch out and roll onto my stomach. A musty, aged smell meets my nostrils as I drag myself across the carpet.

Through the shadows, an opposing four-postered bed looms tall.

Outstretching my hand, my fingers scrape against the wood until I find the energy to jerk myself the rest of the way. Wrapping my fingers around the bed leg and pulling the rest of the way, a loud bang slams against the wall I was recently leaning against. I push myself to hurry, slipping beneath the bed with god knows what kinds of spiders and clutter. The door bangs open just after I've become concealed within the shadows, my heart leaping as I peer back. But it's not Zane's boots I see.

Timberlands coated in mud pound forward, kicking over a few boxes. The creak of the wardrobe door sounds just before four rounds of gunfire are blasted inside. I scream into my hand, the sound mostly covered by the shots, but not enough. The man stills, a swift scrape of his boots preceding his stomps towards the bed.

My nails embedded into my cheeks, fear gripping me so tightly, I begin to shake. I want to look away but my eyes won't respond, tracking the boots movements until they halt in front of my face. I dare not move, but my whimpers can no longer be contained. One knee lowers onto the floor as the glint of the gun appears. This is it. My final moments. The last chance to reflect on all the opportunities I've wasted. If I'd been upfront with the Skulls from the beginning…if I'd been honest about the feelings which are glaringly obvious now. I wanted to be one of them. I wanted to simply be theirs, however they'd take me. A fat finger clenches against the trigger and with a shameless sob, I whisper my goodbye to the Bloodied Skulls.

Bang.

My foot taps impatiently. My ass numb from leaning against the sedan. Maddox sure picked a lovely spot as our rendezvous point, but a girl can only enjoy the view for so long. Parked on the grass verge, over-looking a wide canyon, my star gazing will soon become a romantic sunrise treat for one. If only I could sit back and kick my feet up on the dash, without my side cramping uncomfortably or my impatience getting the better of me.

Still recovering from my injures, I was given the easy job. The 'safest,' although the scraped sides of the sedan would say otherwise. The navy Audi's followed me all the way onto the freeway to the next state over before they started playing dirty. I can only imagine orders came from Trina to run me off the road, and they sure tried their best. At least I have a claim to fame now for all the years I beat Zeke and Zane's asses on GTA. Something I can't wait to bust their balls about, when they eventually get here.

Nope, I can't stand here watching the pinky red of an impending sunrise anymore. That's my signal to leave, but if I don't see it – technically I'm not disobeying any strict orders. Rounding to the trunk, I pop it open and lean over the contents in the back. Pre-packed by Maddox himself. There's two suitcases, each stuffed with brand new clothes in all of our sizes with the tags still attached.

Pushing them aside, I turn to lower myself into the trunk. Yanking my backpack onto my lap, I tear it open and my growling stomach begins to sing. Maddox packed logically – I packed food smart. I'd held off, wanting to keep enough snacks for when the boys return and announce they're starving, but what's a girl to do when stress eating is her only form of entertainment. I bite into a chocolate bar, leaning back on the bags and shaking my feet outside the trunk.

If they don't start showing up soon, I'm going to get back behind the wheel and hunt those shitheads down. There was never a chance of me leaving here alone, to 'start fresh' as Maddox instructed. What am I supposed to do by myself? All I know is looking after idiots who share a brain cell and how to move my body. I've heard of a club called the Thirsty Kirsty a few states over who will literally take on anyone and their moms. Maddox was planning to take us all there for the stag-do he never got to have. Funny how times change.

I'm busy wondering what my version of a hen-do would look like when an engine catches my ear. Jolting upright, I flail like an upside down turtle, grappling with the edge of the trunk to yank myself out. The noise grows louder, a car coming in fast. Elation expands in my chest, until I spot the navy blue Audi heading directly for me. Oh fuck, they're going to ram me straight over the ledge.

Trying to force my body out of the pit I've trapped myself in, my tender ribs ignite with a fresh wave of agony. My arm gives out, smashing my cheek back into the suitcases. It's no use. Even if my ribs would allow me to scramble out the trunk fast enough, I wouldn't be able to dive out of the way of the incoming vehicle. So I do what seems most logical. Reach up with my good arm and heave the trunk closed on top of me. Either way, I'm mostly likely going to die in the drop, but at least this way, my body isn't being flung around the canyon like a weighted boomerang. The Audi screeches, the tyres skidding through the grass. I wince, preparing myself for the impact.

"Aria?" a voice calls out. My eyes snap open. "What the fuck are you doing?" The trunk is released and Maddox frowns down at me.

"Maddox!" I gasp, reaching up to him. "I was just playing a round of hide-and-seek and guess what, you won!" He rolls his eyes, bending low to scoop me out of the trunk once and for all. Clinging onto his neck, I'm risen high enough to see the bloody grazes along his cheek, disappearing into his stubble. The hazel eye above is swollen, struggling to open. Planting me on the hood of the Audi, I look inside for Harlow. There's no sign of her, so I don't waste time on pointing out the obvious.

"So, um, what happened to your face? There's," I brush my finger over the gash in Maddox's cheek, "dirt in your cut. I'm guessing that's not from a fist." Maddox bats away my hand, straightening himself. The sports attire he wore, which doesn't suit him in the slightest, is torn. Along the length of his arm, shards of glass are poking out between his tattoos. Maddox grabs the medical box from the sedan, handing me a pair of tweezers. Setting his ass beside me, I use the rising sunlight I've been trying to ignore to my advantage. "Are you going to tell me or do I need to start guessing?"

"I threw Trina through a window on the second floor and felt like tagging along for the ride," Maddox grunts as I tug a shard free of his bicep.

"You've survived jumping from two stories up?"

"Theo's room is directly above the pool," Maddox peers down at me with a hint of a smirk. "The old man's dead by the way. I heard one of his nurses screaming about it. Gave me enough of a distraction to steal the car."

"Dare I ask about Trina?" I hold the tweezers still, holding his stare.

"Also dead," Maddox nods but the smirk has faded away. "Hit her head on the base of the pool." Looking away, he faces the sunrise, a deep breath lifting his chest through the tattered t-shirt. "Then I held her down to make sure."

"I am sorry," I say quietly, returning to his wounds. Emotion isn't Maddox's forte, but I like to think I'm getting a good read on him now. All this unnecessary pain and heartache is enough to weigh anyone down. "I wish none of the drama needed to happen."

"Maybe it'll prove to have been worth something, after all," Maddox replies hollowly. We fall into a comfortable silence as I rid his body of glass before attending to his face. Cleaning the blood away with antiseptic wipes, Maddox changes his clothes and turns to me with a resigned look on his face. His eyes dart to the sun, putting us at about five in the morning, before returning to me.

"Don't even say it," I raise a finger. Maddox opens his mouth and then snaps it shut, his eyeline shifting beyond my head. Headlights veer along the grass track, not half as fast as Maddox barreled down there. I slide off the hood, stepping into his side to see who it is. A beat-up old Toyota comes to a stop, a shock of auburn hair behind the wheel. The smile that wraps around my face is short lived. Zane, throws his door open from his reclined position, taking too long to drag himself out. Leaning on the car, Zane throws his thumb towards the back.

"She needs medical attention," he croaks. Maddox sprints to the back seat whilst I shove everything back into the medical bag. Joining his side, I get my first look of Harlow. Curled up in the back seat, I'd otherwise presume she was peacefully resting. Yet as Maddox reaches inside to scoop her out, Zane hisses at him to watch her legs. Maddox freezes, retreating to give me a grave look. Nah, I'm not so easily persuaded to stand down. Nudging past him, I crawl into the footwells until my face is inches from Harlow's peaceful one.

"Hey Killer, it's me," I cup her cheek. Stunning amber eyes flutter open, a lazy, lopsided smile playing about her lips as she breathes my name. "That's it, I'm here. Everything's going to be okay now." Smoothing her flame red hair back from her face, I check Harlow over as discretely as I can. There's no swelling or abrasions on her head. Her wrists are sliced in even rings that were most likely caused by rope or zip ties. Working my hands down her body, I peel up her vest to peek at the welts slashed across her delicate torso.

There's only one person I know who used a whip as their weapon of choice, fancying herself as some kind of marvel villain. If said person wasn't already dead, I'd be in the sedan, gunning my way towards the manor to finish the job myself. As it stands, I'm able to shove aside the anger threatening to choke me from the inside, put on a smile and promise Harlow she's never going to come to harm again. That we'll take care of her from now on. Replacing her vest, I watch Harlow's eyes close, the smile still on her face as I shuffle back to inspect her legs.

Through soiled, blood-soaked jeans, I can't see the extent of the lacerations, only that there are many. Whips, like that on her torso. My heart aches, as if being physically weighed down in my chest for the horrors she's had to endure. I chose her because she was strong, resilient and had a death wish. But this? None of this was supposed to happen.

I whisper an apology, pushing against Harlow's cuts to feel deeper within. I need to know if anything is broken. Her left ankle has ballooned to twice the size, coated in a thick purple bruise but other than that, she's lucky – all things considered. The tightness of her jeans has acted like an instant compress, holding her together until we get to a hospital. Not wanting to run the risk of her bleeding out in the back of this stolen car, I leave them in place, bandaging over the top. It'll have to do for now.

"Do you know," I begin to ask Zane as I rise from the car, until I see him slouched into Maddox's side. Bruising shadows his face, his arms hanging loosely at his sides. It's a wonder he could even drive. "Zane?" Without an invitation, I perform the same check on Zane as I had Harlow – just more rushed and invasive.

"There was a gunman," Zane chokes out as I feel the length of his legs, listening for a hitch in his voice. "He'd found her, was this close," he struggles to hold up his forefinger and thumb, "to killing her. If I'd been a second later…" I move upwards to lift his hoodie, and then I see it. A blade protrudes from his side, a slither of blood leaking from the serrated blade. I share a grave look with Maddox, one that silently tells him to keep Zane talking.

"But you weren't," Maddox lifts Zane's head. "She's alive because of you. But now we need to move. We've been here too long and you both need medical attention." Zane shakes his head, trying to stand of his own accord.

"I'm not leaving without Zeke."

"We don't have time," I steady him.

"N-no, it's-" Harlow tries her best to argue from within the car. The paleness of her face and cold sweat beading across her brow speed up the rampant beat of my heart. Scooping beneath Zane's arm, I force him to lean on me and start to head for the sedan. The only car here that isn't stolen, even if the plan was to ditch it first chance we got. My side screams in protest but I press on, only the thought of saving those I love at the forefront of my mind.

"Maddox is right, we have to go. We need a hospital. Zeke will find us," I promise. There's no doubt in my mind if anyone could track us down, it would be Zeke. Now there's just praying he's still alive and able to do so. Easing Zane into the passenger seat, Maddox is right behind, Harlow limp in his arms. I open the rear door and slide in first, holding out my arms to support Harlow's head. Maddox lowers her gently across the seats, her head on my lap. I stroke her hair, soothing her as best I can when the engine roars to life.

Maddox is behind the wheel, spinning us in a wide circle to head back down the grassy bank. His movements are stuck between the need to go fast and the desire not to throw Zane and Harlow around anymore than necessary. In the crooked angle of the rearview mirror, Zane's eyes catch mine. Pools of blue, shimmering with unshed tears. Like an arrow to the chest, my breathing is hindered.

Never have I seen Zane show such raw emotion. Taking him away from Zeke is like separating conjoined twins. The two boys who molded themselves around each other, spend every possible moment together. I've even heard them jacking off together to porn, which is worrying, yet entirely them. With a reassuring nod, I force my gaze out of the window before tears of my own begin to fall.

He'll find us. I'm sure of it.

Speeding down along the grass trail, the sun is now fully risen, casting the peaceful morning in an orange hue. In this car, however, tensions are high and the fear is palpable. Still, I keep my hands relaxed, working my fingers through the knots in Harlow's hair. Her eyes are closed, soft delirious moans seeping from her curved lips. She's an angel, and she deserves to look like one. Lost to her beauty, the car skids to a sudden stop and I'm thrown into the seat in front. Gripping Harlow, protecting her the best I can, I glare towards Maddox. His arm is across Zane's chest, pinning him in place as a tractor rolls across the grass, blocking our exit.

"Where are you fuckers going?!" Zeke shouts, throwing both arms in the air. The wheels are bigger than the sedan, continuing to roll past until the other side of the trail becomes visible again. Turning, Zeke briefly eclipses the sun, before turning off the engine and hopping down onto the ground. "You were going to leave me behind?!" he opens the rear door by Harlow's feet.

"Careful!" I raise my hand, point towards her bandages. They've begun to turn crimson, blood leaking through. All traces of relieved humor Zeke had fades. I'm sure he'd have loved to chase us down the highway on a tractor, had we all escaped last night unscathed. As it stands, even he has small cuts and dirt smearing his cheeks.

"Get in," Maddox barks gruffly. "We'll explain on the way." Slowly lifting Harlow's legs by her calves, Zeke slides in beneath them. He holds her gently, his eyes not once leaving her face. Maddox doesn't waste time trying to be cautious now, speeding us onto the adjoining highway and in the direction of the closest hospital.

"Are we there yet?" Harlow mumbles, her head shifting on my lap. I stroke her cheeks lightly.

"Where are we going, Killer?" She chuckles at me, her hand finding my knee to squeeze weakly.

"I've never been to Miami," she sighs to herself. Zeke smirks, leaning over to join in our game. Whatever it takes to keep Harlow awake, talking and her mind off her pain.

"Really, Feisty? We're free now, we can go anywhere in the

world and you don't even want to leave this country?" Zeke reaches over, toying with her tatted hair. Harlow's smile grows, her eyelids cracking open ever so slightly.

"Fine," she murmurs. "The world is our oyster. Where are you taking me?"

"Bora Bora," Zane replies, shocking us all. He's nudged down in his seat, fiddling with a loose thread on the hem of his hoodie.

"Yessss," Zeke agrees, stretching forward to stroke Zane's shoulder. I don't miss how Zane's head automatically lowers, seeking comfort from the brother we almost left behind. "Stay in one of those water villas, surrounded by crystal blue water. Mountains in the distance, champagne on ice. Nothing to do but swim, drink and fuck." He grins so wide, his dimples pop out while Zeke's eyes sparkle. Even Maddox has the hint of a smile in the rearview mirror.

"Dine on local cuisine," I pitch in, "served to our dining table every night. A masseuse or two on hand for daily girly pamper sessions."

"Fuck that," Maddox says at the same time Zeke moans about wanting to be included in the daily girly pamper sessions. "No one is touching Harlow's body except the people in this car. She won't even touch herself if I have anything to do with it. I'll attend to her massages."

"I'll scrub her body in the shower," Zane lifts a finger as if we're now picking our own Harlow privileges.

"I'll wash her hair!" Zeke and I shout at the same time. I reach out to slap him and we all laugh, Harlow included. She's been silently listening in the whole time. A city looms in the distance, my heart thundering with the need to get her attended too. Not long now.

"Sounds perfect," she muses, snuggling further into my lap. This time, I let her drift into her own thoughts. Giving her time to dream about the life we're going to lead. One day, when she's healed and ready. It doesn't matter where we go, as long as it's just the five of us, I can already tell it's going to be everything any of us have ever wanted. The chance to be a family, to build a future and to enjoy the one we love. I just never, in a million years thought, that would be the same person.

"Hold on just a little while longer, Killer. Our happily ever after is about to begin."

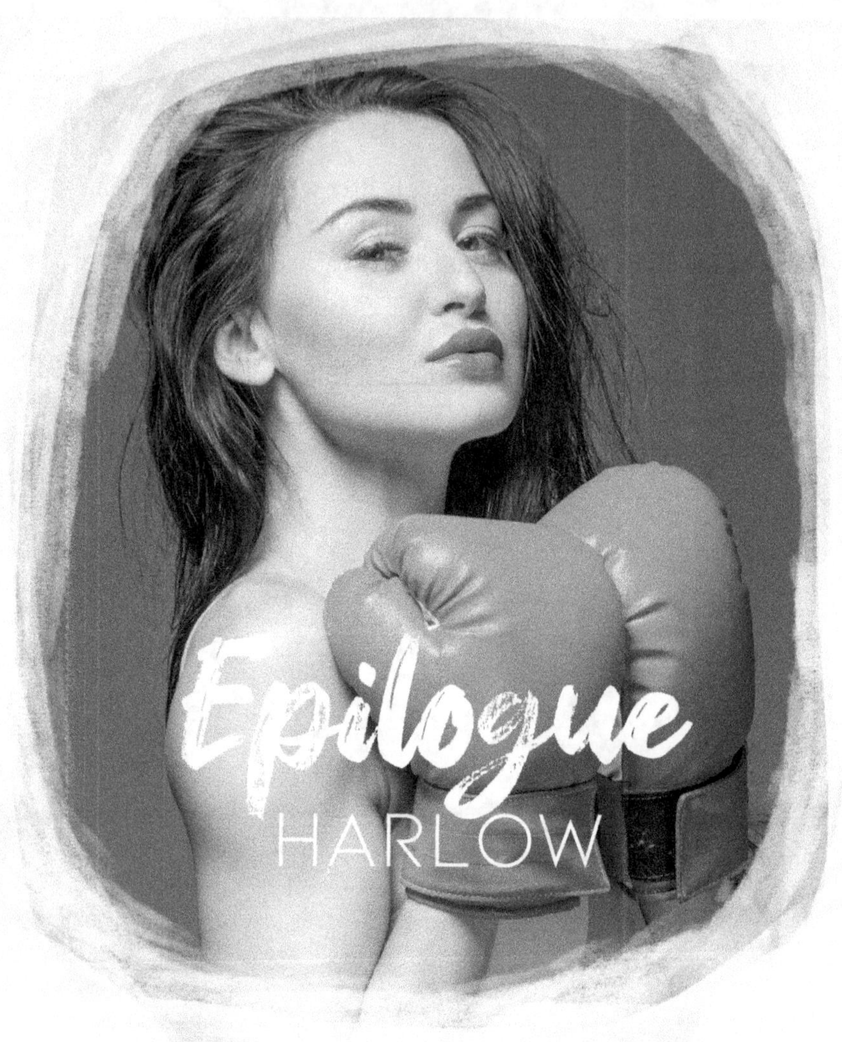

One Year Later

“Mmmmm, just like that. Oh god yes, that's the spot,” I groan, tilting my ass upwards. Maddox's fingers curve along the ridge of my spine, splaying over my shoulder blades to knead into my collarbone deeply. His touch is magical, just enough pressure to work out every kink whilst providing me with the artistry he's been taught by a personal masseuse to the others.

I don't mind Maddox remaining possessive over who

touches me, not one little bit. When he works my body into a languid state of bliss while the others are preparing dinner, there's nothing more I could want. I've truly become a spoilt princess, but I still forbid both him and Zane from calling me that.

"Jesus," Zeke interrupts my moaning. "I thought I'd better come and check you hadn't got started without us." His playful blue eyes await me as I turn and lay my cheek on the massage bed.

"Never," I fake a gasp and he winks at me, disappearing beyond the door he entered through. The thing is, all five of us have yet to have the huge sex fest we continuously joke about. But I gather tonight is veering that way, starting with Maddox limbering me up. I would have missed the memo completely if I hadn't seen the code on the calendar. *RGH.*

It's been one year to the day that we visited the Reverse Glory Hole. The first and last time the five of us have been fully united and with the smells emanating from the kitchen, I can only guess today's being treated as some sort of anniversary.

Working his way lower, Maddox reaches the towel covering my ass and stops. I arch my back, daring him to go lower but he won't. My recovery has been slow, both physically and mentally, and those within this villa have been nothing but patient. Obviously I'm grateful, and incredibly blessed to be their chosen one, but there's only so much missionary a girl can take. Even Aria refuses to go higher than the second speed setting on our vibrators.

Surrounded by four insanely hot bodies every second of every day, my libido didn't seem to get the message I was supposed to be in recovery. Instead I've been forced to crave them, practically salivate over them when all I've wanted to do is tear everyone's clothes off. Well, no more. Tonight I'm going to finally get a taste. I'm going to prove to them I'm ready to take us to the next level, to solidify our harem once and for all.

Especially since we live in our own slice of paradise. I thought Zane was joking about Bora Bora, or in the least, that we'd vacation here. However, it seems without Theo or Trina to chase them down, the once-Bloodied Skulls had full access to a series of off-shore accounts they would funnel the money from their heists into. Their first big purchase – this very villa.

It's stunning, mostly in white to emphasize the blue lagoon passing underneath. Every room has at least one transparent panel in the floor, coaxing us to slip out of the sliding doors from our master bedroom and dive straight in. We share one gigantic bed every single night, yet each of us has a personal space in the water villa for some time alone. Mine is a library, fitted with a hanging swing and leafy house plants. A home fit for their queen, apparently, but I refuse to don such a title.

They've tried to make me their leader, promising to obey the rules I put in place. But that's never been my goal. They've spent too long in a life conditioned by hierarchies and punishments, and I refuse to have any part in that. Whatever we are - a harem, lonely souls who found their purpose in each other - we're all an equal part of this. No one has superiority over another and any decisions we make must be agreed upon by the entire group. That's the only way this will work, and the only way it should.

"Smells like dinner is almost ready," Maddox whispers in my ear, drawing me back from the barrage of my thoughts. His hands smooth over my naked flesh, leaving a trail of goosebumps in their path. I groan, rolling over and making no move to cover myself with the towel.

"I hope you're talking about me," I smile lazily. Stretching my arms above my head, Maddox's hazel eyes latch on to my breasts, his primal hunger filling the air like a shock of static. Easing me up from the table, Maddox guides me to a divider across the room and ushers me behind it.

"There's an outfit on the hanger for you. Take your time

and join us once you're ready." I hear his bare feet pad across the tiled floor, the door closing with a soft click. True to his word, a dry cleaning bag is hanging on the back of the divider by a singular hanger. The mischievous part of me which has been locked away for far too long feels like strutting through the villa naked, putting on a show and making a statement at the same time. I'd like to see them try to deny me then, but it's not in my nature to ruin all of their hard work. Unzipping the bag, my eyes light up at the garment inside and that's when I know, regardless of my doubts, I'm in for one hell of a night.

"Holy shit," Aria breathes when I emerge from the relaxation room. I give her a twirl, letting all four of them feast on the outfit they chose. A silk baby doll nightie in a deep, ruby red. Black lacing trails the low V between my breast and hitches high on my thighs. A matching silk robe rests in the crook of my elbows, leaving the skinny straps exposed over my shoulders. In a similar fashion, the robe just covers my butt, the lace trim tickling beneath the curve and at the sensitive areas around my wrists. Everywhere the silk and lace touches me, I'm alive. Best of all, the outfit my does nothing to hide my scars. In fact, I'm certain it was chosen to accentuate them.

The four of them stand, staring and I bite on my lower lip. Zeke is first to break away from the group, offering his hand. I take it, and squeal when he suddenly twirls me into his body.

"Come eat, quick," he mutters, pressing his erection against my hip. I swear the best part of Bora Bora are linen trousers. All of my men have taken to wearing them, although the unbuttoned shirts are pleasant additions. For now. Leading me towards the kitchen island, I lower into one of the cream puff stools. Platters of food all colors of the rainbow have been laid across every inch of the marbled surface, the smells too delectable to deny. Aria and Zeke take a stool either side of me, Maddox and Zane sitting opposite. They make no move to eat, in favor of watching me tip back an oyster and swallow it whole. A small smile plays about my lips, deciding I'm not in such a rush to fulfill the promise in their burning gazes.

Maddox's hair is in a top knot, waves of sandy blonde escaping. He's let it grow long, like the beard that now covers his inked neck. At his side, Zane's auburn hair has only intensified with the intense daily sunlight. Zeke's had to become a self-taught professional at bleaching and dying his own to keep up. Can't let the façade slip, not when the pair are practically joined at the hip now. More so than they were; they never leave the villa alone and whenever I'm in bed with one, the other sits on the armchair in the corner to watch. I don't mind – I rather like it.

"Are you done yet?" Aria asks, her green eyes dipping into my cleavage. As I laugh, my breasts jiggle, my nipples pushing against the silk.

"You know the point of dinner is to eat, right?" I look around the four of them, thoroughly enjoying the barely restrained hunger emanating from each. I, too, am writhe with anticipation for what tonight will bring, but this is presenting far too entertaining to rush.

"We will," Zane nods robotically. A light blush coats my cheeks and I reach for the bread basket. Carbs. I'm going to need my carbs. Another five minutes passes before Zeke exhales, plucking a half-eaten salmon and cream cheese bagel from my hands.

"We've got you something," he says, replacing my food with an elongated gift box. It isn't lost on me how the black wrapping and red box match my outfit, and I wink to Aria for the feminine touch. Pulling at the bow, I lift the lid and find a set of restraints inside. Curled into the infinity symbol, the mix of suede and leather are soft to the touch. On top, a pair of leather-lined handcuffs have been placed delicately. "If it's too soon, or too much, just say," Zeke fumbles over his words. "There's no pressure."

"They're perfect," I reassure him, my heart fluttering. Relief washes through Zeke's blue eyes, his hand smoothing over my thigh.

"Really?" he beams the biggest smile, his excitement flaring.

"A hundred percent! These will look so good on you," I nod, handing the box back to Zeke. His smile falters, his eyes flashing to the others for back-up. I raise my brow expectantly. "Well, what are we waiting for? Let's go get you set up." I slide off the stool, turning to him with my own smile. A year of wet dreams and longing has sent me a little overboard, and now the opportunity is presenting itself – I'm not backing down. Let's see how far I can push them before they snap and revive their dominating natures.

"Malicious bitch," Aria mutters, falling into step with me. She winks, her arm winding into mine. "I love it."

"Deprived, horny slut, more like," I mutter back. Aria tugs gently, leading away from the bedroom I was steering them towards.

"There is something else," she reveals, leading me past Zane's gym and Zeke's gamer room. I glare at the cunning minx and she shrugs unapologetically. "The restraints were to gauge your reaction before gifting you the real present."

"You know there's no need for gifts. I just want you guys. All of you, together." I pull her to a stop and tug at the traditional style kimono she's wearing, turning her by the shoulders. "At the same time."

"Yeah, yeah, I get the picture," Aria rolls her eyes, pushing open the door of my library. Wait, why are we in here? Leading me straight over to the bookcase, I raise a brow at her secretive expression. Seems like a weird time to read a book, and all of our karma sutra hardbacks are in the bedroom. Aria strokes a finger over my beloved collection, which I quickly accumulated after stumbling across #BookTok, and pauses over a spicy romcom. Pulling the book outwards, it only moves so far before a click sounds and the entire bookcase pops free of the wall.

"What the hell?" I start, inspecting the edges of the wood. The slither of a gap can now be seen just behind, a light leaking from it. My hand runs down the wood, dipping into a groove. Tucking my fingers inside, I'm able to pry the bookcase open further, and discover the hidden room beyond.

My jaw drops at the layout behind me. Large and spacious, with plush carpeting underfoot and walls that are painted in a deep, earth tone green. My body instantly relaxes as I breathe in the scent of vanilla from the candles burning in the holders throughout, allowing a soft glow to circulate. The room exudes sensuality and warmth, but my mouth still goes dry at the four-poster bed in the center, draped in soft sheets and so many pillows. Zeke flings his shirt onto the floor and proceeds to cuff himself to the headboard, while Maddox curses and swoops in to pick it up.

Refusing to believe what I am seeing, I wrap my arms around myself, pinch my own arm and walk further inside. As my toes sink into the plush carpet, I run my fingers along the wall closest to me, smiling at the range of toys artfully arranged in a display case. My lips quirk, savoring the small details included just for me. Soft cuffs and positional pillows. Then there's the items for us to share; double vibrators, blindfolds, a range of crops and paddles - ranging from soft to hard, feathered and even some that feel like sandpaper against my fingers. I shiver, my thighs clenching at the different sex swings hanging from the ceiling, along with light and heavy chains. I can already picture my legs spread wide, Aria's face buried in my pussy while one of my guys fills me from behind.

"What? But...how...and when?" my voice trails off, words failing me. Aria presses herself against my back, her chin resting on my shoulder.

"Zeke noticed there was an empty space in the center of the villa from the blueprints. That's why we bought it."

"You reconned our future home?" I gape at him, wondering why I'm even surprised. No matter how much they'd like to, there's many traits of their previous life they will never be able to leave behind. Come to think of it, I had noticed the how the walls in each room are at an angle, but figured there was nothing in the middle. Now I know better, and the hexagonal room is a hidden trove of my darkest fantasies.

"There are multiple secret entrances," Zane says, entering via a hatch behind the TV in the lounge, answering another question I couldn't quite fathom. "Maddox has been working on it since we moved in." My eyes slide to the hazel ones watching my reactions intently, then down to his hands. That's why he kept appearing with cuts and splinters in his fingers. I thought he just needed to vent sometimes and went out to pick a fight with a tree. Zeke rattles the headboard, checking his wrist is firmly in place, and then realises he has to now remove his pants one-handed. Zane rolls his eyes at the awkward display, stepping into Maddox's side to mirror an arms-crossed stance.

"Maybe we should discuss a trigger word?" Zane adds tentatively. I chuckle at Zeke as he sits on the bed, eyes full of expectation.

"For Zeke? I promise I won't go that hard on him," I try to jest. The four of them exchange concerned looks and I drop my bravado. I guess we're not going to slip into this as easily as I'd hoped. "Guys, It's been a whole year. I'm fine." I purposely avoid peering down at my legs. The recovery wasn't pretty, and I can't say the slashed scars are either, but I refuse to regret what I can't change. We just need to keep moving forward and make sure it was all for a reason.

"You've been through a huge trauma, and we don't mean just physically," Aria says from behind. She's still pressed against my back, her hands winding around to stroke my sides through the silk. Ironically, her thumb brushes the burn mark Zane left on my ribs. The one that started all of this. Pressing a kiss to my neck, she sighs deeply. "If you need more time, the room is finished now. We can come back and try again at any point."

"Stop treating me as if I'm going to break," I say a little too loud, jerking away from her body. Pacing over to a mini bar, stocked with water and coconut milk, I put all four of them in my eyeline. "I'm as resilient as the rest of you, remember? I promised to never set rules, but I'm making an exception." Finding a leather footstool, I step onto it as Aria slinks over to hold my hand. As if I can't stand on a freaking footstool unaided. I do wobble, and keep a hold of her hand, but we're going to ignore that. My declaration deserves the added height.

"New rule – *anyone* who holds back from me will be forced to sit out and NOT watch." I raise a brow at Zeke, knowing he'd be the one to pout the most. The tension around the candle-lit room ebbs away, satisfying everyone's protective nature. Aiding me down, Aria's green eyes sparkle.

"You've got it, Killer," she winks. My heart skips a beat as Maddox suddenly moves, his long legs eating up the space between us. I look up as his large hand grabs my face, firmly yet with a softness that I can tell was paining him. "Just say the word and we stop."

Aria places a kiss to the hollow of my shoulder and I shudder as she gently pulls the baby doll down, exposing my aching breasts to the cool air. Maddox's jaw ticks with barely restraint desire. I jut out my chin, looking directly into his eyes with a dare passing between us.

"I am not going to break. But…" I pause, a smile curling my lips, "I will certainly let you bend, twist, and fuck me until you find that out for yourself."

His eyes flash as he pulls me roughly against him, testing

my words. I don't let him catch onto my sharp inhale, distracting him by arching my chest into his, whispering breathlessly. "Is that all you've got, Maddox?" He chuckles.

"Not in the slightest, *Harlow*," he mutters my name like a sin, his hands roaming over my body before giving my ass a sharp smack. "Before the night is through, you're going to scream for us. You're going to soak each of our dicks with your cum and even then, we won't fucking stop. Just remember, you asked for this."

Maddox crushes his lips to mine, and I vaguely feel Aria ease the robe from my arms. Gone are the days Maddox winced when we touched. Now, he can't get enough. His facial hair scrapes while his lips soothe, drawing me up onto my tiptoes in a bid to get ever closer. It's never quite close enough. A soft pair of handcuffs snap around my wrists as shadows invade my personal space, a mix of hands roaming over my body as Maddox lifts me from the floor.

Not giving me a chance to breathe, his tongue dances with mine and I groan as a hand works its way between us to slide into my soaking pussy. Bucking, Maddox forces my legs wider around his hips. A jingling sounds before he steps back, leaving me fully seated in one of the sex swings hanging from the ceiling. A strap against my upper back and beneath my thighs levitate me in midair, joining above my head for me to hold onto. My legs are impossibly wide and my feet are quickly being harnessed into foot holes by Aria while Zane rounds my back to hold me steady.

My heart is in my throat, my eyes darting to Zeke who's fully reclined on the bed. Having rid himself of his linen pants, he strokes the hard length of his cock as he watches on. Quite the voyeur. It's not lost on me how Zane angles the swing to give him a full view. My exposed breasts rise and fall heavily, my attention on the languid pumping of Zeke's fist as a set of lips wrap around my clit, causing my head to fall back against Zane with a soft moan.

"That's right Harlow, we got you," Zane's voice whispers in my ear, placing soft, open-mouthed kisses on my neck and shoulders. "Every time you think you're drowning, we will be there to save you."

"Damn, she's so sweet," Aria breathes against me, her hands running up my thighs. I cry out as she sucks my clit into her mouth and gently flicks it with her tongue. At the same time, she dips her fingers inside of me, just enough to be a tease. My hips buck, and I whimper as she swirls her tongue slowly, pressing her lips against me. I pant as my chin hits my chest and our eyes clash. Mesmerized by the purest of emeralds staring back from long lashes, I watch as she reaches to grip my ass, and slowly rocks me into her mouth.

"Fuck," Zeke murmurs softly, my eyes flying back to his dick. There's something wholly sexy and naughty about watching him stroke himself over the sight of me. My mouth goes dry as a bead of precum glistens from the tip and when I meet his eyes, he smirks. Zane's chest shifts as he reaches behind the swing's straps, his fingers pressing firmly against my ass.

"What are you waiting for Zane? Fuck our girl," Maddox growls from somewhere in the room. Before I can find him, Zane's arm lashes out to catch a bottle of lube that was about to smash into my face. Aria continues to flick her tongue over my clit, a mischievous smile growing as she produces a vibration wand from nowhere. The device is powered up at the same time Zane presses the lubed head of his cock against my ass, gently pushing, slowly applying pressure.

"Help me out here Aria," he grits out. Lowering the wand onto my already throbbing clit, Aria spits on three of her fingers for show and thrusts them straight into me. My body tenses as I arch back on a groan, until Zane slaps my thigh and tells me to relax. With Aria's thrusts worked in time with the vibrations, I will myself back into the seat, my back flush against Zane once more. Working his dick into my back hole, inch by inch, his arm grips the straps above my head to steady himself until he's finally fully seated. I sag, releasing a built up exhale.

"Such a good girl, the way you take me right in that tight ass. You like being like this, Harlow? As our little fuck toy?" Zane growls as he starts to move inside of me, pushing and pulling my hips, rocking me against Aria's assault. I whimper. Zane bites down on my neck with a rough growl. "We want to hear it. Say you like being our little fuck toy."

"Yes, fuck yes. I love being your toy. Just fuck me," I cry out, my body vibrating with tension as they continue to fucking tease, keeping me on the edge. The entire time, Aria's fingers are buried in my pussy, picking up her pace and then slowing back down.

"Make her come already," Zeke groans. "I need to shove my dick down her fucking throat." His dick is now leaking precum, glistening in the candles that flicker throughout the room. Maddox finally steps back into my line of vision, a smirk on his face as he passes Aria a thick dildo to finish what she has started. It's barely pushed inside my pussy before I'm scream-ing, my body hurtling over the ledge and I feel Zane groan as my body tightens around him.

"That's it, Harlow. Cum for us," he groans. My entire body shakes against the swing with the force of my climax. Not for one second do these assholes slow their thrusting, screwing me through the obliteration of my soul. Screaming all of their names in turn, washes of orgasmic bliss crash through my center, taking my senses with it. I almost lose consciousness, my skin writhe with a fierce flush and my vision still speckled with dots as Zane and Aria pull out of me at the same time. I groan at the loss of sensation, my body going limp.

"I'm with Zeke," Aria moves up my body to mutter against my lips, my own taste coating hers. "I can't wait to ride your face, but I think he deserves a turn, don't you?" Without waiting for an answer, she steps back with a wink, pulling the vibrator away from my clit.

Maddox and Zane release my limbs from the swing, carrying me over to the bed. As I'm settled on the edge, Zane unhooks the cuffs, kissing each one of my wrists, only to replace them with my hands in front of me this time. Maddox runs his fingers down my back, before pushing downwards on my nape and twisting me onto my front. I take my cue to crawl up the bed towards Zeke but Maddox grabs my hips, pulling me backwards so my pussy is level with his dick. Zeke pouts as much as I do, his dick weeping from being stroked. I lick my lips, brimming with anticipation to taste him.

Running his own dick up and down my pussy, Maddox leans over me. "Your hands will remain bound, because as Zane said, you're our little toy tonight. Nothing more than a flesh light created for my pleasure," he says darkly, slamming all the way home inside of me. I scream, his piercing stretching me in a way I can never get used to. Dragging the nightie all the way up, Maddox smacks my ass and thighs in time with his harsh thrusts. I cry out with each one, spiraling back into that haze of painful pleasure. The initial intrigue that bound me to them in the first place. Each sting is soothed, every powerful slam of his thick cock immediately leaving me to beg for another.

"Ahh, come on Maddox," Zeke whines, desperately trying to wriggle down the bed towards me. "Why am I being punished?"

"You were stupid enough to restrain yourself," Aria drops down on the mattress at his side, crossing her long legs before her. "Besides, the view is rather good from up here."

As if to piss his brother off, Zane slides in front of me. Gloriously naked, painfully hard and washed clean. But he doesn't let me lower my head. Instead, Zane lifts my bound hands and slips them around the back of his neck. Leaning my forearms on his shoulders, Zane kisses me. Deeply, passionately and completely. My toes curl even further, the two men at either end of me like polar opposites. I fall into Zane's kiss, my tongue searching for his to cling onto his desire. Whereas Maddox rams into me like a machine, one hand seeking my clit and the other fisting my hair.

"Come for us, baby," he grunts. Working my clit in rapid circles, Maddox forces my body to obey. Zane's skilled fingers seek out my breasts, twisting my nipples hard at the exact moment my pussy clamps down. Twin groans are drawn from Maddox and I as he, too, explodes inside of me. Once Maddox releases my hair, my head drops into Zane's shoulder, pulling on his strength to see my orgasm to the end without collapsing. The thrusting slows, barely a breath between Maddox's sharply spanking my ass and pulling out. A towel is immediately placed over my pussy as I'm cleaned. All I'm focused on is controlling my breathing, the sweat coating my skin making me hot all over.

The cuffs are popped open by Aria and I swiftly toss them to the floor. A bottle of cold water from the mini bar is placed in my hand and I down it, pouring the last over my body in an effort to cool down.

"Is it my turn yet?" Zeke asks hopefully. I smile, shoving Zane out of the way. Hell yeah, it is. Crawling up the bed, I fist Zeke's cock tightly at the base and lower my head, taking him all the way back in my throat. His moan is music to my ears, his restrained hand jingling against the headboard. "Fuck Feisty, I knew this would be so good."

At my hips, a set of hands gently strokes my skin. Not calloused or rough enough to be Maddox, and with Aria watching me deep throat Zeke, it can only be Zane. Unhurriedly, he rubs better the welts Maddox will have left. Rounding my legs, those same fingers feel the ridges of the scars lining my thighs. Not once have I been shy about them, and that's all to do with the four of them refusing to let me be. As soon as we left the hospital with my ankle in a boot and bandages covering most of my body, Zane vowed to worship every one of my scars. My war wounds, as Zeke calls them. Proof of the sacrifices I was willing to take to be with them, and evidence of the strength I've had inside all along.

"So fucking beautiful," Zane murmurs, lining himself up with my sopping wet cunt. He guides through the remainder of Maddox's cum, taking it far more gentle on me. Too gentle, for Zeke's liking.

"Be a good girl and open up Feisty. Don't be shy, let me feel just how hard that mouth can suck." Stroking my hair with his one hand, Zeke watches my every move while I lick, suck and hum around his dick. He asked how hard I can go, and I don't hold back. Creating a vacuum seal with my lips, my cheeks hollow and Zeke melts into the pillows. Aria's green eyes also sparkle as she takes credit for teaching me the true definition of oral. My eyes snag on the clit wand laying across the super king-size bed and I have an idea.

Snapping my fingers, I point to it, beckoning Aria to retrieve it for me. She quickly obeys, excitement passing over her features. Shimmying down the bed, Aria stuffs a pillow beneath her chocolate waves and, without taking my mouth off Zeke's dick for a second, I pull the cord of Aria's kimono open. It's payback time. Ramping the wand to max speed, I jam it against her pink pussy, rubbing the large head in small circles. She cries, trying to close her thighs so I abruptly stop, pulling the wand away.

"Oh I see, Killer," she chuckled. Spreading her legs wide, her thigh pressed against Zeke's, Aria drops her head back to face the ceiling. "You just wait. Two can play that game." I smirk around Zeke, pressing the wand against her again, enjoying her whimpers all too much.

Drawn back to my own pleasure, Zane seats himself inside of me, rocking his hips and prolonging our time together. Maddox is an aggressive lover, accustomed to his pussies being made of silicone and unable to moan back. But Zane, he's surprised me. Once his stoic mask slipped, he began to flourish and watching him find himself day by day is a journey I'm glad to be on.

I moan as Zeke jerks his hips upwards and I swallow him deeper. Tightening my lips, I run my tongue on the underside of his dick before flicking it over his thick head, savoring every drop of cum leaking from his tip. He wraps his hand into my hair harder, his blue eyes locked with mine as he thrusts harder into my throat.

"That's right, keep those pretty eyes on mine. I want to see them when Zane makes you come around his dick."

I groan as Zane works to pick up his pace, tilting his hips downwards before dragging himself out slowly, just to fuck me harder. He can feel the desperation thickening the air, and sense that we're all drawing closer to something incredible.

"This pussy is so damn perfect," Zane slips his fingers to my cunt, feeling his own girth sliding in and out of me. Zeke groans in agreement, his eyes glazing over.

"Fuck yeah. You are so beautiful, taking us both." Spurred on by their praise, I take him all. Swallowing him as far as can, savoring his taste and the feel of his dick jumping in my throat. Zeke's eyes grow heavy and soft 'fuck's' fall from his lips as I quickly bop my head up and down, as Zane fucks me harder. All whilst working Aria in to a frenzy, her nails embedded in my forearm. I focus on breathing through my nose as the boys use my body, driving me higher and higher while I do the same to Aria. Everything, except us, fades into the background as we wring out every bit of pleasure we can from one another. Then, as a unit, we all explode.

This time, I'm certain I blacked out. My nightie is discarded and strong arms scoop me up, carrying my limp body from the hidden sex room. Best gang-bang-aversary gift ever. Water droplets drip onto my face, rousing me enough to peer up and see Maddox's ruggedly handsome face. I smile, pride swelling in my chest. I'm sure there are those who would see his long hair and tattoos, and promptly cross the street, and that's just fine. Maddox has come so far, and the love-filled gaze he gives me tell me all I need to know.

"You missed the fun," I murmur as he places me down in the bathtub. It's empty apart from a sponge Maddox wets and begins to wash me down with.

"No I didn't," he tries to bite back a grin. "And neither will you at tomorrow's home-movie night." My eyes widen then, no words forming as Maddox cleans me all over. Once he's rubbed a layer of body wash over the entirety of my skin, he lifts the shower head from above and sprays the suds away with warm water.

"Mmmm," I groan, contentment and sheer joy blossoming in my chest. "I-" The shower head turns off and Maddox leans into my face.

"You, what?" He asks. My cheeks flame and I bite down on my lower lip. Shaking my head, Maddox gives me a knowing look and lifts me against his bare chest. If it were up to him, I'd never walk again. The whole gang is in our shared bed by the time we arrive, having cleaned themselves elsewhere. The circular mattress is huge, and they're already under the satin covers. Zeke pats the space at his side, rushing me to scramble closer as soon as I'm placed down. It's the same every night – Maddox spoons my back on one side while Zeke, Zane and Aria rotate who gets to sleep closest to my front.

The five of us snuggle down, Maddox's legs following the curve of mine while my head lays on Zeke's chest, tattooed arms wrapping around me as I stare at the huge full moon in the sky beyond our open sliding doors. It's particularly yellow tonight, reflected in the still water below. Our own slice of paradise. I used to question 'why me?' or wonder if Aria had picked another girl at Club Rapture, would she have been here right now. But I've come to terms with, either way, it doesn't matter. Through fate or dumb luck, I've found my place to belong.

"I'm gonna do it." Zeke announces out of nowhere. His voice reverberates through my head, quickly followed by the irritated groans of everyone else.

"Don't ruin it," Maddox grunts harshly.

"Not right now," Aria leans over to nudge his bicep.

"Can't you just leave it be?" Zane adds.

"Nope," Zeke shakes his head, pushing at my shoulders to force me upright. "I'm going to do it - right now. I-"

"I love you Harlow!" The sudden outburst comes from Maddox, Zane and Aria, causing me to flinch. "I said it first! No, I said it first!" a subsequent argument breaks out, accompanied by the petty smacking of their hands. I press my lips together to contain my laughter. Zeke's mouth drops open in complete shock.

"You spiteful bastards," he releases me to dive on Zane. There's nothing like a heterosexual naked bed fight to prove a point. Pulling Zeke back into the center of the bed, I can no longer withhold my laughter. It sort of bursts in his face, tears streaming from my eyes as emotion begins to overrule my head.

"I love you guys. All of you, together and individually. Being yours is...well, it's everything. I just hope I prove to be enough in return."

"You're more than enough," Maddox yanks my body back against his chest. His thick arms wrap around me like a boa constrictor, latching on and refusing to let go. Dragging me down the rest of the way for my head to hit the pillow, I manage to free my arms and reach out. Six hands respond, all claiming a part of me as Maddox's deep breaths fan across my nape.

Everyone finds their comfy spot, encasing me in their warmth. Sleep calls for me, no matter how much I want to relish this moment. Surrounded by those I love and who love, crave and care for me in return. When everyday life is a dream, sleeping seems like a waste of precious time. Yet my limbs grow heavier and my face sinks into the pillow. As my breathing evens out and my mind begins to fog, I cling onto one last thought, replaying it over and over like a broken record.

How the hell did I get so lucky?

Holy Smokes!

Well, I don't know about you…but I need a drink!
Harlow's story has taken me on one hell of journey, into the
depths of the smut cave in my mind I had yet to discover. On
the plus side, my husband is ecstatic! From the trials of Rapture
to the wicked revenge scheme of a jilted ex, I hope you have
enjoyed spiraling into this unique take on crime organizations
with me!
Can we just take a moment to aww over sweet Freddie - who I
refused to kill, no matter who told me I should! I mean…I did
beat him up and throw him down the stairs, but who's
checking? We still need to cheer on the good guys, even when
stripping off and throwing ourselves at the bad ones!

Okay, moment's over. Now where can I find a Reverse Glory
Hole for myself?

Acknowledgments

Gosh – where do I begin? There are so many people who boost me on a daily basis. Especially with this whirlwind of a novel that took even me on a wild ride, I've replied on those close to me for their constant strength and love to keep me sane.

To my Keyboard Whores – Every single one of you is a beautiful, inspirational and incredibly hardworking woman I have the pleasure to write with and talk to on a daily basis. From valuable insights to smut-filled conversations, each day brings me so much joy! I'm forever grateful for the friendships we have formed.

Peas in a Taco – Your beef is my lifeline. Nuff' said.

To Lucy and Lou – Loyal brainstormers, thank you again for letting me beat my ideas against your face and scrape what sense you manage to make of it. This certainly was one of those writes I threw your way in a state of panic, and as always, you guys were there at the drop of a hat! Whether banishing me to the writing cave or talking me down from murdering all characters, I couldn't have done this write without you.

To Mr. Cole and the kiddie Cole's – Pursuing a career as an author was never going to be smooth sailing, and isn't one that brings instant gratification. I cannot thank you all enough for the support I receive at home, for the cups of tea after pulling an all-nighter, for the evenings of family games I've missed to make a deadline. You're all my motivation and my solace when the dark, imposter-ish thoughts creep in, and I could have never achieved any of this without you.

To my incredible readers – It's plain and simple; I'm nothing without the readers that support me! Thank you all for devouring my books, and also becoming my friends. I love getting to know you, seeing your gorgeous book shelves and building connections with so many talented and wonderful people!

If you're a new reader to Maddison – welcome to the Mole's Burrow!!

Maddison is a married mum of two, and a serial daydreamer. As a huge fan of all romance tropes, mostly the dark and deprived ones with more d!cks than h0les, she finally decided to put pen to paper (finger to keyboard doesn't sound as poetic) and write her own.

As a child, Maddison was a jet setter and has lived all over the world, only to return to the south east of England, where she is now happily settled. With a double award in applied arts and art history, Maddison is just a creative chick with a dark passion for feisty females and spicy stories.

Read More by Maddison!

A list of Maddison Cole's other releases can be found below and for up-to-date info, make sure to follow her socials! The Facebook reader's group and newsletter are the best places for reveals, announcements, giveaways and more, and please never hesitate to reach out!

Facebook – **Author Maddison Cole**
www.facebook.com/Maddison.cole.314
Facebook readers group - **Cole's Reading Moles**
www.facebook.com/groups/colesreadingmoles
Instagram and TikTok - **@authormaddisoncole**

OTHER WORKS

<u>Dark Humor RH - Completed</u>
Findin' Candy (novella)
Crushin' Candy
Smashin' Candy
Friggin' Candy

<u>All My Pretty Psychos</u>
<u>Paranormal RH with ghosts and demons - Completed</u>
Queen of Crazy
Kings of Madness
Hoax: The Untold Story (novella)
Reign of Chaos

<u>A Wonderlust Adventure</u>
A Deranged Duet Retelling
My Tweedle Boys
Our Malice (pre-order)

<u>The War at Waversea</u>
<u>Basketball College MFM Menage - Completed</u>
Perfectly Powerless
Handsomely Heartless
Beautifully Boundless

CO-WRITES

Life Lessons with Emma Luna

Haunted by Desire with Emmaleigh Wynters

<u>Up for Pre-order:</u>

Moon Bound – Standalone Shifter Duet
Playing Games with a Bully – Billionaire Badboys Book One
Our Malice – Wonderlust Adventure Book Two
Deranged – Mafia Ties Book One

9 781916 521001